ROYAL HOUSE

Royal House

A Novel

Best wishes,
Marilyn Brown

Marilyn Brown

Covenant Communications, Inc.

For my mother and father

Covenant Communications, Inc.
American Fork, Utah

Printed in the United States of America
First Printing: September 1994
94 95 96 97   10 9 8 7 6 5 4 3 2

Royal House
ISBN 1–55503–706–2
Library of Congress Cataloging-in-Publication Data:

Brown, Marilyn McMeen Miller, 1938-
    Royal house : a novel / Marilyn Brown.
        p.   cm.
        1. Hotelkeepers—Utah—Provo—Fiction. 2. Mormons—Utah—Provo—
Fiction. 3. Family—Utah—Provo—Fiction. 4. Provo (Utah)—
I. Title.
PS3552.R694R68 1994
813' .54—dc20   94-27264
                                                    CIP

Acknowledgments

Many have helped with the writing. I owe special thanks to Darla Isaakson who encouraged me to write a sequel to *The Earthkeepers*, and to Giles Florence, Managing Editor, who was especially supportive. His knowledge of great literature, his kindness and editorial expertise have made it a pleasure to work with Covenant. And the others who worked with him, Marilyn Kofford and JoAnn Jolley, also gave valuable advice. To the generosity of Valerie Holladay who asked the right questions, I owe thanks for improved clarity and power. And to my daughter Simeen and her models, Mike and Cindy DuVall, I owe many thanks for the beautiful illustrations which grace the covers of all three books.

To my friends of literature, especially the *Utah Arts Council* for their first place novel award in 1992, and the *Association for Mormon Letters* for the award to *The Earthkeepers*, let me say that this encouragement helped me stay fixed to my goals. To Mormon writers Bruce Jorgensen, Richard Cracroft, Donlu and Douglas Thayer, Eugene England, Steve Walker, Levi Peterson, Don and Jean Marshall, Jerry Johnston, Lavina Anderson, Sally Taylor, Marden and Dennis Clark, Douglas Alder, Edward Hart, Clinton Larson, Tory Anderson, Larry Ferguson and John Carmack, Todd Hannig, Carol Lynn Pearson, Peggy Bohn, Elaine McKay, Maxine Miller, Veda Hale, Kathryn Gardner, Mary Bradford, Joseph Hullinger, and last but not least, Stan Zenk, and Curtis Taylor–and to my family, and to all who have influenced my hopes to write for this audience, I owe thanks for inspiration.

While studying for my MFA at the University of Utah I gained so much from Francois Camoin, David Kranes, Meg Brady and all of my teachers and classmates, though this work called for a different treatment. And to those who have contributed special support, from my popular Pulitzer Prize idol Wallace Stegner (now deceased), the dear poet William Stafford, my early contemporary Scott Card, and special encouragers Ron Carlson and Patricia Connell, and to those who have contributed by asking me the question, "How is your writing coming?" thank you for your kindness.

Finally, for those who liked the first two books and have looked forward to seeing this one, my heart-felt gratitude! Also many thanks to the bookstores and the marketing people who have made it possible for my work to appear.

Sincerely, Marilyn Brown

FOREWORD

The Roberts Hotel in Provo, Utah, is the model for the Hull House Hotel. While doing my research I explored its wonderful old halls, opened the doors to a couple of fancy "room and bath" suites, and read every word of old newspaper copy in its quaint historical museum. Now, although it is a refuge for homeless people, and has certainly changed from its heyday in 1918, when a delicious breakfast of steak and eggs cost only sixty cents, it is still a place of fascinating reflection and meditation upon a nostalgic past.

The lot on Second South and University Avenue (then called "J" Street), was originally owned by Brigham Young, sold to Warren Dusenberry in 1878, and then to Esther C. Pulsipher in 1882, who built the Occidental Boarding House. The Roberts family purchased the boarding house in 1885 and created the Roberts Hotel, adding its dining room in 1900, its north wing in 1906, a third floor in 1908, and its fountain in 1912. By 1918, perhaps because the war was hard on Provo's economy, the Roberts family was ready to sell.

I have pushed the sales date up a bit, as the hotel actually sold to their new owners in 1919. There was some hitch in the transaction at that time, in which the hotel passed through another set of hands (a bank, a financial rescuer?) for a very short period of time. Because this transaction seemed unclear in the history, I have taken the liberty to make one up of my own. I suppose there is someone who knows what really happened, and it would be fun to find out. But for the purposes of spinning a good yarn, I have merely included a scene of economic wheeling/dealing which, far from being fictional, consistently recurs into our present day.

I can only vaguely recollect the place of the mortician in the hotel's history, although there was one. The steel people are based on truth, although I have changed L.F. Rains's name to Barrington because his real name was confusing with my Indian Rain. Of course the fire at the mill, the economic struggle between the east and west sides of town, the release of the BYU professors for teaching evolution at BYU (1911), and the search of President Benjamin Cluff for Zarahemla are all true. Mrs. Carroll's, and the three houses on Fifth West that belonged to the Eastman family are fictional, although a house like their first one might have been torn down to make way for the present H. and R. Block Building which occupies that corner today.

Aside from giving me another opportunity to express my regard for the difficulties of the Native Americans and the pioneers, it has been a delightful experience to write this novel about the week before Christmas at the close of World War I. Those years in the early part of the century in which our world suddenly turned into a modern machine are a seedbed for some of the problems we experience today, and it has been invaluable to examine the dynamics of shifting economic and cultural values against the backdrop of eternal human needs: the need to love and be loved, and to find a meaningful place in the overall scheme of things.

Marilyn Brown

1

Hanson Eastman,
December 1918

It had been too long since he had slept well. Three, maybe four months. He had never slept more than an hour or two since he had been wounded in the skirmish at Verdun. When he went down he had said, "Now the war is over for me." And then a few months later it was over for everyone.

Now, when he leaned against the glass of the coach window in the train headed home, above the din of war still in his head he thought he could hear people talking. And it was not just the talk of the group of businessmen who had entered the car at the brief stop in Springville. There were no words in the most prominent voices, really, just sound lurking in the metal thunder, as though there were underground forces humming: "Come home." The voice that vibrated most in the sound of steel was the murmur of the old Indian Grandmother Rain. All across the country, in the rumblings between his moments of not quite sleeping, he had thought he heard her humming as she had hummed all of her children to sleep.

But now sleep didn't come.

There were other, more prominent voices in the hum: the voice of his old Aunt Mara, and the voice of his father Ashel and his mother Caroline, and then penetrating all of these voices, a quiet lament from the girl he left five years ago. It was Grace who seemed to be pleading with him now: "I am waiting. We are all waiting for you to come home."

He tried to find some semblance of peace. He prayed. But every nerve in his body seemed shaken. Although he had vowed to leave war behind—crowded on the ship, and on this smoking train across miles and miles of prairie—it still roared in the undertones and trembled along the edges of his consciousness. He was still reeling from its terror. He had seen three different companions shot down in the fields; he had heard their cries, had seen the whites of their eyes rolling back in their heads, heard the rattle of death in their throats; and in lugging their bodies to the camp, he had soaked his own hands in their blood. He still carried bits of the shrapnel that had exploded near his leg, and vivid in his memory was the feeling of his own body lying along the trench, until he felt arms slip under his knees and lift him, then shift him like a bag over broad shoulders. As they had walked, the bobbing had been so painful, he had finally lost consciousness.

"You're going to be all right," the stranger had told him while he crouched against the tent wall, the gas lantern flickering orange light across his full face. Deftly, he dressed Hanson's wounds. "You still got more spittle in you than a blunderbuss." He leaned toward Hanson, his blue eyes large under the shag of straight blond hair. "After we finish this up, man, you and me are going to find the girls on the Marne!" he had laughed encouragingly. When Hanson hesitated, he had said, "You hear me? I said girls, man."

It hurt Hanson to breathe. His wounds responded with needles of pain. "No . . . it's. . . ."

"No, what?"

"There's someone back home."

The man sat back and the light on his cheeks made hollows of his eyes. "You lucky son of a gun. Somebody back home, eh! You'll make it from spite, then. Tell me, what does she look like?"

The words Hanson tried to push out on his thick tongue felt heavy. "She's good lookin'."

"Good lookin'?" the soldier smiled. "Ooooh . . . she's good lookin'! Better lookin' than me?"

Even though it hurt, Hanson laughed.

"Ha! Anybody that can still laugh is in great shape!"

In the rough farmer's cart behind the lines, the stranger stayed with him. "Just call me Alex," he said. He told jokes about the girls he'd known in France. The girls back home. Sometimes Hanson laughed, though he didn't want to hurt so much.

"No one girl?" Hanson had asked, barely able to speak.

"Not yet, maybe someday . . ."

Alex had stayed day and night with Hanson after that, talking for hours. He hadn't left his side until Hanson had been taken to the medical unit. And even then, he visited regularly, racing Hanson around on the back two wheels of a wheelchair, cracking jokes. When Hanson recovered, they walked the streets of Verdun. And then when Hanson found out Alex Hunt had grown up on a huge ranch in Idaho and knew a lot about the Paiute and Blackfoot Indians, he badgered him with questions. As two westerners who had found each other in Europe, they shared stories about the Indians, the settlers, the railroad, until they finally began to share their personal fears and dreams for the future, and what they would do when they got home.

Hanson was unsure of home.

"I'll come and help you with your hotel so you won't be alone. Nobody knows what it's like to suck mud unless you've done some of it. Right?" Alex said.

"Nobody knows," Hanson agreed. He knew he was still suffering from shell shock. "Nobody knows."

"Maybe not even God!" Alex threw his head back and laughed. "Or should I even mention God, eh? He must have been off fishing when you nearly died on that mine."

"I believe in God," Hanson had told him.

"Well, ask him where he was when the shells hit, and would he please take away the pain."

"Maybe God is the one who sent me you," Hanson said.

"Oh yeah? You think so?" Alex Hunt hooted. "That was nice of him."

"Maybe."

"Well, I don't know much about God. I sure didn't see much of him out there in the crossfire."

It was true, there had been little sign of God on that field, and yet Hanson knew he was preparing to return now to a people who knew God intimately, and knew that God had a hand in every beat of every day. And now he would be in the business of reconciling everything—of trying to make a whole of his life again.

If this Alex who had saved his life really did come down from Idaho as soon as he said he might, Hanson knew there would be someone who would understand, and perhaps he could survive. He clung to the hope that his raw nerves would heal. He could not let his family see his pain. No, they must not guess how on edge he felt. He began to pray in his heart, "Dear God, I know you are there. I know I am suffering from the shock of war. When I know what it is, why doesn't it help me to calm down?"

But it did not seem to help. All that he must now face clamored in his brain: finding Grace—did he even know what love was like anymore, or had calluses grown over his heart? He must also face taking over his father's business at the hotel. And what would he find? Even before he had left, the city had been moving toward the east, leaving behind the East House Hotel and making it the secondary hotel in town. He prayed his friend would come to help him. He prayed Grace would understand. He prayed his father and mother and his Aunt Mara would be patient. His tired spirit yearned to rest in the calm presence of Grace's old Indian grandmother, Rain.

When the train had clanged into Provo at half past nine, he stood in the aisle, half dizzy with fatigue. The group of businessmen who had just entered the car at Springville stood in a line in front of him, frustrating his exit, and he wanted to scream. But he bit his tongue. Directly in front of him was a huge heavy-faced dark-haired man with Indian features, dark eyes, dressed in a black greatcoat and carrying a polished cane. As the large Indian blocked Hanson's way, he pounded the cane against the floor in a slow steady rhythm, and the sound jarred Hanson's nerves. Once Hanson managed to step off the car, even the snow along the ground did not prevent him from side stepping and slipping away from the men moving like slow cattle. He did not hesitate to step around the huge man and work his way past the others who were talking in low voices about "the best site for steel." Exiting the empty station, he began to run, tearing along the walks, knowing he would soon be home.

As he rounded the corner along Third South, it was then that he saw her like an angel coming down out of the storm, her dark hair blowing, her cheeks red with the cold. He flew into her arms, trying to ignore his fractured nerves. "Grace, Grace, Grace," was all he could say. And for a time she had been like manna to his troubled spirit.

"Calm yourself. They need you," he told himself. "Act as though you had never seen so much death, because this is life, and life must go on."

Running down the street with Grace, for a few moments he had felt free. Then, when he found his father and mother at home, he held them in his arms and felt a wave of rejoicing that filled him with hope. But when he accompanied Grace north to the old Eastman home two doors away to see her Indian Grandmother Rain—when they climbed the stairs and walked into the bedroom, they had found the beloved grandmother lying pale and lifeless on the sheets. And all his inner efforts to stay whole betrayed him at once. His heart broke at the sight of her.

Grace ran to the bed and touched her grandmother's cheeks. "But I left her for only a few moments!" she said over and over again.

Later, when Aunt Mara had come, she sat quietly, saying nothing but, "She is at peace. She is at peace."

Though he clung to a calm exterior, he could feel his muscles tighten, his nerves shiver. When Grace left to call the funeral director, he could not bear to stand calmly by while his Aunt Mara slowly thumbed through the book in her lap. When Grace returned, his nerves seemed to leap as though cauterized with a hot iron. It was all he could do to hold on.

And then he heard the faraway sound of an automobile horn.

2

Grace Tuttle

There were times when she believed he would never come home and that this was the way it was supposed to be—that they would hear much later—perhaps from a delayed telegram or a bottle washing up on the Atlantic seacoast—that Hanson was going to live in Hamburg on the Rhine, or take a boat to Bangladesh, or climb a mountain in Nepal. Because for five years those were the kinds of letters that came through. First on his mission to Belgium. Then as a soldier helping his people against the German army. He was at Marne. He couldn't come home. He was in the medical unit at Verdun.

And so there were the months and months when she began not to believe in Hanson, nor in her dreams. Finally, as their resources began to wither, as business at the hotel began to dry up and she had only been barely able to pay for her schooling at Brigham Young University with the most exacting sacrifices, she believed she could not believe in love anymore. Going morning after morning to the train station to find Hanson had become a meaningless exercise. She had learned to accept the reality that he was never there. So when the tall slender man with the piercing blue eyes reminded her of Hanson, she was at first numb with disbelief. She did not recognize the thin cheek bones and square jaw under the scrubby beard. But finally the burnished hair convinced her that Hanson was home.

Hanson! Hanson! Oh, Hanson! She ran with him through the snow. Nothing would ever be the same again, she knew. It was as though her universe were cranking up to be rewound for some astonishing new spin. And when she brought him to the house and found Grandmother Rain gone, she was too stunned for tears. And for a moment, too stunned to speak, until Aunt Mara came, and assigned her to call the funeral director. Finally, when she came back from using the telephone, she had leaned on Mara and buried her face in Mara's neck. And let the tears come.

Hanson's Aunt Mara had been the loving caretaker who replaced the mother she had never known. Grace clung to her while she sobbed, "I wasn't here to say good-bye." For long moments, she could not believe what had already happened in a single morning. The sudden shock of Rain's death unearthed so many conflicting feelings, she could not focus on Hanson's presence in the room. He had been so quiet. At one time he took her hand. But now he seemed to have withdrawn from her, and remained stone quiet beside the window while Mara sat quietly holding the cloth bound book on her lap. "Sobe's journal," she said to Hanson. "Rain loved to read in it." Hanson drew back from the window, his face in a grimace, when they had heard the sound of a horn.

The horn shattered the morning and opened a flood of memories. Grace suddenly felt she was in many worlds at once. She seemed to hear the circus blaring into town when she was a child and the family had no money to spend. It had been during one of the first real jolts to their business—when Mr. Hull had purchased Mrs. Pulsipher's Occidental Boarding House on the east side of town, and the new competition had drawn away business from the East House Hotel. Grace remembered watching the colored cars in the street, especially the red one that held the tiger. The children ran beside him, while behind the bars his eyes burned like white fires in his face—with hatred, as though he were not meant to be pent up and he would jump them were the bars gone. And she and Hanson had wanted to go with the children to see the tiger and the man in red trousers, but they could not.

To console them, Grandmother Rain brought out an old

box of her childhood toys. The Indian toys were wrapped in deerskin, and Rain had unwrapped each of them gently and laid them on the porch mat. Awed, the children had leaned over them. "You may touch them," Grandmother Rain had said. Both Grace and Hanson had attached the notched sticks to one another, rearranged the beads, put the beads inside the deerskin pouch, shook them, then took them out of the pouch and restrung them for hours. While they touched the beads laid out on the handkerchief, their hands had brushed. Hanson had looked up at her. They were still children, but it had been the first time there had been feelings she had never felt before. They stared at one another, and she drew her hands away. Hanson had looked up at her with solemn eyes. Then he had taken her hand in his and held it. And she had let him hold it while they sat in silence over Rain's toys. And then it had been not long after that in the hay rack when they rode behind Ashel's horses, their hands and arms bare in the hot sun, that the cart had lurched, and they had fallen against each other, and Hanson had wrapped his arms around her to steady her. Grandmother Rain, sitting against the hay, had smiled at them.

Now Grandmother Rain lay still. With such vivid memories haunting her, Grace closed her eyes while she pressed her hands over her grandmother's still hands. She didn't know if she could quietly accept what had happened without question, though her grandmother was old. She didn't know if she could let go. But the sound of the horn seemed to remind her she would have to try. So she opened her eyes and focused them on Hanson's old Aunt Mara whose head was bent over the journal, her eyes wet. "Do you hear something?" Mara was asking her.

Grace lifted her cheek from her grandmother's gnarled hands. She was going to speak, but she heard Hanson's voice behind her.

"Someone's motor car has a horn that's stuck," Hanson said.

Grace's eyes met Mara's distracted gaze. "Mr. Hull?" They expected him any moment with his funeral car. When she mentioned Mr. Hull, Mara visibly winced. Grace knew the old feud still hurt Aunt Mara. Mr. Hull had been far too successful transforming the old Occidental Boarding House into the Hull House Hotel. And far too successful as a funeral director as well. But he had often been kind. He preferred the funeral business to the hotel business, he told them. "What you Eastmans ought to do is buy me out," he had said. "When you're ready, I'll sell." But Hanson's father, Ashel, had felt the price he asked was too high.

"It can't be the funeral car," Mara said, gazing thoughtfully, smoothing the pages of the journal in her lap. "It doesn't sound like the funeral car."

When Grace turned, she watched Hanson pull the curtains back from the window and focus his gaze on the street below. "There's someone in the street," he said. He looked once more toward the bed where Grace and Mara sat with Grandmother Rain. "But it's not Mr. Hull." As he spoke, his words seemed flat, as though he were trying to keep the lid on some hidden nervousness he could not control.

Grace thought she saw some anxiety in his eyes, but she didn't want to bring it to anyone's attention. She went to the window to stand beside him. "What kind of motor car is that?" she asked him.

"I don't know," Hanson said. He did not look back out of the window. He tossed a pale glance at the room as though it were spinning for him. "But I think the driver might be somebody I know." The moment he said it, the moment he drew back, the blare of the horn seemed to soften as though it were moving toward the south part of town, toward the railroad tracks, perhaps toward Garbett's Garage, where old Mr. Garbett would be able to unhook it with a pair of pliers. "Aunt Mara," Hanson hesitated. "I . . . hope you won't feel I am not concerned about Grandma Rain. But a friend . . . was driving down from Idaho today." He struggled over his words. "That might have been him just now. I need to find him . . ."

In this moment of questioning, Grace saw him standing next to her in the reflection of the window. She looked small beside him; her shiny black curls shimmered like a smear of ink in the glass where daylight was not far away. But her narrow white cheeks, and the red mouth, barely visible, looked like a copy of his face, as though they could have been brother and sister, though they were not related except through living for years with the same family background. She and her Indian ancestors had been adopted by Hanson's Aunt Mara for many years. And after the death of her parents, Charles and Jenny, it had been the Tuttle and Eastman families who raised her. She believed she had lived so close to Hanson that she knew him well, and yet now he seemed ready to be different from anything she had ever known. But of course, this was Hanson's first morning home. Of course he would have had many things to do to get settled, readjusted. But Grace's heart felt cramped somehow, and heavy with more of what she had been feeling for the last few moments in this room—it felt like abandonment.

Mara returned the journal to Rain's bedside table and rose slowly, leaning on the book to get to her feet. "No, no. Don't worry about waiting for Mr. Hull, Hanson. If you need to go, that's fine, my dear." As she said the words her dark eyes observed both Grace and Hanson. She looked at each of them once, and then again.

Grace's heart fell. She and Mara had been so involved with Rain that they hadn't taken a minute to ask Hanson about himself. He looked so thin and out of place in that moment, a man who had just been through a war—who had been wounded. They couldn't possibly have known what it had been like. There had been a few letters. There were so many questions he might have answered for them now. But neither of them had been paying attention.

"Of course, Hanson, you have other things to do," Mara said.

But Grace noticed Mara's eyes were still moving back and

forth between them. "Grace, you go with him. I'd like to spend some time with Rain alone."

Grace glanced at Hanson quickly to see how much he had guessed that Mara meant to stage their exit together.

Hanson's gaze seemed blank; his mind seemed to be a thousand miles away. "Sure, come along, Grace," he said. He reached for her hand. The power of his touch still sent a chill into her spine, though he seemed completely unaware.

"Grace," Mara detained her for a moment with surprising strength in her withered fingers. "I know you loved staying here with Grandmother Rain in this big old house. But now I don't want you staying here alone. You can move into either of the other houses—with me and Will, or with Ashel and Caroline, whichever you'd like. But why don't you move some of your things to Caroline's this afternoon, and help Sissy with the chores, at least for now? I'll be there for supper tonight."

Grace winced, wondering if Hanson would notice that Mara was putting her together with him in the same house. She glanced toward his eyes. But he was still somewhere else. She could not seem to connect. "I'm going to stay here until Mr. Hull comes," Mara continued, "I'd like to do some cleaning up and look through Rain's things. You two just go." Then she looked up at them through hesitant eyes. "This is a happy time, too, you know. Please, Rain would have wanted for you to have some fun."

It was her attempt to put things back into one piece again, Grace reflected, but her words were true. She remembered her old Grandmother Rain hobbling in moccasins to the theater when they had put on *The Pirates of Penzance*. Rain had stared in wonder at the streamers hanging from the balcony. Grace had been dressed in lemon ruffles with thick makeup on her lashes and ostrich feathers on her bonnet. "I like to see you having fun," her old grandmother had smiled. "Having a good time."

And too, this had been during the same time they had

found out that Rain's daughter, Samantha, and granddaughter, Eliza, had died of the flu. And then Rain's son-in-law had come with the terrible news that the little boy Mathew had disappeared in the field at the Eggertson's farm in Salem. Since they had been unable to find him, they believed the Indians must have taken him. They had never seen him again. And it had meant that all of Rain's children and grandchildren—except for Grace—were gone. And yet Rain had smiled at Grace and said, "I like to see you having fun."

Yes, Grace thought, she should try. She paused for a moment. Now she could only faintly hear the faraway sound of the horn.

3

Reginald Summerfield

The short assessment trip from Provo to Springville and back again was over. That was the first hurdle. When the men were slow to exit the car at the station, he brushed the lint from his large dark coat and tapped his walking stick nervously on the floor. There were still the numbers to reconcile. That would be his job as the accountant. So far as he knew the particulars of Barrington's budgets, the possibilities for a steel mill on the acreage between Springville and Provo looked feasible. There was water; there was accessibility to the railroad. Barrington seemed pleased. There was plenty of labor available in the area, fairly adequate roads, two good-sized hotels.

When they had arrived earlier that week, he and a couple of the others had reserved rooms at the East House Hotel, strangely named since it was now situated five blocks west of the center of town. Though less expensive, that particular hotel had not suited Barrington, who chose to stay on the east side of town, murmuring "seedy," though he expected the others to keep up with his schedule, regardless of sleeping quarters a good mile away. They had made the trip early this morning to accommodate Barrington, who had a full roster today, but it meant they would be free this evening. And at the East House Hotel last night Reginald had met someone—and he had not stopped thinking about her startling green eyes.

Nervously tapping, tapping his way out of the car, he thought he should have been feeling some kind of excitement, but there was a rawness in his throat. Ever since Denver, when the girl with the cigars had taken everything but the lint out of his pocket, he had begun to think twice about where he was going. Maybe Ethel was right. It had nothing to do with the fact that he was a half-breed—because he was handsome enough in his own way with his black hair and large cheeks jowlish above the white collar. And his accounting degree and the job had given him status. Yet he continued to feel an unnamed anger or need that beat in his blood. For several years he had believed his needs could be satisfied in only one way, and he had satisfied them with what he could get—and as a half-breed, it had not been much, although he cut a fairly commanding figure with his great size. But lately his needs had seemed only partially satisfied—the result of an impossible pain that lashed at him—as though the more he had, the more he needed. Or that something deeper than the surface satisfaction was becoming more important to him. Perhaps it had begun with his feeling that Ethel was too easy, and he had fallen for the girl who sat on the wall—her white ankles showing. Or perhaps it had begun with knowing that even though he had been adopted by the Summerfields, he was a man without a country. Without a family. He had never belonged to anyone— really belonged.

Coming off the train, Reginald saw a thin soldier leap off the steps from behind him and stumble into the snow. Below the man's cap, his red hair glistened in the sun. Reginald had avoided the war. Maybe that was part of his unrest, as well. Now that the war was over, the boys who came home were heroes who deserved praise. But it was not his war, he had justi- fied himself a thousand times. His own war had been formi- dable enough—making something of himself though his Indian blood had been against him. That had been his war. And he had won. Yet he felt no victory.

There had been two girls at the hotel last night. The one named Maggie who had brought the towels had seemed cold. But it was the other girl who had been with her who had smiled at him—he wasn't sure of her name. Now, as he followed the committee across the yard of the station he cleared his throat. Lately his conquests had seemed empty. Far ahead he could see the soldier boy with the red hair, running. He would have run home, too, if he had ever had a home to run to. The Summerfields had tried. Even his first adopted father, Hawk in the Tree, had tried. But his real home had always been the earth, the sky, a lean-to. And he had fought his way out of that home, until he felt suspended. What had this white man's life done for him?

When the men climbed into the car, Barrington's hat flipped into the snow. Before climbing in beside the chauffeur, Reginald picked it up and gave it to him.

"Thanks, Summerfield," Barrington said briskly. His voice emerged as a husky growl. "Come to my place first. We'll get the figures done in a couple of hours. Then you can take them to Wigginton and Pierpont tonight yourself. I don't want to meet with them at the East House Hotel." At every chance he got, Barrington railed against the hotel, repeating the story about the multi-legged creature in his soup. "You can take care of it. Just report to me if they look like they are doing business this evening." Barrington leaned back in the seat and settled himself when the chauffeur took the car down the road. "Then I want you to stick close by, Summerfield. We're hoping to put something together this weekend so we can be home by Christmas."

The roads glistened in the morning sun. Seeing the lake like a sliver of glass on the left suddenly filled him with wonder. The mountains on the right towered over them dusted by clouds. The surface looked like the warp of some precious fabric. For a brief moment he could not breathe. The land was still inside of him so deeply he could feel it pulse in his pores. He was really still a son of the earth who wanted to run to the mountain, lie on its surface and embrace it, not lower his face into the papers under the stub of pencil he always held in his hands.

The figures went faster than he dreamed. Not much later,

when he came to the East House hotel, he found it so quiet that he thought he heard the water in the pipes. The girl Maggie was seated at the desk. When she looked up, he grinned at her. But her look was wary.

He fingered his keys. "Hello," he said. "You were . . . Maggie?"

"What can I do for you?" She sounded all business. That was how she had come across last night behind the stack of towels.

"You and your friend . . ." he started.

"Sissy?"

So that was her name, Sissy.

"Where's your friend?" he said.

There was a moment of absolute silence, as though she were still trying to decide whether or not to give him the time of day.

Her voice was level, without energy. "She comes this evening."

He smiled his most winning smile. It was Sissy, then, who had seemed to respond to him. Maggie simply turned around in her chair and concentrated on sorting the mail. At the side of the desk stood a stand of newspapers. He had purchased one yesterday. He had read every word of it. He took another today. "If there's anything that goes on in this town, I guess I'll know about it, won't I?" he nodded toward her.

She glanced at him. "What?" She tried to smile. It was the smile they usually gave him for looking like an Indian— although he was not a bad-looking Indian. His nose was sharp, his eyes deep set and the whites very white under his black brows. But his hair was all Indian. Though cropped straight, a little less than shoulder length, his hair was as stiff and shiny as crow feathers. "Oh, yes. There's not much that happens in this town."

He stood for a moment at the desk. It would be a challenge to interest this girl. But she kept her eyes focused on her work. "Well, I'll be back to get this paper tomorrow. You'll see me whether you want to or not!" he laughed. When he turned away, he hated her. He had wanted to reach across the desk and take her little neck in his fingers and snap her head back—in the same way he killed the quail many years ago above the river, in the hills that lay somewhere not far from here—where he and Hawk in the Tree had stalked game and whispered stories about the old Indian man's escape from the destruction of the old village with his mother. Reginald felt suspended between two worlds—the past and the future. And often there seemed no place for him to stay.

He turned away from the girl at the desk, to let her have her white man's world that she didn't want to share with him. He thought it was ironic that just at that moment he heard the sound out in the road of some crazy wailing, gone-haywire automobile horn.

4

Mara Eastman Jones

They were waiting in the upstairs bedroom for the funeral director when Mara heard it. Though slightly hard of hearing, she jerked her head at the sound. From far away, it came—at first halting, then steady, then staccato, as though it were fighting its way through several layers of heaven.

She leaned her graying head over the still body of her friend Rain who lay silent now, her hands flat and cold. Mara felt suspended between heaven and earth, the top of her skull transparent, as though she were floating above herself where Rain still hovered in the room. The occasional words spoken by Hanson or her niece Grace seemed muffled and distant.

She gazed at the large cold head on the pillow. Rain's face was smooth and gray, her white hair pulled back from the leathery hairline. Rain had begun to slip away only yesterday, promising Mara that Hanson would come home soon. And now this morning, he had come running down the walk from the train station.

Still ringing in Mara's ears, the sound of the horn seemed slightly more distinct, now. And for a moment she felt confused. A trumpet wasn't exactly what she thought the angels would have been playing at Rain's death. An old drum would have been more appropriate—a tribal beat to gather her people to carry her home. But no Indians would gather at the sound of a drum anymore. Only ghosts of memories.

If the Indians had only been able to come from their almost total extinction, they would find themselves traveling through the center of a flourishing town—past the fountain on J Street, the Ellen Theater, the Taylor Furniture store, the Chinese laundry, and a hundred other encroachments upon their open land. The sound of a drum beating, beating, beating into this house where the Eastmans had played out their lives for so many years would only echo the changes that had taken place while the Indians had backed away, their own drums pounding, pounding, until the beat vanished into the snow beating against the window. If a drum were throbbing into this room, it might echo perhaps only a vision of Rain holding the baskets of wildflowers high over her head as she ran. Even an angel's drum would have had to rumble along under the ground, to reach the ears of the Indians who now lay along the veins of dust and leaves.

Leaning forward in the chair, Mara brushed open the rough journal in her lap. She had been reading it to remember Sobe, the Indian child she had raised, the boy with the wide dark eyes. The pages lay sprawled under her hand, October 10, 1917. Sobe had written about his Indian loved ones who had passed on:

The old world seems gone. Now Rain's daughter Samantha Tuttle is dead, and her little daughter Eliza. And her little brother Mathew gone too. We do not know how—kidnapped? We fear the worst. It is as though the Indian blood cannot flow into this new world. But it cries out for earth, the real home.

Looking up from Sobe's journal, Mara felt the tragedy of his words. Why had all the native people been destroyed? Why hadn't any of Rain's descendants—except for Grace—been able to stay and prosper in this land? What had become of all of the earth-colored people her astounded father had once discovered through his spectacles that early spring morning? The pioneer families had tried to include them. They had tried diligently. Now sixty-nine years later—it was December, 1918—Rain was the last of them. All of her children, her grandchildren, all had died before Rain—or like little Mathew, disappeared. But all the others had died: Samantha and her daughter, Eliza, had contracted the flu, Clarissa and Charles had died in the storm on the lake, and little Tommy had drowned years ago. Only Charles's daughter, Grace, remained—Grace whose cheek still lay against her grandmother's hands. Rain was the end of an era that Mara had cherished. Mara stiffened. There was that sound again.

The keening sound of the horn blared like a message from an unreal world. Could it have been from heaven? She wasn't sure. At least Rain wouldn't be bothered by it. Unless she was waiting in the room for a few moments, hovering over the three of them, watching with her somber dark eyes. "What do you know now, Rain?" Mara might have said. "What could you tell me now?" She wanted to believe that Rain, and Sobe, too, might hear her. They had probably already found each other in the spirit world. She felt they were still close by.

Mara lowered her eyes into the journal and skimmed the pages Rain had been reading before her death.

Rain told me why our people often went up into the hills to fast and ask for visions. They wanted to find Wakan Tanka, the Great Mystery. Sometimes they gouged out pieces of their arms to give as tokens. . . . They wanted to know what they were called to do in their lives. I will never forget the day I walked along the river from the school late at night under a full moon and I received my witness. It is my calling to grieve that we have been so divisive in our many worlds.

"Sobe has left this part of himself, at least," Mara thought. "They are together in heaven and earth—all of them, now." Perhaps if she listened she could hear them singing. But when she listened, all she could hear was the one clear note of the angel's trumpet.

"It's in your head," her dear old Will would have told her. How she and Will had been married so long and had stayed in such good health often seemed a miracle.

"Do you hear something?" she looked at Grace, then Hanson. Grace was still leaning against her grandmother's hands. How many times had she told stories to this black-eyed Indian granddaughter named Grace, sat with her in church, sang with her in choir practice, talked philosophy with her in the garden while they cut the asters and chrysanthemums for the hotel bouquets? Just behind Grace, Hanson still stood in his uniform, his back straight, his red beard full across his chin. How many times she had tossed bread and jam in a basket and walked with both Grace and Hanson to the park where they peeled off their stockings in little round balls to dangle their bare feet in the canal.

"Someone's motor car has a horn that's stuck," Hanson said.

So it was not in her head. It was a real trumpet, after all, although maybe not an angel's trumpet, Mara said to herself. As the horn drew nearer, she wiped her eyes quickly. Rain would not have wanted her to cry. She carefully watched as Hanson and Grace moved together to the window to see what was happening in the street.

What would happen now? Hanson could not know yet about the financial problems of his father's hotel. He would soon learn that the people who were bringing the steel mills into the town had blackballed their hotel because Mr. L. F. Barrington had found an earwig in his soup, and that the entire town had grown so fast toward the mountains that the East House Hotel was in danger of closing.

Mara had tried not to crowd worries into these final few minutes with Rain. At any moment the funeral director, Horace Hull, would be there from his east side Hull House Hotel. Though Grace was a friend of Mr. Hull, who had married her college friend Julia, Mara didn't like him much. Aware of the Eastmans' financial troubles, he seemed to approach them in a careless manner, as though the problems were not that serious. She never knew if he was joking when he said he'd sell his east side boarding house to them if Ashel and Mara Eastman wanted to buy him out. But every time he mentioned it, his words seemed more like boasting than anything else. "I'm making much better money in the funeral business now."

Mara thought buying Mr. Hull's version of the Occidental Boarding House was a splendid idea, but she had let Ashel run the finances for the past six years, and he thought Mr. Hull wanted too much money for the place he had purchased for much less from Mrs. Pulsipher years ago. Mara wondered if she ought not to find out from Ashel how things were really going. She had known for a long time that there was less and less money for investment—and then less and less money for anything at all.

Grace bent toward the window to see what Hanson had seen. "Do you know that auto?" she said.

"No," Hanson said. He stared at her. "But I think the driver might be somebody I know." At these words, the horn seemed to waver slightly in the distance. "Aunt Mara," Hanson hesitated. "I . . . hope you won't feel I am not concerned about Grandma Rain. But a friend . . . was driving down from Idaho today." He was struggling. "I think . . . I saw him drive by."

Mara saw Grace back away, and her heart fell. It was at that moment that she realized Hanson was not really with them yet, but a thousand miles away. And she wondered what they must do to bring him home. Mara returned Sobe's journal from her lap to Rain's bedside table. The last words she had read were: *The words of Jesus Christ are like the words of "Hunkayapi," our ceremony of "making of relatives." If we are all one we are all his. There are many truths from the old world. Our separate worlds must become one.* Oh, Hanson! Which world are you living in? She closed the journal and leaned on it to get to her feet. "No. No, don't worry about waiting for Mr. Hull, Hanson. If you need to go, that's fine, my dear."

She and Grace had been so distracted with Rain, they hadn't taken the time to include Hanson. And what was he thinking now? Here he had only found more death, when he had already seen so much. He had faced his own death, seen his friends die. Perhaps his friend was the one he had mentioned who had carried him to safety. Mara had been too engrossed in Sobe's words and the space beyond the veil to listen to Hanson. She shook herself into reality when she realized that Hanson was going to follow that horn, and that he really ought to take Grace with him.

When they walked out of the bedroom, Mara stopped to listen. Everything seemed quiet now. When she heard the sound of the young couple's feet on the stairs, the sound of the front door shutting, she could no longer hear the piercing horn. The automobile may have reached the garage, where old Garbett, with heavy leather gloves on his hands would have pulled a wire quickly to silence the blare. But the drum beat, Mara thought. If there had been a drum beat, it would still be pounding along the moving earth, in her own heartbeat, in the rhythm of the words Sobe had written in his journal, in the thump of Hanson's feet beating down the stairs.

Still holding the journal, Mara leaned on the table to get up, and slowly hobbled to the window. She intended to read as much of this journal as she could—this journal of her Indian boy Sobe who had been like her own child, the son of the beautiful Indian girl Blueflower who had died. But she would have to wait until she had time to read it. She believed that Sobe had much to say about reaching out to the Indians because they knew the earth. The native people had been here thousands of years before any of them. It was important to listen to their voices as they spoke from the dust. What had they learned? There would be more they could tell—even more than what was in the Book of Mormon. Sobe had learned a lot from Rain. He had always felt as though he straddled two or more separate worlds. How had he managed? He would probably have many secrets to whisper, and she would discover now all that he had to say.

Mara parted the curtains to watch the young people leave. The light snow melted on the walks, and the morning sun broke through the clouds. In a sudden flash of memory she saw

Rain as a girl, running by with her school books and waving up at the open window, running against the wind in one of Mother Eastman's roomy dresses, the thin yellow flowered skirt clinging to the brown calves. Her black braids flew behind. Rain, Rain. Now both the heaven and the earth claimed her.

As she was lost in the reveries of that old world, the light from the street blinded her for a split second. As she blinked, she saw the new limousine parked below. She had never seen anything like it: Mr. Hull's new horseless wagon—a brilliant blazing display of glass and steel. It glided quietly into the curbway at the house, swiftly serpent-like, stopping even as Hanson and Grace had closed the front door. Mara watched Mr. Hull in his green waistcoat bounce out of the limousine and onto the lawn, just as Hanson and Grace stepped out to the walkway. His bouncing walk and the streamlined funeral car irritated Mara. It seemed to be just another display of Mr. Hull's success in contrast with their own hard luck, as though, like pricking insects, the Hulls were feeding off of Eastman deaths and trials.

Mara couldn't help but think that Mr. Hull had undoubtedly been able to purchase this new hearse from all the business the Eastmans had given the funeral home these past couple of years: first Jenny, then Charles and little Willy, and Samantha and Eliza. This past summer Mr. Hull had helped them reclaim Sobe's charred bones from the fire at the woolen mill and bury them. Mara wouldn't have been surprised if she found out the Eastman business alone had paid for Mr. Hull's new hearse as well as the new Hull House Hotel he had purchased from Mrs. Pulsipher. It was possible he was doing well in both the funeral and the boarding house business at the expense of Ashel and Mara Eastman and the East House Hotel! Mara shook her head and scolded herself for bitter thoughts that were of little use to anyone.

Mr. Hull in his green waistcoat and red vest stepped briskly around the front fenders to greet Hanson who walked to him from the sidewalk. His young wife, Julia, looking slightly pregnant, followed him on cautious little feet through the patches of melting snow. She embraced Grace. In their college days at Brigham Young University, the two had been close friends.

Mara held her breath as Mr. Hull stretched out his hand to Hanson for a hearty hello. If he was into the same bit of conversation he always had with her, he would be saying, "I know your father Ashel hopes you'll salvage the East House Hotel, but I don't think you have any idea how much difficulty he is in. You certainly haven't got the business from the steel people anymore. Say, I've decided to opt for the funeral business. I've been making such a lot of money in the funeral business. What you ought to do is to buy my place and move east where the rest of the town is."

Mara had to focus to breathe. As quiet as she was, she still could not hear their words. But she could see Hanson put his hands into his pockets. He was asking Mr. Hull questions now. They were in deep conversation, Hanson standing loose, turning slightly toward the south, now lowering his head and listening to Mr. Hull's words while he looked at the ground. Grace and Julia stood beside them, busy with their own thoughts, holding each other's hands as Julia probably talked about her pregnancy. The Hulls were having their first child in the midst of all that economic windfall and luxury.

If Mara had not been so tottery and slow, she would have run downstairs to the front yard and stopped all of this at once, or if her voice had been stronger, she might have opened the window and leaned out to call to them. However, she supposed her nephew Hanson would not be protected from the awful truth about his father Ashel's distress for very long. Her worst fear was that Mr. Hull might include the detail about the earwig in Mr. Barrington's soup.

Time seemed to stand still while she waited for Mr. Hull to stop talking. Finally, Mr. Hull's wiry little assistant, Cory Weatherby, wheeled the gurney out onto the lawn while the sun broke through the December storm. Julia and Grace walked around Mr. Weatherby while Julia tucked the blankets around the sides of the cot.

For a moment Mara thought Grace and Hanson might follow Mr. Hull as he turned to come up into the room for Grandma Rain. But they did not. After a few moments, Hanson moved away from the Hulls on the sidewalk and waved good-bye. Again Julia and Grace embraced. Hanson stood still, his muscles tense as if he were straining to hear the sound of the horn that was no longer there.

"I am standing here quite helpless—nearly on the other side of the veil—in the same realm as my Indian friends, while that life down on the front lawn still goes on," Mara thought. "We are always straddling one world or another. Someone leaves us, and suddenly someone else is here in the middle of decisions, appointments, and the problems of making a living. Someone enters the lives of the young people and introduces them to real life, before one has a chance to cushion their fall. And someone drives by outside the window in an automobile with a broken horn that sounds like a warped version of the trumpet from heaven, and suddenly nothing is ever the same again."

5

Ashel Eastman

Ashel stared at the stack of bank books with conflicting feelings. The time had come; Hanson had returned. The first moments of homecoming this morning had been glorious. But now Ashel had to face the real world he had helped to create for his son. He tapped his pencil against his knuckles on his left hand. He sat unmoving, listening to Caroline grind the music box in the next room while she sat by the window in her wheelchair, waiting for Hanson to return from visiting Grace's Grandmother Rain.

He had never told Caroline how bad it was: that he had taken out mortgage loans on all three of the houses to subsidize the woolen mill and the failing East House Hotel. And when the mill had burned down in July, and nothing had come of the mining stock, and the renter he had arranged to lease the Center Street office had moved to the Markham building because it was closer to the new center of town, he had been unable to restructure their assets to satisfy their debts.

He ground the lead of his pencil down onto the empty page that lay before him, making several circles—a series of zeroes. He was too old to start over again. He knew he needed Hanson's help—and he needed it now. His son had come home just in time. Ashel was not sure exactly how Hanson was going to fit into the picture, but he knew the time for decisions had arrived—that something must be done—and soon. At one time Hanson had suggested building a theater in the Center Street space to display the new moving picture shows. But Ashel couldn't fathom it. Then there was Horace Hull's invitation to pay a fortune for the Hull House Hotel. Hanson, in one of his last letters, had encouraged his father to buy it, but Ashel felt angry about the price. When Mrs. Pulsipher had purchased the empty lot to build the Occidental Boarding House, all she had to do was climb up on a soap box and sing a song to get it from Warren Dusenberry who had purchased it from Brigham Young. Then several years ago Horace Hull had purchased the Occidental Boarding house for a few thousand dollars. And now after only a few years, he wanted twice as much. For what? For adding a few bathrooms and changing the name to Hull House Hotel. And yet he had told Will when the steel people came and refused to stay at his place, "They are outdistancing us. We are dropping behind, Will. The woolen mill is gone. Steel is taking its place. There isn't room for an old worn-out hotel on the west side. We'll either have to refurbish it or move."

Mara's husband, Will, had said, "Look, Ashel. When Hanson comes home, if I were you, I'd just buy Hull's hotel."

The light from the blank paper seemed to blind him until he could not see the figures anymore. He stopped and looked up out of the window of the back room to the right of the kitchen, where he was working at the old desk. Far across the yard, across their winter lawn and flowers, across the alley and through the raspberry bushes and the maple leaves of the back lot, he could see the broken-down back porch that barely hung to Frank Corey's small home where their huge family seemed to burst the walls. The door opened and hung crooked on the hinges as Sissy climbed the few broken steps. Looking through the winter leaves, he could barely see her covered head, the loose gray dress under the frayed fringed cape her mother had worn. She looked like a little animal darting in its natural habitat through the gray trees.

""At least I should be grateful we are still living in some comfort in our own home, while people like Frank, whose small job at the woolen mills had been part-time, are scrambling just to make a living," he thought to himself. The only long-term occupation Frank had managed to keep for years was pushing a red wooden cart from corner to corner along Center Street, crying, "Peanuts! Popcorn!"

Caroline's music box slowed to an occasional tinny note and a long series of arrhythmic pauses. "Ashel," he heard her small, high voice.

"Just a minute," he answered.

"Ashel, come here for a moment."

Ashel had believed the woolen mill would last, and so had not been as careful to hang on to their fluid resources. Instead, because he had known for a long time that there were things more important than money, he had perhaps been overly generous to the Coreys, and the Sanchezes, and several other families by making employment possible over and over again, even when it hadn't been financially wise. To help the Coreys, Ashel had hired their mother to do the housework for Caroline. And then when the mother had been burdened with so many small children, he had hired their oldest daughter Emily— everyone called her Sissy.

He watched Sissy cross the yard, picking her way through the burrs. Even now, while Sissy was still working in their house at a cost that Ashel sometimes was unsure he could bear for a month longer, he had agreed to placate her desire to hire on at the hotel if she would learn Maggie's work. And then he had agreed to hire the next daughter, Cherry, in Sissy's place here at home.

"Ashel!" Caroline's voice seemed impatient. "Something's going on! Please come and look!"

He stood from the table just as Sissy reached their back porch and opened the door to come in. She removed her wool cape, shook it out and hung it on a hook by the back door. A tightly wound red and gold bandanna covered her hair. "Sister Eastman!" she called. But when she saw Ashel at the desk close by, she stopped. "Oh! I didn't know you was home, Brother

Eastman. I would have knocked."

"It's all right, Sissy," he said. "Come on in. We need you to fix a nice breakfast. We have a surprise this morning."

"A surprise?" She stayed beside the door for a moment, staring.

"I'll let Caroline tell you," he said and turned back to his papers.

She did not come inside quickly, but took her time. Out of the corner of his eye he watched her. She tiptoed as she moved to the grate to check the fire in the stove, then glanced at him nervously. When she discovered he was looking at her, blotches of red appeared along her neck. She ducked down behind the bin to pull out the flour.

"Are you enjoying your work with Maggie at the hotel?" Ashel decided to make talk to quiet the tension. Then he decided he would take his books to the front room. "I'm coming, Caroline," he called out to assure her he hadn't forgotten.

"Who is that? " Caroline called. "Did Sissy come?"

"It's me, M'um," Sissy called back to her. "I'll be doin' the bread this mornin'. I didn't know Mr. Eastman was home." For some reason she was still flustered.

"Come in for a minute, both of you," Caroline called.

When he waited for Sissy and began to follow her into the hall, he envied her easy walk. His legs hurt him always, now. But he never said anything about legs when Caroline had not used hers for more than sixty years.

"What is it, Caroline?" he said, feeling tired in Sissy's presence. He had not really felt alive since the death of the mill. He had gone with Will to Senator Smoot to apply for government funds to rebuild, and he had seen Senator Smoot's look of despair. "But it's all we can do to host the steel people this year," Smoot had told Ashel.

When he moved close enough to the window to see, he stopped breathing for a moment, almost as if in absolute silence he could hear the answer to his questions. Instead, he found more questions.

"Why is my son—in his first hour at home—talking to Horace Hull?"

Horace was moving toward Hanson and Grace, gesturing and standing first on one foot and then the other, giving them some quick language with his tongue and some language with the tips of his fingers.

"He's talking fast," Sissy breathed. "Why is Mr. Hull on the corner?"

And when Ashel looked at Caroline's face, he saw a bleached look of panic.

"It . . . it's Rain," she whispered. "It has something to do with Rain."

When Hanson and Grace began to walk toward the house, Ashel said, "They're coming here." He waited at the window for a few moments while the young couple stopped in the walkway. Caroline reached out to touch his sleeve and he tightened his fingers around her hand.

"Don't worry," he whispered to himself as much as to the others in the room. "Everything will be fine."

6

Grace Tuttle

"Grace," Hanson stood apart from her a little. "I hope you won't mind. I need to find my friend."

She held her hand over her eyes because the sun was so bright. She couldn't see his face in the shadow. They stood in front of his father's home for a few moments, the pillars of the porch made rosier than usual by the December light. Grace thought she could feel Caroline behind the windows, anxious to see more of the son she had sent on a mission five years ago, the son who had now barely made it home from the front lines.

"I know you need to see him, but are you just going to look in garages all over town? And what about staying with your parents . . . ?"

He looked down the street. Grace remembered the lemonade business they set up in front of the Freshwater Hardware across the street when they were only nine and ten. They had asked Aunt Mara for some of her oatmeal cookies and drawn a sign with charcoal that said, "Eat here for a dime." When his friends had come down the walk on their way to the river, he had told her, "I've got to go fishing now." Suddenly the years melted away, and she was standing on the same street in the same sunshine watching him anxious to go. The light glanced off the Freshwater roof and glimmered in the last leaves on the trees. In that moment she had serious doubts that she would be able to keep him from tramping off to find his friend if he really wanted to go.

He glanced at her. "My friend . . . I owe him my life," he said. "You have no idea."

"He carried you out of Verdun." Grace had read the letter a thousand times. "Can you be sure that was him—the horn?"

"I think so." And suddenly Hanson turned to her, his eyes bright in the shadow. He reached for her hand. "Grace, forgive me if I seem anxious. Alex and I made plans . . ."

Grace felt her knees go rubbery. What about the plans she and Hanson had made? In that moment she felt she did not know him at all. Aunt Mara and even Grandmother Rain had tried to tell her he would probably need time to adjust. He would be recovering. All of them must be patient. But it looked as though it was going to be harder than she thought.

"Things are just so up in the air. I have some things to solve." Then he stopped and took her hands again. "Before we go into the house, I want to tell you about Alex. He wants to help us with the business. I know he can help us get things running."

She wanted to understand. "Of course, I understand."

"Do you?" he asked. The sunlight shone directly on his face now.

For the few moments they stood in front of the house, waiting, Grace felt a wave of nausea from the cold, or from the bright sun reflecting off the glaring snow. Or from knowing that she was feeling alone. This morning she had lost the only blood relative she knew—her Grandmother Rain. And she was not sure about Hanson now. She felt isolated from the many conflicting thoughts in his mind. He was so thin. His cheeks were drawn, and his burnished reddened hair shaggy against his beard.

"It upset you, didn't it, what Mr. Hull said about the East House Hotel?"

For a moment he did not answer. He dropped his head and ran his hand across his hair. "I'll admit I'm stunned. I feel . . . I really need to talk to Alex more than ever now."

She climbed the steps to the porch with very heavy feet. "His name is Alex?"

"You'll like Alex," he said in a voice so quiet she could barely hear him. "Before I got this news, he and I had mapped out some possible changes for the hotel business—things that would give it . . ." But he did not finish his sentence. He was looking intently up the street as though he wanted to get on with his business. Even as he had discussed the hotel business with Horace Hull, Grace had noticed that he seemed already on his way to his own world. She could not catch his eyes. She felt as though she had already been dismissed from his mind, until he totally surprised her by suddenly pressing her hands between his palms. "Tonight. Can we talk tonight? Just wait for me while I find Alex. Tonight we'll talk some more." The sun suddenly seemed bright against the white porch. "Grace, please be patient with me. There's so much . . ."

Her head spun again. She was reeling with apprehension. Then he spoke slowly, as though collecting all of the feelings, the heartaches, the longings into the only few words he could say. His eyes scanned the street, the mountains in the distance. "If you only knew . . . I have dreamed of holding your hands like this in a thousand dreams."

7

Sissy Corey

Awakened by the light through the chinks of the back porch, she felt the tangled blanket gripping her everywhere. And it frightened her for a moment until she saw her twelve-year-old brother, Chub, watching her from his cot on the other side where he was lying with little Eric, trying to keep warm.

"Do you hear someone running?" he whispered.

She listened. "Yes," she said. "Is that what that is? Someone running?"

She never dreamed that it would be Hanson Eastman—the son who had been fighting in the war. And that he had finally come home. She had twisted out of the blanket and looked out on the thin layer of snow.

"It's freezing," Chub said. "Let me have your blanket."

"Are you kidding me?" Sissy frowned. She flipped the blanket out to smooth it. "You've got Eric. All I have is myself." She got up out of the cot, wrapped herself mummy-like, and hobbled into the house. Her mother was seated on a chair at the kitchen table nursing the baby. The other children milled around in the kitchen in their nightshirts trying to get close to the stove. Cherry was feeding it with sticks and a few lumps of coal.

"Good morning, Sissy," her mother said.

"Good morning." Sissy went to the kitchen window. "I have got to hurry and there's snow," she said. "Can I use your shawl?"

"Yes," Lida Corey said softly. "Please get something to eat before you go."

But Sissy only moved quickly to the peg in the front hall,

took her mother's knit shawl, and wrapped it about her shoulders.

"Mother, I won't be home tonight. I'm working out fine with Maggie at the hotel."

"Sissy, Sissy," her mother said. "Let me look at you." And still seated at the table, she had raised her left arm and pushed Sissy's head back, looking closely at her eyes. "What is wrong with your eyes?"

"My eyes?" Sissy said.

Her mother had been quiet for a moment. "Sissy, you haven't been using lamp black on your eyes?"

"Like a common girl," her mother might have finished, for Sissy knew these words were in her mouth. But Sissy did not hear them. She froze, believing she had wiped it away last night before she came home. And that she would always be able to wipe it away. But she would not go without it now. It had made something magic happen when she had gone with Maggie to take the towels to the man upstairs. It had given her power.

By now she had turned to the back door to go, and she glanced in the glass. "The stove at Eastman's is black, and I rubbed the smoke out of my eyes," she lied. Her mother could not stop her. The light from the lantern on the stove in the gray room flickered against her face.

"It looks like lamp black," her mother said. And she looked Sissy through as though she could see everything there. "Oh, Sissy," she sighed. "You are growing up into a woman."

Sissy stayed at the door where she could see her face, her cheeks round and her hair a mound of rusty curls all over her head. She did not turn to speak to her mother. She spoke to her image in the glass without moving anything but her lips.

"As long as I am making money, please, you don't need to worry about me. The hotel will give tips."

"Do they tip you?"

As clear as though he were before her, she saw the light-colored Indian man with the black, black hair. He had smiled at her. But there was no money. Not yet.

"Not everyone, Mother. But some give me money."

Finally her mother had been quiet. Sissy wrapped her hair in a bandanna, still looking in the glass, and then she had opened the door of the house and left the porch. In front of the Eastman home she saw Grace standing on the walk talking with a tall, thin man in uniform who looked weighted under a head of shaggy, strawberry-brown hair. She looked again more closely. There was only one person on earth who would be holding Grace's hand. How many thousands of days had she followed her father's peanut cart into the dusty twilight out on Center Street when most of the men were coming home from their work at the woolen mills, and while her father sold popcorn and peanuts to the hungry workers, she had watched Grace running to greet Mr. Ashel and Uncle Will. And how Sissy had envied her—for always running at her side had been this wonderful fair-haired boy who could ice skate and throw a ball better than anyone she had ever known. He had always been tall and strong and kind. He had befriended her several times, though her family was poor. Finally, after he had left them for so long, all of them had wondered if ever he would come home again. And now! Hanson, the Eastman son, who had gone away when she was only eleven years old—Hanson, her friend! He was home!

8

Mara Eastman Jones

"Being in love isn't what's important. Love can grow," Will said when Mara told him she was worried about Hanson and Grace. "The best marriages in the world were made by Jewish parents who made lists."

Mara knew Will was right, but she had wanted the two young people to "be in love." She looked at Will, his handsome shaggy brows. She certainly hadn't cared as much for him those many years ago as she cared for him now.

He smiled at her. "Don't worry about them. It'll all work out."

Mara glanced at him. "How do you know?"

"I just know." Will was grinning.

"You have something up your sleeve?"

"Hmm." Will was dodging her.

"Maybe something about Ashel—maybe something about the Hull House Hotel?"

Will was cagey. He glared at the paper he was reading. But he could not hold back the grin emerging around his eyes. "Hmm. Maybe. Maybe I think Ashel is seriously thinking about buying the Hull House Hotel."

"Really?" Mara turned to face him.

"Well, he said he had an idea about how we could do it just the other day."

Mara's heart quickened. "You know, that might be good for all of us." She felt excitement, though she knew that with their troubled finances it would be a serious move.

"It's not time to worry about Grace and Hanson. Let's just

take care of what's at hand—get one thing taken care of at a time. First here."

Mara looked down at Rain's boxes they had taken out of the old broom closet and spread out on the floor. Sobe's journal lay on the table. "It seems like Rain was from a different time and place," Mara whispered. It seemed to be a world she strangely wanted to hold to, because she wasn't sure anyone else would care. But she knew life was a series of hellos and good-byes. Now she must somehow find the strength to say good-bye to her Indians as she knew them, and "hello" to some new struggles she knew they would all have to face—struggles she could not yet name, that seemed threatening: the world moving so rapidly that it promised to leave her behind. A sharper world—of machines, loud noises, and speed. A world that no longer needed Rain—or her.

As she lifted one of the boxes, the musty smell threw Will back with a scowl. "Whew!" he said.

"Just look at this! This is Rain's life," Mara said more to herself than to Will.

Uncle Will retreated almost as far as the kitchen door and made a comical face.

Mara separated each of the old cigar boxes that stood in a stack—Red Seal Cigars and Duke's Mixture, along with Del Flora de Juan Portuogo. Below the cigar boxes under a pack of books, pamphlets, and magazines was the wooden apple crate. The words on the crate had been worn away.

First, thumbing through the stack of old papers, she found a 1917 copy of the *Breeder's Gazette* decorated with a picture of two horses that looked like they were talking to each other over a short barn doorway, and an April 1916 copy of *The Relief Society Magazine* with an article by Eliza R. Snow entitled "The Mother of Mothers in Israel," a sonnet by Alfred Lambourne, and "The Wondrous Woman's Book" by Ida Harper.

"Look at this, Will!" She thumbed through the papers quickly.

"I'll just stay here!" he called back.

"Oh my goodness! Who would have thought Rain's things would have lain here all these years!"

After she put the stack of magazines on the table, she leaned to look at the crate. Through the slats she could see there were only two foot-high metal cans packed inside—one that used to contain Sego Lily Brand Pure Refined Lard and the other, Calumet Baking Powder.

The crate wasn't heavy—about twelve to fifteen pounds. She lifted it easily by herself to the table. When she shoved the empty cigar boxes back into the dark broom closet where she had found everything, she closed the door and called out to Will, "I've shut up the closet now; you can come back."

"Never mind. I'll read *The Wall Street Journal*. I think something too old is still in the air."

Well, old Will wasn't much good at straddling the old and the new, Mara thought. She hovered over the open crate, and reached inside to slip the cans out to the table. So these were Rain's treasures! She felt a sudden start touching the cans, as though she were still sitting on the hearth with Rain's deerskin pouch on her lap, the beads in her fingers.

"Oh look, look, look!" she murmured, mostly to herself. When she lifted the lid of the lard can, she found an old deerskin pouch she had remembered in Rain's hands years ago, worn and withered, lying across the top of everything else, with two blue beads still tied into the leather thong. It was the same little purse Rain carried when she had first come!

Rain! The vision of Rain as a young girl came so forcefully into the room, she half expected that when she raised her eyes, Rain would be standing there before her. But it was her old Will. Curious, he had hobbled back into the room and leaned on the table.

"Oh look, look, look," Mara whispered. "Do you think I dare?" She stroked the deerskin with her fingers.

"She'd rather have you look it all over than Mr. Seedham in

the Deseret Industries."

Mara looked up at Will. "Do you know how valuable some of these things may be?"

"Artifacts," Will said, coming around the edge of the table to peer into the box. And he added, "Ooof! It still smells mighty strong."

When she lifted the deerskin pouch out of the can, she took the blue beads in her hands and drew the top of the pouch along the leather strings carefully so as not to break the deerskin—now almost a transparent gray, like paper. She brought out a couple of old thorns and feathers that had been inside the bag and lay them on the table. "These are the old things from Rain's childhood, all right! She had saved the beads and thorns that had broken off Blueflower's necklace."

Under the deerskin bag, Mara found a large, dried, brown seed pod with two circles or horns that looked like circular knitting needles, a bottle of Gombault's Caustic Balsam, and a package of Crystal White Soap. In another little bag was a collection of arrowheads, a necklace of beads and a shiny black arrowhead, a whistle on a leather string, and a stick attached by a string to the tiny white skull of a bird.

"I remember this!" Mara whispered in wonder. "Rain taught us to play this game! The Indians played it. You bounce the little skull on the string until it lands on the top of the stick."

She felt Rain's eyes somewhere close and visible. Below the bag of arrowheads was a small enclosed watermelon-shaped basket tied on the outer two points with leather string.

"What is this?" Uncle Will said, still with Mara, though he appeared to be suffering, sometimes wiping down his watery eyes with his handkerchief. But Mara was glad to have him here.

"One of their baskets," Mara whispered. "I don't know."

Around the tiny mouth on the side of the basket was a rim of dark-colored straw of some kind woven around the frame for decoration. She held the little basket in her hands like a ball.

They had made baskets for hours each day, Rain and Spirit of Earth, working while Mara and her mother had pulled weeds or washed and hung sheets out on the lines.

"Do you remember what kinds of baskets they made?" Will asked.

"Some of them were much larger," Mara said. Perhaps this was the only basket Rain had saved.

Under the basket Mara found a small hard painted leather cup, a comb and a stone ladle. In the Calumet Baking Powder can they found a flat smooth stone, a small pair of beaded moccasins and a beaded bag wrapped around a strange-looking root, bulky and dark, with small wiry roots growing out of it like sharp wire or thick hair. Mara believed the tiny bag was a medicine bag. Had she seen this bag? She couldn't remember.

Against the side of the can was a notched stick with another stick attached at the top, like a toy propeller. She had never seen most of these things.

"Not much there, really," Will said.

But Mara disagreed. She carefully laid the treasures out on the table. "To Rain they were precious. Because of what they meant to her. She loved the ways of her own people. And it is things that remind us of others."

Now she remembered seeing the medicine bag in Rain's hands one day after Rain had become a polygamous wife and lived in the canyon with Mr. Richard's insensitive family nearby. When Rain's boy, Tommy, had drowned in the water hole, Rain had carried this little bag in her hands for a long time. She had been carrying it when they came to the house to take Tommy's body away. Her belief in the medicine had been what gave her strength. And because she had the strength, how had it mattered how she had received it? The physical world connected the spiritual. Words and books, the temple—even the sacrament could do that. Substance simulated life.

"Well, of course they meant something to somebody," Will leaned over and peered through his spectacles. "But to most people they just look like a bunch of old things."

"Say," Mara said, "if you ask me, to most people you look like an old thing."

"What, eh?"

"You're water and mineral deposits. A little salt. Well, a lot of salt."

"Well, I haven't left this old thing yet." He pounded his chest.

"Well, I haven't left these old things," Mara covered Rain's treasures with her hands. "And as long as I don't, there's still something valuable yet in them."

9

Grace Tuttle

Exhausted after helping Sissy with the morning meal, after Hanson's departure to find his friend Alex, Grace lay on the small bed in the back room to the south of the kitchen meant for the hired girls—if they had not lived so close. Yes, she could stay with them in the back room, Ashel had said, smiling. And Caroline had nodded and held Grace in her arms.

Without taking off her dress, even her shoes, she lay on a coverlet she had seen a thousand times in Grandpa Eastman's home, and she covered her eyes with the back of her hand to block out the gray light. The sun had come out and the snow in the garden outside the back window had melted. The raspberry bushes, the tangled vines emitted a feeble December glow, as though everything alive promised to wait.

She was surprised to find that she had slept the afternoon away and that Uncle Ashel was standing at the door. She could hear his words only vaguely. He was saying Sissy was still here, but would Grace mind helping with the potatoes? "Are you awake?" he was asking.

Her door opened. Grace sat up quickly. Through the doorway, beyond Ashel in the hall, she could see two men talking. Hanson, and . . .

"Ashel!" It was Caroline's small voice from the front bedroom where she had also been napping. "Please help me into the wheelchair. I'll supervise the supper."

"He's here," Ashel said quietly.

"Who's here?" Grace felt her heart pounding.

"Hanson's friend, Mr. Hunt."

"Grace, darling!" Caroline called out. Grace could barely hear her. "Help me. We need to get the supper."

Grace rose out of the bed so quickly she blacked out behind her eyes. "Okay, Uncle Ashel. I'm coming."

When he left the doorway, she could hear Caroline's voice, still. "The potatoes. They are in the cellar. Is Sissy here? She can make pie. We had some pumpkins and a bushel of apples. Fry the hominy." Caroline was in the hall now.

"Sissy already made pies," Ashel told her. "We don't have hominy. Hanson ate the last of it before he bathed."

Grace thought she was hearing things. Had she really slept through a couple of hours while Hanson had returned to the house and bathed? She waited for a moment to orient herself, to find out where she was. She felt a new sense of self-possession when she came up from sleep, as though she were reborn from a deep sea.

"Bring in the corn and put it on to boil. We'll have corn."

But before she left the room, Grace stood at the mirror. Her eyes had swollen in her sleep. She used Caroline's brush to smooth down the wings of her burnished hair. The only hint of Indian in her face manifested itself in the high cheek bones and the wide swollen mouth. Her hair had been black for years, but was softening now into a reddish tint like that of her father, whom she had never known. The hazel eyes were deep-set below heavy dark brows. She smoothed the sleep from her eyes, but it still looked as though she had been crying. She brushed the wrinkles out of her dress.

"Hello, hello, Mr. Hunt, I'm glad to meet you," she could hear Caroline say as Ashel wheeled her into the front room. "We're so glad you could be here on this special day. Set the table for seven. Mara and Will are coming, too," she instructed Ashel.

Ashel left for the kitchen while Caroline drew close to the boys in the parlor. Grace could hear her small gentle voice. "Tell me about yourself," she was saying.

Grace hesitated at the door of the bedroom.

"Come on in, Grace, darling," Caroline called. "Come and meet Hanson's friend."

The room seemed to rock with light. When she looked up, the first person she saw was Hanson. He had shaved his beard. He looked so different. Slick against his brow, his red brown hair gleamed with the light from the window. His ruddy cheeks glowed beneath his brilliant blue eyes.

Both he and his friend stood up from their chairs when Grace came into the room. She forced her eyes away from Hanson to take in his friend. The young man rose quickly. Out of habit, Grace extended her hand. He was very tall—a large young man with a fair complexion, a head of bright shining hair. From the moment she first looked at him she saw something in his eyes she had not often seen, and she was afraid to look too closely, for the power in his eyes moved her.

"So this is your Grace, Hanson?" Alex Hunt said. His voice, thick in his throat, startled her. When he cleared his throat, his voice resonated with something like music. "She's absolutely beautiful."

For a long moment all of them stood in the room locked into a breathless instant, staring at Alex. He had been forward, yet there was a hush as though magic hovered in the room. Grace felt something so powerful that she imagined Alex Hunt was reaching out to her to hold her hand.

"It's the eyes. Something is in the eyes of someone who is in love," Alex Hunt smiled.

Hanson looked at Alex while Alex looked at Grace. "Yes, she's beautiful," he said.

"Our princess," Caroline said swiftly, watching Hanson's face. Hanson seemed puzzled by the thickness in the room while his mother continued in her tiny voice. "Shall we be seated? Now, Mr. Hunt, what is this I hear about you and Hanson? Has Ashel talked to you this morning?"

"We've talked, Mother," Hanson looked directly at his

mother. He walked to the sofa when Alex let go of Grace's hand. Grace stepped back and sat on a chair. "If we can make it work out, Alex is going to help me manage the hotel."

Caroline did not respond at once. She gazed at Alex and smiled. "Where are you from, Mr. Hunt?"

When Alex began to answer, Hanson interrupted. "His father is the largest land owner in Idaho—some three hundred thousand acres. His father is interested in investing in Utah."

"My father is a friend of L. F. Barrington," Mr. Hunt spoke softly. If the name should have registered with Caroline, it did not.

"Remember, Mother?" Hanson seemed nervous. "He was the one who found an earwig in his soup and got angry at our hotel."

"My father is an investor. Mr. Barrington is in steel," Alex said.

There was a moment when Grace saw his eyes flicker as he met her gaze. Then he looked quickly away. Her face felt hot. She looked at Hanson. He was hanging on to every word from Mr. Hunt's mouth. "My father was reared in Idaho, but nearly lost his life as a child. He was so ill they thought he would die, but he fought back and became a millionaire."

Grace could not tear her eyes away from Alex's face as he spoke. His mouth worked slowly; the husky sound in his throat mesmerized her.

"And he wants to invest in Utah County?" The silence was thick with anticipation. Caroline rubbed the arm of her wheelchair with her thumb. She looked at Hanson. "Do you know this man in Idaho?"

Hanson seemed uncomfortable. "No, Mother. But I know Alex. He's my friend. He carried me out of the front lines at Verdun."

Caroline nodded. "Yes! Yes, Alex. I cannot tell you of our gratitude to you," she began. But even in her moment of gratitude, Caroline seemed preoccupied not with the past, but with the future—perhaps because the future was facing them with such force in these few moments of planning—more forcefully than it ever had before. Because the hotel was dying, Hanson and Ashel would have much to recover, many decisions to make about how much to remodel, what kinds of services to add or maintain. And in the midst of their problems there were conflicting feelings: about this unknown Alex Hunt becoming an employee at a time they were trying to keep from hiring anyone new, about Barrington with his plans to bring the world's problems here with the steel industry. Economy was one thing, but the inundation of the elements of the world was another. Already—even since the army had camped too close—there were unpleasant problems in the city: numerous saloons, robberies, vagrants.

Caroline took one thing at a time. "Does your father know you are going to work with Hanson?"

Alex Hunt was charming. He broke the tension in the room with a smile. "In spite of a shifting center of town, Mr. Eastman is known to be very knowledgeable about the hotel business. My father would be thrilled to learn that I will be his student for a few months."

Hanson watched his mother. She relaxed a little. She seemed more impressed with Alex by now. She had even been "honored" to introduce "Hanson's rescuer friend" when Mara and Will came to the door. When Mara and Will seemed impressed and excited to meet Hanson's friend, Caroline's last reservations subsided.

At that moment Ashel called. "We're ready to set up the supper now," he said. Grace rose, puzzled at what she could not put her finger on in that crowded room—a feeling, an intensity. She excused herself to set the table.

Ashel had supervised the supper with the help of the Corey girl who had taken her mother's job at the Eastman house. She was not very efficient, really, but she worked doggedly. As she stood over the stove, Grace could see that she was sweating beneath her bandanna, the drops running down into her eyes and onto her cheeks. As soon as the table was set, Grace offered to help Sissy carry the food into the room: pickles, a large pan of scalloped potatoes, ham, and cheese. Grace finally set the salt and pepper shakers on the table, hurrying to finish before Hanson and Alex wheeled Caroline to her place.

Ashel sat at the head of the table and asked Sissy to bring the Brigham tea before she was excused. After she set the tea tray on the table, she stood beside Ashel and asked if there was anything else. "Not now, Sissy," he said kindly. "You may go."

But for a moment Sissy did not go. Standing at the buffet beside Hanson's chair, she stayed for what seemed like forever, her eyes fastened on Hanson. It was almost as though she wished to speak to him, but could not say what she wanted to say. Then suddenly, seeing Grace's eyes on her, she ripped the bandanna from her head. Grace was embarrassed. The girl's snarled mass of hair fell around her hot face. When she finally backed away, she untied her apron, rolled it into a ball, and stuffed it into the bureau drawer there in the dining room. Everyone was silent. When the back screen door banged shut, Mr. Eastman explained to Alex, "Her father is a street vendor. Seven children and nothing but popcorn and peanuts." Without skipping a beat, he looked around the table until his eyes rested on Hanson. "This is the moment we have hoped to share for years. We are so grateful. Hanson is back with us. We are going to improve the hotel." Ashel was smiling broadly. "We have so many thanks to give." He bowed his head and began to pray. "Dear Heavenly Father. How may we thank you for this day? Our hearts are filled with gratitude for the safe arrival of Hanson."

Grace opened her eyes during the prayer. She couldn't resist it. Alex Hunt was looking at her. He shut his eyes at once and Grace felt the blood pound under the roots of her hair.

At the table, Alex Hunt was charming. He spoke easily, sometimes boldly, approaching subjects the others had learned to avoid. However, he graciously deferred to Ashel and Caroline when they spoke, asked to be pardoned, and used impeccable manners. Most of the talk was about business.

"The steel industry in America has tripled during the war."

Will sat at the corner of the table beside Ashel, hiding behind the bouquet of leaves. He was still notoriously against building steel mills in Utah. Everyone knew he was still hurting from the summer fire that had destroyed the woolen mills, and though his dream was to rebuild, his petition to Senator Smoot for government money had not been gratified. Sometimes it seemed Uncle Will could talk of little else, so no one liked to mention it when he was around. At the mention of the steel mills, Ashel, too, stiffened. The fire at the mill had destroyed him also, and the steel people weren't helping, especially when Barrington had boycotted the East House Hotel.

But Alex Hunt did not choose his words to placate Ashel or Uncle Will. "The future is in steel," he said, taking another helping of scalloped potatoes. "Maybe Brigham Young wasn't successful in Iron County, but Pierpont and Barrington will be successful here." He spoke of the Iron Mission near Cedar City which had failed in 1858. "You have the ideal situation here— plenty of transportation and labor."

There was a profound silence until Caroline said in her small voice, "Have you been to the park yet, Mr. Hunt? Did you take him to the park, Hanson? There are ducks in the pond. Mara, will you please pass the corn?"

Mara passed the corn and said, "We have an empty house where Grace took care of Rain—the old Eastman home. If you like, Mr. Hunt, you are welcome to stay there."

"Oh, thank you, Mrs. Jones," Alex smiled graciously. "But since I drove Barrington down, I think he has reserved a place for me at the old Occidental Boarding House."

"The Hull House Hotel?"

Alex Hunt ascertained the situation at once. There was a rivalry here. "You needn't worry about the Hull House Hotel,

Mr. Eastman. It doesn't compare with your facility. Barrington is eccentric. He knows it." In a moment, dabbing his napkin to his face, he quickly looked up at Mara and said, "Well, of course, I don't know . . . I would not want to cause any inconvenience."

"You would be welcome there. You could use it for a headquarters. Grace—and of course Rain—will no longer be living there. Grace is staying with us," Caroline said.

"The Hull place is either fixing to be remodeled into a mortuary or becoming a branch of the East House Hotel." Uncle Will tipped up his soup spoon. The words and the sound of the soup startled Grace, who looked at the faces surrounding her.

"All it will take is a little foresight and a little of our cash too . . ." said Uncle Will.

Ashel's face suddenly turned white. "You've spoken to him again?" he said to Uncle Will. "That ambitious scoundrel Hull," he added quietly.

Grace looked at the others. They were used to Ashel's refusal to give up on the East House Hotel or to entertain the thought of buying out Hull. But the tension was something no one could get used to. For a moment she wished she were far away from here. She thought about her Grandmother Rain. Rain was lying in Robert Hull's special quarters at the Hull place at this moment, her hands stiff by her side, her large face broad and pale. She was saved from all of this now, her dear Grandmother Rain.

"Which reminds me, we have a funeral to plan," Mara said. "Yes, we should drop these touchy subjects and be talking about what we will do tomorrow." Caroline put her hand on Ashel's arm.

Alex Hunt, perhaps unconsciously, perhaps consciously, Grace could not tell, moved his chair back an inch. He flourished his napkin. He was still smiling, his face smooth. "I have a feeling I'm here at a bad time. Maybe I'd better not stay.

Anyway, I need to get with Mr. Barrington. I just feel I'm in the way of some important family business that . . ." He did not finish.

Hanson quickly moved his chair closer to Alex's and half standing, put his hand on Alex's arm. "You'll do nothing of the kind. You and I still have our plans to talk over. And our family problems don't have anything to do with it."

Ashel put up his hand. "Sit down, Hanson." For a moment there was a cloud in the room.

Grace felt it. She got up from the table and began to collect the dishes. "Would you like pumpkin or raspberry pie? Pumpkin pie, Mara? Or raspberry?"

"I'll have raspberry, thank you, Grace. No, Alex, we are very serious," Mara continued. "There is no one using the house right now. Please. I will feel very sad if you do not use it. You are welcome also to offer it to Mr. Barrington."

Will's head, lowered over a last bite of potatoes, bobbed as he choked lightly. "I guarantee you will hear the ducks in the morning."

But Mara laughed. "The ducks won't squawk if you feed them!"

Some of the tension went out of the room. Alex gazed at Aunt Mara as though he was taken back with her fervor. He had pulled his chair close to the table again. "Well, if you insist, then. I think I'd like that."

"Then it's settled. Mr. Hunt will stay at the house. And if Mr. Barrington wants to stay there, he is welcome." Mara was smiling. She gathered up the last few plates at the table and handed them to Grace, who ducked into the kitchen.

Grace stoked the coals in the stove and set the pan of dish water over the fire. She sliced through Caroline's delicious pumpkin pie with a sharp knife. She was not sure what was happening. But the day of Hanson's return was not as she had always imagined. Her heart was leaping around inside of her as though it were not attached. When she walked back to the table with the pie, Alex Hunt was looking directly at her, raising his water glass to the chandelier and toasting the meal.

"I want to express my gratitude for this delightful company, and for the meal," Alex was saying. "It has been a wonderful supper. To you, Miss Grace, and to your fiancé Hanson, and to his delightful parents and aunt and uncle. This has been a most profitable day."

Grace suddenly felt warm. The color that came up into her cheeks ripened in her lips. She looked at Hanson. He was concentrating on his pie. She turned back into the kitchen to get the rest of the desserts. Alex had said Hanson was her fiancé. But they were not entirely engaged yet. Hanson had said nothing.

"We shall make a toast to Grace's Grandmother Rain," Aunt Mara said. "I wish you could have been with her these last few years, Hanson. She reminded all of us that the earth is where we live—the land with its grass and flowers. She was used to wresting her living from the land itself." Aunt Mara paused. "That time is fast disappearing."

Where was the earth now? Grace thought to herself on her way back to the table with the last pieces of pie. It was somewhere below layers of gravel and macadam, and floors of wood and steel—somewhere too deep to be experienced, except perhaps in their own heartbeats, like the drums she had heard the Indians beat in the hills when she was small. She had heard from her Grandmother Rain of the legends of a fourth world for her people. It was a world above the underworld which they inhabited for a long time. Was there now a fifth world—a place safe from all that stood between them and the ground—all this industry and steel?

"Give the earth the credit that is due. It is just yielding more of its gifts to us now—ore, glass, grout, and tile." Hanson raised his glass with Alex. Grace's heart raced when she looked at them both. They were laughing as they tapped their glasses and the water leaped at the impact. No, she didn't know Hanson at all anymore. He was different. The war, no doubt. This was the first day. Give him time. Give him time.

Ashel smiled and nodded. He raised his glass reluctantly. "You cannot stop progress," he said dryly.

Uncle Will and Aunt Mara nodded. "As long as our progress is really progress," Aunt Mara smiled.

10

Grace Tuttle

Grace was uneasy, not knowing when Hanson would talk with her that evening, or if he would talk with her at all. Alex Hunt stayed and stayed. Finally, as the sun sank behind the piece of wall that had begun rising in the west, Hanson asked her to walk with him and Alex to the park. She was frustrated he had forgotten they were to talk. But she would never have thought of excluding Hanson's friend.

First they stopped at the shiny new Ford parked out on the street, so Alex could make sure his valise was still inside of the car, and the doors locked. He and Hanson inspected the motor and kicked the tires. Then Alex rummaged around in the back seat of the car and pulled out a raccoon coat. Grace watched fascinated while he juggled it beneath his chin. It was so large that it buried him.

He followed Grace and Hanson to the porch of the big old Eastman house on the corner, where Grace unlocked the door and inspected the linen in the rooms while Alex and Hanson reviewed the war. Finally, at about the time the sun set, the three of them bundled up in their wraps and walked out into the cold. Grace thought Alex Hunt looked like a bear.

The snow that had melted in the afternoon left the streets washed clean. Grace carried a bag of old bread in her hands.

"The sky is the color of peaches," Alex observed. "It reminds me of your cheeks." He turned to Grace and smiled. "Ever heard of the old saying 'Your face is like a sunset, your eyes are like the sun . . .'" It was a poem, but he left it unfinished. He was laughing.

"No, but I've heard the saying 'Your nose is like a river; it runs,'" Hanson teased.

Alex broke into laughter, slapping his thigh with his glove. He changed the subject. "Have you ever been on a river raft? They use these river rafts in Idaho that bob downstream like a cork. You don't ride on them without getting wet."

"We had enough wet here to last several lifetimes," Hanson said. "Too much lake—swallowed up people." Grace had been a baby when her parents were killed on the lake. Though it had been the most terrible event of the family's history, it was perhaps now a sign of healing that Hanson had mentioned it only in passing.

Alex's face took on appropriate expressions at once with no time wasted. "Oh, I'm sorry," he said quickly. "And so you were raised by this Grandmother Rain Hanson told me about?" he turned to Grace.

"Oh, everybody," Grace said. She had never known anybody like Alex Hunt. He was intensely with her in every word he spoke. His eyes were riveted to her for this moment. She drank in his attention, not knowing why. Hanson was walking beside her with his hands in his pockets. "Everyone. My Grandfather Sobe—and Aunt Mara and Uncle Will, too. Caroline and Ashel, Hanson's parents. Grandma Nancy and Grandpa Sully, who have passed away."

Alex began to smile again. "Well, if they raised you, they did a good job," he said. He reached out with his fingers and pinched her cheek lightly. Grace backed away from his touch, surprised. She was not sure how she felt, though she thought he was funny. And yes, a little bit wonderful.

He was not finished saying all he wanted to say. When he focused his smile on her, it was a very genuine smile. "Hanson, what a lucky dog you are," he said. Then he turned swiftly and leaped over the irrigation ditch. "I can tell this is going to be the time of our lives!"

At the park, Grace hugged the bag of bread close in her

arms. She was fascinated as she watched Hanson and Alex Hunt. They were both so intensely interesting to her. She watched them walk to the cannon where they read the words slowly in the twilight. "In commemoration of the long years of hostilities with the Indians, and the Utah War."

"Give me a home, where the natives don't roam!" Alex sang at the top of his lungs.

"Do you remember that time we heard the German girls on the Rhine singing 'America the Beautiful,' Hanson then said, reminiscing, "and you took one of them to the parsonage and gave her a scare?"

"She thought she was going to marry me!" Alex hit his thigh with his gloves again. He put his head back when he laughed. His white teeth shone in his mouth like big pearls. "The problem was that the father who owned the saloon wanted to shotgun me."

"She wasn't . . ."

"I know it. But did her father know it?" Alex's mouth opened again, and the laughter pealed through the trees.

At the pond, Grace took the bread out of the bag. "They were wild ducks at first. They ate the bugs in the water, and the moss. They used to leave in the winter. As soon as we started feeding them they stayed around."

"Oh my gosh," Alex leaned down at the edge of the pond. "They're tame mallards—very pretty, green-wing teal! Look at that. They're coming up to you! Do they know you? Good-bye, they look like cousin Henry and his boat crew! Here, ducky ducky. You have names for them?"

"This one is the mother. But she's smaller than the others now. She used to be the largest one. We fed them grain. Then we fed them bread. They grew so fast."

Grace broke off the bread and gave pieces of it to Hanson and Alex. Hanson threw his piece into the water. The ducks smashed heads with one another as they leaped for it.

"Oh my gosh. Look at that!" Alex exclaimed. "They all

wanted it. They bashed heads."

"That's life!" Hanson said philosophically, his hands back in his pockets. "The more ducks there are after the same piece of bread—the more heads crash."

"I could make a verse out of that. Bread heads. Dead heads. Here ducky, ducky. Look at the broad bill. And the color of the lower jaw—the distance in the mouth!" Alex broke his bread into small pieces and tossed them into the black water one by one. The ducks skirmished for each piece with absolute terror. If one of them had it, another would follow him until it disappeared into his gullet. "My grandfather was a wizard, he always used to quote that scripture 'Cast your bread upon the waters. . . ,' you know the one. He used to say 'Cast your bread upon the water and the ducks'll eat it.'"

"It's supposed to be 'Cast your bread upon the waters and it will come back to you.'"

"What the heck does that mean?" Alex said.

Grace broke the bread again, and Alex took it out of her hand without looking at her face.

"It means whatever you give will be returned to you," Hanson said, tossing another large piece into the water and watching the scramble.

Grace tore up the bread in her hands and tossed the pieces in all at once. The ducks turned around swiftly in the stream, backing up and ducking to retrieve the bits wherever they landed. There was no way to keep them from jabbing each other. The bread disappeared as soon as it hit the water. They lanced one another with their sharp bills after an extra piece.

"Why did you start feeding them? Why didn't you let them just keep eating the mosquitoes?"

"I think there's a Christmas dinner or two here. Am I right?" Hanson looked at Grace furtively.

Grace laughed, "Maybe." She tossed her brightest glance at him. It was a strange time of mixed emotions. She had never been so ill at ease as in the presence of the two young men, yet she had never felt such excitement.

"Not a good Christmas dinner!" Alex got serious suddenly. "You ever eat duck? Tough as leather. I'm gonna get you a turkey. Turkey's got it all over duck. You ever had grain-fed turkey?"

"We used to have turkey." Hanson looked at Grace. In a brief moment he was caught up in her eyes. "You had turkey the last few years?" he asked her. He was looking at her now. He was smiling. He reached out and touched her fingers when he took another piece of bread.

Grace could feel the touch in her head. "Dr. Hopkins sells us his turkeys," she smiled. "We'll have a turkey. Hold your horses."

"Hold your turkeys." Alex tossed another handful of bread into the pond. The ducks went wild. "Give me turkey! Turkey, turkey!" The ducks bobbed and lashed out, and squawked.

Grace laughed at Alex. "They don't like being called turkeys."

When the bread was gone, Grace walked to First North and E Street with Hanson and Alex to show Alex the exterior of the East House Hotel. For a few moments they stood outside of the broad doors and watched the people inside the large windows. A few pine boughs decorated with holly were looped in the curtain rods. The tables, set with silver and glassware, glowed under the crystal lamps. Two large men sat near the window in high sheen wool waistcoats. One smoked a large cigar. The other was bent over some papers on the table, writing vigorously with a quill pen.

"That's him," Alex said. "I'll be jeebered. That's him, all right. You ever knew a man with the first name Wigginton?"

"That's his name?"

"His mother named him Wigginton," Alex said. "And the fellow signing the papers is old Pierpont as sure as I'm Hunt."

"So, what's up?"

"Pierpont is the only one at the present time who is making

steel in Provo."

Grace waited, holding her arms with her gloved hands, beginning to feel the cold. She watched the employees of the East House Hotel through the window, remembering when she worked for Ashel. She was glad to see that some of the local steel people still frequented their East House Hotel, even if Mr. Barrington would not be there. Maggie Hammond, who waited tables, was taking orders from the two gentlemen near the street. Feeling uncomfortable staring, Grace moved toward the door.

"Do you want to go in?" She looked back at Alex. He had taken off his gloves. He held them between his teeth. He was warming his hands by hitting the palms together, blowing on them.

"Do you want to go in?" Hanson asked Hunt.

"I don't think so. No. I don't want to interfere with what Wigginton Creed and Pierpont are doing."

"What are they doing?"

"Rumor is they're drawing up the documents for Barrington—who is determined to purchase four hundred acres between Springville and Provo, to build the rails, and in short, undertake all the tasks that go into the production of steel."

"Are you sure?" Hanson asked him.

"Not sure of anything. Just sure I don't want to be in the middle of it."

From where she stood closer to the door, Grace saw Maggie in the front corner of the dining room. She was waiting on a girl with a mass of straw-colored hair. Grace pulled back. The girl looked familiar! And across from the table, with his back to the girl, was a huge man in a greatcoat and boots tapping on a walking stick. She was struck at once by the thickness and the blue-black color of his hair.

She could not see the man's face, but she would have recognized Sissy Corey anywhere. Sissy Corey was having dinner with a stranger! Her heart leaped up into her mouth. She didn't want to believe what she was seeing. Sissy was too young for these steel men. Her mother would have been sick with worry. But she realized she was making assumptions. Quickly drawing away, she remained at the door, puzzling at the presence of Sissy seated with such a large strange man in the dining room of the hotel. She thought about it until Hanson spoke.

"Are you ready to take a tour from the Freshwater Hardware to the Schwab?"

"I've seen the Freshwater and Schwab about three times driving the streets all afternoon looking for you," Alex said.

"Maybe it's just me. I want to see what's changed. What's changed, Gracie?"

Grace brought herself up out of her reverie. "They were going to transform the Opera House into an armory," she said, trying to sound matter-of-fact. "The high school finally has grades up to twelve."

"And you were seven!" Hanson smiled at her.

"Seven?" Alex asked.

"I was seven."

"What on earth does that mean?" Alex said. "I was seven once."

The way he looked at her made Grace laugh. "I taught grade seven until Rain was ill." Grace smiled at him. She slowed her step. "And now I'll probably teach again in January."

He turned and clapped his gloves together. "Well, I'll be . . . I didn't know you taught school. A woman of many talents." He looked far down the street as though getting perspective. He bit his lip. "Say, I'm impressed," he said.

After they had returned to Center Street, their walk took them along Center to J Street—ending in the legendary east side of town. The east side seemed busy, bustling; it was fresh and new, all right. The empty lot for the new city center building sat on the southeast corner covered with lumber stacked under canvas, and a bulb of a cement mixer dripped with lime. There were people walking by the lot; a family with a baby buggy strolled by. There was a fountain in the middle of the street. Alex strutted around the fountain. An older couple parked on a bench, and a seedy-looking bum sitting on the curb stared and grinned.

As they passed Frank Corey, Grace wondered if he knew his daughter Sissy was having dinner with a strange man. He was still at his post, just folding up his motorless cart, removing the decorative Christmas wreath, and about to put away his sign: "Peanuts and Popcorn." One of his sons, Chub, sat on the curb behind the wagon wheel carefully straightening out used paper bags. The bum with a curved pipe squatting near him was Reb Stuart—one of the Stuart boys from the houses down by the railroad. Seeing his squalor, Grace felt distaste, but she was too filled with excitement to let it spoil the fun.

Alex didn't ask who wanted what. He made a great gesture out of furnishing his purse and buying three sets of two bags each. Frank Corey grinned. He glanced back at his son and at Reb Stuart. Little Chub rose quickly and fished in the side of the cart for paper bags, new mixed in with the old. Mr. Corey looked at them sheepishly, but filled every bag. He nodded and smiled at Chub, saying "Thanks, son." Grace knew the family was a special project of the Eastmans and Jones. They would be present at Mara's party Christmas Eve for—if no other reason— the food. Knowing as much as she did about the Coreys, Grace felt uneasy. Frank seemed so intent on teaching his son this business. But what would following such an occupation mean for his son?

Grace wondered if Frank knew where Sissy was. Did he know she was in the hotel with an Indian man—a stranger? Did he know where any of his other five children were, for that matter?

"Well, thank you, gentlemen," Frank said, his face red from the ears to the eyes. "I don't believe I know you. Do I?" He smiled and extended his hand.

"Alex Hunt," Alex said over a mouthful.

"And you are . . . ?"

"Hanson Eastman."

"Hanson Eastman! Ashel Eastman's soldier boy? My daughter has been working for your father. Best employer in town. Say, Grace, I can see you got a winner here." Frank Corey pumped Hanson's hand.

Grace was glad the dusk hid the color in her face. She pulled the scarf up around her cheeks. *I don't have him, Mr. Corey,* she would have said if Hanson had not been beside her. *I don't have him. I am not sure what is happening, but something about his return is different from what I had dreamed.*

Alex threw a kernel of popcorn or two to the pigeons in the middle of the boulevard. They danced around in the water of the fountain, flapping their wings, bashing their heads over the same morsel.

"My good night! These birds do the same thing as the ducks!" Alex laughed.

"Competition!" Hanson observed.

"They'll be gone before Christmas," Grace said quietly. "If it snows again they'll be gone, if they don't end up at the wrong end of someone's ax for dinner."

"I thought they stayed around here pecking around Utah Lake at Bird Island."

"But they'll be gone from here," she said, standing against the edge of the fountain, watching.

"I haven't started getting into the spirit of Christmas time!" Alex suddenly exclaimed. "What do they do here for Christmas time?" He turned around in the street and looked at the lights down Center. "I think I do want to stay, Gracie. You don't care, do you?"

Grace didn't answer him. Instead, turning to the south, she said, "And next spring they'll start to build the new City Center. The design is classic—the most elegant Greek architecture in the West. Right on that corner." Grace pointed to the southeast plot on the avenue, across from the tabernacle, standing gloriously regal in imaginary splendor.

Alex stood throwing popcorn into his cavernous mouth. "Maybe I'll want to see this Greek wonder. Maybe I'll stay until they finish it. What do you say, Hanson?"

"You can stay as long as you like, Alex. You know that." In enthusiastic answer, Alex pounded Hanson until the popcorn jumped out of the bag and the birds clamored at his feet. Alex turned the rest of his own bag over and the birds went mad. "Oh my, I've had a good time," he said. He looked at Grace, then, his eyes piercing hers. "I've had such a good time. You don't want to go home do you, Grace? We should have a barbecue right here on this spot in the middle of the street. But not ducks or pigeons. Let's roast Hanson Eastman. He's the best thing that's happened to Provo, Utah, since General Cradlebaugh burned." Then Alex broke into song. It was the same song Grace had heard Sister Priscilla Pollard of Tom Pollard's meat pies—tamales at five cents each—sing once at a church social. She had told them it was something the prophet Joseph Smith sang when he was a boy.

They took him to the graveyard
In a rubber tired hack.
They took him to the graveyard
But they did not bring him back.

And they sang a song the whole day long,
Poor babes in the woods, they lay down and died.
And when they were dead, the robins so red
Brought strawberry leaves and over them spread.

So bury me both wide and deep
Place a marble stone at my head and feet.
And on my breast place a snow white dove
To show the world that I died for love.

"The robins so red," Alex repeated. "To show the world that I died for love."

Uneasy, Grace glanced back to see little Chub and his friend, Reb. Stuart, follow Frank Corey's wagon down the road. Thank goodness the street was empty at this moment, she laughed to herself.

"If I didn't know better, I'd think you were drunk," Hanson was laughing.

"I'm drunk with happiness. This is where I belong, Hanson Eastman. I never thought I'd be where I really belonged. Something in my bones, in my heart and bones here, tells me this is where I really belong."

He lengthened his stride—his heavy fur coattails flapped from side to side. He held his peanuts high over his head.

"Grace, hold my hand," he said, reaching for her. "I'm going to fly if you don't.

On my breast place a snow white dove.
To show the world that I died for love."

11

Grace Tuttle

Something had happened. She wasn't sure what. She had looked at his eyes again. And had felt his hands on her waist. She loved Hanson, didn't she? Yet some consuming clamor in her blood cried out for more of Alex Hunt. She stayed awake funneling each threatening word and touch through her mind. What was happening? Why couldn't she sleep?

Several restless hours had passed when she heard the noise outside the window. The moon shone through the glass with a pale green glow. The bare fingers of the sumac tree beat uneven taps on the pane. When she heard the cry, she believed it was cats. She rolled over and pulled Caroline's satin sheets over her hair. But after a moment she believed it was more than cats. It sounded like someone far away was running and crying.

Moving the rosette knots of the glacé curtains to the side, she peered out into the large moonlit yard. The withered flowers stood in impeccable rows like school children. The willows bent far over into the small pool under the fountain. Ashel and Caroline's mansion and yard were lovely. It had been like magic here. But now there was no hiding the fact that they were having financial troubles. In fact, it had been because of their financial troubles that they couldn't hire a full-time employee to help Caroline. They were lucky to have Sissy who lived close by.

Now she wondered about Sissy. Why had Sissy been sitting at that table with the large gentleman in the overcoat at the hotel? Where was Sissy now?

Outside her slightly open window, she heard the sound of

rapid footsteps coming from the direction of the hotel. Holding the quilt around her shoulders, she stopped and listened. Then there was a sound as though someone had come to the front door, and again she heard Ashel's deliberate step in the hall. She crawled back into the sheets and held the quilts up to her chin. For a moment she could hear muffled voices beyond the heavy sound of her own breathing.

Then there was a tap on the door. "Grace. Grace!" It was Uncle Ashel. He opened the door to her room. "Honey, do you know where Hanson is?"

Still groggy with the dark morning and a lack of sleep, Grace asked, "What time is it?"

"Four-thirty. Where's Hanson? I've looked in his room."

Grace felt disoriented. She had no idea it was that late. She must have slept some. Now she could not remember what had been happening. Even the images of Alex and Hanson from the night before seemed far away. "Hanson?" Ashel could not find Hanson. One of the reasons she wanted to stay here was because Hanson would be here. But he was not here. The boys had walked her to the house under the street light. And then Hanson had turned to her and said, "Alex has to drive to the Hull House Hotel to talk to Barrington. I'm going with him." Where was Hanson, then?

"Maybe he stayed with Alex in the old house," Grace said without knowing that the words would not come easily. She cleared her throat. "What's wrong, Uncle Ashel? Who's at the door?"

"Never you mind, Grace. You need your sleep. Thank you. I'll find Hanson." As he left, she could hear him murmuring. "Just what we need—bad publicity at the hotel!"

When Ashel turned away, Grace got out of bed and pushed her feet into her slippers. "No, I'll help you." She walked to the door of the bedroom and peered out. But she could not see far enough. So she moved into the foyer. Whoever it was still stood in the doorway. The gas light across the street that stood in front of the Freshwater Hardware shone through the oval screen and through a huge head of matted hair. For a moment she thought it might be Sissy. Sissy had hair like that—dirty blond matted curls that looked like good nests for lice. But it was not Sissy. The voice was from someone older.

Grace drew closer. The woman turned as Ashel drew his overcoat over his pajamas. It was Maggie Hammond from the hotel.

Grace raced to the front of the room. "What is it, Uncle Ashel? Can I help?" When Maggie saw her, she turned quickly and gasped. Her face was streaked with tears.

"A man was stabbed at the hotel."

Grace drew a sharp breath.

As Ashel crossed the threshold and swung the heavy door behind him, he said, "If he's not dead yet we may be able to save his life." Dr. Taylor at the Aird hospital would help. Ashel hurried Maggie out and Grace pulled the door open behind them. "I'll be there," she said.

"You stay here," Ashel said. "There's no point in waking the entire neighborhood."

Grace stood in the door, dropping the quilt around her. No, she would come, she thought. She could not sleep now. She raced into her bedroom and pulled her housefrock over her nightgown. She put her keys in her pocket. It took half a minute. When she raced out into the night north past Mara's and Will's to the old house on the corner, Ashel and Maggie stood knocking at the door.

"I have the key, remember?" Grace said. After all, it was her house where she had lived for many years with Grandma Rain. The door croaked on its hinges. The noise scraped against the quiet.

"I had to go to the hotel early to start the bread this morning," Maggie was crying. "I went to open the kitchen door and there was a man lying behind the trash barrels."

Grace held the door for Maggie and Ashel. As Maggie

brushed past her, she could smell some vague perfume in Maggie's hair.

"Wait here and I'll see if Hanson slept here," Ashel said. For an elderly man, he fairly flew up the stairs, the panels of his greatcoat flying like huge dark bird's wings. The pictures on the walls shook; the chandelier lamp in the stairwell winked with the breeze.

Grace and Maggie waited in the foyer. Grace was praying.

"He said 'Help me, I got cut bad' and I didn't want the people in the hotel to hear him, so I said 'Don't wake anybody. I'll fetch help.'" Maggie was clutching her own fingers and wringing them.

"Do you think he's dead by now?" Grace asked.

"His feet wasn't dead. They moved when he was behind the trash barrel. But I never saw his face. I don't know. That's all I saw."

Both Hanson and Alex were indeed staying at the old house. Once they were aroused, both of them clamored into the hallway, pulling on trousers and coat sleeves. Hanson had tried not to wake Alex, he said, but Alex had heard the word "murder."

Alex appeared at the top of the stairs with the whitest face Grace had ever seen. "Who's murdered?" he said, pulling on his coat.

"We don't know," Ashel said. He was out of the door before Alex reached the first landing. Grace and Maggie waited to go behind.

"We ought to call the police," Hanson told his father.

"And get more unfavorable publicity at the hotel?" Ashel shook his head. You didn't tell anyone else, did you, Maggie?"

"No, sir." Maggie was still gasping for breath.

"Well, see you don't breathe a word of it. I don't need bad press. Every time Mr. Barrington and his people come into town . . ."

Moving as quickly as she could behind the men, Grace raced

with them to the back of the hotel in the dim light of the gas
street lamps and the hollow moon. In the alleyway on the north
side, she stood shivering in the cold while Ashel pulled out his
keys at the iron gate.

"It's open," Maggie said.

But Ashel had already discovered it. "My goodness! You left
it open! You could have lost us everything in the hotel!"

Behind the iron railing at the back, the trash barrels
crowded into the pen like huge fat clams with empty gaping
mouths.

"Get more light," Ashel said as he leaned down and fumbled
behind the trash barrels. Pulling them out one by one, he
revealed a painted trail of dark blood across the stones. But
there was no one there.

12

Sissy Corey

She could still smell apples on her hands when she put her hands to her face and ran. Nothing looked the same at this hour in dead quiet. The moon made a sliver of silver out of the distant lake. There were no birds chattering, only the occasional scrappy caterwauling of a tom. She was shaking when she reached the house. Shaking with fear, horror, and cold. And she tightened her arms around her chest, breathing with difficulty. *Oh God, please.* Yet tears had not come until she reached the door of the porch and felt in the darkness for the cold knob. For a split second she felt another apple in her hand. Apple or no apples, if only she had never let him in. And the memory of the way he had held her still beat, beat, beat in her brain. "Oh please, please, please," she sobbed, but under her breath. The lights of all the houses on the street were blind. And there was nothing from the porch, not even the sound of Chub's breathing, though she knew he was there with Eric curled on the cot.

She would not dare to wake her mother. Nor Chub, nor anyone. Not now. Not with her sleeves torn, and the lamp black smeared on her cheeks. If there was a way she could wash it out she would. Her mother would never believe that she had cut her finger making applesauce in the hotel kitchen, though it was true. And the necklace. It was so beautiful, and he had . . . How could she have guessed he would. . . *Oh, dear God.*

She sat on the stoop and covered her face with her hands. The raspberry bushes looked like wild hair in the dim light, the Eastman garden like a field of graves. Her heart thumped

against her breast. She could hear it. It shook her body out of
rhythm with the pulse of her shivering. She leaned forward on
the stoop until her head rested on her knees and the deep sob of
her throat throbbed in her skirt. No, no, no.

Because it was cold and she was in nothing but her dress,
she could not cover her legs and her arms with her hands. And
soon she could not feel her fingers. So, remembering, she
reached under the stoop for the ice skates and felt the cold
blades in the dark with a sob of relief. They were like old
friends. When she tugged at them, the leaves and grass stopped
her from pulling them away. And when they finally came they
were covered with dried sticks and burrs. For a moment she
squatted on the stoop clearing the weeds tangled in the laces.
*Oh dear Hanson. When you left me your old skates before you went
away, you never dreamed I would still love you when you returned.*

She had been only eleven years old, and it had been a foggy
day, with the ice of the lake hidden under a cloud cover that
came down and sat in the hills. And she had watched Grace and
Hanson at the fire by the lake. They had been laughing together
while he was untying her skates. Then Grace fell against him
and stayed in his arms for a moment while Sissy watched them,
burning with hunger to be as rich and as beautiful—the light
from the fire shimmering against Grace's black curls. And Chub
and Cherry and Eric and Margaret and Susan, and all the
others, if they noticed that moment between Grace and
Hanson, they said nothing. But Sissy had waited until the
others had gone to the road, and she had stood near them to
feel the warmth of their fire, and her heart had beat crazily
under her dress when Hanson had turned to her and said,
"Sissy, you are pretty good on your father's old homemade
skates."

She had not said anything then, only stared at him in
wonder because she could barely breathe, she admired him so.

"What could you do with a pair of blades, eh?"

And she had untied her father's crude wooden blades from

her shoes while he talked.

"I won't be needing my skates while I'm gone. If I gave some to you, would you . . .?"

And Grace had tossed her head back and laughed. "Hanson, Sissy will never have feet as big as yours."

He paused, hit his gloves together. "I have an old pair of smaller ones." He smiled and blew on his gloved fingers, and like smoke, his breath covered his face.

Emily's heart raced. "Sure," she said. "I'd take them," believing as she said it that she might explode with joy.

Clearing the last of the grass off the skates, she ran with them through the front gate to the road, and then south to the railroad tracks toward the Barbars' pond. The trees leaned over in the dark as though they were reaching for her. Their fingers looked gray without leaves, without apples, without buds, with no life now, as though they would take hers, too, if they could. The silence seemed to shriek to her. She could not bear its heaviness and she wished for nothing in an instant. Wondering how it would be if suddenly there were nothing—no knife, no body, no inquisition, no people, no earth, nothing.

Her mind raced in a thousand jagged circles as she reached the dark pond, a black gash of shimmering light under the moon. She looked across the fields warily. She had prayed no one saw her on the railroad tracks—certainly no bums the likes of Reb Stuart. And as much as she liked a few of the working boys in town, like Hammersly Potter, she prayed he would not see her now.

She leaned forward to test the ice on the pond, pressing her hand against the surface until it dipped into the cold water. Then with a little pressure, the ice cracked and broke, and the water sucked up from under it until it swirled like a black sea under her fingers. The ice was too thin. The water was so cold that when she drew her palms away, she rubbed them against each other to get them warm. She rubbed and rubbed. Then, feeling the tears slip down her cheeks, she dipped her hands into the water and rubbed them against her face. She rubbed and rubbed at the lamp black until there must have been nothing left at all, and she could no longer smell the apples anymore. Feeling tears crowd up now like the water of the pond, she pulled back and cradled the skates in her arms.

13

Reginald Summerfield

The light happened when the girl screamed—just before he felt the blade of the knife cut against his ribs, before he had backed up quickly and tripped on the steps, hitting his head on something as he fell. Then the blackness seemed to be something he understood. But the light? The light had happened only a few times before. It seemed to happen most at times when his oldest memories came to him—sitting wet and cold in a dark circle with the soft lady who made her cookies round by cutting the dough with the shaving mug, the flying boy, and Hawk in the Tree. Most of the time he remembered Hawk in the Tree. When he sat at Hawk in the Tree's feet in his mind, he saw the old man's face over the fire. He heard his voice then, the voice that talked truths over the fire.

He knew he should never have touched Sissy Corey in the first place—not while she was paring apples and a knife lay close by. He picked himself up enough to move between two sheds on the north side of the street. His body ached. No one must know, except the girl Sissy Corey. He caught himself sobbing. It began in his lungs and came from so far away he thought it was not from his own body. But it climbed into his throat and it shook his wound. He clamped his mouth shut. He did not want them to hear where he was. And then again he saw the light.

At first he thought it came from his oldest memories. He remembered he was sitting around a fire in a storm. Only vaguely he remembered there had been a boat—and a wrenching sound on the lake. He had hit his head and swirled down into the water. Someone pulled him out and he found himself sitting at the fire. He was wet and everyone around him was crying. It was all he remembered. He was sitting around a fire and many people were crying. He did not know what it meant. In the other of his oldest memories, he saw himself standing by a cliff, and a boy was standing beside him. The boy suddenly fell off the cliff and flew without wings. Sometimes other brief pictures came to him easily; most of the time they did not. But he could see his adopted father Hawk in the Tree very clearly.

Hawk in the Tree, a Hopi in a Ute land, was a recluse. Because he was alone in the mountains, the Utes left him alone. His mother had escaped her village with him in a basket at the time of the destruction of Awatovi. Awatovi had been a village of the old world destroyed by white men. The Castillas—the priests—had come to the village, washed the heads of the people, broke the Kachinas and ridiculed their ceremonies. Their new stories turned the people against each other. The people, torn between two worlds, lost their faith in the old one. They didn't understand what the Castillas told them. They saw no Bahana—the white person in the legend who had only half a stone tablet. And then because they had two worlds, suddenly they had no stable world. Was that where he was? Without any world at all they became suspended, without their feet on the earth. The people killed each other and the girls were raped by the Kwitamuh—the lusty men. The Chief of Awatovi begged the Walpi to send warriors to bring Awatovi to an end.

When Awatovi came to an end, the mother Anangtana, named for the place of hearts where the Tewas buried the hearts of their enemies—this Anangtana—placed her baby in a basket and escaped with him until she reached the high mountains where she could make her own world. Hawk in the Tree kept her world for his own, and taught this world to the little son he had found. He had named him—Moon Hawk.

"We live with Masauwu," he could hear Hawk in the Tree

when he returned to that life in his mind. "He is the spirit of death. He is the master of fire, and he owns this world." The little boy had learned to fear Masauwu.

When Hawk in the Tree talked of the great light, he could see the light, but he was also able to see blackness of Masauwu. He was never sure why. The blackness seemed to be of his own body. He could not control the blackness that seemed to be of his own body. He was never sure why he could not control his own body. But it screamed at him, and he had reached out more than once and held the scream in his hands.

"The people climbed through the opening to the fourth world of Masauwu to escape the evil powakas. But they found evil here also. Evil is always with us. It came with a young girl, the very last to climb up the stalk of bamboo through the Sipapuni. When they discovered she was a powaka, it was too late. She had already contaminated the fourth world with evil."

Yes, true to the stories he had heard from Hawk in the Tree, it was always a young girl. He too had known this to be true.

He stopped breathing to hear the voices in the street. There were many of them. He curled up more tightly between the two sheds so they would not find him.

Hawk in the Tree's eyes glistened in the firelight.

"What did you pay for me?" he always asked Hawk in the Tree.

"Are you sorry?" he said.

"Tell me again. What did you pay for me?"

"A piece of stone. It was little to pay for a boy. The Utes who came to bother me believed it was the other half of the broken tablet the native peoples always searched for. But it was not. There is another piece to the broken tablet. But it was not my piece of stone."

Sometimes he dreamed he was back in his true mother's arms, for at the time he was taken, he was old enough to remember her. She was warm. She was soft. But he could not remember her face. He thought he could remember that she held a small baby in her arms. But he did not know.

"All of them came through the opening of the earth to escape the evil ones. All of them departed to their places in the fourth world. When they saw that the young girl was a powaka they tried to leave her behind. The Bahanas, the white man, took her with them.

"Beware," said the kikmongwi. "Because the powaka went with the white man, the white man will know both evil and good. The white man will grow strong because they will have secrets we do not know."

All the stories of Hawk in the Tree's world twisted into the stories of his first world, and the present world. Which stories were true? Or did it really matter if he could not reconcile them? He believed he was still sobbing deep inside himself. He could not hear himself, but he could feel the wound pumping blood out into his clothes. He believed his first family was named Ickerson. Or something like that. As soon as he had come to the white world he had tried to find anyone by the name of Ickerson. There was no one in Provo by that name. He must have waited too long.

"Because of their knowledge, Bahanas will be strong," Hawk in the Tree would say. "Listen carefully to the Bahanas. But do not follow their ways."

He should have stayed with Ethel. She had asked him to stay with her during the break when her roommates had gone home. Tall Ethel, with her washed-out brown eyes, was from a Mormon family, but she didn't live her religion. She wanted to, but she couldn't. She loved him too much, she said. She had been loyal to him. He told her: "I have to work with Barrington for at least a year. Then I will come back, and we will see how we feel." He had never felt that he would honor his promise to return. Promises were only words—they meant nothing.

"Yet it is promised in the old stories that in some distant day there will come a Bahana from the direction of the rising sun. His name we do not know. But he will bring harmony, friendship, and good fortune to our people. Bury the dead with their faces to the east so they may watch him come."

When he fell backward against the metal frame around the garbage boxes, he had been unconscious for just a short time. Then when he tried to turn over in the small space, he could feel hot tears on his cheeks and the pumping of blood in the wound. When he had told his white mother, Mrs. Summerfield, about the white Bahana, she had said "So your people are looking for a white Bahana? Our culture is looking for the return of Jesus Christ. Seems everyone is looking for a white Bahana."

After Hawk in the Tree had died—at the time Reginald was with Mr. Summerfield and his wife—he had never talked about the white Bahana with anyone outside his home until he came to the university. A very fair girl with pale hair sat next to him in his English class. Outside of class she sat on a wall with her white ankles dangling. There were no shoes on her feet.

"What are you reading?" he said.

"The Book of Mormon," she said.

Mother Summerfield had told him, "Talk about a white Bahana. There's your story of Jesus coming to the Indians! But it's all poppycock." He remembered her words. "That is poppycock," she said.

"It is the record of your people. They were waiting to see Jesus," the girl told him.

He listened carefully to the white girl with the white hair. Her name was Laura. He had already been with Ethel and had promised her . . . They were intended, but Ethel had been easy, and so then he decided he did not care that much about her. He fell in love with the white girl. But all she gave him was the book. She told him all about the pioneer people and their book. She told him to read it.

He carried the Book of Mormon back to his home that summer. But he never opened it. Finally he carried the Book of Mormon back to the university in his duffle bag. While he slept in the train station, someone took his duffle bag. He never saw it again. After that he saw many other copies of the Book of Mormon. He saw many other people who had read the Book of Mormon. And he talked with them about it, though he never read it. He believed his own book would come back to him someday like the lost half of the broken tablet.

Hawk in the Tree would not tell him much more about the piece of stone. "It is a legend," he said. "All of these are the old stories of the earth people who climbed through the Sipapuni to the Fourth World. When the children grow older, they will tell them the truth—that their ancestors came from across a great body of water. Our ancestors are the Patki, which means 'dwelling on water.' They escaped a place of wickedness by making houseboats and floating the houseboats across a great sea. And no one knows how long it took them to come to this land." Was this the true story, then? Which story was it necessary to know? Could he live with many different stories?

Most of what he heard about the stories of the gods and ancestors came from the words of Hawk in the Tree.

Now he could hear the people in the street. He could hear what they were saying. "We cannot find him. Perhaps he is all right and has crawled somewhere." He could hear the sounds of the feet dying in the clear morning. There were no other sounds on the air. There was a pure cold chill around him. His great-coat was not heavy enough to keep the moisture from seeping into his limbs.

The girl Sissy who said her name was really Emily Corey had been friendly with him. She would know she invited him with her eyes. Oh, his body had felt such longing. He could feel the longing shake in his blood. She knew she had looked at him. She too was at fault. But he had not had a good reason to reach out. Why couldn't he have kept his hands in his own keeping? He thought about Ethel. He was Kwitamuh, also, no better. He could feel the wracking in his wound. It had stopped beating. He did not think there was that much blood pouring out of the wound now.

Sometimes the most vivid thing he could remember was the fire in the storm and the crying people sitting around the fire. When he remembered the fire, why did he also see the eyes of Hawk in the Tree? The eyes were very wide. They were shining with the reflection of the fire. His mother must have been there, but he couldn't remember her.

Hawk in the Tree told him the story of his own mother, Anangtana. Some Tauramuri Indians found Anangtana under a tree. She hid her baby high in the branches. But the baby squawked like a bird. They looked up and saw the baby in the tree and laughed. They called the baby Hawk in the Tree. They were friendly Indians from the Sierra Tarahumara. They were Tauramuri—footrunners. He was raised with them until he was a young boy.

Anangtana lived with the friendly Indians until a terrible war destroyed them. But she was lucky enough to run away and escape across the frozen water. When she ran away, her son Hawk in the Tree was old enough to run with her, and they lived alone together in a hidden place in the hills until she died. Then, alone, Hawk in the Tree lived for a long time until the Tonoquints came to him. They had captured a young boy as prisoner. They wanted to sell him to Hawk in the Tree for a gun. But when they walked into Hawk in the Tree's house, they saw the precious piece of carved stone. One of the Utes believed it was the other half of the broken tablet. He wanted to take it. Hawk in the Tree remembered how afraid he had been when he was in the captivity of the Utes. He looked at the young boy. He wanted to save the life of the boy. So he let the Utes have the stone for the Indian boy in white man's clothes. That boy had been Regi. All of these stories were stories that Regi, named Moon Hawk, then heard from the mouth of Hawk in the Tree—the stories of the other worlds that seemed lost.

For many years after Regi mourned Hawk in the Tree's death, he was forced to live in the new world. Mr. Summerfield, a hunter near Strawberry who had shot near Moon Hawk into the brush, had been horrified to have almost killed a boy. When he brought him to his house where he and his wife lived alone, Mrs. Summerfield loved the boy at once, and they cared for him as though he were their own child, eventually sending him to the University of Utah to become an accountant—as though his years as an Indian had never existed. And afterward, he had gone to the university at San Jose for a short time. But he could never forget his other worlds: Hawk in the Tree, and before Hawk in the Tree, the faraway world. Sometimes he thought he could remember something about the faraway world when the water fell from the sky and Mr. and Mrs. Summerfield said "Rain. A good Rain." Always, when he heard the word "rain," he thought he remembered the world farther away than the world of Hawk in the Tree. He thought he remembered hearing something about a good Rain when he sat by that fire by the lake with the lady who made cookies with the shaving mug. When he never found anyone by the name of Ickerson, he took the hunter's name, Summerfield. "I am no longer an Indian," he thought to himself. "Then why do I see the eyes of Hawk in the Tree and hear his voice? Why do I hear his stories? Why does my blood sit up in my head and begin to make noise when the man Dawes in the hotel says to me that in today's newspaper there is a notice about the burial of an Indian this morning named Rain?"

14

Mara Eastman Jones

Mara was not sure how the young people felt about the funeral, although she knew Grace was nervous because she was going to sing. But the occasion was a time of renewal for Mara. Friends of the Eastmans, members of their ward, and dignitaries from the political and business community as well as many from the Brigham Young University where both Mara and Grace had graduated with teaching degrees, began to flock to the tabernacle by 10:30 A.M. to pay their last respects to Rain. Many of the most prominent citizens were there because of Ashel and Will. Some of the viewers were from the poorest side of town: the Coreys filed beside the coffin in ragged shoes, the father herding his children from behind. Maggie Hammond from the hotel came with her bearded father, the junk man and die-hard polygamist who had been essentially ostracized from Provo society for his insistence that he should have the right to maintain his two wives—a fact everyone in the Church knew, but no federal official could ever prove because he was entirely circumspect where he lived with his daughter—alone.

Some of the visitors were people no one knew. Mara noticed one large dark-haired man with Indian features stepping through the south entrance to the circular stairwell that led to the balcony. He looked ill, almost pale beneath his dark skin. She wondered who he was, and why he had come if he were as ill as he looked. Dressed in a large black coat, he did not take a seat for a while. Yet he did not go through the line, but stood just inside the door folding his thick arms.

Many of the people who came seemed not to be paying

respects to Rain alone but to an outlook upon life that had suddenly seemed to have ended with the armistice at the end of the World War, the upheaval of the Church community with the death of their prophet Joseph Fielding Smith on November 19, just seven days after the armistice, and the changes in their world as a whole.

Foremost in the minds of Bishop Wesley Morgan and his counselors, Martin Jensen and Caleb Hyde, was the recent scandal at the university concerning their professor friends. Two sets of brothers, Henry and Joseph Peterson and Hugh and William Chamberlain, had been called to the office of the president by the Commissioner of Church Education, Horace H. Cummings, and summarily dismissed for destroying the faith of the students by teaching evolution, modernism, and higher criticism. President Brimhall had told of his dream that the faithless teachings of professors were preying upon the students like a huge black machine fitted with baited wires like fish lines that climbed into the sky to catch and haul their faith-loving victims, who were flying high like birds, down, down into gloomy jaws.

The dismissal of the teachers had rocked many members of the Church in the area who, though strong in the faith, saw themselves beginning to take their place in a larger world and found themselves, instead, somehow unable to make the necessary adjustments to the new modes of thought. The world required their acceptance of evolution and some of the modern philosophies, and they were reluctant to let go of the scriptural versions they had accepted. Rain's simple faith became a symbol of not only her own people's death and elimination from Western society, but a representation of something basic and primitive that was dying.

"This seems to me the end of an era," Bishop Morgan said, his voice resounding in the tabernacle. "Rain was a woman who perhaps understood more about the laws of the earth and its spirit than those of us who are caught up in the tide of the affairs of men will ever know. She began in the lap of nature. She understood the work of the sun and the mystery of the ground. She was one of the last native Americans—and a way of life." He paused. "A way of life we regrettably found incompatible with our own."

Mara noticed how slowly he spoke. Outside the windows of the tabernacle she saw a jab of what looked like lightning and a flurry of powdery snow.

"I would like to read a passage from Sobe Eastman's journal that Sister Mara Jones gave me. Sobe wrote: *It was Rain who taught me to be quiet, to wait, to listen. She said, "Our people know there is a spirit in the earth that moves inside the water and the wind. It will heal us if we but listen. We must not underestimate the power of waiting, of hearing the quiet, or of communicating with the earth." She was the last of a people of the earth who might have had something to teach us. And I wonder—did we learn?*

Suddenly, as he spoke, a gust of wind rose up. The electric lights in the ceiling of the tabernacle snuffed out. The noon light, crowded out by black clouds, hung in the eaves like smoke.

"Is that our answer?" he said, looking away from his papers on the podium. A good-natured rumble of laughter stirred through the congregation. "The intellectual, the quest for thought, has always clashed with the basic primacy of man. Just as we think we have learned something and we are comfortable with it, something like a war or a controversy or a death churns our lives. But in our turmoil there are times we must look at the stability of a Rain.

"She gave to everyone alike. She nursed the Indian child Jenny, Grace's mother. She became a second wife to Sully Tuttle to give him children, only to lose them all—except for her grandchild Grace, who is with us today." Everyone knew of Rain's sacrifices. Everyone knew that they had never found the body of little Mathew Eggertson after he had disappeared when he was four years old.

Mara took Grace's hand in hers and held it tightly. She leaned over to whisper to her. "Did you see how many are here to hear you sing? All of these good people loved Rain."

When Grace turned slightly, Mara followed her with her eyes. And as she turned her head, she saw the large black-haired man sitting in the back by the door, his head clearly visible above the crowd. He looked so pale, she thought he would fall over. He looked very much like an Indian. And it puzzled her. She had never seen him before.

"It is time to say good-bye. Perhaps not to someone who has made any outstanding political contribution to education or the community. We have recently suffered tribulations over the encroachment of modern education, the darkness of modern thought which seems bent upon destroying our faith. It seems to me that Rain's contribution to our lives has demonstrated the truth of the gospel in our lives, the miracle of simple faith."

When Priscilla Pollard began playing the introduction for Grace's song, Mara clutched Will's hand. She knew Grace was not the singer her mother Jenny had been, but she loved to hear her try. Hanson and Alex both smiled as Grace walked to the stand.

As Grace sang, Mara closed her eyes. "For a wise and glorious purpose, Thou hast placed me here on earth." Mara felt a great simple love flow through the room. And when Grace sang, "You're a stranger here," she could not help but catch a glimpse again of the stranger sitting so obviously near the side door.

As soon as the song ended, the clouds cleared and the sunlight shone from the upper windows through the colored glass on the side front row. As the light fell on the family, Mara saw the images of the rest of the crowd diffuse into blurred colors of flowered hats and shawls and white collars. Then she could see no one in the room but Grace as the girl sat down. She was beautiful. The room was hushed while there was another minute of tribute, and then a prayer.

Priscilla Pollard played quiet majestic chords on the organ while the congregation stirred gently. Mara expected only a few to follow them to the cemetery. As Grace stirred, Mara saw that Hanson took the girl's arm. "That was beautiful, Grace," he said. And then he said almost inaudibly, whispering, "I can't believe how beautifully you sing. You were marvelous."

In that moment Mara saw Grace's eyes meet Hanson's gaze, and she said a quick prayer for them. "Oh, please God, help them see one another."

"Let's get out of here before we're trampled," Ashel said, wheeling Caroline toward the south side door. Caroline was dabbing at her eyes.

When the crowd stood aside to let Mara and the family through, and they reached the side door, the large, strange man, favoring his side as though he were in pain, stepped forward and laid a huge hand on her arm. "They told me you are the family of the woman Rain."

"Yes," Mara paused. "Yes, we are." She could not help but notice his large jowls, his jet black hair.

"I am not sure. But I believe I had an Indian grandmother whose name was Rain."

For a moment Mara felt weak. Leaning on Grace's arm, she felt her legs begin to buckle under her. Oh no! It couldn't be! But yes, he even looked like Rain. Grace leaned close to her, and Hanson took her arm.

"What is it, Aunt Mara?" Hanson said, holding her steady.

It couldn't be, but it was!

"I believe I am somehow connected to your family—by the name of Ickerson."

"Eggertson! Yes, Mathew Eggertson!" Mara leaned on both Hanson and Ashel now. Will also stayed close to her.

"Mathew Eggertson! Is it true!" Ashel breathed.

Is this real? she thought. If so, then it is a miracle. And then she breathed to herself: "You are here, Rain. All of your love has filled this room. You may know more about what is real than any of us will ever know. We pretend to be wise with our reading and arithmetic. But we are not good at hearing real life pulse through the veins of air. We are not good at hearing the drums of life in our heartbeats that still echo underground."

To the Indian man, she said, "Yes, yes! We have wondered all these years, Mathew! We did not know what happened to you. I am your Aunt Mara. Can you come with us to visit for a while? And we'll also introduce you to your father's Eggertson cousin who is still our neighbor! This is wonderful!" and she leaned against the man as he awkwardly folded her into his arms.

Mara had never felt such a spiral of ecstasy as she felt now. She knew Rain's presence. She thought, "I can feel your love that is warmer than light in this dark place. It is more real than any substance here. Perhaps it is true. Now you have also brought Mathew home."

15

Grace Tuttle

That night after the long day of the funeral, when Grace lay in the Eastman's narrow room, she thought she could hear the sound of breathing in the trees. But it was only the snow falling.

Yet there was a rumble from the north side of the house—from Mara's house next door—the sound of furniture moving. She lay awake for a long time, wondering what was happening at Aunt Mara's—or if the rumbling sound came from the old house on the corner where Hanson and Alex would still be staying.

She lay awake for hours. She could not shut down her thoughts about all that had happened after the funeral today.

When Mara had reached the door of the tabernacle after the prayer, the huge man with the black hair had stopped her. Her knees had buckled slightly. In one astonishing moment they had regained their long lost cousin, Mathew Eggertson.

Mara was smiling. "Ashel, Caroline, Grace! We have good reason to believe this is our lost Mathew Eggertson. He has come home!"

When Grace took the big Indian's hand in both of hers, she felt the solid strength in it. The large sinews made his hand twice the size of a normal person's. He was very tall, pale beneath a face that looked burned by years of sun. His eyes were almost hidden behind the swollen lids. He leaned to one side, as if in pain.

"Are you sure?" Caroline was asking. "Are you sure?"

He nodded, his white teeth shining through dark scarred lips. "I'm sure. I was four years old. I came from a town near here, but I never knew anyone's name, except for a grandmother Rain. I tried once looking for Mr. Ickerson, but I never found anyone by that name. I was a captive," he said. "Now I know my name was Eggertson. I was sold to an Indian when I was a young boy, and after his death, the Summerfields of Heber found me, gave me a name, and took me in. I studied accounting at the university and I work for Mr. Barrington."

Barrington, the steel magnate. Grace held her breath. When Mara invited the stranger to ride with them to the cemetery in the large funeral limousine, Hanson steered Grace away from the giant man, and maneuvered him into the back seat with Alex. Through connections with the steel people, Alex had already become acquainted with Reginald Summerfield. He now made a particular point of saying he had heard from cursory conversations with Pierpont that Summerfield was a loyal employee of the steel people, a man who would fight for the proposal of the Ironton steel mills. Neither Ashel nor Will breathed a word of protest.

"There will be enough money for the mills," Reginald Summerfield said. "We've got several investors." At one point, he leaned forward on the seat in the limousine. He looked very pale for a moment, as though he would faint. Mara reached back toward him quickly. He did not seem at all well. Seated close to Mara, Grace asked Mara questions with her eyes.

"I talked to him briefly. He shrugged it off," Mara whispered. "He says he is not well because of a condition left over from an attack of the influenza." The flu had hit the whole community hard in the spring of 1918, though careful quarantine and the hot summer had dried it out sufficiently to stop most of it after almost everyone had suffered from it. Last year it had taken Samantha Tuttle Eggertson and her daughter Eliza. If Mathew knew it now, he did not say. He looked through them.

"I don't think it's the flu," Mara said.

Grace and Ashel exchanged glances, remembering the blood,

the knife, the man who had disappeared the night before. That Mr. Summerfield was involved seemed obvious.

The confusion, the effusive greetings, the high color of the flowers, the ride in the limousine and the dedicatory prayer at the cemetery, the presence of the Hulls, Julia Hull's whispers of friendship into Grace's ear, even the presence of Hanson and Alex Hunt standing at the sidelines at the family luncheon after they had walked to the church house—all seemed to fuse together into a blur. The ladies of the ward brought pans of good cheese and potatoes, slices of roast beef and apple strudel—all of it paled beside the truth of Mathew Eggertson's identity and the reality that Rain's lost grandchild had been found.

The Relief Society ladies in the church kitchen smiled and whispered while the family ate the large meal provided for them. In spite of his apparent weakness, Reginald Summerfield ate portions that surprised even Mara, who had seen the Indians eat at the banquets in the park. He loaded his plate with scalloped potatoes and laid eight or ten slices of beef across the potatoes. When one of the slices threatened to slip off the precarious load, he lifted it to the level of his mouth, sucked the offending slice off into his teeth, and with a weak grin, made it disappear.

Not long after that, Hanson whispered to Grace that he would be back, that he was going with Alex to look at the property where Barrington planned to build the steel mill. He did not ask her to go along.

After the lunch at the church was over, Grace walked with Mara and Will back to the tabernacle to Ashel and Caroline's automobile. She said good-bye to Julia Hull and promised to visit her soon.

As they stood to get into the large car, Grace stopped and felt a wave of panic flood through her. In a flash she could suddenly see that she was to sit with the half-breed cousin on the way home. She did not like herself in that moment because a shudder of revulsion swept through her. She fought it, but still, she held back. Mara came to her while Reginald Summerfield was on the other side of the car and squeezed her hand. "Honey, be kind. He's your cousin. If his own people are not kind, who will be?" Grace had heard these words from Mara before.

The large half-breed Indian climbed into the back seat with her, and from a great distance above her said: "So, you are my little second cousin. I am very glad to be home."

She could not breathe for a moment because of the garlic on his breath. He was very close. He smiled a wide smile pulled back from startlingly white teeth. His eyes were broad and round, the pupils like ink marks—or black stones.

"Do you remember the name of your mother?" Caroline asked him.

"Sally, Sally. I think it was Sally," he said. "I called her Mother. But I knew Mr. Summerfield loved me. They sent me to the university." Grace winced inwardly. She knew his mother's name was Samantha. For a moment she hoped this was not her cousin at all, but she corrected her feelings with energy.

"You graduated from college?" Grace asked.

He nodded, still smiling. "Yes. In accounting." His large lips curled outward when he enunciated carefully. "I was educated in Utah, but by a school that is not afraid to teach the truth about what the world really is."

It sounded like a statement to cast disrepute upon the Church school. Grace knew it was. How many times had she heard words just like it from people educated in the modern sciences at universities seemingly more sophisticated than Brigham Young University? President Brimhall's unabashed attempts to maintain Karl G. Maeser's prayerful approach in the classroom had limited the world's acceptance of the university curriculum. Their graduates could not get eastern jobs. They could not enter eastern universities. Outsiders did not want "students who saw the world through colored glasses," though another name for the colored glasses was "faith."

"You are . . . not a Mormon, then?" Grace asked him.

"I . . . Mormon?" he laughed, and then paused, looking out the window into the street. He was guarding his words. "I . . . don't know," he said suddenly. He seemed uncomfortable. There was a moment in which his eyes and his brain seemed to be processing the most recent information. "I . . . guess I was when I was Mathew Eggertson, wasn't I?" He seemed to experience a moment of revelation. "I believe in everything."

Grace peered carefully toward him through narrowed eyes. "Do you?" she asked him.

"Sure. I just accept everyone's view. I give everybody credit for creating their own world of belief."

Grace sat back against the upholstery of the back seat in Ashel's auto. It sounded like all that modern thought. She had never heard it expressed quite like this before. She saw the people on the street as though they existed in another world. "Did you serve in the war?"

"I passed off Indian," he said, smiling. "I worked lumber camps in Alaska."

Grace could not face him for long because of his hard breathing. She turned to look out of the window. He had not asked her any questions about herself. Suddenly the light changed in the trees. Then suddenly, it began to snow.

"It is nice of you to offer me your home for a couple of days," he said, leaning forward to talk to Mara. "I work tomorrow. I hope there's time to talk." His body was so large the wool was tight across his arms. When he leaned, there seemed to be less room, and Grace resisted crushing herself into the corner.

"Think of us as your home," Mara said from the central seat. "We all want to hear your story. Tomorrow at supper? You'll all come?" She spoke to everyone. "Caroline, Ashel . . . Grace?"

When he moved back against the seat, he looked at Grace again with a strange predatory smile. Then he suddenly leaned forward again and said to Ashel, "If it's not too much trouble, could you drive past the East House Hotel? I left my bag and my walking stick at the hotel."

16

Grace Tuttle

It was early Thursday morning when Grace heard someone in the kitchen. It must have been Sissy cleaning out the ashes in the stove. Lying under the quilts, thinking about the funeral, about Mathew, about Sissy and the stabbing at the hotel, Grace did not want to get out of bed. She knew there would probably be a lot of cleaning for her at the old house later on this afternoon, so she had told herself she would take a leisurely morning to think through plans for the next few days.

On the table beside her were new novels she had wanted to read by Edith Wharton and Theodore Dreiser. She thumbed through them, but she could not read. If she were really going to teach school in January, she would have to begin a serious reading program of the books her pupils would be studying, but for now she could not look at the words on the page. At the funeral she had glanced through Sobe's journal when Mara drew it out of her bag. He had written: *Books are my friends. I wish my people had kept written records. I read the words of Emerson, and John Donne, and Milton. They speak to me of the spirit of every man.*

On the other side of the books was the wardrobe. The door was slightly open. She could see the white satin of her wedding dress crushed against their clothes. Many months ago Caroline had offered to help her work on it. Now it seemed a strange foreign object, like a white bird locked in a cage that would never be opened. Hovering around the cage would be dangerous black spaces and large bodies. She thought she could feel the bulk of Reginald Summerfield's big body where he lay in the house on Mara's guest bed in the back bedroom. He seemed like a heavy black weight clutching at them, weighing them down. For a fleeting moment she saw the dream described in the newspaper—President Brimhall's hulking black modern thought machine spiked with the fishing lines like wires reaching into the sky. She mused: she was dreaming the President's dream. When the birds saw the bait on the wires, they grabbed it and the dark faithless thoughts hauled the birds down to the ground. The birds lay devastated. In President Brimhall's dream, when he found the very sad students he said, "Why, students, what on earth makes you so sad and down-hearted?"

"Alas, we can never fly again!" they said.

How strange that she had ever begun to sew on her wedding dress. She thought she was all right, but she suddenly felt an unexpected pain. Most of what she felt was confusion. She could not stay in the room. She could not read. She thought she could quilt. The pieces she had been embroidering were at the house on the corner, stashed in the hall chest. If she went to the house just to fetch the pieces, she could assess how much cleaning time she would need this afternoon. She would not need to wake the boys—although the fleeting thought crossed her mind that she might see Hanson before he left for work at the hotel.

She dressed quickly and went into the kitchen. Sissy was not there. A younger girl with a rat's nest of black hair tied at the top of a red bandanna was scraping the ashes out of the stove. It was Sissy's younger sister Cherry, a spitfire of a girl with long legs and arms as thin as handrails. She did not gaze at Grace. She glared at Grace, her eyes daggers.

"Cherry!" Grace said. "Where's Sissy?"

"At home." Cherry disappeared inside the stove. She did not stop working. Her voice echoed from inside the black hollow.

"Is she sick?" Grace asked.

"She doesn't feel good."

"That's too bad. Is there anything I can do?"

"She don't want nobody botherin' her."

"Can I help you?"

"No. I got it," Cherry said. Cherry did not look her way. Deep in concentration over the stove, cleaning the lids in a bucket of water, she said what sounded like "Hmmmph."

For a moment Grace stood at the back window and looked out on the yard. The snow lay in filigree on the smallest branches. The world was white. Caroline would not be up for another hour. "If Caroline wants to know where I am, tell her I'm running an errand," she told Cherry.

Grace took the key to the house. She slipped on her tallest leather boots and wrapped her neck in a scarf. The street was empty except in front of Mara's house. She stepped back a moment. Parked at the curb was the sleek new Hull limousine. She looked again. She was sure. She had been in it on the drive to the cemetery yesterday. Ducking to take a look inside, she peered at the driver for as long as she could before seeming rude. It was not Mr. Hull. It was a man with a gash of black mustache under his nose. She looked away. She did not know him. She wondered if Mara knew him. But at that moment she believed it might have been the big steel man, Mr. Barrington. But it was only guessing; she did not know.

The door to Mara's house opened and a large figure in a black greatcoat backed out onto the stoop, wielding his walking stick. It was Reginald Summerfield. Grace stayed inside the door frame, still out of sight. The Indian got into the car with the man that must have been Mr. Barrington, and the Hull limousine drove past. She was puzzled. For a moment she saw something in Reginald Summerfield's flat cheeks of their Grandmother Rain. The man did not see her. He had not turned back. His large head on the passenger side was intent in conversation with the driver. If it was Barrington, he had borrowed Hull's big car.

Grace stood still inside of the door for a long time. She

waited until the street was empty again before she made her way past Mara's to the old Eastman home on the corner. She hoped Mara or Will would not see her. As she stepped along the walk, she could not help but narrow her eyes in the glare of the bright snow.

For a long moment she stood at the front of the large east veranda of the old home. The glass in the door winked in the light, reflecting the day in its beveled silver. She looked through the door at the dark red curtains in the foyer, the carpet and railing on the stairs. In the curved front bay were the dining room windows. She smiled. The house seemed like an old friend. She hadn't ever remembered seeing the house as something particular that had grown around her like her own bones and skin. But that was how she felt in this moment. The house was a shell whose form had shaped her somehow. She had breathed her life into its corners. She had seen Grandfather Eastman grow old in it and Grandmother Rain pass away. She had often thought she could never be sure which came first— the house or the people who lived inside the house. It was entirely possible that the house made the people. An elegant house made elegant people. If it was quiet and charming, whoever felt its mantle around their breathing rested in its peace. The old Eastman home where Rain had passed her last days was such a royal house—an old buff brick with its splendid add-on pillared porch. Grace had always swept the stone steps clean. They were now white with snow.

From where she stood she could see how much the windows needed to be wiped down. On the porch, piled up against the dining room walls, she saw leaves. There were chips of wood from kindling lumped under the snow.

As quietly as she could in her leather boots she tiptoed up the walk through the ice. She had the key, but the door was not locked. She moved the door quickly to prevent a creaking noise.

When she stepped inside, she could smell a strange sharp odor like gasoline. When she looked around, her heart sank in her breast. The furniture pillows lay scattered on the parlor floor, the chairs were in different positions, one of them on its back in front of the window. Torn magazines, newspapers, and books lay on the floor by the sofa.

For a moment Grace stood without moving. She had known she would face some cleaning, but her heart sank when she saw how much. She knew the boys had been preoccupied, and that Alex had been having trouble with his car. The gasoline smell came from the kitchen. When she walked into the kitchen she saw the gasoline can on the table, a handful of very filthy rags beside it, and a pair of gloves black with grease. Large black handprints appeared on every white cupboard door. Scattered on the sideboard were dishes and cups rinsed and turned over. An unwashed pan sat on the stove, thickly coated with lard grease. It was hard to believe that only the day before yesterday she had finished putting away the dishes and left only Rain's cup and saucer still wet with tea.

She walked out of the kitchen, through the foyer, and into the street. For a moment she stood in the street and thought about what she ought to do. Cherry Corey was probably still working at Caroline's. Uncle Will was at Mara's. And she thought Hanson and Alex were here in the house asleep, though she couldn't see Alex's car. She felt alone. She had looked forward to sewing this morning, but she had often noticed that if she maintained a proper attitude about the work she was expected to do for others, that she felt sustained when she created order out of the residue of other people's lives—especially if those others were sacrificing too. But there were questions she could not answer—whether there were any sacrifices on the part of the residents who had left this disarray.

She felt very heavy when she turned around and walked back in. Upstairs she found the picture the same: dirty towels spotted with grease lay on the bathroom floor amidst stockings and slippers and shoes. The bedroom doors were open. The beds lay unmade—more than unmade; tortured with sheets and blankets skewered into knots. No one was there.

For a moment she stood at the window and pulled the curtains aside to look at the street below. Everything was quiet. A bowl of half-eaten apple cores had been spilled at the edge of the carpet. Standing by Rain's bed where the covers leaned over to the floor, she picked up the dish of large cores and cradled it in her arms. She looked at the bedstead, at nothing, at the empty air.

Just putting things away took all morning. Grace had been careful to keep after the corners in the house every day she had lived here with Rain. But as soon as Rain was gone, and as soon as she had moved her things out to Ashel and Caroline's place, it seemed the house was going through a grieving process of its own. It had torn its hair, she thought, as she bent and picked up newspapers, towels, and Hanson's duffle bag turned inside out. She placed personal things unfolded inside drawers for the boys to take care of themselves. It was the look of order she needed. She believed she had moved to Ashel and Caroline's because she wasn't supposed to be alone after Rain died. But now, returning home to find the house disturbed, she felt so alone. The disorder characterized some deeper disorder in all of them. And she gritted her teeth to commitment, to holding things together, as she had learned women often do.

She left the house only at lunchtime to tell Mara and Cherry and Caroline where she had been. Mara had offered to help, but Will needed her to go over some more papers he wanted to submit to Smoot asking for the funds to rebuild the mill.

The afternoon passed slowly. When the kitchen was finally clean, she heard a motor car stop in the street, and she felt someone tramping through the door and up the stairs. She held the dish rag, listening for a moment, hoping it was the boys coming back from work.

"Ye cats! Snow white!" It was Alex's voice.

"Someone's been here!" Hanson said.

It was Alex bounding down the stairs. When she saw him

she could not help smiling. From head to toe impeccable Alex was alive, and without his raccoon. He wore a neat navy driving hat with gold buttons and braided trim. The collar of his white shirt gleamed. He was in a short red driving jacket with piping on the lapels, knickers, handsome wool socks, and alligator boots.

He stopped when he saw her and backed up as though her light stopped him, burned him, laid him bare. "Look what you've done!" He spun his finger, dressed out nattily in the sharp leather glove. "Cleaner than clean here!"

"Grace!" Hanson said. "Dad got us early . . . so we couldn't clean up. Sorry."

She smiled. The words seemed almost enough from Hanson, although she would like to have scolded him. Instead, she wiped down the last dust on the top of the stove. Her body felt sore, numb with fatigue, but she was beginning to smile behind her eyes, and then, because she saw that they were done with their work, and she was done with hers, she couldn't hold back her smile.

"And now!" Alex announced, "for helping us out in the house—a big evening! Where do you want to go?" he said. He grabbed a chair, turned it around, straddled it in front of her. "You name it. It's all yours!" He looked at Hanson. "Any flicks in this town? You seen *Birth of a Nation*?"

Hanson looked at him blankly, as though wheels were trying to grind to a stop in his head. He shook his head slowly. There may be three theaters, but none of the big films ever made it to Provo, Utah, he might have said. But he was watching Grace. She was searching his eyes. "Whatever we do, let's do something big!" he said. "Nothing's too good. Grace, do you want to go dancing?"

"Dancing? Dancing? It's Thursday. Is there dancing on Thursday?" Alex said. "No dancing until Friday. We'll go dancing Friday. Where do you want to go, Grace?"

The new electric light in the room—a convenience recently

installed—buzzed. The buzzing seemed to tie all of the words in the room together. The moths had come in out of the cold. They were dancing around the light, fluttering their wings.

"This is some beautiful girl. Can I have her, Hanson?" Alex said, climbing so hard over the chair that it tipped. He put his arm around Grace and put his face in her neck. "Beautiful, beautiful." The words drowned in her hair.

Grace's head leaped into a thousand needles of light. The feeling zipped down her back and into her blood. She could feel the electricity from her head to the soles of her feet. It was a feeling unlike any she had ever felt before. She saw Hanson lean his head back. He was laughing. "Be careful now! You've really fallen for my girl, haven't you, Alex?"

"I fell for her!" Alex said, looking into Grace's eyes now. "And I'll have her, too." He was close. His eyes were close. His mouth was close. Grace, tingling and laughing, felt his presence jar the very center of her nerves.

"I love you, Grace," Alex said. He kept her tightly circled in his arm and suddenly leaned close to kiss her on the mouth. It might have been only in fun, but it was a genuine kiss. Totally surprised that she was accepting it, she let her lips linger on his. Shocked at her own lightheartedness, she felt every jolt of this man's power. The lights above her head began to spin. What was she doing? She didn't know.

"You lover boy, Alex. Grace, you need to know about this Romeo," Hanson was grinning. "Let's go before you get serious." He was smiling. "Anywhere you want to go, Gracie? Name it." He put his hands into his pockets.

"Have you been kissed since Hanson left you alone?" Alex said. He still held her to his side with his arm. He turned his head to look at her. She was surrounded by his face and his arm. There was magic in the room—everywhere: in the feeling of his body close to hers, in the laughter beneath the electric light where the moths curled and batted their wings. She didn't back away from him this time. She smiled.

"Come on, Gracie. Where will it be?" Alex said.

She shrugged her shoulders.

"We'll have dinner at Mrs. Carroll's on State Street," Hanson said. He moved his hands in his pockets. He stood awkwardly while something magic seemed to happen in front of him.

"They have ribs?" Alex said, not moving his head an inch further away from Grace's hair as they walked from the room. "I need something to stick to my ribs."

"She has lamb, I guess," Hanson said good naturedly.

Grace still tingled. Alex's nose was again in her ear. "I love you, Grace," he said. "Hanson won't say you can't be mine."

Hanson was still grinning. "You dog. Reminds me of that time on the Marne."

Alex leaned back and laughed at Hanson's words. "Nothing like this, Hanson, buddy," he said. "Nothing like this. He doesn't know how serious we are, does he? I love you, Gracie."

"Don't listen to him, Grace. He can't be trusted," Hanson laughed, then turned. "Let me get my other shoes. I'll hurry." He bounded up the stairs. In the bedroom next to the landing Grace heard the door open and close. She looked up. Alex was standing above her, his eyes so close, she could not see. He had his arms around her in a moment and pulled her in quickly. Folding her close for a long moment, he placed another kiss on her lips. She had never felt anything like it. Not ever: the softness, the pounding blood, the leap in her limbs. He held her close for a long time—until they heard Hanson on the stairs.

Hanson did not seem to notice. Without moving away from her, Alex nodded to Hanson to get the door. "You never had an evening like this, Grace. Hup, march!" He gestured for Hanson to stand on the other side of her.

Hanson came to her left and took her hand. "Well, I'm back. Time to go." He lifted her hand in both of his and gazed at it for a brief moment. Grace was totally aware of his presence. When he looked into her eyes and said, "Thank you for taking care of us, Grace. Alex can't appreciate you more than I do," she felt even more of the same spinning.

"You're welcome," she said.

17

Mara Eastman Jones

When Mara saw how sick Reginald seemed at the funeral and after the dinner at the church, she invited him to stay in her home until he felt better. He had hesitated only a moment. Though he did not want to be any trouble, he would appreciate going to a place he could get some good rest. Mara could see a hunger in his eyes not just for rest, but for someone to care. She promised herself she would do everything she could for him. After showing him to his room and giving him a moment to rest, she returned to ask if there was anything else.

He wondered if he could move the bed closer to the window. Because there was not much she could do to help him with this heavy task, she stood by uncomfortably while he pushed and pulled—even though she could tell he was still in pain. She glanced at the way he had wanted the bed to lie. It had something to do with both the outside and the inside light. The table by the bed was skewed so that the lamp shone over his pillow. Then she noticed she had left Sobe's journal on the books that were lying there. She might have reached for it to take it out of the room, but she was thinking of other things.

"I'm not sure you're well enough to do all of this, Mr. Summerfield."

"I'm all right," he said, holding himself up on the bedpost. "Do you have some baking soda?"

Mara got the baking soda in a glass of water. When he turned toward her to take the glass out of her hand and lifted his head to swallow it quickly, she saw that his eyes looked red and weary.

"You're not all right," she said, holding his arm. "Your eyes are terribly bloodshot. Please lie down."

He slowly lowered himself to the bed, trying to maintain control. When he tried to lie still, his body continued to shake; the cold must have seeped into his legs. She brought another blanket and lay it over his feet. As she looked at him quietly she thought she could see the Eggertson on the bridge of his nose, Sully in the high brow, Samantha in his mouth. But the broad flat cheeks and the eyes were Rain's.

It seemed a long time that he held the covers very tight. She sat quietly with him until he was warm. He lay up on the pillows, but held the blanket high to his chin. "I can't miss the business meetings tomorrow," he said without looking up.

"You'll be all right if you get some sleep," Mara whispered. Then she heard nothing but quiet. She chose not to move, staying close.

"I think I remember you," he finally said in a low voice that sounded far away.

"I remember you, Mathew," she said. She reached for his hand. "You were a dear four-year-old boy who had survived that terrible night on the lake."

"My mother saved our lives. I wanted to find her. All of my young life I wanted to find her. Now I know she is dead. My baby sister, Eliza, is dead. My father is dead." His voice was almost indistinct.

Mara thought she could hear the snow falling. "Mathew, can you remember anything at all about that day you never returned?"

". . . a boy was flying," he said. "I was four years . . ."

With her other hand, Mara stroked his large wrist. "I am so grateful you are here again. We can make plans for you."

"My father remarried? Then he died?"

"Yes."

"Do I have any half-brothers and sisters?"

"Don't you worry about it, Mathew." She still stroked his

hand. "You are a Summerfield. And you'll probably always be a Summerfield. That is all right. Mathew," she spoke slowly. "Do you remember your name Mathew?"

"I think so. Mr. Summerfield wanted me to have his name. I was his only son."

"Reginald Summerfield," Mara said.

"I also have an Indian name." He smiled a broad smile for the first time since he lay on the bed.

"Oh?" Mara felt the time growing late, but she could not leave him while he seemed to want her to stay. He was not really well. She did not know why he was weak, but she was afraid. Now, because he wanted to talk, she let him talk. "What was your Indian name?" she asked.

"Moon Hawk," he said. He smiled, and with his free hand drew a circle on the window glass that was now situated beside his head. "Moon Hawk."

"Who gave you the name Moon Hawk?"

"Old Hawk in the Tree." He was looking out of the window now, and Mara thought he was closing his eyes to sleep, but, with his voice sounding far away, he continued to talk. "Some of the Indians were still close by," he said. "They were still close by."

In strained words that seemed to come from somewhere very deep, he began to recount what had happened when he was a child. His mother told him not to leave the field when he went to play. While his father was working at the woolen mills in Provo, he chased butterflies on the meadows that led to Elk Ridge. Sometimes he saw the elk standing in great herds on the hills. He did not always do as his mother had told him to do. He left the meadows and followed the elk up into the hills.

The boy named Bud Kunz was only a few years older than he was. He led Mathew high into Loafer Canyon and leaned too far over the ridge. He flew like a bird.

"Now I remember his name was Bud. But I called him Butter." Reginald was looking out the window still, his face frozen.

"When Butter fell I was never so frightened in all my life. He cried out, and then I heard a crush of bones on the cliff below."

Mara continued to look at this man's face, searching for the little boy she had known inside this large body. She could not see him there.

He had lost his way, Reginald continued. Two Indian braves had found him sleeping. They must have believed they could sell him. And in fact, they did trade the boy for a flat carved stone an old Hopi Indian gave for him—an old Indian who knew what captivity was like because he had been captured by Utes at one time many years before he made his home on the high trail to Strawberry.

Hawk in the Tree lived in a lean-to on the Scatterback Mountains that looked west to Mount Nebo. Many years ago his mother had escaped the destruction of her village and lived with the footrunner Indians until they were captured by the Utes. When his mother had escaped, she had run to the hills. And after her death, he had lived alone. "Hawk in the Tree called me 'Boy' until one night under a full moon I found a rabbit near my bed and caught it. Old Hawk in the Tree laughed and said, 'We call you Hawk in the Moonlight. Moon Hawk,' he said."

They learned together how to survive the winters and avoid the traffic of cattle drives and encroaching settlers.

Hawk in the Tree had been stubborn about not leaving to go to the reservation. He wanted to stay in the mountains, so he stayed in the mountains, taking care of the little boy Moon Hawk until he was nine years old. Moon Hawk thought his Eggertson name was pronounced "Ickerson" and he was never able to find his grandparents, though he knew they must have lived somewhere beyond the black mountains. It was much later that he remembered there had been someone named Rain.

One morning Hawk in the Tree went out to hunt and never

returned. Moon Hawk found his Indian father dead, lying peacefully under a cedar tree. From the cedar tree Moon Hawk could see down the ravine for twenty miles; he could see the back of Mount Nebo and the miles of cedar and aspen that had begun to turn yellow in the autumn sun. He thought to himself "Hawk in the Tree does no more running. Now he is flying in his own heaven."

He knew winter was coming, so he followed some trappers down to a camp to find something to eat. Because it was autumn, he saw men hunting deer and heard shooting in the trees. One shot grazed his shoulder.

He pulled the collar of his shirt open to show his wound to Mara. There was a scar at the top of his shoulder.

"A man with a little gray beard came through the draw with his gun," Reginald whispered. And when he saw the small boy Moon Hawk lying on the rocks with blood all over his body, he began to cry, terrified that he had killed a boy.

Mathew knew a little English as well as the Indian language. When he told the man his Indian father had died, the man put Moon Hawk on the back of his horse and took him home. His wife Rachel made so much over him that the boy never left them.

He was happy with his white folks in their little home near Heber, Utah. He thought someday he might try to find his family, but he never did. The Summerfields saw that he went to school and to the university. When he was looking for a job as an accountant, he learned about a Mr. Barrington who came through Heber on his way to Denver in a train of mules. At work for Mr. Barrington, he was a faithful employee for several years. He wanted to be a credit to the only parents he knew, but he was always trying to reconstruct his past—to remember names, like Ickerson and Rain. When he followed Mr. Barrington to this town, a man in the hotel talked about the funeral of an old Indian named Rain. And then he had read the notice in the newspaper. He wondered if this Rain were someone he knew from long ago. He wanted to know.

The light from the falling snow had completely gone now. Mara held Regi's hand in her own and warmed it, still. She was a thousand miles away in her mind—somewhere in the miles of mountains between Salem and Strawberry, somewhere in the blue hills now covered with snow.

"Regi, your Grandmother Rain was brokenhearted when you disappeared. When she died, she mentioned your name."

"I have heard my grandmother's voice talk to me. But I have not listened for a long time. But I believe I heard her when she died."

Mara thought she could see tears. But he did not cry.

"I am sure I remember you. You are Aunt Mara who made biscuits with a shaving mug."

Mara laughed. She remembered little Mathew so well. "Mathew!" she said, overcome with emotion. "Reginald," she corrected herself. "If there is any way we can help you to feel at home, please let us know."

While she talked, she realized she was gazing at a man who may have been Mathew, but that now he was a man she did not know. All she really knew about him was what he told her. She knew little Mathew would have been about twenty-nine years old, that by now he could have grown very large, and he had survived by himself for all of these years.

"It's getting late," she whispered, still holding his hand. He clasped his fingers more tightly around hers. "You'd better go to sleep. You'll feel better in the morning."

"I'm all right now," he said slowly. Though his eyes seemed to be closing, he suddenly looked directly into her face and said, "I also remember Sobe."

Sobe. Mara started at the name, not knowing why. "Sobe? How did you remember Sobe?"

He looked at her and then over at the journal on the table beside the bed. "I hope you do not mind. When I first came in I thumbed through the pages, reading some of what he wrote.

May I keep it a while longer?"

Mara looked at the journal on the table. "Of course, Mathew. You are welcome . . ." she began, though she noticed that his eyes seemed to be closing. In a few more moments he was breathing heavily through his nose.

Mara thought he was asleep when she reached to turn down the kerosene lamp, but he said to her in a quiet voice, "Please leave the lamp on."

Mara walked out into the hall and shut his door. For a moment she sat down in the chair outside of her room, listening to Regi's heavy breathing. And yet she was concerned that the lamp had been left on. For a moment she sat in the dark, but when she stood and peered through the crack in the door, she could see Regi holding Sobe's journal in his hands. When she left him to go to her own room, he was still reading.

Finally in her bed, she lay awake for a long time hearing what she thought must be Reginald's breathing. She believed she did not sleep, but she must have, because when she finally rose in the morning, Reginald was gone.

She fussed around in the kitchen awhile before she went into Will's room to wake him. The sun was bright on the snow. When Will rose he wanted hot camomile tea right away because he was having stomach pains. After she fixed the tea, she sat with him at the table and told him about Mathew.

"He was reading Sobe's journal. I left it there by mistake. He and Sobe—they are a lot alike in many ways."

"I don't think so, Mara," Will said.

"It's true there is still much I don't know," she said.

Will was quiet. When she stopped, he said "You're unrealistic, Mara."

She looked at him, surprised.

"He's not connected with us in any way. A quarter of a century has passed."

Mara watched Will's eyes. They were behind his thick glasses darting around on the headlines of the newspaper. He could read only the headlines now.

"You are right," Mara said. "There is still a lot we do not know. We don't know him. But we do know he has worked hard to become educated. He is working for L. F. Barrington."

"Seems to me he's got some of those modern philosophical scientific ideas. To the exclusion of faith."

"I wonder why? Perhaps he has been through too many unhappy experiences," Mara said. "We could help him."

"Mara." Will peered over his spectacles. "Sounds to me like you're fishing around to adopt a project."

"Maybe."

"I thought one of these years you were going to retire."

When Mara didn't answer him, Will returned to his newspaper. "Hmmmph," he said quietly to himself. "You never give up, do you?"

18

Reginald Summerfield

He breathed hard when the door closed. For a moment he stared without moving. He had probably spoken more words to his old Aunt Mara than he had ever breathed to anyone! Deep in his body, down below the pounding wound, the blood and the sickness, he felt panic.

Still suspended in so many different ways of looking at things, he was exhausted. Because he had never planted his feet firmly on any ground, he had grown used to being at sea. Now he saw Mara's kindness with wariness. In one short day she had sucked him in. When she listened, he had told her all. Well, not all. There were still dark spaces that crowded his heart—places he hoped no one would ever see.

His panic was underlined by a sense that he was still as vulnerable as a child. And he had tried too hard to become a man. But there were so many holes in his childhood that had never been filled. Sometimes he was riddled with emptiness, and suddenly he was afraid. He was still himself, whoever he was. And if these people truly knew him, he believed they could not accept him. He hovered suspended in the terrifying vacuum until he forced his eyes to the journal on the table.

Earlier when he had glanced at the open pages of the journal he had seen the words *Hunkayapi was the ceremony of the "making of relatives."* And the words had aroused his deepest interest. Intrigued, he could almost feel some energy in the book reach out to draw him into its bewildering pages. And he had waited until now to discover what was there for him—what voice seemed to know how to speak both the Indian and the white language so well. Now, when the shadows from the kerosene light danced across the walls and ceiling, he could pick up this book and discover what it was that beckoned to him. He held the book for a long moment, as though it were a treasure—perhaps the other half of the stone tablet no one had ever seen.

Nawduh'gwenup are true stories of how God communicates with man. Joseph Smith knew the truth. If one learns reverence for it, there is contact with that world. God. Tovuts. Does it matter what name we use? We are not alone.

Reginald paused and looked up at the ceiling. We are not alone. That was what he believed! He read on.

I . . . have seen the shapes of all things in the spirit and the shape of all shapes as they must live together like one being. . . . Anything less than one . . . is outside the universe.

His mind reeled. He knew this was the Indian boy Mara had told him about. His words were so vivid, he could hear the Indian speaking from the dead to him. He pulled the lantern closer and continued to read. Sobe was talking about prophecy.

I know my people talked with God. They continued to talk with God long after the great wars destroyed most of them.

Rain told me of Pawdookoots—the prophets—either men or women, who fell on the ground. Their minds went out of this world for a time. When they returned they spoke wonderful things. Our earth is older than thousands of years—even hundreds of thousands of years. And our ancestors are as old as the earth. We, as earth's children, can reach out to touch the spirits of others in the universe only if we learn reverence—reverence for life itself and all the ramifications of growing. Every new horizon rises after some darkness.

That's right, Regi said to himself. He wondered if Sobe had ever had spiritual experiences of his own.

As he continued, he now read of stories Rain had told Sobe. One of them was about Pawdookoots, the woman of the Shivwits, who, hungering for spiritual experiences after dark times and periods of great confusion, mounted her horse and rode out to the plateau. There she fasted and prayed until she received the light. The light would always come. And then she would speak. There were always answers. *We are all together in this world: the living and the dead. We will always feel the love from the dead, and the quest of all lives for continuing life. And inside of our own life we must give everything we have. When my daughter died, Rain took me in her arms. "You have now given everything," she told me.*

Reginald put the book down. He did not know this Sobe, but he was dazed. After reading only these few words, he felt he knew the voice of this man who understood him—who understood the Indians.

I am not an Indian as much as I am a human being. My loved ones are not child, man, woman, Mormon, protestant or Jew as much as they are mankind. Will they see who they are and accept the other ones' unusual stories?

Reginald turned the page.

Our people will always have the ceremony Hunkayapi, the "making of relatives." And it is to Hunkayapi of the world that I plead.

Then Reginald's eyes caught some sentences that startled him, because they so well described his own reality.

I have been suspended so long between so many worlds.

That was how he, Reginald, felt. He had never belonged to anyone or anything: a family, a particular creed. He could never recite a particular story of creation, because he had heard it differently from Hawk in the Tree, and then from Mrs. Summerfield when she came home from the Bible class at Heber.

I sincerely believe it is best to follow one way, to give everything to one story of life so that our feet may stand firm and we are grounded enough to give real service. How can we help anyone if we are so loose we are blown from one way to another so that we never dig in roots enough to grow? And so I have chosen the words of Jesus.

Reginald felt dizzy as he continued to read—not only from the displacement he felt because of the wound. *I might have chosen Tavuts, or even the spider woman. But it must be someone. And I have learned of Jesus from these people. And I love his word. I wish to live how he pleads for us to live.* Reginald felt as though he were being scolded by someone who knew him. This man believed close to what he believed and yet he was anchored to something. Reginald was only reminded that he had simply not chosen to anchor himself—yet.

Sobe had reconciled how Jesus's stories fit the language of the old people. He wrote, *Because it is all the same truth.* He continued by quoting Rain's story that Pawdookoots of old had seen the world as a sea of glass. Not as though there were lakes of glass everywhere, but that through glass everyone would someday see other people so that all the world would know that all in the whole world were essentially the same. *And we must learn to embrace all of it at once in Hunkayapi—making everyone our relatives.*

This is a true prophecy. There is a clarity coming in which all of us will see everything. And be able to love the preciousness of mankind that we see.

Sobe's words continued to fascinate Reginald as he read. *The Mormons say the world will reach its paradisaical glory. That is another way to say it. But we are all—no matter our creed—pressing toward the millennial day. Soon we will have the knowledge to reconcile all the stories and all the languages that tell the stories. We will know we are one.*

Reginald felt the flickering in the lamp warn him there was no more kerosene. He had been flying with these words of Sobe's, and now something practical brought him breathing—though unsteadily and still painfully—inside reality.

I have read of the Pawdookoots who foretold that the white man would come to take all the land away from the Indians and cut it up and fight over it.

But I have also read of the Pawdookoots who foretold that

someday the white man would see the land as something he can never own, but only borrow for his life. For he and the Indian both return to the great light and the land breathes under them and over them—the same. And knowing this, everyone can feel peace in sleep.

That day hasn't come, Reginald said to himself. That day certainly hasn't come. Yet it seemed closer, somehow, after he read this man's words. Sobe would have understood how Reginald swung suspended above words of any kind. And he felt his eyes growing heavy now as though he could find a moment of that peace.

19

Grace Tuttle

When Grace saw Mara come to the house with the Indian just at the moment she and Alex and Hanson came out on the porch ready to leave for Mrs. Carroll's, she caught her breath. Only twenty-four hours had passed since the funeral and the luncheon at the church had ended, yet it seemed as though she had known this Indian man forever. And it wasn't a pleasant thought to her. One more moment and she and the boys would have been in Alex's car and gone. Grace gasped when she realized she had wanted to escape Mara and her half-breed cousin. She couldn't believe her own selfishness. She was stunned.

"Well, hello, Summerfield," Alex shook his hand vigorously and asked about Barrington.

Aunt Mara came to Grace and folded her hands over hers. "Will and I . . . with the funeral and all yesterday, we are very tired tonight. Please, Gracie. He's your cousin. Get to know him."

Grace's heart came to a stop in her throat. Everything had changed so suddenly. She looked at the Indian. He knew she was looking at him, because as he was talking with Alex, his eyes were directly on her own. She felt very sick in the pit of her stomach and she did not know exactly why. "All right," she said.

"I hope it's okay. He'll enjoy you young people." Mara smiled and squeezed her hand. "Ask him about his Indian name Moon Hawk. He has quite a story to tell." Then she whispered softly so no one would hear her: "Be patient with Hanson, honey. He has some adjustments to make." When she turned to the others, she spoke up to everyone. "This is wonderful to see you young people having a good time. Will and I won't be able to see you tonight." She did not say why. "I hope it's all right to include Mr. Summerfield in your fun, Hanson?" she asked.

"Of course, Aunt Mara."

Grace saw that Hanson, too, was hesitant. But he did not hold back from smiling and including Mr. Summerfield.

Grace was embarrassed that she had reacted with distaste. But she drove away her disappointment. She would be kind. Laughing, the boys climbed into Alex's two-seater. Alex and Hanson took the front and she climbed in beside Reginald in the back. Her heart broke in two. This was not how she had wanted it to be. The presence of Reginald—the faint odor of something musty—was all blackness. He was casting a shadow on everything. "How did your day go, Reginald?" she forced herself to say.

Reginald was staring at her. "You remind me of someone."

"I do?" Grace asked.

"You do." He leaned back against the side of the car to get a broader perspective. "The dark hair, the dark eyes. Do you look like Grandmother Rain?"

Grace was grateful Hanson had turned to the back and leaned over the seat to talk in that moment.

"Have you ever been to Mrs. Caroll's?" he asked.

"No," Regi said. "Is that where you're going?"

"She serves supper in her farmhouse for money. Delicious supper. There's music—an organ."

Hanson had turned back to Alex now. They were talking about an organ they had heard in a cathedral in Germany. She would like to have heard what they were saying, but Reginald was leaning closer. It seemed that she could smell the sweat that lay on his face. She backed away.

"The Summerfields never had a piano," he was saying. "I would like to have learned. You know, I was telling you that you reminded me of someone? It was the girl I . . ." He paused. "A woman in Salt Lake City . . ." He seemed unable to finish much of anything. "You've been in Salt Lake City, haven't you?"

"No."

"I went to school there."

He talked about small nothings. Grace listened to him. She forced herself to be kind. She wanted to be fair. But Reginald Summerfield was driving her to distraction. She could not hear the conversations that were important to her. She tried to lean toward the front seat. When she asked a question, the boys laughed and gave her only a couple of words when they consented to explain. But the short explanations were only crumbs.

"It was in Sebastipol I saw that organist. We saw a street musician in Sebastipol," Alex turned slightly toward her. "The old man had fought in the revolution." He did not say which revolution. He turned to Hanson and they began to laugh privately: "Remember his boots. They had ripped apart at the seams."

Grace sat back against the seat. It was no use. She was with Regi by some terrible default. She was not sure what had happened. She sat numb, thinking it through, watching the gas lights in the street, the windows of the homes pass her by. She began to pray silently, "Dear Heavenly Father, this is a lost evening. Let me get through it without being unkind." Moon Hawk. Mara had said his Indian name was Moon Hawk. What did it mean?

Mrs. Carroll's was crowded for a Thursday night. The farmhouse sat back from the road on South State, its windows facing the south valley. Its cupolas and eaves were painted a cheerful white, the stone walk lined on both sides with a small white picket fence. At the porch two large poinsettias stood on pedestals. The door was an oval of cut glass.

Grace knew the people ahead of them were dignitaries from the Brigham Young University. She thought she recognized President and Sister Brimhall, the older woman with her hair sleek gray against her head, her peach-colored beads flowing in ropes from her neck. She was in the latest décolleté—a hanging, waistless, scoop-necked dress that stopped just above the ankle, showing pretty feet in beige silk shoes. Grace felt very out of style in her long blue gingham tied at the waist with a white satin sash. She thought to herself in that moment: "I will have to have some new clothes."

On the way to the door they could hear music. "There it is!" Alex cried out. "First dance, Grace!" He took her by the arm and pushed her ahead. She stepped fast to catch up. She felt a welcome relief with the touch of his arm. When the men followed her into the dining room she suddenly felt insecure. She wondered what her teachers from the university would think if they saw her out with three men? When Mr. Peterson saw her, she turned to him and smiled. "Hello, Grace dear," he said. Grace smiled back and offered him her hand.

Alex said under his breath, "Whoa! She knows some swell heads. How about that, fellows?" He grinned. His face was animated. Her greeting to the Petersons had made a visible impression on him.

At that moment, from the back of the dining room, from the French windows that looked out over the winter garden, a man in a sharply pressed gray flannel coat came forward with a tiny lady on his arm, and on the other a young woman whose face was almost overpowered by a thick shower of long blond hair. Grace had never seen her. She thought this man could have been the new science teacher from Logan's Utah Agricultural College. The university people had talked about him, a Robert Adamson, who was a grandson of the Kate Wright Hunt who had worried Mara so. He was slender and tall, with very straight gray hair pomaded against his temples. But it was the girl who paralyzed the entire room. Her hair was almost white gold, and it fell in perfect waves across her cheeks and lay gathered in a large comb at the nape of her neck. Her gown dropped in the new waistless fashion, shimmering in silver thread. Her throat was almost as white as her hair.

Grace was not the only one startled by the beauty of this girl. The others in the room were watching her as well.

"Oh, heaven on earth," Alex said under his breath. "Do you know who it is, Grace?"

Grace was not sure. "I believe a Mr. Adamson."

Alex rubbed his chin. "Hmmm. Adamson," he mused. "My grandmother was an Adamson."

Grace said she thought Mr. Adamson had a daughter named Laura. This beautiful girl could be Laura.

"Can you introduce us, Grace?" he asked.

Grace's discomfort passed through her like a knife. She stared at the girl and felt Alex's eyes were intent upon the girl as she fingered her father's cuff, her hands lightly locked around his large fist. They were greeting the Brimhalls. There was a flurry of gracious talk and the uniformed waiter ushered the party of educators toward a small private dining room. Grace watched them go.

She watched Alex's eyes. He was in a trance. Gone. She expected him to be gone for the rest of the evening. Maybe forever. Suddenly her feelings slammed into a stark reality. She gazed at all of the faces around her. They were in the presence of a bright star—this Laura Adamson. Hanson was watching, though there was something reserved in his eyes. Reginald Summerfield was totally stricken.

As soon as the Eastman party had seen the Adamsons, Reginald had surged forward. Now he followed the adults into the dining room. Grace felt an instinctive pressure to reach out to him, to draw him back. But he seemed to know this girl. Grace watched, puzzled. The giant man bent at the waist and took the girl's hand. She smiled a vague recognition. The father smiled graciously, edging her toward the opposite side of the table, and nodding at Regi. Regi's eyes followed the girl. He stood like an ox in the way of the other men and women. Grace was startled at his insensitivity. Yet, in spite of her earlier feelings, she felt pity for him when he finally turned away from the room and came toward them, his shoulders hunched forward.

"She was at the university with me," he said when he reached them. He spoke as though he had not chased down the elite of the faculty, or as though chasing down the faculty was as everyday an occurrence as common as chasing buffalo.

Grace could barely speak. She stared. "You know her?"

"She introduced me to the Book of Mormon."

Grace felt his discomfort for a few moments as though it were her own. The room seemed very small while the waiter asked for their order. While the others ordered, Alex and Reginald talked in curt sentences to each other, and Alex and Hanson talked in low tones. There were scattered bits of conversation over the soup and the lamb.

"But I never read it," Reginald Summerfield was saying.

"You're a gutsy Indian. You think anybody in Barrington's employment has a right to throw himself around after pretty girls?" Alex was short with Regi. "Going to get your tomahawk next?"

Grace tried to ignore the sharp tone in Alex's voice.

"I know her."

"Didn't look like she knows much about you," Alex snapped.

Grace looked at Regi's eyes. He was so deep in thought about the girl with the white blond hair, that he was completely oblivious to the cruelty in Alex's tone. He was watching her through the doors, his eyes fastened to the figures far away.

From where Alex sat he could also see through the swinging door when the waiter kicked it open. Like Regi, he too was trying to catch a glimpse of Laura through the same swinging dining room door. Grace heard him whisper to Hanson: "Tell me where you'd get details about the new faculty and family."

Grace spooned the vegetables out of the soup and picked at her lamb. She was not hungry. She noticed that Reginald sucked the soup out of his spoon and pushed the basil leaf with his tongue. When he caught the leaf between his fingers he said

"Basil. Poison." Embarrassed, Grace turned her head.

"Have you ever grown basil, Miss Grace?"

She was silent for a moment. Suddenly she saw Reginald as someone who may never become aware. She had a sudden feeling of compassion for him, and a hope to shed her selfishness. After all, he was her cousin.

"We grew peppermint and made tea," she said to him, turning to him, but not really looking at him, avoiding his portly flat face.

"Ah, we also grew mint. And camomile, and rose hips. Have you ever made tea with cranberry?"

The question about the cranberries was so innocent, she found that her eyes suddenly met his. "Cranberry?"

For a moment Regi had stopped ogling the crowd in the dining room. He was focused on Grace. She wasn't sure how she felt. Suddenly he leaned his head back and laughed. "You've never heard of cranberry tea?" He leaned toward her. "Do you like to try new things? You ought to try cranberry tea." Then he whispered, "and cranberry color."

When she dared to look at him, she saw that he was smiling. She was not aware of the look of surprise on her own face.

"Not that you need color," Regi said. And without a pause he touched her lip with his finger. As she drew back, he laughed. "You have a cranberry mouth."

The touch confused Grace. She could feel the heat come up in her cheeks. She blushed because she was aware that Hanson was watching her, too.

"Do you want cake?" Hanson offered.

Grace shook her head.

"I'll have cake," Reginald spoke to the waiter. He said he had caught sight of the cake on his way into the room and it was magnificent. "Bring two large pieces and Miss Grace will eat one of them."

Grace sat, numbed by the lights, numbed by the touch on her lips, by the glimpse she caught of the girl in the room, numbed by her responsibility to be kind. When the waiter brought the cake, Reginald leaned over her and cut a tiny piece from the corner. "It's delicious," he told her. "Try it. This is Boston cream."

Grace had never seen a confection like it. It stood very high with layer after layer of delicious white cream and sugar. It melted in her mouth.

"Now that's what I call cake," Reginald said, enjoying it.

But Grace could not concentrate for long on the cake. She saw that Hanson had begun to keep his eyes focused on her. He looked at her with a mixed uncertainty. He directed questions to her, but she tossed them off in a mysterious anger toward him that she could not quite understand.

"Are you teaching in January, then?" Hanson asked her.

She could not look directly into Hanson's eyes. She looked askance and kept aloof. "I'm applying." When she realized her tone of voice was almost cold, she tried to make up for it with a coda: "I just hope they'll have me," she said in softer words.

"They need teachers."

"How do you know?" she asked.

"Well, I heard they let a lot of them go while I was gone. Why?"

"Some of them were teaching evolution."

"Is that why Brimhall is resigned to leaving it a Utah training school rather than opting for a nationally accredited university?"

Alex and Regi began listening to Hanson while they spooned in mouthfuls of food. "Who is this Adamson?" Alex asked, expecting enough time had passed that he could get a thorough answer now.

"A science teacher from Logan," Grace said. "He and another teacher, Franklin Harris—they are both strong in the faith. Now for the training school they are hiring only people who believe."

Reginald sat up very straight. His eyes grew dark. "That's

what I thought, no academic freedom," he said.

"There are other universities to teach in," Grace said simply.

"You mean if they want to teach something a little off center from Mormon doctrine, they can teach elsewhere?"

Grace nodded. "There ought to be one university that teaches faith."

"You can't believe there's no evolution?" Alex said to Grace, surprised.

"I don't need evolution to live a good life. But I need faith in God," she said.

"You know there's evolution. Or else how can you teach that man evolves into a god?" Regi was sitting back against his chair, grinning.

"I'm not saying no to evolution," Grace whispered, feeling outnumbered. She appealed to Hanson in a brief flickering glance. But he seemed far away.

"There's only one truth," Regi said. "The force toward creation." The smile on his face flickered.

"Is that what you learned at the University of Utah, or California, or wherever you went, Mr. Accountant?" Alex sneered.

"There is one great truth," Grace said. "Love has to be learned. There should be one university on the earth that can teach it."

"And what is love?" Regi placed the tips of his fingers together.

Grace moved back from him and smiled. She tossed her head and the curls bounced. "Why don't you come to classes at the university and find out?" she said.

"That's such a lie," Alex laughed. "I've heard plenty about the precious close-minded Brigham Young Academy. If they really knew how to love, wouldn't they open up their portals to all the peoples of the world, all of the ideas of the world, and share with everyone?"

"The best way to love is to find the truth and guide others

to it," Grace said.

"What's the truth?" Regi grinned at her.

Hanson was watching Grace.

"How can we find joy if we don't learn to do God's will?"

Alex laughed. "You would make a good missionary, Grace Tuttle!" he guffawed. "A tiptop top-of-the-batch missionary."

Grace forced a smile when she felt she might cry instead. "We're all missionaries, aren't we, Hanson?"

When he heard her question, Hanson turned his head as though he came up from a deep reverie. "Missionaries? Maybe." He looked at her and smiled a vague smile. "We all spread our work and our word—but for good or for ill." He leaned forward at the table now. "And no one is exempt from spreading a good share of both, I don't suppose. Although it is the goal of our lives to spread more good."

"You preach! You preach," Alex said. "As if there are ever any final answers!"

"You're a missionary of sorts. But maybe the devil's advocate! And quite inspired! I never saw so much fire and brimstone in one soul," Hanson tried to joke about Alex.

"Hah! I'm inspired. But not by creeds! Love inspires me!"

"I know. You're inspired by gold hair," Hanson teased Alex now.

The atmosphere had changed to lighthearted sparring. It seemed Hanson had forgotten Grace's serious words of only a few seconds earlier. Or he was being careful not to go too deeply into the spaces where Alex would have felt somewhat uncomfortable.

Alex was cocking his head, shamelessly trying once more to look behind the swinging door, but it shut before anyone could catch a glance.

"The blond head, the blond head," Hanson chanted.

"Whoops. There is that confounded door again! Shut before we can take a look," Regi sneered.

"Hey! Don't get personal, man," Alex stopped him coldly.

"I know her, and she's not interested," Regi snapped back. The world was filled with voices and birds flying against the wires snapped to the black machine, and the wires pulled and the wings beat.

Grace was silent. She couldn't go on. She looked at Hanson's eyes. She thought she saw surprise in them. His lips opened slightly, as though he wanted to speak. Yet in a moment he turned his eyes to Grace, and as he looked at her now, there seemed to be worlds of words being said in the air between them. Suddenly there was a warmth she couldn't explain—as though the only agreeable forces in the room had electrified them. She felt a sudden hope she had not yet had since he had been home. She half expected something about the evening to change. But she had not expected this change.

Regi drew back from the table in that instant. "Now we'll have music! I happen to know Laura likes music. Grace, play for us. No more serious talk!" When he rose from the table, the entire table setting almost went with him. The glassware rocked. A few drops of water spilled. He did not notice the near catastrophe. As if he were used to glasses dancing whenever he moved, he extended a hand to Grace and pulled her up with him. "Play, Grace. Play a hymn if you're feeling your faith. Play anything!" He led her to the organ and tested a key. It was on. "I love music. Play 'Camptown Races.'"

Grace, still stunned by the seriousness of the argument during the dessert, played a few chords on the organ. It was not "Camptown Races." It was "Oh give me a home, where the buffalo roam." Regi stood over the console, beating the rhythm out with his hand. When she was finished, he raised his giant arms and clapped very loud. He was obviously looking toward the small dining room. Grace saw that he was hoping to get someone's attention there. Everyone in the large room was clapping with him. Grace could see through the glass in the door of the tiny room. President Brimhall and Mr. Robert Adamson were in a different world. They never turned their heads.

She played "Brown Bird Singing" and "White Wings." The sound from the organ rolled into the room.

"You're good, Grace. Very good," Regi said. But when Grace looked up at him, his face was lifted toward the dining room.

During the rest of the evening little changed. Most of the attention—both visual and verbal—rested upon the diners behind the swinging door, whose world, because it was mysterious, seemed somehow more desirable than their own.

After the meal ended, Alex and Hanson took a great deal of time discussing how the bill should be paid. And when it had finally been decided, they walked together out of the front door of the farmhouse restaurant. Grace found herself trailing behind with Reginald Summerfield, such a large man that he crowded her on the walk. In a few short seconds, however, Grace realized he was crowding her not only because of his size, but on purpose to be close to her—to touch her with his shoulder.

"You have a good dining place here," he said. "Good people, good town." He paused. "Pretty women."

Grace felt his eyes on her. She stiffened. When they made their way out into the street, one of the men started up his auto and the horse in front of it tugged at the bridle, broke it, and kicked. When Grace came to the walk, she sidestepped, but not in time. The horse reared up again. With its forelegs high in the air, it rocked and whinnied and came down over Grace. She leaned back and cried out. Just in time Regi lifted her and carried her back a few feet. The motion was so sudden, he tumbled with her to the ground. Grace gasped. She wasn't really sure what had happened.

When Regi leaned over her, she sat up immediately. The others in the road came quickly to see if they were all right. She sat in a daze for a few moments while the light from the sky and the lamps on the farmhouse seemed far away. Regi was a shadow, his giant body hovering over her.

For a moment she could not say a word. She heard Regi's

breathing. "Well that was lucky, little cousin." He was slow to move away from her. "I'm glad I was here."

Still, she could not speak. She held her hand over her throat and closed her eyes. When he lifted her to her feet, she finally breathed. "Thank you, Regi."

While Hanson and Alex were drawing the horse back out into the street, she suddenly felt Regi's arm around her shoulder. "Are you all right?" For a moment she was too stunned to protest. Then she quietly but firmly slipped away from him.

"Well, I guess that's one you owe me." Regi turned away from her and put his giant hands in his pockets.

As they got to the car, Reginald climbed silently into the back seat beside her before the boys came. She slipped against the window, every nerve in her body tense, though he did not move across the seat or make any move to touch her now.

Soon, Alex and Hanson had reached the front seat, and the automobile began to move. "That was a close call!" Alex was impressed in spite of himself. "I never saw that kind of quick thinking before, Regi."

"Are you all right, Regi?" Hanson said slowly, turning in the seat. "I thought you were hurt yesterday," he added.

Now Grace could feel Regi's body freeze. "I'm fine," he said.

"Grace, you're one lucky girl this Indian here is quick as an animal," Alex said.

Grace sat close against the corner of the back seat, still nervous, as though at any moment he would draw his giant body closer to her. But he had grown thoughtful and quiet. In the light of the street she thought she saw fresh blood in his clothes.

Neither she nor Regi said another word.

20

Ashel Eastman

On Friday morning, Ashel woke very early with a great deal on his mind. Before the funeral Will had said, "One thing at a time." Now it was time.

He had been grateful to get through the funeral. His friends had rallied graciously—really as a tribute to their own struggle to absorb the native American people, though they knew their efforts had not really succeeded. The Indians were virtually gone.

The focus was now on another vigorous undefined bunch— the young people. Ashel knew it was time for the young people now—who must, like the Indians, somehow become established or "civilized." He had seen promise in Hanson and Alex these last mornings at the hotel. But . . . whether or not it was his age (he might have to admit it) or simply the state of their economic distress, he had ascertained how much tutoring they still needed, and he felt tired.

He was much more than a day behind with his books. He tied the rope on his dressing robe into a knot and shuffled in his slippers to the back office. His books lay in a formidable disarray. All he felt he could do was to stand at the door.

In a moment, Grace was behind him. "Father Ashel," she whispered.

When he turned, he thought he could see some unusual distress in her face.

"You're up early," he said.

"Yes, I . . ." She looked away from his eyes. "Is Cherry coming this morning?" Are you going to be all right with

Caroline if I leave to clean up the other house?"

"You're in the hotel business too, eh?" he grinned.

She lowered her eyes. Then she smiled. "If I let it go it just gets worse."

"That's the hotel business, all right," Ashel said. There was a long pause. He felt he needed to give her some excuse for Hanson and his friend. "They're concentrating so much on what needs to be done now." But as the words came out they sounded very lame, and he wanted to change the subject. "And how was your dinner last night?"

"It was fine," Grace said. But her voice wavered.

He waited for a moment before he spoke. "You're concerned about Hanson, aren't you, sweetheart?" When he put out his hand to take her slender wrist, he felt uncertain how much he should open up the subject of Hanson and his friend Alex. "It's not what you hoped for, is it, darling?"

For a moment Grace met his eyes with a frank gaze. Yet she could not let go of herself. She could not speak—to perhaps tell Father Ashel, "Yes, Hanson seems changed."

He could see through her house-cleaning excuse, and so he smiled, assuring her that Cherry would be there. There was a great deal to do before Christmas next Tuesday, and Cherry had promised to stay until Emily could return. And then he let her go. "Hanson has a lot on his mind right now. Things will get better."

As she turned, she looked back briefly and he saw a brave smile.

When he turned back to his books, he felt a weight of concern. He wasn't sure what he could do to ease the situation. But he suddenly felt cramped in the office, angry at the burden of their misfortunes, and weary of trying to hold all the disparate parts into one piece.

When Cherry came to tend the fire in the stove and he went upstairs to dress, he continued to worry about how much there was to catch up on. He had told the boys he would meet them this morning to go to the hotel, and he hadn't even begun to gather the figures he had hoped to go over with them.

When Caroline woke, he took more time to help her with her breakfast and settle her in her wheelchair beside the window in the front room. Then he continued to fuss about carrying some of his books and papers out to work with them at the dining room table. At one time, when he crossed the front door and happened to look out on the cloud-covered morning, he could see Mara on the street with her small arms linked in the huge elbow of their new charge, Reginald Summerfield. He was carrying his valise. For a brief time he watched her to see what was happening. She walked him to the Eastman house and ushered him in.

Ashel went to the front room and continued to look out the window, puzzled for a long time. Mara had been so thrilled over finding Rain's grandchild. She had always lamented the white man's passing off the native Americans to someone else— shoving them off, passing them around. From what he could see, though she had been smiling and attentive to the huge Indian, it looked as though she were now moving him from her own home. Ashel did not completely understand. But in a few moments, when the large guest appeared to be safely inside the big house, Ashel saw that Mara was now headed for his house. And he was surprised.

"What's happening?" Caroline said in her small voice.

"Mara's on the way here," Ashel said.

Caroline put her needlework down and asked Ashel to wheel her closer to the front window.

Ashel watched Mara's determined walk. She was still strong. She seemed undaunted for her age, but when he looked at her now he saw an interval in her footsteps that looked like weariness. When Mara arrived on the porch, with some of his papers still in hand, he was already there to open the front door.

Mara looked surprised. "You saw me coming!"

"What's happening?" Ashel said.

Mara's eyes did not waver from his face except when she nodded to Caroline across the polished wood vestibule, acknowledging Caroline's wave of greeting from her wheelchair. And she did afford one quick glance back toward the kitchen where Cherry was moving from the bin to the grate.

"Ashel, can we talk?"

Ashel, still with his papers in his hands, stared at her, feeling his tongue tied at her briskness.

"Are you very busy? Can I see you for a few minutes?" But she did not wait for an answer. She slipped out of her coat and hung it on the coat tree. Then when she saw that he had been putting his books on the dining room table, she nodded toward the dining room and began to make her way there. "You were watching me."

Ashel followed her. "You took Regi to the old house this morning. At least that's what it looked like."

"Yes. Yes, I did." Now she paused for effect. And with her eyes almost popping, she knit her brows and pressed her gloved forefinger against his breast bone. "Look lively now!"

Ashel was used to his older sister's occasional outbursts. But he had not seen one for a long time.

"Ashel, how old are you? How old am I?"

He opened his mouth, though she began to cut off his reply. "You'd like to think you're a spring chicken the way you waltz down that street," she said, "but I suppose we are both getting up there."

She still directed her gaze toward him. "That's exactly right, Ashel! It's about time we admitted it. I've struggled with it. Heaven knows I've struggled with it. But I had to admit I was in another world after young Reginald Summerfield came in noisy after his night on the town and woke me up just after midnight. I was so disturbed, I could not go back to sleep, so I just lay awake mulling and mulling everything over."

Ashel pulled out a dining room chair for her while she peeled her gloves from her hands and pulled a small notebook out of her purse.

"Well, then? What have you been mulling over?"

Before she continued, she pulled the small hat from her hair and pulled the gray strands of hair back from her face. "I've been thinking and thinking, and this morning when I took Reginald Summerfield over to the house, he said something to me that made me sit up and take notice that we ought to act as soon as we can."

Still standing, Ashel placed the books on the table. He had known for a long time that one of these days he was going to be much too old to balance these books, much too old to run around in his usual manner. He felt his son Hanson had come to rescue him just in time. When Mara took the chair and sat down at the table, she stayed quiet for a minute. Then she glanced at Ashel until he shuffled to the table. Finally, he too sat down.

"Don't tell me," Ashel said, looking directly into her eyes. "It's about the Hull House Hotel."

Mara had opened the notebook in her hands. "How did you guess?" She looked up at him.

"Rumors are thicker than flies," Ashel said then. He leaned forward and put his elbows on his knees. "First Will, then Hanson, who talked to Mr. Hull. Now you. I've still got ears, haven't I?" His words seemed measured.

Mara pulled back. "So?"

"Mara, you don't know." He picked up one of Mara's pencils and almost broke it in two.

Mara went on. "Hanson wants to stay in the hotel business. You told me yesterday that he and Alex were good workers. And we have others we ought to . . ." But she paused. Ashel knew she was thinking about Reginald's future, but that she would not bring up Reginald for a while. "If Hanson wants very much to stay in the hotel business, we ought to move to the east side of town. It's the only logical thing to do." She did not look at Ashel while she spoke.

Ashel lowered his eyes. "I know. You don't think I wouldn't have done it long ago if we had the funds?"

Mara fixed her eyes on him now. "We could mortgage something. Or sell some stock."

Ashel didn't answer her. When she got nervous, she began stacking the papers on the table into a pyramid. Then she told him: "This morning when I dropped Regi off at the Eastmans' we were talking about his accommodations and I had apologized all over the place for moving him. But honestly, Ashel, I am just too old and weary . . ."

Ashel nodded slowly. "I understand."

"And we were talking about Barrington, and he said, 'Well, if he buys it I guess I can stay there.' And I said, 'Buys what?' and he said, 'It's for sale, isn't it?'" Ashel's head spun as she continued. "I have every reason to believe the steel people are about to put in an offer for it, too."

She hadn't intended to put the pressure on Ashel with this hunch, she said. Because it might have been wrong. It was something, after all, that she had heard in passing from Regi. She didn't want to swear by it. She just wanted Ashel to realize that it was probably now or never.

Ashel heard it as though it were a stab of lead. The pencil snapped in two. He jerked up and gazed steadily. "No!" he said. "Is that right?"

"He just happened to let it drop by accident," she whispered, nervously making marks on the wooden top of the table with the tips of her fingers.

"He just happened to let it drop!" Ashel sat back against the dining room chair with the two halves of the pencil in one hand. He let the pressure of the moment sink into him. He could not hold it all in—not now. Too much was happening. He would have to tell her. "Well, Mara," he said. "I guess you'd better know, Mara. I've mortgaged everything."

Mara leaned forward. "What, Ashel?" Her eyes gaped, as though surely she hadn't heard right.

"I've had to mortgage everything to keep afloat."

Ashel watched his sister's face whiten. She couldn't seem to open her mouth to speak.

"We don't have the woolen mills anymore. Where did you think the money was coming from? The hotel isn't pulling its weight."

But she put her hand up to stop him. "Ashel," she protested with a serious gaze. "The houses? Everything?"

Ashel cleared his throat. He hung his head. "I didn't want to tell you. I didn't want to worry anyone. But yes, also a little on each of the houses."

Mara pulled away. She looked stunned. Ashel knew this was the first time she had heard, the first she knew. And her reaction was the one he had feared. How well he remembered those evenings during the depression of the nineties, when they had sat on the porch with Papa Eastman drinking ice cold glasses of lemonade and telling each other, as though taking solemn oaths: "Whatever happens, we'll always have the house. Never risk the safety of the house." Ashel had told him in the strongest tones: "You need never worry about us, Father." And it had been true. Until now. Though Papa had never needed to worry, because he was dead.

"All we have left is the stock in the Tintic mine."

If Mara had been wearing loose sleeves, he imagined she might have rolled them up at that moment as though to get to work. She was completely out of breath.

"Careful," Ashel thought to himself. "We are both walking a tight rope that could break into the abyss of a quarrel, and we are too old to quarrel now." He felt weak with anguish.

Mara could barely speak. "You allowed yourself to get over-mortgaged to pretend like we're not in trouble? You keep buying cars."

"Caroline . . ." Ashel murmured.

Of course it had been for Caroline that he had done it! She could not hear them now. He had always tried to protect her.

He had never been able to forget her pale face when she lay on the cot after the accident, when they told her she could no longer use her legs. Rain and Sully had brought her in on the back of her horse; Sully had cradled her in his arms. He looked on her face and pulled the hair out of her eyes. "She is going to be all right." She was going to be all right, but at what cost? At what cost was the truth? Mara had stood at the door into the studio where the girl lay on the couch with her head at an angle along the needlepoint cushion with the temple in its embroidery and the words "Glory to God" under the all-seeing eye, and she had leaned against her own hand and felt the bones beating with her blood. It had been Mara who blacked out. Ashel had watched her as the doctor said, "The girl has been paralyzed," and it had been Caroline who moved her head and said, "Mara, please help Ashel put the horse in the barn." It had been Caroline who had been strong. Still, he had always protected Caroline because he had known deeply all along that when Hanson came home things would be better, that it would be merely a matter of time. Yet—perhaps Caroline could have taken the truth all along.

"I've been expecting the Tintic Mine stock to go up any day," Ashel raised his eyes. "It will, Mara. I just have a feeling."

She pulled back. "How much is it worth now?" Ashel was reticent to say, but she held her ground. "I want the truth, Ashel."

"Not what we paid for it."

"How much? Fifty percent? Seventy-five percent?"

Ashel tried to fit the pieces of the pencil back together again. "I'd say seventy-five percent."

"Then sell the Tintic Mining Stock and we'll get back into the hotel business," Mara said.

Ashel leaned forward onto the table. He lifted his graying hands and spread his fingers over his eyes. He wasn't used to losing with stocks—even twenty-five percent.

Ashel watched Mara's frozen face as she looked for a long

time out of the windows of the front lawn, to the December sky. A few late birds perched on the limbs of the maple tree. Perhaps they had believed there was still going to be some warm weather. But they were wrong, now. His heart ached.

"I'm sorry, Mara. I had no idea. I was sure Hanson would get the hotel back on its feet and we could make the payments from the mine stocks. He would never have had to know."

It was not long before they saw Hanson and Alex through the front window. They were sauntering up the walk, laughing with each other. For a moment Ashel hesitated. This was the critical time of decision. Once Hanson knew they were interested in the purchase, it would be extremely difficult to stop the ball from rolling.

"Can you borrow from the bank on the stocks?" Mara asked Ashel.

"I've already tried, believe me. But we could always try again."

"Can you sell the stocks today?" she asked.

"I know that Mr. Grable in the bank has asked me about them. He would buy them today for seventy-five percent. He won't tell me, but I think he believes they will go higher than a kite in just a little while."

"We'll be open with Hanson—except to mention the other mortgages. Just tell him we decided to sell the mining stock for the purchase." They could hear the front door open. "Now we'll talk it over with the boys," she said. "Are we ready for that, Ashel?"

Ashel looked at her. Then he leaned his head into his hands. He was in turmoil. But he felt she was right. And he looked up at her again. "Sure," he said. "Sure. Let's do it."

When the boys saw the papers on the dining table, they stopped in the hall. "What's up?" Hanson asked.

Ashel glanced at Mara. "We need to talk to you," he said.

When Caroline called to them from her chair, Hanson went to her first and kissed her cheek. Then he wheeled her into the dining room slowly. Alex followed him. "So, what are you doing?" Hanson asked.

Now Ashel's tongue seemed completely tied. He was leaning into the wind, like an old fence pole. He was still holding up the fence, but it was sagging. The wind seemed to be blowing him over, and his wires crossed and swinging against the sky, almost crying, but perhaps crying like music, like old hymns that were no longer intelligible. "We've decided to purchase the Hull House Hotel," he said.

Hanson's eyes widened. "What?" he said.

"We've got to act now," Ashel said.

Hanson looked at Alex. He looked back at his father, as though the information had finally registered. "Whoopee!" he cried out. "Well, I'll be. Whoopee!"

"We have some details to discuss. Sit down and we'll talk it over," Ashel said.

The light in the room passed from muted to glaring as the morning progressed. When the light left the front windows and seeped through the colored glass in the stairwell, they were still at it. The group at the table seemed to turn in a magic frozen moment of time while they discussed every detail. They discussed both mortgaging or selling the Tintic Stock. They discussed the possibility for the division of management. They discussed procedures. Ashel seemed nervous. But when he saw Hanson's excitement, he began to smile.

When the sun stood high in the noon sky, Cherry Corey brought little cakes and sandwiches with hot milk and camomile tea. She came shuffling with small steps across the polished wood, her loose sleeves half torn at the shoulder. As Mara looked at her, she said quietly to the others, "We are not talking about pennies, but things are so tight, are we making room for Christmas?"

As they put the ink to the paper, it was true there wasn't much room for the gifts they would like to give. So Mara suggested that they might make handmade gifts this Christmas.

She could make pincushions from the old shawls in the attic boxes, where the mice ran interminably, spoiling everything that had been left behind. And on each pincushion she would tie one of Rain's precious blue beads as a reminder that there was still a place for the old with the new. "We will never forget this Christmas, because it will be the beginning of something lasting for everyone," she said to the boys. "All we really need is money for the food for the party on Christmas Eve. I will not give up our special neighborhood Christmas Eve party. But that's it. Everything else must wait." Everyone agreed.

Ashel nodded amicably. "You're right. If Barrington's group is interested, we can't wait," he said.

Mara looked up and spread her hands out on the notebook in front of her. "We can make it for Christmas if we hold tight. If you will promise me to borrow a few hundred dollars on your car, I will use my pin money. But our main present—to be announced at the party—will be our purchasing adventure. Agreed?"

Ashel looked up directly into her face from his position at the table next to Hanson, where they were going over the figures they had scratched on numerous sheets of paper. "It will put Hanson into the hotel business full tilt. We'll have a chance with one hotel in the busy part of town." Ashel paused. "Though it's a gamble, Mara."

"It's no more of a gamble than living," Mara said. "Right, boys?"

"Right, Aunt Mara," Hanson grinned. He and Alex were scratching and adding and subtracting. "We can do it! I know we can do it!"

"Living, eating, every breath we take is a gamble." Mara shut the notebook and smiled. Ashel followed her gaze to the sunlight outside the window. "It gives me an idea." Her eyes gleamed. "I'd like to call it the Royal House Hotel."

"Royal House Hotel?"

"Let's somehow do away with 'east' and 'west.' You know—

all the opposites: Indian and white, bond and free, male and female!" Ashel grinned inwardly at his sister's constant philoso-phizing, and her love for the Indians. He knew she was also probably still thinking about hiring Reginald. But she hadn't mentioned it yet. And probably would not for a long time. "Royal House. It would mean a kingdom—for everyone, from both east and west. Everyone who comes would be treated like a king."

"Hmmm," Hanson said.

"I think that sounds bully." Alex Hunt stood up and doffed his tea like a toast of champagne.

"As long as it isn't Royal Flush. You don't really want to gamble, do you, Mara?" Ashel said.

"It's a gamble for stakes that are very high. After all, we are all kings and queens, or have the potential to become them," Mara said absently. Her thoughts seemed far away. She stood slowly. Finally, as though she came awake for a moment from a dream, she lifted her hands, held the little notebook high over her head in a gesture of triumph. "It is the gamble for life itself—that everyone who pays the price will come into the kingdom."

Ashel chuckled softly. "Mara, you think life is a game! You think you are a girl again."

"I'm a wise old girl," Mara looked at him out of the corner of her eyes. Then she raised her arms again, waving the note-book in her hands. And she leaned her head back and smiled.

21

Reginald Summerfield

"Take this down," Barrington said when Regi came into the meeting the morning after Mrs. Carroll's. It was Friday.

Moon Hawk, Moon Hawk. Never never. Sometimes I go crazy. Seeing Laura . . . But that was no excuse—I should never have put my arm around Grace after the dinner at the restaurant. She's beautiful. But she's my cousin. Why are you weak . . . Reginald Summerfield?

Focusing on Barrington's voice, he tried to write down what he heard. "A Springville man in connection with the city will sell us four hundred acres between here and Springville, west of the road. Four hundred acres is plenty. Adamson here says his cousin has connections with the Denver and Rio Grande."

He scribbled words along the outside margins of the last accounting of money Barrington was getting from the investors. Martin Drucker was the one who would invest twenty thousand dollars in a Provo hotel. Martin Drucker. He smeared his name with the pencil lead.

No. No. Why? I probably deserved to be knifed by the girl at the East House Hotel. It has been a year and a month since I have been with Ethel and no one since that time . . . I am on fire.

Two men were seated at the table in the corner with Drucker. One was L. F. Barrington. One was Robert Adamson, the new professor at the BYU whose wife's cousin in Idaho owned stock in the Pullman car. It did not seem relevant that it was his wife's cousin from Idaho who had the money instead of Robert Adamson himself. The gray-headed gentleman looked like a millionaire—he was suave, his clothes sharply pressed, his collar and cuffs so white they made sun spots in Reginald Summerfield's eyes.

Reginald bit the tip of the pencil in his teeth. He wanted to scratch the paper clean through and stab his pencil into his hand. He wrote calmly all that Barrington told him to write until Martin Drucker said, "The key is to control the unions. Carnegie couldn't."

"He got the peace medal for something else besides keeping his steel workers happy," Adamson added.

"There's unrest, all right," Barrington said. "But not here. You'll not see a Haymarket here in Utah."

"Are they controlling Gary? I heard there was trouble in the middle of the war."

"More trouble now that it's over," Barrington said. "More unrest. But not here."

"Unrest everywhere. First thing democracy does is destroy the status quo."

"Destroy the old to nourish the new."

"But you'd have thought democracy was more human. I was shocked the Bolsheviks shot Nicholas II, his wife, son, and four daughters!"

"Not just them. But William II in Berlin. The Hapsburgs."

"Not everything's coming apart. November 29, they tied up that bunch of countries and called it Yugoslavia."

"And just how long will that last? The Serbians, Croates, and Bosnians hate each other."

"Let them destruct. Steel is still going to be good. I don't care if half the world kills the other half. They'll do it with steel."

Regi bit the end of the pencil and thought he tasted lead. Get to the point, he thought. Four hundred acres in Springville.

"Creed ought to meet Pierpont," Drucker said. "He'd know they could do it here."

"He'll come along," Regi said.

Barrington was a florid man with thinning hair. He sat

forward with his elbows on the table, his black satin tie crushed up against his chin. "See to it he does, Drucker. You're the man for it." Then he pulled back. "Did you make a decision if you were going to invest in the Hull House Hotel?"

"If we pool resources, we can help this Mr. Hull. He talks like the east side of town does big, but he's losing his shirt." Drucker drew back and bit his thumb. "Who wouldn't, mixing the hotel with the dead body business?"

Barrington smiled and looked out into the tile lobby. "Not on account of me is he out of business. I've been a faithful client since I found the smallest living reptile in my soup on the west side of town."

"You ever thought what would have happened if you'd have bought this hotel a while ago, Barrington?"

Barrington looked around the dining room. "It was in better condition then," he laughed.

"The Hull House is dying," Adamson said. "No aspersion implied upon his new profession as mortician." He said it behind his hand and glanced in Reginald's direction. "You're not taking all of this down, are you, Summerfield?"

Reginald laughed, looked at his notes. "I stopped at 'the key is controlling the unions.'"

"That's the key, all right," Drucker said.

"No problem in Podunk, USA," Barrington snickered. "I can promise you there's no problem here with unions."

"Well, I'll throw it in, then, for Wigginton Creed and the Columbia Steel Mill, and maybe the hotel to boot." Drucker drew away from the table.

Adamson looked very intently at his hands in the long white cuffs. "I learned a thing or two. I didn't come back from that expedition to Book of Mormon country for nothing."

"You went all the way with those suckers?" Drucker said.

Barrington leaned over the table closer to Adamson. "You mentioned once following that BYU President Benjamin Cluff fellow all the way to South America while he was taking time to court that little school teacher in Colonia Juarez."

Adamson had a distant look in his eye. "Educators don't have any money," he said. "Industry makes money. But looking for Zarahemla, I found out you don't always find what you're looking for."

"Sounds like he found it in the little woman!" Drucker said.

"Never found Zarahemla," Adamson repeated.

Regi held his pencil above the minutes. He wasn't going to write "He never found Zarahemla" on the paper. In the flash of the moment he wondered which of Hawk in the Tree's villages they would have named Zarahemla if they had not already all been named.

"I say that the Ironton operation'll be about as close to Zarahemla as you can get," Barrington said. "Mark my word, it'll bring industry into Provo, Utah, and you'll have a thriving metropolis in less than twenty years."

"No union troubles?"

"No union troubles. The people here are docile—even about competition."

"I'll recommend it to my wife's cousin."

The men talked for what seemed like hours. Reginald wrote until his fingers ached. At last Julia Hull came into the room with coffee and hot mint tea. She circled the table and filled the cups with sugar or cream as each man requested. Regi noticed she was going to have a baby. A baby born in the hotel mortuary, he thought. At least you would be ready for death if it happened. It was easier, he supposed, to have everything ready for death. Unlike life, which often lacked the possibility for planning and organization, death clarified things. No foolproof plan was simple as a four-sided box. Plans for death were black and white. Like the words he was writing on the page.

Regi watched Julia's hands pour the coffee. Then he could not help but watch her gentle sway as she briskly moved from one side of the table to the other. The lace on her bodice revealed the soft curve of her throat. He stopped himself. He knew he was always watching a woman's body. If he was serious about wanting to change, he would look away. He forced himself to withdraw. *Reginald Summerfield, learn something. Make a Ben Franklin list.*

He leaned over the paper and focused his eyes on the letters he made: "Unions are the key." "I believe that's true," he thought to himself. "I always believed in unions—even believed that controlling unions is the key. Unions are the key." He couldn't take his mind off of Laura Adamson all the while. He tried. In his memory he saw her white ankles, and he forced himself to write "Adamson will contact his wife's cousin in Idaho—the Pullman Car cousin." He had been wordy. He erased what he had written after "contact," and wrote "his Pullman Car cousin in Idaho. Then he scribbled "Let's have some contact right away," and he rubbed it out as quickly as the words appeared on the page. Pencils and numbers had betrayed him. He coughed and cleared his throat.

In the doorway of the dining room, Julia had stopped to talk to someone. Regi looked once, then looked again. It was Laura with the long bright curls, her white ankles hidden now in a sweeping cascade of yellow lawn. She peered around Julia and into the room. "Papa," she called.

As soon as she had come to the door, Adamson had seen her. He laid his cup in its saucer and put both hands on the arms of the chair. When Julia stepped aside, Regi felt Adamson move the chair. It scraped the floor and he bounded to his feet. "Excuse me," he said.

Barrington and Drucker turned round in their chairs. The sun shone through her hair, through the open door. When she moved toward them she was a silhouette surrounded by light. Regi watched her move. He thought to himself of a poem he had read: "If she were coming toward me, how would I begin? How would I pause and how should I presume?"

It would not be to leap for her as he had for Sissy or Grace.

Of course not. That was not it at all. He must learn. He pulled at the pencil in his hands and it broke between his fingers.

"We'll make arrangements with Boshell Real Estate. We'll go through the Security Bank. Reginald contact."

While Barrington spoke, Adamson met his daughter and surrounded her with his embrace. He held her in the circle of his arm. Her eyes flickered, opened and shut rapidly, as though she were speaking a code with her eyes. Regi could not see her mouth.

In a moment Adamson turned back to the table. "I must be excused; it's my wife. She has been ill with . . . influenza." He stumbled over the word. He turned to Laura and said in low tones, "The funds. The hotel. I should never have suggested to her that we use her family's . . ." His face was very white. He turned to the others. "I'm sorry. If you'll please go on without me."

Suddenly everything changed. The hotel room seemed cold. A dampness came up into the sweat on Regi's hands. He rose up and walked them to the door. "Is there anything we can do?" he said.

Adamson was so pale, Regi feared he would pass out in the foyer of the hotel.

"Get the hospital," Adamson said in a low voice. "Bring the hospital. She's in danger . . ."

The boy at the desk said "The hospital has been called."

Holding to his daughter's shoulders, Adamson leaned against her, put her off balance as they went up the stairs. "She'll be all right." The daughter was crying now. Her cheeks were wet. She rubbed them with the back of her hand. Regi followed them, holding the man's left arm from behind, staying close in case Adamson should fall.

"She took a sudden turn for the worse."

But it was not that. When they climbed the stairs, they saw Julia had been there with towels and hot tea. She came swiftly down the hall carrying a large bundle of laundry tied in a huge pair of men's dungarees. Her hair was pulled back under her bandanna as though she had replaced it quickly in a moment of stress. Her eyes were glazed and her face was white.

"Mrs. Hull," Reginald began. He wanted to ask her if she was all right. Since he could not hold Laura, he knew he wanted to touch Julia Hull, to hold her and let her cry. But he repressed the violence of his need when he looked at her. "Mrs. Hull, what has happened?"

She stopped to be polite. "I don't know," she whispered.

"Are you all right?"

"Yes, I'm fine." Julia moved out of the way. She clamped her lips in a thin line.

Reginald stood in the hall outside the room while Adamson shouldered his way through the doorway and shut the door behind him. He did not allow Laura to follow him. She stood against the wall with her hands behind her back. For a moment she looked like a butterfly pinned against the flowered paper. She leaned her head back and closed her eyes.

Regi's body began to shake. He could not control it. His imagination swooped upon the soft vulnerable wingless flesh before him, shimmering in white and lemon-yellow lawn ruffles and long bright curls.

He wanted her. And he would have dipped into her now— as he would have violated frosted cake or lemon ices: delicious. But he knew his weakness and he was fighting it. He had resolved. He pulled himself back with his sheer will. He would pull all of the charms from his repertoire.

"You look tired, Miss Adamson."

For the first time she looked directly at him, as though before this she had not known he was there.

"Let me take you for lunch while your father is with your mother."

The look she gave him drove a spike into his heart. She lifted her chin and narrowed her eyes.

Reginald did not allow the look to daunt him. He absorbed

her pure presence as though it were clear water. She was so lovely—the curve of her white throat contrasting with the blush on her cheeks. He tried to ignore her coldness. "Hah! So you don't go to lunch with just anybody! But you ought to go with me. If your father's cousin is joining the steel people to purchase the hotel . . . I juggle the figures . . ." But his voice sounded ineffective, dull, his half-sentences inane. She looked at him again, her eyes chips of blue ice that began to melt. "Don't you believe the doctors can do something for your mother's influenza?"

"It's not influenza," Laura said so far under her breath that Regi barely heard her words.

"What?"

"You heard me," Laura said. "You heard what I said."

It was at that moment someone screamed. They both froze. Never had Regi experienced the same cold chill he felt in his neck when he heard this curdling scream. It surprised both of them—a long, guttural wail that sent shivers through him. It came from behind the door of the room. Like a small animal in the brush, Laura jumped and quickly turned away. Giving a quick excuse, she pulled a key from her pocket, unlocked the door to the room next to her parent's room, and disappeared into the darkness. Now the yell became very harsh, garbled, and without sense.

Astonished, Regi found himself in the hallway quite alone. He made a note of the number on the door: 206. He made a note of the number on the daughter's door: 204. He heard voices in the hallway and slipped down the back stairs. There was a boxy enclosed wagon standing in the back yard in which the motor was idling rapidly. He paused. A young man with a dirty yellow cap quickly gathered a stash of chains that lay on the floor of the wagon box. With a set of large keys he unlocked some huge links from the floor and pulled up a tangle of chains. Carefully winding them around his arm, he shut the door of the wagon and bolted it.

After the door of the wagon had closed, for a moment Regi followed the boy's bobbing yellow hat through the window of the door to the hotel. Alone again, he stood on the hotel's back stoop, staring at his hands and the notebook in his hands. Because the lunch hour was almost over, he hadn't time to grab anything to eat before meeting at one o'clock in the foyer with Barrington. He pulled the notebook up under his arm and walked across to the shadowy side of the street. There wasn't much sun. It was a dry December day. The black leaves scuttled along the walk and raced in the curbway.

He felt the tall homes lean in around him. The people who lived on this east side of town were trying to see that the main part of town moved east, while the people on the west side were bitterly regretful. He had seen the look on Mara's face this morning when he had mentioned the possibility that Barrington, who hated the west side of town, would find an investor to purchase the east side Hull House Hotel. He had not been thinking when he said it, and Mara's face had clouded over when the words escaped his tongue.

He did not know where he was walking, but he walked west. When he looked back over his shoulder to the hotel, in the corner of his eye he saw two orderlies in blue gray uniforms holding between them the body of a woman with a grizzled mouth and black fly-away hair. She was struggling as the men brought her to the wagon. She screamed and kicked and bit the men's wrists, bending down into an awkward cramped position, bringing her knees upward, and pounding the pavement with her slippered feet. Her torn skirt gaped open at the waist and revealed the glaring white disorder of her petticoats and chemise. The bodice of her dress was torn open and the white of her breasts visible as they fell forward.

Regi's body felt numb. He was terrified of his own feelings and the possibilities of the events surrounding this spectacle in the dooryard of the Hull House Hotel. As soon as the woman was shoved into the wagon, he saw Mr. Adamson, head bowed, leaping through the doorway, following the boy in the scabby yellow cap.

None of the men entered the wagon box. As soon as the woman was locked inside, the three men—two orderlies and Mr. Adamson—sat on the front seat. Left out, the boy stood on the back step and clung to a rail.

Regi waited until the wagon had turned around in the street. He saw the driver hit the brakes, then the gas pedal. The exhaust bloomed and choked off, bloomed and choked. They turned around in the street and headed east toward the mountains.

Feeling the taste of his late breakfast in his mouth on an empty stomach, he turned back toward the hotel and began to negotiate his way into the back yard through the low scrabbled marigold and winter mums. The frost had strangled the flowers into brown heads drooping with the fuzzy webs of spiders and gray mold. Without being able to change his direction, he kicked his feet against the rock on the wall. His hands shook on the notebook as he entered the back door and climbed the long stairs. Each step was fraught with a scream of need in his body. Seeing him coming, hidden onlookers in the upstairs rooms retreated behind closed doors. The tall airy hallways reeked with the smell of tobacco and soap. He came to room 204 and stood fighting himself, but he moved toward the door all the same, and knocked lightly with the corner of his notebook. He was silent for a long moment. There was a rustle of sound inside the room. For only a second, he hoped she would not hear.

"Who is it?"

He heard her voice as though it were a thousand miles away. "Mr. Summerfield. It's a message from your father," Regi found himself saying. "Open the door."

The lock in the door cracked and, metal against metal, the door opened slowly to reveal her white face. Her cheeks were wet with tears. Regi moved toward her slowly, and closed the door.

22

Grace Tuttle

Although Grace had hot rolls and steaming hot milk ready for Alex and Hanson when they came into the kitchen Friday morning, they didn't stop to talk to her. "We have to hurry," Hanson said.

Alex gulped his milk, and folded the roll into his handkerchief. "Sorry, but we're late," he said.

"We should have met my father half an hour ago." Hanson seemed to look through her. "See you." That was all there was.

It took her all morning to launder the sheets. Swinging like giant flags along the rope across the stairwell, they billowed like ghosts when she walked through them, reminding her she was alone.

Not until noon did she hear the front door open. The sun streamed through and brought a breeze with it. The sheets billowed and snapped.

"Grace!" someone called.

When she hurried through the sheets from the dining room, she saw Hanson at the door. She hadn't believed she could feel as much as she was feeling now. Her heart stopped beating.

He did not come in, but hung on the door knob and yelled to her: "Don't let your housework keep you from missing the big event this afternoon!"

"What big event?" she said, hurrying through the ghosts all about her, moving them to the side, wiping her hands on her apron.

"We're buying the Hull House Hotel!"

Grace stopped to test her own sanity. Besides everything else that had happened this week? Her head spun. "What?" she asked.

"Want to come with us to the bank this afternoon? We're mortgaging or selling the Tintic stock to buy the Hull House Hotel!"

The outside light was a blur. When she walked to the door, Hanson stepped outside again. He had come by just to tell her, he said. He had to get going. Before he shut the door, he yelled "Hurry." And then he was gone.

Grace stood away from the sheets in the hall and leaned against the banister for a moment to catch her breath. Was the world coming to a stop? She wondered.

When she got to Ashel's house, Ashel and Mara and Caroline and the boys were still at the dining room table.

"Well, hello, Grace!" Ashel turned to her when she came in. "I guess you heard the news?"

Everything seemed to have wound down to slow motion. It seemed like a hundred years passed before everyone was ready to go. Grace felt out of place, even though Hanson had made an unprecedented sprint to fetch her. She wasn't sure what was happening—with the businesses, with Hanson, with her own heart. There was so much going on in her life in this moment, that she felt numb. She helped Cherry with the dishes. She stood on the outside of the conversations while she heard them talking. She did not know how much she should enter in. When Uncle Ashel saw her, he did not offer to fill her in on any details. He kept his eyes on her, and he smiled. She thought he could see her suspicious, shocked, narrowed eyes. "Since this concerns you, too, Grace, if you want to come, you're welcome to join the crew of the new Royal House Hotel," he added, tossing it out as though he were inviting her to go shopping.

The Royal House Hotel. Grace let the name settle on the back of her tongue. "Well, I do want to come," Grace said. She noticed that Caroline looked at her—perhaps as though she didn't look ready. She put her hands in her hair. "When are you leaving? Can you wait a minute?"

"We have an appointment for one-fifteen," Ashel said. Pulling out his fob, he glanced at his watch. "Well, it's just about that time, isn't it?" he said, surprised.

Alex and Hanson got up and put on their topcoats. Their shoes echoed on the polished wood floor.

"We'll wait outside," Alex said, pulling on his tie.

Grace ducked into Caroline's bedroom to comb her hair. Caroline followed her in the wheelchair. "It's only eight minutes to one, honey. Are you sure you want to go with the boys? They'll be back. I really haven't had a chance to talk with you."

Grace saw her own face in the mirror. Her eyes had narrowed. Her cheeks were white. She looked like one of the china figurines on the mantelpiece—her face white and the thick dark curls a frame. The excitement had begun to put color into her neck. She pinched her cheeks to make roses.

"There, Grace," she said under her breath to herself. "You look good. You are every bit as capable as the others of seeing to the business of the Royal House Hotel."

The Royal House Hotel. Grace was reeling under the onslaught of so many surprises when Caroline drew her chair near to the mirror. Her eyes were wide. "Has he said anything to you yet, darling?" she whispered in a small whisper.

"No," Grace said. She didn't want to talk about Hanson. At least Hanson had come for her a few minutes ago, even though he left without waiting. No, she didn't want to think about Hanson. Caroline did not need to know about the triangles.

Caroline was watching her. "Grace, sometimes I feel just as confused by Hanson's behavior as you must be."

Grace stiffened. She loved Caroline. But she didn't feel there was anything Caroline could do. Things could blow apart at any point. "He's trying to adjust, honey. Just remember, it's only been a few days and he feels obligated to this Alex . . ." Caroline wasn't born yesterday, so she was aware his friend Alex was more than half the problem, Grace guessed. "Let's see what happens now with their decision to purchase the Hull House Hotel. It could change everything." Grace didn't want to count on changes. She didn't want to think very far ahead. All she knew was that she would take every opportunity she could to be with Hanson if he felt he needed her. At least Hanson had come to the house to fetch her, so she was going to go.

In the car, Alex and Hanson kept up a constant chatter. Although Alex sat with Grace in the back seat, he leaned forward to talk to Ashel and Hanson every minute of the five block drive. It was talk about mining stock, possible three percent interest loans on stock, quit claim deeds, and escrow.

When she followed them into the bank, she was surprised because the first person she saw was Julia with her husband. They were standing with the banker, Mr. Grable. The first thing Grace thought was that now she wouldn't have to go to the hotel to see Julia. But then her heart seemed to stammer. The bank wasn't really the best place to visit. She hadn't really thought about what she would say to her, except that she felt right then she needed a friend. She might have told Julia how exciting it was that her family was thinking of making the purchase of the Hull House Hotel, except that on the way into the bank, Ashel had said sternly, "Keep any mention of our purpose here to yourself."

Julia stunned her with a surprise of her own. Just as the Eastmans turned to open the swinging gate, Julia spotted Grace, rushed to her, and grasped her hands. "Oh Gracie! We are here for the most exciting thing!" When she glanced at her husband, he knit his brows in disapproval. "Oh," Julia lowered her voice. "We are going to have the money now to build a mortuary of our own! I wish I could tell you now." She glanced back at her husband. "But I can't. Not yet. But I'll tell you soon. Where are you going to be on Christmas Day?"

Grace was surprised at the question. "Ashel's . . . probably Ashel's."

Then Julia took Grace's hands in hers and looked over at

Hanson and Alex who were busy together, concerned about one thing only. The assistant banker, Mr. Harper, had invited them to sit at the desk in the front window. In front of him was the Eastman safe deposit box, the keys still in the keyhole, dangling. It was Ashel who dug the papers out of the box, tied at the top with a string of red yarn.

Julia whispered, "How are you really doing? I mean . . ."

Grace nodded and smiled wearily. She whispered, "Hanson? Oh, Julia, I don't know."

Julia's eyes darted to Hanson.

"So many things are happening. You know Hanson's friend is here, Alex Hunt. And my cousin Reginald Summerfield is staying in the big house. I feel like I am a one-person hotel."

"Oh, Grace," Julia squeezed her hands. "Isn't it true! We are always the 'hotel!' Which makes me want to tell you! It's about . . . but I can't."

Horace Hull looked at her sternly out of the corners of his eyes.

"I really must go. Please, Grace, come to see me on Christmas! It will be decided by Christmas Day. And I want to talk to you. You must tell me what Hanson is doing, too."

Grace pulled Julia close to her by her hand and whispered, "Shhh."

"It's not working out?" Julia's eyes widened.

"I don't know," Grace said between her teeth. "Oh, Julia! I need to talk with you. I don't know." She fought the tears that sprang to her eyes. "Something big is happening with the men. I guess it's larger than our lives."

Julia drew back, her eyes brightened. "What could be larger than your life?" she asked.

"I . . . I'm not sure I can say, either," Grace whispered, meeting Horace's eyes. "I guess we'll know by Christmas Eve."

Julia shook Grace's hands in both of hers. "Men, men, men. They think they make the world turn around. When really we do quite a bit of it ourselves." She smiled. "We'll both have something to talk about on Christmas Day. You must come to see me, or I will come to see you. Please have faith, Gracie. This weekend anything could happen."

Grace nodded.

Horace Hull took his wife's arm and they moved through the gate toward the door.

23

Hanson Eastman

As soon as he got into the automobile with the others to go to the bank, Hanson rolled the window down. Inside, the car seemed stifling—even though it was December.

"Do you need to open that?" Alex asked from the back seat where he sat with Grace.

Hanson watched the street roll past like fast moving picture film. "Just for a minute. Sorry. I feel hot."

"You must have a fever!" Ashel turned to him.

"He's got a fever all right!" Alex said from his place behind Hanson. He put his hand on Hanson's shoulder. "I'd call it a fever, wouldn't you? Smart pants—going to be the owner of the Hull House Hotel!"

"Don't count our eggs before they hatch," Ashel said.

"I have to hand it to you, Ashel. Not everybody has the brains to make this work in the first place," Alex said.

"Or the mining stocks," Ashel said.

"Did you say three per cent interest?"

"Is that high?" Hanson asked his father.

"I know my father bought a commercial building in Franklin with ten percent down, four per cent on the contract and had to sell it because the payments were more than the rent. But he bought low and sold high."

"Exactly what Hull is doing," Ashel said.

"Was that the building your father wrote about that day we ended up in the farmer's barn—and you wished . . . ?" Hanson turned to look at Alex.

Alex laughed and hit Hanson's shoulder. "We wished we had

the wreck to sleep in. I remember!"

While they kept up the constant talk about mining stocks, interest, and quit claim deeds, Hanson looked in the mirror at Grace. Her face betrayed no emotion. He watched her for a moment as he talked, thinking to himself, "I haven't said enough to her. She'll just have to understand." This was the moment he had long hoped for—the moment in which the disparate elements of his future—theirs if she were patient enough to wait for him—would jell. He would spend some serious time with her this evening at the dance.

"It was so cold. It was snowing that night. We're lucky to have more than a barn now!" Alex said.

The bank looked alive with light. Even the gray morning sky was peeling back in the wake of the sun.

"The farmer didn't run our kind of hotel, is that what you're trying to tell me?" Hanson grinned.

"We'll have room service. We'll give them chocolates, turn down their bed covers." Alex spread his hand across the vision he saw in his imagination. When Alex painted it, Hanson could see it, too.

When they stopped, Alex opened the door for Grace. Hanson brought the packet with the stocks and the bank notes. His father shut his door hard, his eyes on the surprising crowd seated around at different desks in the room.

Inside the entrance, Hanson was surprised to see Mr. Hull. He glanced toward his father, but Ashel was not communicating. His eyes up for only a brief hello, he walked past the Hulls. Only Grace stopped Julia for a few moments to chat.

Once they were inside the bank, the secretary ushered them away from the main room to Mr. Harper's office. Hanson looked warily at the groups of people standing in the hall. Some of them he had never seen before.

Without any hesitation, Mr. Harper agreed that he and Grable would commit to buying the stock at seventy-five percent. But no, he wouldn't hear of loaning money on it. He could purchase it outright if they could wait over the weekend for the funds. Ashel was very positive. He flourished his pen. Grace sat in the background saying nothing while the men filled out the papers.

"This is the fastest money I ever saw in my life," Alex laughed to Hanson.

"It's only the beginning," Hanson said uneasily. "I'll need lots of help."

"Help! You've got me, don't you?" Alex said, grinning. "I'm the best help you've ever had. And Grace, there, she's ready to help, aren't you, Gracie? You ready to be Miss Queenie at the Royal House Hotel?" he said. "Got your scrubbin' brush ready?"

"Hmmm. Royal House Hotel?" Mr. Harper said. "You planning on changing its name?"

"It's just a figure of speech," Ashel said. "You say we can pick up the funds Monday?"

"I'd say around eleven o'clock," Mr. Harper said.

As they shook his hand and turned to leave, Hanson said, "Monday is the soonest? Are you sure we don't need to make the offer now?"

"Not wise. Not wise," Ashel shook his head. "It's the best policy to make the offer from a position of strength, knowing exactly what you can do."

"Can't we at least offer tonight?" Hanson said. "I'd hate to think . . ."

"Harper has to consult with Grable. And I don't want a slip. We'll have the money Monday at eleven and we'll make the offer at noon."

"Hey, hey, my friend!" Alex pounded Hanson's sleeve. "Just like always, my friend. Worry, worry, worry."

Hanson looked directly into Alex's face. His smile had always put him at ease. From the moment Alex had leaned over him in the orange light of the tent, through to their escapades on the Marne when the innkeeper had taken down his shotgun to discourage Alex from kissing the daughter, Hanson had received his strength from his friend. "You're a good friend to see me through this," Hanson smiled.

"Hey! What other choice would I make?" Alex's arm was around him now. "We're lifetime buddies. Don't forget it."

24

Grace Tuttle

As they left the bank, Grace noticed that the clock on the wall said ten minutes after two. She remembered, because after she looked at the clock, she looked out of the window and saw Laura Adamson with her father hurrying into the bank. Laura was bent close to her father, clinging to his arm. Her head was bent. Grace was startled. The girl had let someone cut off almost all of her hair! Someone—maybe Jimmy the barber—had cut it and waved it with an iron.

Grace had never seen anyone with the modern haircut, though after the war there were daring pictures of models and movie stars in the newspaper who had been brave enough to subject themselves to what looked like destruction. Actually, Laura looked as though she were making a statement. Her dress, like last night's, hung boldly above her ankles, the shining material swinging back and forth on weights in the hem.

Alex stopped the girl inside the door.

"Let's go," Ashel said.

"I'll be with you in a minute," Alex said. "I believe you're Laura Adamson," he began. But with Hanson at his elbow, he included his friend. "Did I tell you we're related? I found out at the party last night. Laura's my cousin."

Hearing his words, Grace paused. Hanson stopped, too. His face held questions. But he responded to Mr. Adamson's friendly offer to shake his hand.

Grace wanted to hear what Alex had to say, but Ashel, also smiling and greeting the father, was anxious to get to work at the hotel. She thought she heard Alex say, "Was it the Wright sisters?" Laura looked at him with a surprised face. Then her eyes took him in. And then she began to focus on him.

Grace strained to hear the conversation, but she was an outsider. Ashel held the door open for her and ushered her through. In that awkward moment she obeyed him, though Hanson had stayed behind. He was smiling and nodding at Laura. His eyes, like Alex's, were riveted on her face.

Grace thought Laura's face looked pale, her eyes blank. She clung to her father's arm. She did not smile at Alex's words. Her father put his hand on hers, and after smiling and nodding at Ashel and Alex, tugged her away. The Adamsons seemed in a great hurry. Mr. Adamson kicked the gate and hurried to Mr. Grable, who conducted him to the clerk at the window. Grace watched all of this while she stood by Ashel outside, looking in.

Ashel opened the door again and called to Hanson. "Let's go, son."

Hanson's face was gleaming. Alex looked smitten, his face spreading with a bemused smile.

Grace cowered beside Ashel. She forced herself to walk forward, though she stole glances at the boys. No one must know how hurt she was.

"She'll be there," Alex said gleefully.

"What did you say?" Hanson asked him.

"I said, 'I hope you're at the bowery at the Christmas dance tonight.'"

"What did she say?"

"She nodded her head."

"It didn't look to me like you made her very happy."

"No, maybe not. But she'll be there." Alex was in another world. He walked forward with Hanson so swiftly, the two overtook Grace and Ashel in a moment on their way to the car.

On the way home Grace sat with Ashel in the front seat. Hanson and Alex sat in the back.

"What do you know about Adamson?"

"He is one of the new professors at the Academy," Ashel

said.

"Did you know he's related to the Hunts?" Alex said.

"How did you find that out?" Hanson wanted to know.

Grace sifted through what she remembered of Scott Hunt, his wife Kate Wright, and his son Bret's wife Hannah Wright.

"After the party last night," Alex said.

"I don't believe you," Hanson said. "You're making it up."

"I called my father. He told me my Adamson cousin was in town."

So both Alex and Laura were her cousins! Almost everyone seemed to be cousins. Grace did not turn her head. She looked out on the street. Frank Corey was lighting a candle on his popcorn cart. Again he had tied his wreath to it. It would be Christmas on Tuesday.

Mara had told her once that Scott Hunt was also her great-grandfather. She did not care. It seemed like a terrible mistake. Scott Hunt's people had abandoned her mother Jenny. But now she didn't care.

She stayed quiet while all of them gathered at Ashel's place for a supper of beef noodle soup while they rejoiced over the good news that on Monday Harper would deliver the money to purchase the Royal House Hotel.

It was hard for Grace now to look at Alex, knowing she was related to him. He seemed loud today. He slapped Hanson on the back, and grinned through the entire meal. He pomaded his hair and donned spats before he prepared to go to the Friday dance. Hanson slicked his hair also. But Grace said she didn't feel well. She didn't want to go.

Hanson's reaction took her by surprise. His jaw dropped. "Grace," he began. "I . . . was counting on it."

But she knew he had never mentioned it.

"You remember we said on Thursday we wanted to go dancing, and we said there wasn't any dancing until Friday?"

Grace remembered they had only said the dance was on Friday so they couldn't dance Thursday. She had never been asked.

Hanson looked stricken.

Grace looked over at Aunt Mara's eyes. They were twinkling. She was smiling slightly.

"Oh, I don't believe so," Grace said. "I've had a very busy week cooking and cleaning for three men." She was forcing a smile, though her statement bore so much truth. "I don't believe I'll go. You'll find someone fun to dance with, Hanson. You and Alex have fun. I'll have to cook for Mr. Summerfield when he gets home."

When the three of them left Ashel's together to go to the house on the corner, Grace walked ahead of them in silence. No one said much of anything. When they reached the porch, Hanson let Alex go into the house to get ready for the dance while he stayed behind and took Grace's arm. "Grace," he said, "I don't want you to think . . . That is, I . . ."

Grace stood very still. She did not respond to him when he touched her arm.

"Please. This is my first dance since I've been home." He stopped. She saw his face in the moonlight and the lamplight across the street from the Freshwater Hardware. "Things are so confusing. I wanted you to be patient. I think I might not have made it clear with Alex here and all the confusion about purchasing the hotel."

Grace was quiet. "It's all right, Hanson," she said honestly. "You have to feel right about what you do. And I have to feel right about what I do."

As she opened the door and left him to walk to her upstairs room, she felt tired, but she didn't care. When she reached the bottom of the stairs, she fumbled to find the switch to turn on the light, and she felt a hand on her arm. She gasped and turned. She thought it was Reginald Summerfield, and her blood turned cold. But when she turned around, she found Hanson standing over her.

"All right, Gracie. Let's have a talk right here," he said. "I'm not sure what is going on, but I told you I needed time. So why can't we at least go to the dance together?"

She stopped and stared at him. He was all she had dreamed of for five years. They had not seen each other for five years. Five years ago, she had stood at the bottom of these stairs with the light barely flickering in the hall, and he had said, "I will be back, Grace. I can't say what is going to happen, but with everything I can promise . . ." Her Aunt Mara had come back into the hallway with a can of gas and poured it into the lamp. "We'll be having electric lights here someday," she had said, and Hanson had grinned. "By the time I come back, you'll have light." What had she expected in four days? She looked at him. The light in the upstairs rooms went on where Alex was busy getting ready. She saw Hanson's face. It was the same face she had always loved. What had changed?

"It's just different," she said, searching her feelings and finding nothing. "I don't know why it's so different."

"Well, it is different," Hanson said. His hand still gripped her arm. "But that doesn't mean we can't work it out until it is good."

Grace asked the harder question. "Do you want to work on it?"

"I'm working on it now."

"All right. If you want to, I'll work on it with you." Although Grace wouldn't let herself feel glad in that moment, in her heart she felt a sudden rush of relief.

For a moment Hanson's hand maintained its grip. He looked at her for a long time. "Maybe it won't work out," he said, "but unless we try we'll never know."

"I agree with that," Grace said softly.

"I still care about you."

She wanted to leap into his arms and tell him, "I love you. I more than care about you, Hanson. I love you." But because she cared about him, she also wanted to give him enough space and enough time. "I have never stopped caring about you, Hanson."

It might have been too much. But he leaned over her, and he touched his lips to her hair. She added: "I do care about you so much that I want to give you plenty of time. Both of us will need time."

"Yes," Hanson said. "We both need time."

25

Reginald Summerfield

He knew the pen was not alive. But he was so nervous that it seemed to be alive, to jump on its own in his fingers. He could barely see through the blur in his eyes as he scratched: "Friday. To L. F. Barrington: Don't look for me. I'm taking the afternoon." He chewed on the top of the pen. Then he added: "I don't know how long I'll be gone. But I'll be back."

He leaned on the counter as he wrote. He knew the clerk was watching him with a sidelong glance. He felt uncomfortable under his scrutiny. He folded the note and watched the clerk slip it into the right box. Then he gathered his greatcoat under his arm and began through the door and into the street, his vision still hazy, the sunny December light slanting against the blue mountains. He did not know where he would go except that it would be away.

The Hull House Hotel was on the southernmost edge of town. He began to walk south and he walked against the wind stinging his eyes, the sand carving his face. He did not care where he walked—only that he must move as far away from this place as possible. He knew that if he did not return, the committee would send someone to find him. He leaned into the wind, his head bent against the cold. He pulled his coat on and tightened it around his shoulders, tied the scarf around his neck. If he had his way the world would never find him in the hills. "Oh Father of Gogyeng Sowuhti. Tawa. Oh Tawa, God, please, Father God," he raged, gritting his teeth against the wind. He looked up and cursed the sun. "What have I done? Will this battle inside me never end?" He felt evil. He cried.

The tears smarted in his eyes, ran into the cavities of his nose and throat, choking him. The memory of the girl who cried out in his heavy arms stung him. For a moment the pain was more than he could bear, and he began to run to forget it.

"Run. Always run," Hawk in the Tree had told him. "There is always running with your own feet." Hawk in the Tree had learned from the footrunners—always run. Reginald ran for half a mile; his feet seemed to follow him clumsily, barely holding him upright. The toes of his shoes caught on stones in the road.

When he leaned into the wind he thought he heard the clatter of an engine on the track. He saw the tracks laid out below him like rows of fallen fences. The leaves had fallen; the grass had fallen. At one moment he leaned forward and skidded in the dusty road against the sharp gravel, cutting the palms of his hands open until the blood bloomed like a field of red flowers. He made a fist.

He walked swiftly to the south across the tracks toward Springville, toward the hills he had known with Hawk in the Tree. He was going to someplace under the sky where he could retrieve his innocence, where no hungers drove him, where he could sit under the dark sky over a roast on the spit; where his belly and his heart would be full; where he alone was kikmongwi, chief; where the stars would sing.

It was still daylight, he guessed about two in the afternoon. By nightfall he could possibly find the hut above Spanish and Nebo. It would be to the east toward Strawberry. He strained his eyes, but still, he could not see. A mist of clouds came down in the south below the sun and he recognized the look of cold—the haze surrounding foggy light. Buried for a week in his papers—while he was looking at the figures scratched like the tracks of birds on paper—he was always dreaming of finding his old mountains. He had always dreamed they would still be standing as he left them, under the same blue sky. He stumbled forward, hoping the farmers in the houses along the road to the south would not watch him from their windows. He beat his body against the long road, deliberately punishing himself for the barbs in his flesh that burned brighter than fire.

He had never dreamed he would come so close to violating the girl with the white hair! Oh, how could he have even touched her? He cursed the power in his limbs, his shoulders, the power in his legs. He lowered his head into the wind, hoping to drive away the terror of his mind. He wanted to blow away the memories of his power, away from the beating beating beating of the blood in his brain.

"They have taken my mother away from me," Laura had sobbed in the closed room. He had approached her and put his arm around her shoulders. Distraught, she had leaned into his arm. And then it had happened so quickly. And she had responded—at first. As he remembered, the tears came hot from his eyes. He had taken her into his arms without his own body's permission. The miracle was that he had let her push him away, because all that was in him had screamed for relief. Only when she had sobbed and pushed him away, had he been able to force himself to move back to the door. He could have . . . It had been a miracle that he had managed to wrench his body away and slip quickly out of the room.

When he met her father on the stairs, he had cried out, "She is distraught over her mother." But that had not been all. She had been trembling from fear. Now he pressed his hands to his head and grimaced. What had he been thinking? Oh, he wished he were dead. But he had said in the note . . . that he would return. He had been thinking about Martin Drucker and L. F. Barrington, who wanted to be home on Christmas Day. He knew Barrington was counting on him to be with them on the way home on Christmas Eve.

He felt a fresh wave of shame while the images of his unchanging mountains crowded into his head. He had promised himself. And how short-lived his promises had been! Though he came from these sturdy hills, he felt shifting, weak, like sand. He wanted to die. Waves of anger shuddered through his body when he tore his hands from his brow and pounded his fists through the cold air. His feet tore up the ground. He burst forward at times, putting long strides of distance between him and the hotel, between him and everything about the white man's life he had chosen: the paycheck, the binding clothes, the figures that marched interminably on the long pages. Ethel's tears.

Ethel had wanted him to stay and he had promised her he would make the job secure. But then he had never returned. Instead, he had found the woman in San Jose. He had followed his heart, which always seemed to lead him to a ragged edge. Always on the surface, his desires drove him into constant ecstasy, but the ecstasy had changed into an addiction which he could not control. And he found himself continually without reality. He had never settled into a resolved love.

He leaned toward the teeth of the hills that loomed south. There was the canyon along the Hobble Creek River. He ran sometimes, still stumbling into the wind and the mist ahead of him. He would abandon himself into the mist. He would fold it over him like a quilt and sleep forever if the hills would accept him. He believed the hills would take him. They were his mother and his father. He belonged to them. He ran southeast across the stubble, cutting a triangle to the canyon road. The hills began to stand up beside him, eating the sun.

Nothing seemed real. The farms nested at the foot of the hills seemed like toys. The mountains closed in on him, narrowing and then widening as the sun slipped behind him into the dusk. He came upon the open valley in the canyon road he had seen a hundred times in his dreams. It opened into rolling oak and brush surrounded by hills. He knew he could make it through this time of year, knew he could climb the back hills keeping Nebo in his view. Back up against the canyon, following the river and climb . . . anywhere.

He ran again. The weary hours of moving began to drain

him. Lately he had given in to the soft life. He pounded himself against the dusty road until his body could no longer feel anything but its own pain. And the fear and the heartache seemed to be driven out on the cold air.

He ran holding his arms high to the hills. He saw only one cart returning on the road from the Jolley ranch. The farmer waved: "Do you want a ride?" But Regi shook his head. He must have been a strange sight, running into the hills, obviously unprepared for a cold night in the mountains, his thin greatcoat flapping, his thick Indian hair in disarray. But he pounded on. No one else was on the road, no cart, no wagon. He knew there was logging in Hobble Creek Canyon. But he saw no one on a late Friday. The rest of the roads were empty and cold. He would climb the alligator-backed hills. He ran up an incline and sobbed out his anger to the dipping sun.

"Oh Father," he cried out to the sky. "I have tried everything. Nothing has been so driving as my need. Did you create me knowing I could not do without? I am suffering even now, and the sun is leaving me here alone."

He climbed higher and he could see the farm and the wagon on the road below him, the size of a fly. The sun glared on the high rocks, and the pine and oak blurred under the mist that blew away, leaving the air sparkling cold. The coat and the scarf no longer protected him from the chill. He sat on the ridge and spotted a herd of elk on the far side, and suddenly the elk and the slanting sunlight filled him with a sweetness he could not explain.

It hadn't done any good to resolve to give up his hungers. He had tried to explain them away as the answers to his needs—not as weaknesses. It was the emptiness that had claimed him, but in this moment he suddenly felt a sweetness fill his limbs. It would freeze tonight. He would give himself to the earth as the earth had always given to him. He would be the fodder for one of these magnificent animals. He would go to sleep forever on this hill.

He sat for a long time, listening. He sat without moving. A buck and two does glided over the ridge below him and stopped, alert. They faced him, surprised. Their large ears stood sharply up to catch the sound of his breathing. When he listened he heard himself breathing so hard, he was almost sobbing.

"Yes, Father of my spirit," he whispered, "I need to die." And the tears started up behind his eyes. "I need to return to you to find out who in the world I am. What is my hunger? Where are my mother and my father?" The elk stared at him. "Where are my people? Who are my people?" He murmured without making a sound in his throat. The animals watched him without moving—breathless, waiting. "I am as much a child of this earth as any child who walks this earth." The sun flickered off the water of the lake twenty miles in the mist, beyond the valley, the farms like jewels in a vast checkered fabric of brown and gold.

At that moment, the elk bounded away, and Regi sat in stunned wonder. He could hear the beating hooves against the ground as though there were drums under him. "Oh God. The world is too beautiful to leave. How can I live without dishonoring it? Tell me how I can take myself under my own power." He leaned his head into his hands and the tears began to flow.

He prayed none of the Eastmans would ever know how weak he had been. He could only hope that Laura would never tell them. But it was not Laura, not the Eastmans. It was himself. It was finally himself. He knew it. He had given himself up to needs of the moment without considering the world he had glimpsed through Sobe's eyes.

He found a boulder on the side of the hill toward the setting sun. He curled his back against the shelter of the rock and watched the deer scamper into the dark trees. He would return to his father, the sun, and to his mother, the earth, where he belonged.

26

Grace Tuttle

On their way to the dance, the threesome from the old Eastman house drove past Frank Corey at his popcorn cart. He was wrapped in a red wool scarf, urgently ringing a large bell. Tonight neither Chub nor his friend Reb Stuart from the railroad tracks was there. But it was Sissy Corey who stood beside him now, shivering in a thin sweater. She hunched her shoulders and looked down the road. She looked cold.

"He looks like Santa Claus," Alex laughed.

Frank Corey stopped ringing his bell. The lights in the clock tower above them said 8:00 P.M. The bells on the clock began to chime.

Grace leaned forward from the back seat and put a hand on Hanson's shoulder. "It's Sissy Corey," she said, her voice almost inaudible. "I haven't seen her for several days."

"Shall we stop and take her to the dance?"

Before Grace could answer him, Hanson slowed to a stop in front of Corey's cart and got out of the car.

Grace got out also. She straightened her skirt and felt a sinking feeling. She was not really sure what she had started. She was surprised at herself. Perhaps the greatest surprise was her own awareness of how selfish she really was.

While Hanson approached Sissy, Frank Corey saluted Grace with an admiring smile. "What can I do for you, Grace?" he said. "Popcorn? Peanuts? Take some peanuts with you to the dance, why don't you?"

"Oh, thank you, Mr. Corey, but no thank you. I don't believe . . . we just stopped by to see if Sissy wanted to come with us to the dance."

A strange blank moment of caution passed through Frank Corey's eyes. "Oh, you don't say," he said. "How nice of you. Say, Sissy, weren't you thinking about going to that dance?" His ruddy cheeks seemed to glow.

She backed against the building, shaking her head.

"No, please do come with us," Grace pleaded.

"I haven't anything to wear," Sissy said.

"You look fine," Grace said. "I'm all right with this skirt and blouse. Why don't you wear my jacket with the velvet collar. Look, it goes perfectly with your dress." The floral pattern in the dress matched the periwinkle blue. Sissy looked at it out of the corner of her eye.

"I have my comb with me," Grace continued, discovering herself moving without hesitation down a path that would more than likely ruin her evening. "We can get you looking beautiful. We knew you weren't feeling good for a while. Come with us and we'll see that you have a good time."

Grace held the jacket up against her skirt. The blue velvet collar blended perfectly with Sissy's flowers. When the girl reached out to touch the collar, Grace smiled. "Just put it on. You'll look fine." She opened her bag and took out her comb. "Sissy, you really are very pretty. Isn't she, Hanson?"

"I always thought so."

Sissy looked up at him while Grace drew the comb through the tangles of hair. "You haven't seen me since I was eleven years old," she said.

It was true. He had seen Sissy when he and Grace had walked to church on a summer day when Caroline had been too ill to go. She was riding on the top of the Corey wagon in a pink dress her mother had made out of an old shawl. Hanson remembered that day because Sissy had kept her eyes fastened on him while the cart moved down the road. Then she had waved.

"She's getting to be very pretty," Grace had said.

"She is," Hanson had whispered. "But still not as pretty as you are."

They had walked behind the cart all the way to church, while the Corey children had begun to sing "In Our Lovely Deseret." It had been the very next day, on a Monday, that Grace had been present when Hanson gave Sissy his old ice skates, as he had promised that winter. He had left for his mission during the following week, and now all he had seen of her was the glimpse he got at the house on the day he had arrived. She was even more beautiful now.

Though it was dark on the street, there was enough lamplight to reveal the sudden glow in Sissy's eyes. She pressed her lips together tightly, but she could not stop the beginning of a smile.

Grace gathered the profuse walnut-colored curls at the nape of Sissy's neck and drew away the little blue silk scarf from her own throat to tie the hair into a knot with a large bow. "I can't believe how your dress goes perfectly with these things," she said. "You really look beautiful, Sissy. Doesn't she, Hanson?"

She saw a stunned look of gratitude in Frank's eyes. "Oh, don't she look grand," Frank Corey said. "She do, don't she?"

"She really does," Grace said. And she wasn't just forcing words. She turned Sissy around and then stood with her hands on her shoulders to peer into the reflection in the shop window. Sissy Corey was beautiful. The dress with the velvet jacket was perfect. The scarf tied in a large loose rosette looked like the flowers in her hair. She was transformed.

"All right, let's go," Grace said. She opened the door to the front seat of the Chevrolet that Ashel had allowed Hanson to drive, and as though she were a princess, Sissy climbed into the front seat. Only her shabby shoes detracted from her fine new appearance. But she did not seem to notice.

As Grace climbed into the back seat, Alex followed her. He had been standing around on the corner beating his hands together to keep them warm. Now he was watching her carefully, not trying to suppress his grin. His eyes were very bright. Grace felt his eyes on her as she ducked into the back seat. She had only her white blouse and the fox stole now, and had not noticed the cold until she sat down and moved to the far window. When Alex climbed inside in his big raccoon coat, he put his animal arm around her and whispered in her hair, "Do you want me to keep you warm?"

She saw his eyes and his grin and felt the same sharp delight she had felt at Carroll's, but tonight she knew how much it meant. It meant nothing. It was a momentary thrill.

"Sure, Alex," she laughed. "You do the job and I'll pay you what you deserve."

"Meaning a kiss or a kick?" He leaned close to her.

"You try to do the job and you'll find out."

"I hope you'll be warm enough," Hanson said.

"I hope . . ." Sissy turned around in the front seat.

"No, no, Sissy. Don't you worry a minute. All I need is my fox stole," she told them.

"Or your raccoon Alex," Hanson grinned at her.

In a moment they were inside the gymnasium. The walls had been covered with large white snowflakes cut out of old sheets. The inside pieces hung from threads all over the ceiling—the room looked like an ice palace hung with snow. Festoons of holly and Oregon grape clung to wreaths under the windows. It was cheery and light. Even when they were inside the gymnasium at the Academy, Alex followed Grace as though he were attached by a kite string. Now she knew he was playing games, yet she could not seem to stop playing them with him to get just a little bit under Hanson's skin.

Nevertheless, she was frustrated when Hanson gave Sissy the first few dances, and took her with him to the punch table a couple of times. Sissy was radiant. Grace could not have created as pleasing a combination for a dance dress out of her own wardrobe. At one point Hanson and Sissy stood in the middle of the floor to talk while the dancers swirled around them. After only a few moments Hanson then took Sissy by the elbow and over to the punch table again where he bent over her intently to listen to what she told him. She was gesturing, moving her hands as though she could not speak without them, until Hanson put a cup of punch in her fingers, and she hid behind it for a long time, draining it slowly. When Sissy let the cup down, Grace thought she saw tears.

Alex was intent on Grace. When the polka blared, he spun her away from the dancers. He leaned close to her when she spoke to him. Grace began to feel crowded in the room. She felt the oppressive air and smelled body odors. The widower Peter Jeffrey, who also taught at the high school, came to say hello to her. He was small and heavyset with a stiff white collar at this throat that seemed as though it were choking the cherry color into his cheeks. He was a rather pitiful figure who had lost his wife six months before and had not seemed able to choose a new woman. Perhaps he was interested in Grace. He said hello and began to ask her a few questions when Alex moved in his way and virtually blocked him off. Just as Grace moved to another position to smile at Mr. Jeffrey again, the clock on the tower chimed nine, and suddenly Grace saw visible expectation in Alex's face. It was the most amazing moment. In one instance he was leaning near to her, blocking her from the venerable Peter Jeffrey, breathing in her hair, and as soon as the chimes had ceased, his eyes were fastened upon the door to the gymnasium and the blood had drained from his face.

Grace quickly turned toward the direction of his eyes. Laura Adamson was standing in the door.

Suddenly Grace felt inadequate. More than inadequate— alone. As she backed up, she felt herself against the outermost flesh of Mr. Jeffrey whose waistcoat felt like a stuffed settee. Startled, she excused herself to the powder room.

"Grace!" Mr. Jeffrey began. "Will you save me the next dance?"

"Certainly," she stammered. "I'll be right back."

But she wasn't sure when she would be back. It was obvious no one would know she was gone. Just this evening Hanson had promised her he would work something out with her, and he had ignored her completely.

She did not even tell Alex where she was going. He was already moving toward the door. And she would never hear what passed from his mouth to Laura's ears, for in just a split second after the nine o'clock chimes, he was spinning in a totally different orbit, reeling with the proximity that had smitten him so completely last night and this afternoon.

Grace bolted to the powder room and sat down in front of the mirror. There were two rows of tiny electric lights up both sides of the mirror. She did not really see the lights, shaped like candle flames. But she saw the light they cast upon her flushed face. She saw the blotches in the corners of her cheeks, the blue cast of the veins along her temples and on her eyelids. She touched her cheeks with the palms of her hands. She pressed her face hard between her hands. "So what is happening to continually place me at arm's length from anything real?" she asked herself. "There is some craziness here. A terrible craziness. Some insanity I can't explain." Where was Hanson? Why had she, Grace, made sure Sissy Corey was here?

While she stared into her blank eyes she saw Sissy behind her. She did not know how long Sissy had stood behind her there, peering into the mirror at her own beauty.

"My name is Emily," Sissy said. "My real name is Emily. Nobody calls me Emily."

Grace started from her own reverie when she heard Sissy's voice. "What, Sissy?" she said clumsily. "What did you say, Sissy?" she repeated.

Sissy was not looking at Grace. She was looking at herself. She leaned nearer to the mirror with a new radiance in her face Grace had never seen there before.

"Will you help me put my necklace back on?"

Grace rose quickly to help her, to lift her heavy curls. "Are you having a good time . . . Emily?" she asked.

"Uh . . . yes . . ." Sissy was hesitant.

Grace looked in the mirror.

"Hanson is very nice to me. But he likes you the best. I wish you'd dance with him. Do you think Hanson would mind if I danced with Hammersly Potter?"

Grace felt the electricity of Emily's hair in her fingers. "You want to dance with Hammersly Potter?" she said quietly, drawing her hands around the profuse curls.

"Yes, I do. Do you think Hanson would mind? How can I tell him?"

So. Emily Corey had something going on her own! Grace felt an overwhelming relief but controlled her voice. "Well, sure, I'll tell him, Sissy."

"Would you call me Emily?" Sissy said to the glass. "It would be all right if you called me Emily."

To her surprise, Grace found Hanson waiting for her outside the powder room. Behind Hanson, she could see Alex with Laura Adamson's hands lightly resting on his shoulders.

"I just want to walk out to the road to enjoy the night. There's a little bridge over the irrigation canal," Hanson said. "Will you walk with me?"

Grace looked at him. Then she smiled.

As they left, Grace saw the tall gangling figure of Hammersly Potter, the young farmer from Covered Bridge. He approached Sissy Corey and leaned close over her hair. She sailed away with him, wearing the velvet collar like a queen.

Grace and Hanson were silent walking away from the lights to the canal.

"It seems like we're having a time of it," Grace laughed.

"I thought you were having a good time with Alex."

She stopped in the middle of the bridge and looked down into the black rushing water that reflected the moon. "Not really."

"I didn't know."

"The moon is in little pieces," Grace said.

"That is only a reflection," Hanson said. "If you look up at the real moon, it is still whole."

He looked up at the moon, and she followed his gaze. "Do you remember when we used to ride the hay wagon to the lake and watch the moon?" Grace whispered.

Hanson looked at her. "I have thought of that a thousand times, and everything else we did together."

"Is it just me? I feel there is so much different about our being together this time."

"It's not just you. I have too many obligations. And I'm sorry. I wanted you to show Alex a good time."

For a few moments they walked in silence. "I just want to know one thing. Am I being impatient?"

He reached out and took her hand. "I think so." There was a moment of startling quiet now. Though Grace could feel tension in his hand, she didn't want to spoil this moment for a long time. Finally, Hanson spoke again. "Are you ready to come to this dance with me now?" he said.

The gymnasium had changed from a place of dark frustration to shimmering light. She walked back into the room in wonder, holding his arm. When she heard the music, she stared at his face. He had caught sight of Alex and Laura as they held one another at the edge of the crowd. Though he took Grace's hands and held them together between his flattened palms, she could see that he kept his eyes on the beautiful couple whirling in rhythm in the middle of the floor.

"Grace, you don't know how lucky we are. I'm alive because of him."

Grace watched Alex and Laura turn slowly as the music blared. While everyone around them moved in a rapid whirl, they were paying no attention to the rhythm or the step. They had drawn closer to one another, lost in one another.

"He's so good with people, Grace," Hanson said earnestly.

"Even Pa says he's doing a good job at the hotel." He paused. "I hope he doesn't get so involved with Laura that he forgets how much we need him in the new venture."

When he turned to Grace, he took both of her hands again. "Isn't this wonderful? Alex is going to us get back into making a success with the hotel business—a big success!"

Grace still felt uneasy. "Hotels aren't everything," she said, trying to smile.

"Well, no. His father's got a construction business. He can help us in construction—he knows how to build."

"Remember, once you had the idea of starting a moving picture show house in the office on Center Street?" Grace looked up at him.

He turned again and looked at Alex. "You know, I bet he'd be good at that, too."

Grace felt the music grow softer, and the dancers swirling around them slow to the faint sound of a violin. "You'd be good with or without him," she said.

"But aren't we lucky he's here!" Hanson turned with her toward Alex and Laura, and they greeted one another with nods and smiles. All Grace could think about for a moment was that at least she was in Hanson's arms. When Alex spun away with Laura, Hanson followed them with his eyes, but he finally turned to her. "Well, it looks like he's off somewhere else for a while." For a moment there was quiet while they moved on the floor. "You still dance good, Grace," he finally smiled. "Do you still ride as good?"

Now she saw his eyes. "Of course," she said.

"I was thinking we could take King Pin out tomorrow and break in that new bridle."

Grace's heart stopped. "I'd like that."

"I asked Alex to come, but unless we can borrow a horse from someone, there aren't enough horses for four."

Grace was inwardly glad in this moment that their economic difficulties had diminished their stock. "That would be fun. I'll make a lunch."

"Would you? We could spend some time together. We haven't done much of that yet."

I know, I know, Grace wanted to cry out. But she just smiled.

He did not kiss her when he left her at the door, but only said "We'll have a good day tomorrow." And that's what Grace wanted: many good tomorrows.

When she woke in the morning, she was almost afraid for a few moments that she had been dreaming. The sky looked brighter than it had ever looked before. She hurried to the large house before some of the nightmares of her worry about Hanson's love threatened to come back to her. She remembered Regi was staying here now. But when she passed his door, she saw that his room was empty—that he had not returned home.

Puzzled, she began packing the picnic lunch and fixing breakfast, trying not to think about Regi. She wanted no interruptions from last night's magic. When she heard steps on the stairs, she turned fully expecting to see Hanson. But it was Alex. He seemed to be in a good mood. When he came into the room, he was tossing his wet hair in a towel.

"Pretty Grace," he mused. "Will you make me a sandwich? I have business today."

She turned to look at him. He had rubbed his cheeks red. He looked fresh. He smelled like cologne. The collar of his shirt was open.

"You're not going riding with us today?" she asked, though she knew.

"I have business," he repeated with a smile.

"Oh, really? What kind of business?"

"For me to know and you to be sick with envy," he laughed. Pouring himself a tumbler of milk, he threw his legs over the chair, straddled it, and drank with eagerness.

Grace turned back to her silver. "I don't need to know. I can see it all over your face."

"You mean Laura?" he asked quickly. When he finished drinking the milk, he slammed the tumbler to the table. "How'd you guess?"

She turned, grinning. "You're as easy to read as a headline."

"Am I?" He flicked the towel at her apron and ran two at a time up the stairs.

Finally Hanson came down slowly, pausing on the landing. She could see him from the reflection in the window in front of the basin while she spread the bread with mustard and sliced the ham.

"There is nothing that says you have to feed us at this hotel," he said. His lips curved in a smile.

"Only a book of about fifteen hundred pages featuring 'Thou shalt' and 'It came to pass.'" Grace turned with the mustard knife in her hand. Then she laughed.

Hanson's hair, still uncombed, was standing straight up on the top of his head; his eyelids drooped. "I look that ridiculous?" he grinned. He tried to smooth his hair against his head with his hand, but it sprang back up.

"I could butter it to make it stay down!" Grace lifted the knife with the mustard on it.

"Try it and see!" He caught her wrist with his hand and suddenly the room reeled.

"Go easy, girl," Hanson said. And without warning she saw nothing but light. The room pulsed with light. Her heart bumped to a stop in her breast. She thought she could not breathe.

"Do you want me to make you a sandwich too?" she asked, telling him with her eyes that she loved him and she knew what was happening between them, but she would talk about sandwiches because that was what she knew he wanted her to do.

He stopped for a moment with her wrist still in his hand. His eyes saw into hers and he explored her heart with them. Then he looked at the mustard knife she was holding under his nose and he grinned. "I'll make a sandwich out of you," he said.

"Try it," she laughed, and pulled away.

When he released his grip he turned to the sideboard where she had laid the bread in rows. "How can I help?" he said. Once more he slicked down the rusty-colored cowlick on the top of his head with his hand.

"Keep your hair off the bread," she said, giving him a little nudge with her hip.

He slipped a larger knife out of the chopping block and began slicing the ham.

Just as it had last night, the five years they had spent without each other rolled away like a breach of air. The clouds parted and there was nothing but light in all the corners of the room. She was standing with him as she had stood with him years ago in this same house, with Grandma Rain rocking in the front room, the curved legs of the rocker beating, beating against the wood floor. Mara had come in one day and said, "We'll have live music at your farewell dance, Hanson. Ashel has hired a string quartet. The Partridges. Do you believe it?" And Mara and Will had circled both Grace and Hanson with their arms, their love like a river of fresh water that rolled into both of them once more. When they brushed against one another, their laughter, their smiles, the way they moved in the room in a dance without any jarring rhythm, gave them life.

Grace was radiant with joy. This was how she remembered him—dancing with her against the sideboard, smiling, joking about the ham. When she looked at him she saw his heart in his eyes. There was no need for words.

"Want to go saddle up King Pin?" Grace finally said, wrapping the sandwiches in newspaper.

"I'll be right out," Hanson said. "I've got to get Alex out of here and make the bed." He paddled her with the back of his hand. "So you won't make it."

She grinned at him.

The December air was pure cold light. It looked like one of

those Christmases they often had without snow. Though Hanson had trouble getting the new bit in King Pin's mouth, both he and Tar Boat were ready in half an hour. On the horses at last, they began trotting down the street in time to see Alex drive down Center in his car. He grinned and waved, gave Hanson the okay signal, and sped to the Hull House Hotel.

"He's gone," Hanson grinned. "I hope he knows what he's doing." His gaze was wistful. But his eyes returned to Grace.

"It was funny to see him fall so hard." Grace leaned her head back and laughed, breathing up the sun. Then she leaned forward and kicked Tar Boat's withers. "I'll race you to the Barbar farm."

Hanson turned the bay horse sharply and sat hard on the saddle. "First time I've been on a horse since you and I did this right before I left," he yelled. But his words, and the sound of his voice, and his laughter, were absorbed by the wind.

27

Reginald Summerfield

Regi did not know how long he had been lying on the side
of the mountain. It had been cold, he remembered, but he did
not feel it now. Instead, he felt a pressure on his arm, and a
rocking, rocking. Some outside force was grasping him and
rocking his body, but on the edge of blackness, he could not
respond. He was rocking as though he were coming up from a
dizzying pit, spinning and rocking toward some light—first
away from it, then tapping into it. The light hurt his eyes. He
reached out. Beyond the light was a field of flowers blowing in
the breeze, the heads of flowers rippling in waves like a meadow
of milk. Above the meadow were two figures blazing with light.
They walked toward him, figures in dazzling white clothes. As
he saw them he suddenly felt a diffusion in his spirit—an astonishing wordless peace. He had never felt such peace in his life.
They walked slowly toward him. They held out their hands to
him. He was flooded with absolute joy.

"Mathew," one said to him.

And then he heard the music. It was music such as he had
never heard before. It touched him in the very inside walls of
his body, shimmering, vibrating in every cell. All the galaxy was
singing with him. "Oh Tawa," he said. "Let me come home."

"You are not ready," the other one spoke to him.

The white Bahana! They stood before him, billowing with
light. The flood of peace filled him; the music sang inside of
him. Reaching, reaching, he reached out.

But suddenly his hand hit substance. He spun away from
the light so rapidly, he reeled. He zipped up from the dark. A

shadow stood over him, heaviness touched him, rocked him. He heard a dog bark. He was rocking, rocking, but he could not respond.

"Wake up. Do you hear me? You'll freeze to death."

It was a language he could understand. Yet only faintly, for it came from very far away in the darkness and he was fighting his return from the tunnel and the light. He hung on the edge. He fought in his entire body, but he could not turn one way or the other. A rough hand slapped his cheeks, but he was unable to open his eyes.

In a few moments he felt a large black cloud of some heavy canvas-like material floating over him, rustling and crackling like fire. The noise frightened him. He felt something alive and large moving up against him and settling on his legs. He fought to return the blood to his limbs, but even his lips were frozen shut. Reeling, he wanted to leap away from his own body and the strange heavy body near his legs. He struggled against his own limbs that would not move, when he felt the cold muzzle of an animal against his jaw. Sensing the dark space around him, he felt the cold canvas cracking and cutting him off from the air. *Oh, dear Father, Father of Gogyeng Sowuhti.* He could not move. He began to hear the hiss of the dog's breathing, and he believed he opened his eyes. But there was no color. He heard the sound of a gun cracking against the silence. Someone in the distance was shooting.

His limbs did not belong to him. They were dead, like sticks of wood ready to hack off and be thrown into the fire. And then began the burning in his dead body. He had never felt anything like it in reality. Every cell of his body stung painfully, and he turned away from it in terror. But the tunnel and the light were cut off from him, and the figures in the white clothes were gone.

From below the breaking canvas Regi heard the shots. The shots moved away, further and further away from him. And now they were gone. There was only silence. And pain.

In spite of the excruciating fire of his limbs, he inched his torso away from the wagon cover, out from under the canvas, and away from the rocks. He moved forward until he was in a position to look down the mountain into the valley. It was almost dawn. He could see only the black outline of the hills on the sky, and the stars. He knew he must get out of there. Pulling the canvas around him for protection in the devastating cold, he began to scoot on his belly down the hill. Some stranger had put this canvas over him, and it had saved his life. Slowly the fire in his veins pumped blood into his extremities. He could feel the liquid open up the small passageways of his body as life flowed back into him. The air on the mountain was so cold and so still that he could sense—as though it were a tangible substance—the light of the moon.

He scooted into a gully at the base of the hill, still numb. When he reached the road he could hear the trickle of water and he hunched up, still trying to get his legs under him. Finally on his knees, he crawled to the stream. He dipped his hands in the freezing water. He fell face down with his lips against the stones and let the water tingle on his skin. He lay for a long time. He did not know how long. But he let the water stay cold on his tongue, felt the water on his cheeks. He felt the water wash against his eyes and he writhed with the pain that struggled in his limbs. While he washed he saw in his memory the white bahana reaching with his outstretched hands. He heard the music in his bones. It would be talavai, light he would never forget. *Dear father, oh Tawa, spirit of my people, why am I not with you now?*

Still weak, Regi clawed his way back to the narrow gravel road as the sun began to uncover the outline of the eastern hills. He knelt on all fours, the canvas wagon cover wrapped around him keeping out some of the chill. Painfully and awkwardly he crawled down the road, inches at a time. In a while, when he heard the rumble of a truck on the road far away, he ducked into the trees. He heard the truck stop. It stopped where he had been this morning above the road, lying against the rock on the hill. He heard the bark of the dog staying close to its master. The sounds were far away. He was half a mile from where the truck parked. He could see a man get out of the truck and move to the spot where he had been a few moments ago, reaching out to the figures in the light. They were looking for him. Had he not climbed out of unconsciousness, they might have found him—dead.

For a long time he stayed off the road, scuttling as best he could through the oak brush and the dense trees. As large as he was, he still had his native agility and earth sense. He could smell the wood smoke from the farm houses below. He skirted them, feeling an odd combination of embarrassment and anxiety to get back to the hotel soon to keep his job.

Though he had courted death in his vision, he knew he was not dead and that his best chance for survival in today's world was not in his old hills, but on the plains of his scratched figures, the papers of his books, and the columns of addition and subtraction that blew constantly across the canyons of his life. All he could hope was that Alex and Hanson had not missed him, or had thought him to be working late at the hotel. If he could make it back to the hotel he would freshen up in the lavatory as best he could, and he could attend the Saturday meetings Barrington had planned, and no one would ever know.

Now in this daylight he could only trust that in her own terror and embarrassment, Laura would never tell. Thinking about his weakness, he cringed with self-hatred.

But his fear for life seemed to pale beside his dance with death. He had never realized there was a life in his own body that seemed to have a will of its own.

Shuddering, he began to run across the foothills toward Springville, still away from the road. But his limbs were warming and he could see the roofs of the toy-sized houses taking shape in the dawn.

It was a long walk to the city and he was hungry. But a power not his own spurred him on. It was as though he now leaned toward a light he could understand. He knew Barrington would be meeting at 10:00 A.M., and he guessed by the inner clock that often ticked in his head that it was about 7:00 A.M. Two hours would give him time to be dressed and alert at the conference table.

He felt as though in the last twenty-four hours he had been in several different worlds. First, in the world of the figures he had made on the pages, and after it, the world governed by his shifting appetite which he had tried to satisfy. Third was the world of his stable hills. His heart beat with this land. He had read the sun and the stars and the cold chill of the December day. He had read the tracks of birds and the flight of gulls who wrote across the sky. And now, at this moment, when he was coming full circle to the world where the earth lived, he saw a vision of the civilization that seemed real, but was not real to him now. Without pausing, the world of men seemed to encroach upon the land like a scuttle of millions of crabs climbing out of the sea. In droves, in magnificent numbers, they were eating up the land.

He, too, was a part of that hunger. He had written furiously with his pen on the white papers stretched interminably before him without pausing, without hesitation, eating up the hills with its barren blank expanse. If there was any one hunger that ate away the hills of his youth, it was the appetite of paper. When he thought about it, paper seemed a product of man's destruction, an insatiable plunder of the trees. It had proliferated, choking off the leaves. It lay between him and the sky. In his mind it suddenly became a huge encroachment upon the natural world. And yet, artificial as it seemed, like the earth upon which life spawned, it carried the life of numbers and words. Without paper he would have no employment—and he would never have heard Sobe's cry: to reach toward the most sustaining visions. He realized he must now embrace it to save his life.

Regi began to run. The dawn was cold, but the day brought with it a sunny light that warmed the earth. He found himself inside the tiny city of Springville within a half hour. He jogged down Fourth South past the bones of houses being built on the thoroughfare, past the multiple dwellings with one sign that said "Johnson Family Residence." It looked as though the man was still keeping many wives. When he rounded the corner to State Street, he was feeling the blood beat in his frozen limbs.

He ran feeling light-headed and hungry. But he let nothing stop him. The Hull House Hotel was only two miles away. He made it almost twenty minutes before ten.

Weary, he stepped into the lavatory and tightened his graying collar. He washed his face with his hands, brushed his coat. In spite of his worn look, he was alert and exercised, the blood red in his cheeks.

Out in the foyer he greeted Barrington with the cool greeting of a man about to begin work. At the front desk he asked if Julia had seen his portmanteau. He had left it with the boy.

Julia looked at him with careful eyes. "Did you stay here last night?" she asked. "I thought you had never checked into a room."

"No. I was at the East House Hotel."

Julia rummaged below the counter and produced the leather paper holder. "Did you get breakfast?"

He was hoping she would ask.

"It's been hectic with Horace out of town," she added. "He's in Salt Lake City until Monday. So we haven't the usual bakery order filled. But I made bread."

She whipped into the dining room, tying her apron again about her waist. Not long after he sat at the table, she brought a delicious hot loaf and several pads of butter which he devoured crazily.

"And I don't know what I'm going to do without him," Julia

rambled cheerfully. "A secretary called that someone had died at the hospital, and I told them the family would just have to bring the body on their own."

While she talked she cleared up the tables around him. His ears heard what she said, but his mind seemed far away while he sat chewing and gulping. And with his left hand on the white tablecloth, he fingered his change.

The steel committee met in stifling steam heat in an upstairs room belonging to Drucker. The flies on the sill hopped about in the room as though half dead with frost. He heard the buzz of the flies better than he heard Barrington's droning speech. "We won't be able to leave here before Monday evening. And Drucker has business with the bank Monday afternoon."

Reginald wrote the figure automatically. He added and subtracted with studied habit. He noted Adamson was not there. But no one said much of anything. No one discussed it. "He was called to the hospital to see about his wife," one of Drucker's men said, and the others never blinked when Barrington asked for the quorum to vote, though Adamson's position was in danger of being overridden.

When the meetings were over and he was finished with his work, Reginald ate again hurriedly, gathered up his papers and retired to the lobby, where he sat for a long time in the slanted light from the afternoon sun. He did not want to return to either the Eastman House or the East House Hotel. What questions would they ask? He wanted to stay here, although he had already paid at the East House Hotel—even before he stayed at Eastmans'—and he did not have enough money left to pay for another room. He hunched into a leather chair behind a newspaper and chewed on his lip. He waited for Julia to finish up at the desk, and when she had finished, he ducked down the hall hoping to find not only the restroom, but an open closet or a room where he could wash up and lie down. He was exhausted. At this point he did not care, but anything would do. Most important was that he hoped no one would know. And at that point he saw a door open down the hall and a gauzy lawn skirt swing out on the other side of the door.

His heart stopped. His hands grew clammy and cold. It seemed he could still see the flashing lights and the field of flowers where he had felt whole. Now his limbs seemed to melt. His physical body reacted with a surprising degree of pain—a tension not unlike the trauma of his freezing limbs early in the small hours of the dawn. The draped baize floated against the open door. He was sure it was probably Laura. Without a moment's pause, before the figure in the dress had a chance to come into the hall, he leaned all his weight against the door on his right. He pushed it open, breaking the weak lock with his physical strength. The darkness and the emptiness of the room came into his nostrils like a black gas.

He ducked into the room quickly, his breath beating hard against his heart and his lungs. He closed the door immediately and flung the chain lock into its hasp with an involuntary yelping sound in his throat. He stood with his forehead against the door while he heard the figure on tiny slippered feet pass in a whisper of lace down the hall.

Breathing more softly now, he felt the gathering darkness of the room behind him and turned slowly to open the shades at the windows on the other side of the room.

Without his consent his body did a double take of a shock-step back against the door. He was closed in a room filled with silver and dark shadows, and lurking in the shadows a half a dozen coffins. He remembered someone had said that the manager of the hotel was a funeral director. He was in a supply room. But it was not the coffins that took the breath from his body. In the center of the room was a table as high as his breast. Lying on the table in the half light was a figure in a white dress. The blood drained from his face. It was Laura!

When he leaned against the door and sucked in his breath, his lungs hurt. The taste on his tongue was like metal. He had thought he saw Laura in the hall. How could this be Laura? He fell weakly against the door and slipped down against it, feeling his legs buckle under his body. Standing with his palms flat against the door, he strained his eyes in the darkness. When the light clarified the figure on the table, he thought the face looked older, ravaged. When he dared to walk closer, his heart pounded. Oh Laura, he breathed, unable to face the body lying as though it were asleep. But he knew the smell of death, and there was a lingering odor in the room.

So sure that it was a devastated Laura who lay before him, he came closer now and leaned over the threatening silence. She was almost unrecognizable. There was no peace in the features. A tortured look warped the cheeks. Large deep lines furrowed the brow. The hair was . . . he paused. He collected his memories, his pain. He tried to sort out the historical evidence in the body before him. The hair was a deep color of white, almost gray. And he remembered that morning—yesterday morning—Friday morning, Laura had bobbed her hair. This was her mother. He swallowed. His spittle still tasted like metal.

Regi stood staring for a long time. He did not notice the shadows deepen in the room. If he heard footsteps in the hall he stood with his back against the wall beside the door so that if it opened he would be hidden. He knew Horace Hull was out of town until Monday. His eyes darted into the corners of the room toward the closet and up and down across the collection of coffins stacked in monumental splendor on every side of him. At the back beside the small bathroom, complete with basin and chipped ceramic floor, lay a large black metal box with brass handles and an engraved inscription on the lid: "Vita Maxima."

One of Hull's tools glittered in the faded light of the window. It was a scalpel with a mother-of-pearl handle. He weighed the scalpel in his hand, lifted the lid of the large coffin and cautiously rolled his body into it, holding the lid high above his head. Carefully, he settled the scalpel on the lock, with the handle generously inside so the tool would have fallen inward at a surprise shutting. He would take a chance that no one would come. If someone did come he would shut the lid against the scalpel and he would have air to breathe. He lifted the lid back against the wall. He closed his eyes; the white satin smelled new and sweet like the bed of a baby.

28

Mara Eastman Jones

On Saturday morning Mara heard the scoop of a shovel. Half awake, she turned to the window. Down below in the back of the garden, Will bent over in the potatoes—Will, grizzled and humped, dressed in his old tattered sheepcoat with the red patches on his sleeves. His hair, looking like uncut grass, was tucked into a piece of underwear he had tied around his neck to keep out the cold. He was shaking slightly, leaning on the shovel. At his side in a half bushel basket were those big old potatoes that he had left in the ground since summer, not yet frozen. There were a lot of them.

Something about the curve in his back, the determination in the jabbing motion he made with the shovel into the ground surprised her. "Good, Will," she thought. What could have frozen and died, he was saving. Every few minutes he stopped to rest and lean on the shovel. The sunlight struck his head. The top of his scalp shone slick as some of those potatoes nested in fuzz. His ears looked as though the cold had bitten them red.

Mara flung up the sash. "Where's your hat, Will?"

But he was concentrating on those potatoes. When she repeated the question he took his left hand from the shovel and swiped a never mind gesture without ever turning his head. In a minute he was on his knees pulling a big potato out of the ground. He held it up to the light and inspected it before he tossed it into the basket. Then he dug around in the ground with his bare fingers that poked like sausages out of the frayed knit glove. When he was sure he hadn't missed another one, he raised himself up again and drew his sleeve across his forehead.

He looked up at the sun and rubbed the top of his bare head.

Mara saw Will as he always had been—determined, stubborn, a born example of perseverance, frugality—too frugal to wear out his hat. She hurried into the closet and grabbed his cap from the shelf. She tightened the sash on her nightgown. She tried to hurry, but her hurrying seemed much slower lately. She pulled a brightly printed mackinaw over her nightgown and scuffed into an old pair of open shoes. Going downstairs was not as easy as it had been. She fairly bumped down, leaning every step of the way on the banister, praying as she always prayed, that she would not fall.

Once in the cold garden, she gave the hat to Will, who reluctantly pulled it down over his eyes without a word. She drew her own scarf and coat around her ears. "Did you get all those potatoes this morning?"

"Every one of 'em," Will said, standing now. He looked down into the basket. "Didn't want 'em to freeze."

"I swear I didn't know there were so many."

"I smell that snow coming. Do you smell it?" Will said, raising his head and sniffing the breeze.

"No. I don't smell snow. You don't smell snow before it comes."

Will looked down at her and grinned. "It's a ways off yet." He was grizzled and slow. His face was arranged in hard lines the years had deepened. But his blue eyes were still bright.

"You're dreaming. You want snow for Christmas so Santa Claus can get here," Mara said.

"Well, mark my word. I had enough experience to know what snow smells like a ways off." He grinned at her. "The old man's got one foot on the sleigh."

Mara smiled to herself this time. He was usually wrong. She changed the subject. "You think it's smart we offer all that stock money on the Hull House Hotel?" She stood looking out across the garden for a moment.

"It's the boys that's got to think so. Sometimes we meddle

too much. And it's the young ones who are going to have to take care of it."

"Hanson? What do you think Hanson will do?"

"Don't know," Will said, leaning over his shovel again. "I saw that little Gracie early. She walks over from Ashel's to get breakfast for those boys in the big house. I hope he doesn't break her heart. If he knows what's good for him he'll make a commitment and see to it she's happy for the next eighty years."

"You going to live to be a hundred, Will?"

He turned to her, his leathery face a smile. "What's stoppin' me?" he said. The light danced in his eyes and on his face.

"You've been fun to share it with, Will," Mara said. She meant it. He was grinning, still.

"We've had it good, Mara, didn't we? In spite of the mill and that little mortgage Ashel took out on our place. I never should have given the house up to the trust, thinking I was old. I really ain't old. But in spite of all of that, we've had it real good."

"In spite of the mill and the mortgage," Mara said. "I'm glad I'm not the one starting out. We're about through."

"I ain't through yet," Will said. He leaned over and the red patches split across his arms. The sun was dancing out of the east like fire. Nothing about the sky promised snow. "You've still got lots of spit left in you, too."

When she looked up she saw a couple of young people walking across the back field by the barn, and for an instant she thought they were Grace and Hanson. She hoped it was. But after a closer look she saw Sissy, the red bandanna tied at a rakish angle, attempting to hold back the mass of brown curls. This morning her usual torn gray blouse had been replaced by a freshly-ironed white one. Even her skirt had been ironed, and her boots polished. She was wearing a nice-looking paisley jacket with a blue velvet collar. It looked exactly like a jacket Grace had often worn.

The young man with her looked like Hammersley, that boy of Clem Potter's who lived on his father's large farm at Thistle and Covered Bridge. He was following her, his hands in his pockets. She was carrying a covered basket. Mara could see they were headed out back to the west road where a nice-looking limousine was parked by the fence. She was wondering why the Potter boy hadn't driven it around up front on Main when she caught them looking toward her. When they ducked behind the barn, she thought she understood what was happening. They had parked the limousine in a place where they hoped no one would see them get away. In a few moments they moved from around the edge of the barn, glancing Mara's way sheepishly. They knew they had been found out. There was no way to get from the barn to the car without being seen, and so they decided to make the best of it.

"Hello, Mrs. Jones," Sissy waved.

Mara smiled and waved back.

Before they separated the barbed wire to climb through the fence, Mara was close to them. "What's going on, Sissy?"

"Mrs. Caroline says I can take off for this morning."

"She knows you're with Mr. Potter?"

Sissy hesitated. "No'm."

"Does your mother know?"

"No'm."

"It's all right, Mrs. Jones. I can drive," Hammersly Potter seemed very tall and very thin. He reminded Mara of a poplar tree. But he only looked fragile. He was tough with the horses, the sheep on the hills in the Spanish Fork Canyon in the south of the county.

"Well, it's none of my business except as it affects Ashel's family, and I know Miss Caroline needs somebody with her."

"We were going to drive by and get Cherry to come again this morning." Sissy was subdued and quiet, and she looked from time to time up into Hammersly's stoic face.

Mara stopped and looked at Sissy's clothes. She looked almost beautiful. Something was different about her. She looked at Hammersly. "Does your father know you have his car?"

His eyes were hesitant. He was guilty of something. "He didn't need the car. He took the truck back up Hobble Creek to where he was huntin'."

Mara explored his gaze. "But you didn't take it without his permission, did you?"

"No'm."

She guessed he lied. He seemed confused. She had caught him leaning on one foot and then another.

"I don't know . . ." Mara began.

"We'll go back up to Hobble Creek and ask him if it's okay this time, won't we, Hammersly?" Sissy decided.

"Can you find him if he's fetching game down?"

"It wasn't game."

"Whatever it was."

"Early this morning he said he stumbled across a froze-to-death Indian."

Mara's blood pumped out of her heart. A knife seemed to pass through her and she felt a sudden dizziness. "What did he say?"

"He was takin' the truck up to pick up a froze Indian."

Mara's heart felt as though it skidded to a stop and she reached out to steady herself on Sissy's arm. The girl gave her a hand.

Will had dropped the shovel by now and had come from behind. He stepped hard on the big clods of dirt and was grinding them down into the winter furrows. "What's up?" he said, smiling at Hammersly. The boy looked a little like a pine board with a few knots for eyes and mouth in his face. His look was gaunt and blank—now with hesitation and discomfort.

"Did he say anything about the Indian's name?"

"No, he didn't, ma'am." Hammersly stood on the other foot. He changed feet every time he spoke.

Was it Regi? Mara didn't know. "Regi didn't come back last night," she said to Will.

"Regi? I thought he went back to Salt Lake City."

"Mr. Potter found a dead Indian."

"Dead? Was he dead, boy?" Will said.

"I don't know. I think so. He said froze. Froze Indian. He was too big to carry out without the truck."

Mara leaned against Will now. She leaned hard against him. She had a thousand questions. What she really wanted was for Hammersly to drive her up the canyon with them. The thought crossed her mind, but Sissy's open face stopped her. It took no fool to discover in Sissy's eyes that she wanted to be with Hammersly alone.

"It sounds like it might be our Mathew. We wondered why he hadn't returned yesterday afternoon, although I thought he would have come into the house late." Mara clutched Will's hand and his legs shook holding her up. "What's next, I wonder. A froze Indian. If you see your father," she instructed Hammersly, "tell him to hang onto the Indian, that we will be up to Thistle to fetch him this afternoon."

"Unless he's dead and he takes him back to the hotel."

Mara looked at Will. "The Hull House Hotel?" She shuddered.

"I think so." Hammersly looked down at Sissy as he spoke to all of them. "If it's all the same to you, my father won't be missing the car, and we was planning on driving to the lake."

Mara breathed noisily. She sighed. She let her breath out and still hung tightly to Will. "Of course, of course."

Sissy took Hammersly's arm. They turned and began stepping through the potatoes to the back lane. As they passed, before Mara turned to walk back to the house, she saw them driving away. Once she was inside, she watched through her kitchen window as the car moved into the distance. Smaller and smaller, it was soon lost on the west road to the open fields and the lake. She stood for a long time watching when there was nothing more to watch. She clung to the table top holding to her worry about Regi. Where was Regi? He was too big to carry without a truck.

When Will came in, he made a lot of noise putting away the shovel.

"I'm going to check beyond all possible doubt that Regi did not stay at the house, Will," she said. She buttoned her gloves again and pulled her scarf around her neck. As she stepped out onto the walk, she looked back into the yard and saw Grace and Hanson starting up on the horses. With their faces up to the sun, they were laughing. Their hair was flying in the wind. They did not seem to see her on the walk. Perhaps they saw only each other. She hoped that was so.

29

Grace Tuttle

It was six o'clock Saturday evening by the time Hanson and Grace led the horses to Ashel's front post. Hanson dismounted first. When he came to Tar Boat, he pulled Grace down from the saddle and held her in his arms for a moment before he let her feet hit the ground.

"I'll tell them," he said to her, his lips tangled in her hair.

Eyes luminous, she kept both of his hands in hers. "I'm so happy, I think I might burst apart."

"I'd rather you stay just the way you are," he grinned.

When Grace saw Caroline's face pulling away from the window, she knew Hanson's mother had been watching for them. As they entered the door, Grace heard the clock begin to chime. In the dining room and in the large hallway, Grace could see Cherry Corey moving back and forth from the dinner to the kitchen. The table was set with china, the silver gleaming. She thought she smelled roast pork. A tureen of little apples baked in lemon juice sat on the sideboard. For a moment she drank in the beauty of their lives in this home. It was rich with damask and shining cherry wood. The floor shone. The west light above the first landing on the stairs shimmered through the cut glass, a dance of colored sunlight.

Caroline wheeled in from the front room and opened her arms to both of them. "Did you have a good time, dears?" she said, holding Hanson for an extra moment as he leaned over to her.

"A wonderful time," Grace smiled at her.

Hanson stood, still holding his mother's hand. "Well—all in

one week. The Royal House Hotel . . . and Grace too." He smiled at her, too.

Caroline stopped short. "Does . . ." She stammered in her tiniest voice. "Does this mean . . . ?"

Her son was reaching for her hand.

"Even if we don't get the Hull House Hotel, we've got each other." Grace spontaneously buried her head in Caroline's perfumed hair.

"Well, we're going to have the hotel and each other—both," Hanson said with confidence. "We thought sometime in February." He tightened his grip on his mother's hand.

Caroline held her breath. "Oh, my dears!" she whispered in her smallest whisper. "I knew it. I was just hoping! You're going to do it after all! I'm so happy," she said. "Now I know what we'll be doing for a couple of months. Oh, I am so happy for both of you." She let go of the two young people and clasped her hands. The light from the window shone in her hair.

Cherry, who was back at work now, stood waiting for Caroline in the kitchen door. "Ma'am," she hesitated. "Should I take out the baked yams?"

"Yes, dear." When Caroline nodded and began to wheel into the dining room, Hanson took the chair from her and pushed it. She smiled at him and again clasped her hands. "Hanson! There couldn't have been more wonderful news."

A knock at the door at that moment brought Mara and Will into the hallway. Laughing, Mara was carrying a large brown bag plump with little wrapped packages in embroidered foil ribbons. The papers were colored red and blue and green and embossed with white stars. Mara let Grace take the packages from her arms and asked her to set them for the time being out on the hall table in the spray of Christmas evergreen Caroline had set with the candles. Hanson took the pies from Uncle Will.

Caroline was alive with excitement. "Just wait until you know what I know," she said.

As she took the packages from Mara, Grace whispered in her ear, "We have some news for you, Aunt Mara."

Mara looked up. "What? What's going on? Hanson?"

Hanson, loaded with two pies, stopped and grinned at her from the kitchen door. "It's true," he smiled.

Mara looked as though she were seeing him as he had stood in the same doorway before he left on his mission. Grace remembered that day long ago, too. With his suit pressed, and his shirt so starched that it had rubbed his neck raw, Hanson had helped his father to clear the ditch. They had gone out in the morning before dawn, and the sound of their shovels had echoed against the other houses. The light had come over the hill slowly, and Grace had found time to get dressed before she went down to the house. The family was kneeling by the table, Mrs. Corey standing still over the stove with the spatula in her hand and her head bowed, when Mara had come in the door. "Bring this boy back, if it be thy will," Ashel had been praying. "I'm sorry. I came at a bad time," Mara had whispered. "No, you came at a good time. This is the beginning of Hanson's journey home."

"We're getting married in February," Hanson smiled.

"Oh Gracie, Gracie. I am so happy for you," Mara said. "You have made us happy." Though she still had her gloves on, she held Grace's hands, then held Grace's cheeks. She pressed her palms against the white cheeks, the tears wet on her own mouth.

"Didn't you believe?" Grace said.

Mara nodded, still crying, unable to speak again. Hanson went to her and she held Hanson too for a long time. "You darlings. You are darlings," she finally said weakly. "I was hoping. I was so much hoping. Yes, I always knew. I always believed I knew. But so much . . ." she paused. "So much has always happened from the beginning to stop our fondest dreams from coming true." She paused again, wiping the tears from her cheeks with the back of her glove. "How many years it sometimes takes—to make things right at last." Then she whispered very quietly, "Now I truly feel as though you have come home."

Will came and stood beside her. She had knocked her hat askew and the acorns and feathers were dangling in her eyes. He tipped her hat and Mara scooped it off her head. When Will took it gently and laid it on the top shelf of the hall wardrobe, her hair fell down into her tears. While she stood for a long time in the room, everyone waited until finally Cherry brought the yams and set them on the table, curtsied, and backed away, peeling off her apron.

Caroline said "Yes, that's fine for now, honey. You may go. Take a loaf of bread to your mother. Tell her hello."

As Cherry left through the back way, Ashel made a production of coming in through the front door. He banged around knocking about his umbrella, hanging his hat on the hook of the umbrella stand, and puffing and huffing out of his greatcoat before he began to realize how many people were in the dining room and how still it was.

Before she left, Cherry had lit the candles on the buffet. As the dusk began to fall, the light from the candles began to flicker in the high corners of the dining room against the chintz coverings on the walls, against the sconces, and the tea set and punch bowl festooned with holly and ivy and a few grapes from the arbor that reflected the candlelight.

"Eh, what?" Ashel said as he entered.

Never had Grace believed that Ashel could remind her so much of his Father, Papa Eastman, during the glorious old Christmases they had always shared together in the big house: the hot cider, the wreaths of blue spruce, the old red tablecloth. The memory reminded Grace for a moment of how much she had to do there to clean and decorate in preparation for their Christmas Eve party. When they had decided to invite the Coreys and a few other poor families, Mara had mentioned that it might be better to move the event to the old place.

Ashel looked from his wife's glowing face to his son's grin to Grace's smile. In a reflexive action he pulled the watch on the fob from his pocket and checked it, shook it, listened to its tick. "I'm . . ." He hesitated. "I'm not late, am I? Well, not that late, am I?" he questioned.

Hanson laughed and came to him quickly. He was glowing; his eyes reflected the light. "No, father, you are not late. That's not it. We have something to tell you." He leaned down impulsively and kissed Grace on the mouth.

Ashel blinked. He looked at Grace and she felt weak in her knees. He had guessed, but he said, "You look like you're going to eat her, son."

He stood back for a moment and Grace thought: "Papa Eastman, Papa Eastman," though she could only remember his blustery laugh from long ago because she had been very young.

All of them laughed, and Hanson took his father in his arms. For a moment father and son held each other. Ashel, still joking, said, "Well, son, I'm glad you didn't wait to decide until Christmas. For a minute there I wondered . . ." But after he held Hanson, and the others clasped their hands and talked among themselves, he drew Grace in with his other arm and drew them both close into the circle of his embrace. "You have made all of us very happy," he whispered to them both.

Grace had never been so close to Ashel's cheeks, to the smooth roughness of his face. He smelled tart like very rich cologne, and there was a stubble of whiskers on his otherwise smoothly-shaven chin.

"I love you both and you two will be happy. You've been an obedient son and daughter. And that's what it takes," he said, drawing away a little. "I am so glad we can share this time with you."

"Speaking of sharing," Hanson tightened his grip on Grace's hand. "You were in town—and at the hotel today. Have you seen Alex? He doesn't know yet."

Ashel paused as his eyes met Hanson's gaze. For a moment

there was a heavy silence.

"Is something wrong, Ashel?" Mara asked.

Ashel still stared at Hanson. "I was going to ask you the same question, son. No one has seen Alex, I'm afraid . . ."

"What is it, Ashel?" Mara said.

"No one knows where he is, and . . ."

"There's a possibility he is with Laura Adamson. No one can find either of them."

Mara drew her hands to her cheeks. "And Regi is missing, too," she said softly.

"Son," Ashel spoke carefully, "Laura's mother is in the hospital . . . Think back carefully. Did he tell you at all where he was going?" As Ashel looked at Hanson, he leaned forward as though he hoped to hear helpful information.

But Hanson seemed to draw a blank. "No . . . no. I can't be sure. He said something . . . he had decided . . ." But he stopped, unsure. "No, I can't imagine."

"Where would he have gone?"

Hanson's eyes registered a flicker of grief. The wheels of his memory turned and ground. "I . . . I'm sorry, father. He didn't say. It could have been . . . anywhere."

Ashel stood, tense at his son's words. He stiffened. "There is news. Laura's mother may have passed away . . ."

"Oh," Mara let a sigh escape.

"She died in the hospital?" Grace asked.

"And Laura doesn't know." Hanson spoke slowly, deliberately, pausing to let the message make terrible sense in his mind.

Now Grace put her face in her hands. "Oh Laura, Laura," she said softly.

For a moment no one spoke. Their eyes were on Ashel. When his son had finished speaking, he deliberately took himself into control, and settled himself into his house coat. He pulled at his tie, releasing it from his throat. His face seemed very deeply furrowed. He was not young anymore. He was in his eighties, yet he was the strong one all of them had depended on all these years.

He leaned over and took Caroline's hand. "Well, I guess I've done all I can do," he said in a low resolute whisper.

Hanson's face looked bleached with worry. Mara put her arm around his shoulder. "Please don't worry about your friend, Hanson. Surely we'll hear soon," she said softly.

"But we can't let it stop us from rejoicing at our own happiness," Ashel continued gruffly. He patted Caroline's hand. "This is a time for rejoicing, eh?" He took Hanson's wrist with his other hand, then slipped it downward until he closed his fingers about Hanson's fingers. He looked around the room at the faces he loved. "We have heaven here with us. And though they are welcome, we cannot force the others to come."

Grace felt her heart sinking. Ashel's words were so true. She could not help but watch Mara, who folded her hands under her chin while tears started again to her eyes. Then she dropped her hands suddenly and laughed. "Well, are we going to have cold yams?" she said.

Taking her cue as an invitation, they broke into small bits of conversation, arguing with one another about who was going to have the privilege of drawing back the chairs to seat the ladies at the table. Hanson finally seated his mother while Ashel seated Grace at Hanson's side. A simple meal of yams and a little dried pork, biscuits, and cabbage glowed in the candlelight. At Mara's instructions the star-wrapped gifts were brought from the hallway in to the table and set one by one beside the silver. "They are tiny books to write in—about Christmas," she smiled. "You must begin tonight and write every day until the holiday's end." The candelabra was set in the middle of the table and the flickering candlelight glowed from the bright eyes and white cheeks of everyone in the room.

"And then are we going to have a contest to see who wrote the most accurate notes?" Ashel asked.

"They will all be different," Hanson observed.

"That's what makes it so exciting," Mara said. "Everybody is so different. And then we can share our differences."

"We'll hope our friends will all be here on Christmas Eve," Caroline said. But her tiny smile looked faded. "Oh, my heart goes out to the family whose mother . . ." She grew quiet. "We are so fortunate. How many blessings . . . we must take each other's hands and thank God we have one another as a family."

"Our dearest Father in Heaven," Ashel began. A hush fell in the shadowy warmth. "We have so many blessings. How can we thank you? We have so much to give. Help us to bring what we can of this joy to others. Bring the needy to our door and help us to share." Ashel paused for what seemed like a long time. There was such a great silence that Grace could hear the wax crackle under the flame of the candles. "We rejoice in our love for thee and for each other, and pray we may strive always to be worthy members of thy royal kingdom. We love thee, our Father in Heaven. In the name of Jesus Christ our Savior, amen."

There was a hush when the prayer ended. Ashel looked around. "Well, I hope we're as happy in God's kingdom as we are in the little one we have here," he said.

"Well, this is God's kingdom," Mara said, surprised. "We are the Royal House!"

"You and your Royal House Hotel," Will Jones grinned.

30

Reginald Summerfield

Late on Sunday morning, Reginald was still sleeping inside the coffin. Amused by his quarters, he thought to himself he had certainly slept the sleep of the dead. When he woke and felt the December light through the north windows, he noted the small clock on the table in the room which gave him the time: 9:48 A.M. He did not know if it was accurate.

In the first moments of his waking, he remembered slowly where he was. It was after these few moments that he sensed pouring into his consciousness another awareness—that Laura's mother lay on the table above him and he had slept with her in the same room. But he had not grown accustomed to the odor of death. He was still reeling with the effects of his night in the canyon. A sharp pain flickered behind his eyes.

He rose very slowly out of the satin case and stumbled to the small lavatory. Moving from the toilet to the sink, he stopped and looked at his face in the mirror. His cheeks appeared swollen and blotched with red patches of inflammation, where the frost had bitten him the night before. Splashing water on his face, he looked in the mirror directly into his eyes. He wanted to see if he could look at himself and discover how he felt about himself, knowing he was still alive and an accountant with U.S. Steel. He paused to see the narrow eyes nearly hidden above the large cheeks. They were the eyes of someone who seemed like a stranger. He looked away from the mirror and felt a stab of emptiness and pain. What would he have felt if he had been a child in the Eggertson family and grown to be a man in Salem, Utah? He would never know.

He walked sluggishly to the windows. He moved the dusty curtains to the side. There were people on the street. It was the Sabbath. He knew little about the Mormons except that they were strictly religious, or pretended to be. He knew that close to a hundred years ago the prophet Joe Smith wrote that new Bible, the Book of Mormon, and a lot of people came west who believed in it and wanted to live the way they wanted to live. Regi had always imagined that this Joe Smith was an attractive man who believed in living always open to the possibility of love. That was heaven to Joe Smith—to love when he felt its power in his blood. And he had attempted to create a type of society that would support his choice to love broadly. That kind of social acceptance would have been all right with Reginald Summerfield, too. But Mr. Smith had admitted there were necessary responsibilities that accompanied that kind of continually new joy. In order for this high feasting to furnish stability for children—for all members of the society—there were taxing commitments necessary to organize so many families. The system hadn't worked for long when the United States Government had stepped in crying "barbarism," and quelled their polygamy.

Reginald believed in love, but he couldn't fathom taking the responsibility for more than one family. He felt uneasy when Mara once told him that his grandmother Rain had been a second wife to Sully Tuttle. When the government interfered with the natural families, Rain had given up her place in the Tuttle household. She had been unable to enjoy a large posterity after all, for all of her children and grandchildren had died before her, with the exception of his cousin, Grace.

He paused at the window, watching the bleak Sabbath-keeping figures in the street. So now their basic religion—the possibility for so much love—had essentially been taken from these people. He wondered why they stayed with such a religion now—so much like any protestant sect, and so far away from so many realities. In fashion, in education, in everything, they seemed years behind California. Dressed in rather dated clothes, full Victorian skirts at a time when skirts were growing shorter and slimmer, small feathered bonnets, the women stayed sedately beside their husbands (now there was one for each) and called to their surrounding children to behave. The boys who chased ahead in their knee pants and thick woolen socks squatted on the walks to smash ants with a rock or the heels of their shoes. The girls swarmed around their fathers, competing to hold their hands. It was a picture of some nostalgia reminiscent of Christmas cards he had seen printed on creamy card stock and decorated with silver glitter or embroidered with gold thread. Such cards came to them from Chicago where Mother Summerfield's cousins lived. Putting them away as keepsakes, he had given them to Ethel when he left to work with U.S. Steel. He remembered seeing some of them pinned up along the crown molding in her room.

"Will you keep my books?" he had asked Ethel.

She had gazed at him with vacant eyes. "I would rather keep you."

"When I am situated I'll be back for you. I told you."

"And I told you I can't promise I'll be here . . ."

He took her fingers in his hands and kissed them. "It's different this time. I will find you." But he had a feeling he was lying.

"It seems you are always hell bent on destruction."

"First I've got to find . . ." He stopped. "It is only natural I'd want to make a place for you."

"It's natural that two of our kind stay together. It's greed for material things that tears us apart."

"It's just a short time." He mumbled the words.

"We could stay together now," she said simply, backing against the chintz and lace, the cushions plumped against the white iron of the bed.

"Come on, give me your promise," Reginald whispered, holding her hands tightly.

She had leaned her head back against the bedstead and breathed, "I have given everything else," and he saw tears staining her cheeks.

He believed both of them—with their various appetites for joy—had deserved as much as they received: separation and pain. His intentions had been fair. He had stood on the platform at the depot in the rain, with the water pouring down his hat and into his eyes and vowed that someday he must take control of the future. There would be someone pure and committed who would love him and give him direction, in spite of all of his sins. It was a long time before he came to believe that he may not deserve someone pure and committed, but someone more like Ethel who may or may not hold herself for him while he was gone. But then, immersed in his work, he had never returned. Instead, he had found himself enamored of that woman in San Jose who had said she loved him and would leave her husband to go with him. And now . . . Laura.

Still at the window, he dropped the curtains and backed away. In a brief moment he remembered the two figures in the blazing light who reached for his hands. He had never felt such a consuming love. At the time he had been quite sure they had been Father and Son. But now he wondered if in his yearning for parents, he had imagined them—could it be possible—into a father and mother. He backed away, because he felt the flesh of Mrs. Adamson's hand against his spine. He turned swiftly because for a moment he believed she had touched him. A chill moved from the small of his back into his neck and gripped the center of his brain. For a moment he believed he could see farther than reality. He had always believed that it was love that drove him. And it was always so powerful—the joy—the burning. He knew it was love. But love with a voracious hunger. Without consideration of everything else—the entire world that went on around it. A hunger without control.

He backed away from her body and a horror ripped through him. He half stumbled across the coffins on the floor of the room and into the wardrobe on the wall beside the lavatory. He fumbled awkwardly into his coat, tearing it from the hanger, pulling the lapels to straighten them as best he could. His clothes were not in the best condition by now, having spent a night against the mountain, and a long morning through dusty roads, chaparral, sage, and wheat grass, the mists of December, the cold light. He pressed his hands against the wool pockets, feeling the paper inside of them, not remembering what papers they were, but clinging to them as though they were the only reality that could come between him and the awful self-disintegration he imagined rippling out from his violence on every side. He was coming awake in the sunlight as he never believed he would come awake, not sure what was happening or what had happened, but fighting the sense of his own imagination and the possibility of what he might have done—no, what he had done—by tearing hungrily like an animal into Laura. He thought he would so much rather have gone into the tunnel of light toward the figures of overpowering love. His body ached for it. He needed someone, and now there was no one to help him heal his wounds. He cried out, an involuntary jerking cry, as he put his hand on the knob of the door and leaned against it to hear if there was anyone in the hall. He felt the hunger—both physical and spiritual—move into his limbs. Every inch of his body seemed to be trembling with weakness.

Straightening his tie, his sleeves, he breathed once or twice in rhythm, trying to clear the insanity from his mind. He closed his eyes, and when he opened them, he attempted to gain control, to become a man for the world, as though he were a guest in the hotel.

He gained strength in walking down the hall to the dining room. Only Drucker was there in a cloud of smoke, dashing his cigar against a pewter tray. He was leaning over a raft of papers, checkbooks, a few black folders tied with leather. His white collar under his dressing blazer gleamed as though it were on fire. Uncannily, it reflected the room's gas light. Reginald still felt half-paralyzed, his gaze pierced by the white collar and his eyes swimming in smoke. When he drew a chair from Drucker's table, he barely saw Drucker pull his lips back from the cigar in his teeth and grin. "I'm getting it put together," Drucker said. "It'll be easy in the morning."

Reginald barely heard him. Julia came through the door in lace and chambray, her hair loose around her cheeks, and he could not see her face in the shadows that blocked out the light.

"Can I get you something, Mr. Summerfield?" she said. Though kindly, her eyes seemed to glance to the side to avoid taking in his rumpled appearance.

"Yes." He was as hungry as he had ever been. He ordered hotcakes and berry syrup, fruit, coffee, date-nut breads and the omelettes, the sausages, and cheese.

"We have a nice piece of pork for the stew. It's getting time for lunch. Would you rather have lunch?" Julia asked him.

He wanted breakfast, but he told her she could bring the pork with it and also the stew.

Drucker sat in the veil of smoke and grunted with disgust or the anticipation of pleasure. "Sounds like a Sunday meal," he remarked with irony. "I usually can't eat until I get the particulars resolved."

Reginald regarded him through hollow eyes, not allowing the world an entry into his consciousness, yet abandoning death in every cell of his being. "You're welcome to any of this food, sir," Reginald murmured to Drucker as Julia put a hot muffin before him spread with melting butter and a pool of honey. "It seems to me you had the purchase of the hotel resolved by the time the banks closed on Friday afternoon."

Drucker raised his faded face, the tiny mustache a dark mark on his curled lip. "Oh, we made the agreement on Friday afternoon, all right," he said. "But there was another party who entered into it on Saturday—a relation, it seems. The money was coming from Adamson's wife's brother, who just happened to be this man's father. As well as a cousin of the Hulls.

Confusing, with some complications attendant. We pay the money. We own it. But he brought in a share of funds from Idaho to purchase an option in two years, and he wanted to take over the management of the hotel now."

"Julia's cousin? From Idaho?"

Julia nodded pleasantly.

"Yes, Julia's cousin and his wealthy father from Idaho."

When Julia set a bowl of fruit at his place at the table, Reginald saw the color of the apples as though it were a message he must read, and he could not read it. He breathed deeply. He was still tired. He did not want to understand all the ramifications of Drucker's investment.

Drucker was of a different world—the world bordering on some strange greed that was always in the process of fixing and adjusting properties—a world out of the orbit of the free hills. Yet it was a world that loomed ever more and more critically on the horizon—the necessary order. But Drucker seemed lost in it. Even now the man was massaging the papers in his hands and grinning as though he had hold of a beautiful woman whose perfume made him smile. He smiled and smoothed his hands over the papers, adjusting them carefully, grinning upon them, breathing in the breath of new ink, the dust and the exhalation of milled wood. He gathered the papers into a sheaf, thrust them vertically, and hit them on the table. "Well," he said finally, "in the morning, the trust will own the hotel."

31

Grace Tuttle

When she dressed in front of the mirror, Grace could not easily see herself in the glass. Not only because the light in the room was oblique, but there was a strange blur from the luminosity in her own light—the light from her eyes. The mist of all the light came between her and the image of her face. Through that mist she saw her own beauty: skin without blemish, eyes alive with fire. The tension in her brow and on her cheeks had been replaced by a pale, seamless sheen. This was her own body staring at her from the deep fathomless reflection of distance—a place where no living person had ever been, yet which spoke to the spirit more than most of life as it was lived day by day.

Who used the first mirror? And how many centuries of memories were swimming in the deep cells of the unconscious recesses of her mind—memories of her ancestors who had looked in mirrors—Nefretiri of Egypt, Cleopatra, and Antony? Even Abraham and Sarah and Jesus Christ. She wondered if Jesus himself had ever looked into a mirror. What did he see? It seemed that what he himself saw was more important than what anyone else saw. In such a way, Grace looked at herself today. She was filled with light and it was causing a mist to come over her eyes, a veil-like gossamer mist that filled every corner of the room with joy.

She could not help humming. It came from inside of her as though the sound flowed from her blood. This moment was what she had wished for all the days of her life. She knew this joy could not continue with such intensity forever. She knew it must of necessity break down at times into reality. Yet she believed it would always cycle back to a greater joy, into a new and higher realm, always higher and more glorious, closer to the Father of all, closer to the union with the Father. She clasped her hands before her face and breathed deeply. "Oh, dear Father," she whispered, "how could there be so much . . . love?"

She shook her hair before she slipped the brush through it. She paused and leaned to the side, letting it fall. It shone like slick, burnished metal. She wondered how it would look if she were to bob it short. Like Laura's. She pushed away her thoughts of Laura—the worry that no one still knew where she and Alex had gone, the fear that Laura's mother had died in the hospital Saturday morning and that her daughter did not yet know. And what would Laura do when she discovered this news? Beautiful Laura. But all of the unhappiness and darkness of the unknown could not touch her in this moment of her own joy. And it should not. It was time now only to wonder if she too, like Laura, could cut her hair.

She held her hair again in a cap against her head. The bob was the latest style. But would she dare? She gathered it up in her hands and pulled it to the side. She twisted it and held it in her hand. Then she turned, she looked down, cocking her head, peering at her image in a black-red cap, sleek as firelight and ebony. There was an effect, all right. Something different, something evasive smiled at her from the other side of the glass. She laughed at it. She was as daring as Laura, wasn't she? She could cut her hair, too. She tossed her head back and laughed at the world. There was time for all of these things. There was so much time and so much joy.

She hummed to herself as she dressed, smoothed the magenta faille collar, the smart fitted black velveteen jacket. The faille skirt was shaped and shorter to fit the fashion. She had chosen it because she felt daring. She pinched her cheeks and clutched her bag. Maybe next week—she would talk about it to Hanson—she would bob her hair.

It was almost half-past nine when Hanson—now living in

his parents' home—came through the front door. Many of his things were still at the big house, but since both Alex Hunt and Reginald Summerfield seemed to have gone elsewhere, he had decided that he should move back to his father's place.

Hanson's shirt, which Grace had pressed and starched, glared. His rust and blond head shone. "Are you ready?" he said. He pulled at his collar and moved it away from his neck. He would have to get used to this kind of formal dressing again.

Caroline wheeled into the kitchen and raised her hand. "Let's hurry. If you haven't eaten, Hanson, have a little breakfast. There's a Christmas program at the church this morning and it should begin on time."

There was some flurry of preparation as they offered him some breakfast: a muffin and some hot milk. When the chimes rang at half past nine, Mara and Will came to the door.

On the walk to the meeting house, Hanson and Grace fell behind. The joy she felt earlier seemed diffused by his quiet. She knew why.

"Alex never came?" Grace said softly, knowing what they were both thinking even as she spoke.

"No." Hanson was preoccupied. "And I don't know why." He pushed his hands deeply into his pockets and hunched over in his scarf, protecting his neck from the cold. "All I know is what I feel. He must still be with her."

"With Laura?"

He nodded slowly. "And no one knows where they are."

"What can we do?"

Hanson was slow to answer her. "After church," he looked down at her, "do you want to come with me? I am going over to look for him at the Hull House Hotel."

So many at the chapel gathered around Hanson to welcome him home. It was a glorious homecoming, though brief, for by the time they arrived, the meeting was about to begin. No one asked Hanson or Grace if they were engaged. There was no ring. But those who looked at the couple knew without saying anything what had happened when Hanson had come home.

The meeting itself seemed long. There were several talks by members. A group of young people sang "Hallelujah Chorus" from Handel's *Messiah*. The rafters of the building rang with a loud powerful sound. Mrs. Grable played the organ. Hartman from the BYU led the choir. Grace could not listen to the music without feeling the same joy she had felt early this morning. Hanson held her hand during the closing prayer. Afterward, he whispered in her ear "We'll tell them we'll be getting married in February. Go ahead, tell them."

"Anyone?" she asked.

"Anyone. We're on our way now."

"We shouldn't tell them about the purchase of the hotel."

"Not yet. It hasn't happened yet. But it will. We just need to find Alex."

Grace hesitated. Alex still seemed to loom in a giant way between them. But she felt more amenable to the idea now. She was embarrassed—though she would not admit it—that Alex's absence had actually given her hope, while it gave Hanson grave concern. Her hope was that although Hanson thought he needed Alex, Alex did have a life of his own.

"Shall we mention to anyone that we are looking for Alex?" she asked, still knowing Hanson's thoughts, hoping to stay with him somehow.

"No," Hanson said. "It wouldn't do any good. No one knows him here." He was silent for a moment but then turned to his father Ashel, who stood bent with his hands deep into the pockets of his top coat. Ashel nodded gravely as Hanson spoke, and Grace waited for Hanson to report what they had discussed.

"I've told him I am going to go out and look for Alex," Hanson said. "He doesn't really think I should interfere. But I am worried."

Grace raised questioning eyes to him. "Doesn't he know Alex was with Laura all day?"

"Yes, I told him." Hanson wouldn't say more. He took her hand in his and they began their walk east along First South away from the chapel, then south along J street to the hotel.

Mara called back to them, "Be careful what you tell anyone about our plans. We agreed to wait until morning when we have the written offer in our hands."

Grace heard her words with an uneasiness she could not understand. She thought to herself in her own mind that some ill-fated dread may still be hovering in the air. She believed it entirely possible that she might let the excitement of the hotel purchase slip from her mouth. And that this might change everything. She stayed close to Hanson, clinging very resolutely to his hand. She believed Julia might have suspected they had plans, because Ashel said he had tried to make an appointment with her to talk about some "business proposition," and she had declined. That was the way he put it. Ashel said she had seemed very concerned that Horace was out of town and would not be back until Monday on the early train. Julia was not naive. She had heard them talk about a purchase before. She would be surprised when they came into them with the funds at noon.

They walked briskly, keeping off the cold. The street was alive with both foot traffic and automobiles, carrying people to their homes from the church. Many of the members waved. They were happy to see that Hanson was home and that he kept Grace close to him. The young couple was radiant. No one could have mistaken the future for them. Everyone seemed glad, and everyone seemed to know. Grace thought to herself—though she scolded herself for being a shade unkind—"I am glad I am the one who will take this place by his side. And Alex is not always going to be here."

At the hotel Grace looked into the foyer from the window before she walked in. She saw a very large man turn the corner from the dining room and duck into the hall. She did not see his face. Something about his walk betrayed who it might be. Yet she made no absolutely certain connections, nor did she anticipate knowing any of the guests. When she and Hanson entered the foyer, it was empty. The lights seemed dim and sputtery as though a thunderstorm or electrical short were flickering them. They waited for a long time under the indistinct light.

Finally Julia came through the doors of the dining room, wiping her fingers on her apron and smiling apologetically. There was something tentative in her eyes. And as welcome as she tried to make them feel, her voice seemed somehow slightly forced. "Hanson and Grace, you two! I'm so glad to see you," she said. "You look wonderful." She did not pause long before she said, "What can I do for you?" There was a note of anxiety there.

"Are you all right, Julia?" Grace said.

She took Grace's extended hands and leaned away from her only slightly. "It's . . . I will just be so happy when Horace returns."

"He'll be here in the morning?"

Julia nodded. "They brought Laura's mother here."

Grace thought she heard a small audible gasp escape from her own throat. "Yes, we heard about her mother," Grace said, tightening her grip.

Julia did not face them. She turned slightly away.

"My father said something about coming to see you at noon tomorrow."

Julia's eyes darted to Hanson's, and she removed her hands from Grace. "Yes. I guess so," she said, looking off toward the lobby. "Horace will be here," she repeated.

"Julia, do you remember Alex Hunt?" Hanson asked.

Julia looked at Hanson curiously. Her hands clutched the pockets of her apron. "Yes, Hanson. He's my cousin."

"Your cousin?" Hanson said.

"Yes. We're both from the same Hunt family." Then quickly she turned to Grace and put a hand on her arm. "You knew that, didn't you, Grace? I told you long ago. Your Aunt Mara didn't particularly care for my Grandmother Hannah."

"I knew it," Grace said rapidly. She breathed hard. Her eyes searched Julia's face. Julia would not look her squarely in the eyes.

"But we've always been friends, haven't we, Grace?" she said tentatively.

"What's happening, Julia?" Hanson said.

"With Alex?"

"Yes. He never returned last night to our place."

"Oh well," she began to explain. "We put him up here."

"You put him up here?" Grace asked her.

"Ah . . . yes," Julia said, her eyes darting across the foyer, her hand still tight in her pockets. "It was getting late here. He didn't want to disturb you. So he put up here." She sounded off key.

Hanson was taken back. He looked away from Julia and looked across the large shiny wood floor and out the front door. There were still quite a few members in the street going to or from the chapel. He was watching them carefully as though he were not able to make sense of what they were doing in front of the hotel.

"I wonder if I could see him?" he asked.

"Oh, he's not here now," she said coyly. But it didn't sound convincing. It sounded unreal.

"Are you sure?" Hanson tried.

"Yes, I'm sure, Mr. Eastman," she said. She did not say they could come back later on. "He'll be with all of them right here tonight, too. They are all here and they're planning to drive back to Salt Lake City tomorrow evening."

"But I thought Alex was going to stay here and work for the East House Hotel," Hanson said. "His things are still at our house. Why hasn't he told us anything?"

"Oh?" Julia avoided the last question. "I didn't know he still had things at your place. I'll be glad to tell him when he comes in."

Grace felt an uneasiness she could not explain. Above them the lights in the lobby continued to flicker. She raised her eyes to them, watching the bulbs sputter and burn.

"Oh, Horace will fix those lights when he returns." Julia attempted to give a small laugh, but it turned out to be a pitiful half-weary concession of some kind. Her eyes darted from the couple before her to the door at their backs. Grace saw this movement of her friend's eyes, and she could read it clearly.

Julia also knew there was something hidden between them. "I'm sorry to be so . . . there is just so much going on. And I can't seem to handle all of it while Horace is gone."

"Can we help you?" Hanson said, standing on one foot and then the other one, seeming to work up some suspicion of what had happened to Alex.

"Oh, no," Julia said swiftly.

Seeing the pallor in her friend's face, Grace could not bear her own thoughts. She wondered if something dreadful had happened to Alex. At the worst, imagining that his body at the moment might be atrophying in the hull of this hotel. It was an eerie thought and she tried to put it out of her head.

"Will you tell Alex we were looking for him?" Hanson finally said.

No one thought to ask about Regi, and Julia didn't offer any more. "Good afternoon," she said, though it was darkening, like evening. Without further trouble, they left through the front door.

"Didn't you think she was trying to hide something?" Grace asked Hanson on the way home.

"I don't know," Hanson said. "She's your friend."

Grace stopped for a moment in the walk. "She was trying to hide something," she said.

There was a cold wind in the trees as they made their way back to Ashel's place. It seemed to darken very early in the afternoon. The gas lights on the street flickered as they burned. The lamps were trimmed with holly wreaths tied with large red bows. The street looked like a printed Christmas card, an illustration. The shops were closed but there were still lights behind the silent windows. The whirring sound of the wind, the misty light, brought the distant shops close to them as they walked. It seemed a narrow road surrounded by Christmas, with somewhere the tinkle of wind chimes and the sound of a horse jingling bells on its harness—perhaps on a wagon making its way home to a warm hearth on the day before Christmas Eve.

"I smell goose," Grace said, looking into the shop windows. Alex temporarily forgotten, she smiled with anticipation. Her eyes sparkled.

"Goose?" Hanson said. "Why goose? I say it's turkey."

"No," Grace teased him. She put a finger into his ribs and he leaned back, pretended to be jostled.

"You are the goose," he grinned at her from his distance above her, looking at her out of the corners of his eyes.

"Well, then, you're the turkey," she laughed.

And they giggled and chased each other as they had always done as children. All the way home.

When they returned to their street they found Mara and Will on the walk carrying a bag of holly wreaths and the Spode soup tureen.

"The Coreys have cousins from Scipio—the Russells. If it's all right Grace, honey, we made a decision without you: thought we ought to take the party to your house."

Grace thought for a moment that it wasn't her house. She had ended up keeping it for Rain. She looked at Hanson. He smiled at her expression of hesitation and she realized that it was going to be theirs.

"It's fine, Aunt Mara," Hanson said. Grace believed he was in reality speaking for all who had gone before him, for his Grandfather Eastman who had built it and loved it into a spacious country Victorian home with added porch and rooms. The cellar had been reamed out and fitted with rows upon rows of spacious shelves. And it had been theirs for a long time. It had belonged to all of them until Papa had married Mrs. Hilda, who finally left him to live in Salt Lake City with a friend and her poodle.

"If they're going to the bank we can't get the men to help tomorrow," Mara said, peering over the holly in the bags. "Besides, you wanted a few extra bits of adornment, didn't you? We will make the old place look like home again."

Grace was afraid things had not been cleaned. She hadn't had a chance to do anything since early Saturday morning. She knew Alex had probably left a disaster. Relieving Mara of her holly, she hurried ahead to the door.

"Oh, we've already been there, honey," Mara said. "We just piled it in one spot on the front stairs. Don't get excited. Tomorrow we'll all help until it's done."

Inside the door on the step were Mara's silver bowl filled with plums, her Belleek pitcher, and a stash of dried flowers. Two other bags held sprigs of evergreen and musky cones with sharp little points and hidden winking pinion. In one carefully tied box she read "Tudor Crystal." Just the words gave her a chill under her hair. Some of this would be passed down to her and to her children and to their children if succeeding generations cared enough to keep everything new.

Something smelled wonderful—a bag of potpourri—mostly roses—in the holly Aunt Mara had been busy arranging for Christmas Eve. Alongside the potpourri were little tea-sized treasures of verbena, lavender, and hops, the herbs Mara put in her annual homemade sleep pillows, with the fragrance that she claimed sent you into dreaming. But Grace believed she wouldn't be sleeping this Christmas Eve.

The dappled light from the stained glass in the stairwell played over a collection of plump peach and cream towels from Mara's storage, a large Lenox vase bursting with dried honeysuckle, and a basket of soaps, old Lavande, and one of her favorites, Roger and Gallet.

Grace breathed in the fragrance of the treasures, feeling intoxicated with their loveliness and the excitement of tomorrow.

"Everything's happening!" She clasped her hands under her chin. "How could it all come at once?" She could not wait to dress up the house tomorrow.

"We'll try not to do much on Sunday," Mara warned. "Come back to my place for supper and we'll plan everything."

Grace turned to rejoice with Hanson. But he wasn't there. She was not sure where he was. He hadn't said anything to her when he left. She felt the first little twinge of disappointment she'd had since they had been together so much both yesterday and today. But she stopped herself. She was being possessive. Hanson had always been independent. And she wasn't going to change that. She just felt a flat feeling in her stomach that he had slipped away without saying a word.

But she wasn't going to let it bother her. He wouldn't be far away. She removed the holly from the bag, dusted the mantel with her sleeve, placed the holly under the mirror and stood back to look. She added evergreen. "It's beautiful!" she whispered. Then she added more evergreen and closed her eyes to breathe the piney fragrance. But in all her movements, she began to feel a grave quiet crowd into her heart. She wondered where Hanson had gone—she thought he had gone upstairs for only a moment, but he did not return. Then she thought she could hear him in the upstairs rooms.

When she excused herself, Mara and Will slipped out the door. "Hurry to dinner, honey," Mara said. "We'll have the rest of the pork roast."

In the upstairs hall Grace called to him. She waited in the light that played through the grates over the silent bedroom doors. She waited, feeling a sudden heaviness that seemed to come down all around her as though it were a tangible air. Finally, she heard the knob of the door on his room rasp in the lock, and he came out and shut the door behind him.

"What are you looking for?" Grace asked cautiously, though she believed she might have guessed.

"I was checking to see if either Alex or Regi had come for their things."

"Are their things still there?"

Hanson paused and gazed at Grace with serious thought. "Yes, they are. Nothing's been changed."

Grace moved through the hall and the bathroom, carefully picking up towels and hanging them on the racks for a few moments just to gather herself together. But she could feel a darkness that had not been there before—a darkness that had not been there when they were at the Hull House Hotel where they had discovered Alex was staying. It was Hanson's worry. Once you gave yourself to someone, she thought, you could feel their pain—great or small. You were vulnerable to their hopes and sadness. And she knew Hanson was hurting.

"Did they have keys?" Hanson asked her.

"No."

"Then I should stay again tonight."

"I guess so," Grace murmured.

Hanson looked serious. It was no mystery that he was deep in thought and that he was deeply concerned about Alex and Laura and what had happened to take them away. "I wonder what's going to happen now? Alex was supposed to be with us tomorrow at the bank when we pick up the funds and make the offer at the Hull House Hotel."

Grace could hear her breath and the quiet beating of her heart. More than she wanted her own peace in that moment, she wanted Hanson's happiness. "Well, then, he'll be back, won't he?" she stated, forcing some lightness into her tone.

But that wasn't it. Hanson had already been feeling distress. He was quiet when he paused to gaze at her. His words seemed heavy. "I can't believe . . ."

Grace hated this subject of discussion. She wanted to erase Alex from the darkening house. But she knew his things lay in the next room. "He's at the hotel," she said quietly. "He'll be there. He'll probably be there and you can still pick him up to go to the bank."

Hanson's brow knit. "I don't know." It was a heavy statement. It was true, now. He really did not know.

"Do you really need him?" Grace sat on a cushioned chair in the hall. She leaned on the sewing machine. Suddenly she felt very tired, and the buoyancy of her excitement seemed like a part of something long ago.

Hanson was no longer thinking about her—about the two of them. There was a darkening cloud in the house as though the darkness of the afternoon had a substance and it had seeped into the walls and curled under the windows like smoke. It was apparent that Hanson could not stop thinking about Alex Hunt. He stepped toward the sewing machine, leaned his knee against it, pushed his foot on the treadle, and his hands deep into his pockets. He looked off into the lights of the stairwell. He looked off as though he were seeing nothing at all in place of something that had been there before. "We had made plans," he almost whispered. The sound of his voice, a breathing guttural sound, seemed to stick in his teeth. "I thought he was with me."

Grace spoke gently although she felt like shaking him. She controlled her voice. "Maybe it is just . . . Laura. You saw how hard he fell for Laura."

Hanson did not answer for a moment. He pushed at the treadle and its unproductive movement clanged in its empty chambers. Where the needle went up and then down, it echoed inside the closed box. There was a hush, then. He slowly shook his head. "But it shouldn't have made any difference—Laura. It should have motivated him. He needs employment. If he should decide to get married . . . he still needed the job."

Grace still felt very tired. She thought to herself that Hanson made entirely too much of Alex, and she had now given enough time listening to his need to mourn for someone who had let him down. And she would have guessed that this was Alex's style, anyway. She was torn for a moment between wanting to take care of Hanson's feelings, and letting him know how she felt. "Hanson, Alex is . . ." But as soon as she began this tack, she knew it wasn't going to get her anything but Hanson's anger. She breathed in and calmed herself down.

"Hanson, why do you need Alex?"

That was the crux of the matter. Hanson turned to her now, his hands deep in his pockets. And though he looked at her, his thoughts seemed to be very unfocused. "Grace," he began. He stopped. His voice wasn't strong. He turned his head to the side. "Alex knows so much about everything. And especially people."

For a moment Grace did not say anything. She heard his voice like the cry of a small child in the dark. She had always looked at Hanson as though the world swung in his hands. Suddenly she realized what worlds of unknown quantities lurked in his words. "Well, you know things, and you know people," she began.

But he was still very quiet. "Not like Alex," he whispered, shaking his head.

"Not like Alex?"

When Grace repeated the words, Hanson laughed. He shook his head. "Not like Alex," he repeated. Then he became more animated, though he did not look at her. "You don't know, Grace. He is really . . ." Though he could not finish, it seemed as though he believed he could explain it. At least it seemed he believed it was important enough to explain. He shook his head and removed his foot from the treadle. He moved back from her, his hands still in his pockets, his eyes at the light in the stairs. "You should have seen him here. Just two days at the East House Hotel." He looked down. "He was amazing. He had the help organized better. He was holding Mr. Dawes in his hand." He cupped his hand and tightened it in a strong fist. "He is really something, Grace. If you watched him."

"I have watched him."

Hanson looked at her obliquely. "You don't know him very well."

"But I know him enough—just enough to know that he makes a remarkable first impression."

"Yeah. You saw it. You saw the magic at work. But you don't know the half of it." He turned on his heel.

"Maybe you don't know the half of it," Grace dared to utter.

Hanson turned toward her. He noticed her now.

"I mean . . ." But she couldn't finish for a moment. She bit her lip when she thought about it. "First impressions don't mean very much when there is nothing to depend on—no dependability."

Hanson laughed another sharp laugh. "Hah! You think I didn't notice how he took to you! You would have gone with him if he had followed through."

Grace couldn't believe what she was hearing. She looked sharply up at him. She was still tired. This was getting nowhere. But she kept her voice under control. "I didn't mean that, Hanson." She would pretend not to realize all the ramifications of what he said. "I meant that if you can't count on him, nothing else he does could help that much." And then she added quickly, "I don't think you need him. You are good with people on your own. What makes you think you need him? You are so much more responsible. You are so good." When she ended her words she looked up at him. Her voice was softer, but her eyes said everything.

Seeming only to half-hear her words, his arms at his sides, he stayed tense under the hall light. For a moment he would not accept what she said. He shook his head when he looked at her. "He's not that undependable," he argued. "He has honored his commitments before . . ."

While he continued speaking, Grace stayed very quiet. She continued to look up at him. She saw in him someone who had been a little afraid to stand on his own. "Isn't it good that you find out about him before you go into business with him instead of after you do?" she whispered. "When it's too late?"

Hanson looked at her now. His eyes didn't believe, but he saw hers for what they truly were. "You didn't like him, did you, Gracie?" he said now. He sounded like an old man. "I wish you wouldn't talk that way. There's still a good chance he'll be my business partner in the Royal House Hotel." He turned around and paced the floor. "In fact, I still want it that way." Then he stopped in front of her and looked at her face fully. "You don't mind that, do you, Grace? If Alex and I are business partners? I'll find out what happened. I'm sure it is nothing serious. He'll explain."

Grace felt the weariness fill her up. "It's all right, Hanson," she said. "Sure. We'll find him. If that's what you want—if that's what is going to happen. You know I'll be there with you."

Something had filled Hanson. It might have been whatever Grace had given him, but that was immaterial now. He seemed stronger. For a moment the light in the hall seemed stronger. He reached for her hand and pulled her from the chair. "I'll find out what happened. He'll have an explanation. Let's go to Mara's and forget about it. What do you say?"

Grace noticed the firm line of his jaw. The muscles still flinched when he closed his mouth. Though he had settled into a position, his body seemed still uncertain about it. But his hand was firm. Grace felt the strength of his fingers. There was power there.

"Did you ask Alex to come to dinner on Christmas Eve?"

He moved quickly now. At first he did not admit that he heard. There was so much between now and the holiday that had to be done. "That's yours to plan. You and my mother and Mara," he finally said. Then when he came to the door, before he opened it he turned to her and enclosed her hands. "Gracie, I want you to know that tomorrow, Monday, December 24, the day of this transaction, is one of the most important days of my life. Please don't worry if I seem to be preoccupied or thinking about something else. This purchase means more to me . . ." He paused. His eyes flowed to the light behind her, to the large house, the fading walls. A mist had seemed to gather in the stairwell, or a dusty beam of light. They had stirred the dust hurrying down the carpeted stairs. "More to me," he repeated "with or without Alex." He measured his words. "More than you will ever know."

"I understand, Hanson," she said.

He smiled briefly. "You have faith in me?"

"I have faith in you."

He smiled, satisfied, and tucked her hand under his arm on the way out the door.

32

Reginald Summerfield

Reginald Summerfield did not move from his place at the Sunday dinner table with Drucker for several hours. As Drucker continued to ask him to perform an occasional addition or subtraction, Reginald continued to order from the menu. He assured Julia he would be paid in the morning and that his bosss, Mr. Barrington, would settle the bill. He ordered the kidney pie, the stews, the soups, and biscuits. For desserts he did not stop with one piece of pie. He continued to order pie while the afternoon dragged on. He finished several large pieces of the cherry pie, and would have had another piece, except that at about two o'clock he turned to the foyer and thought he saw Hanson Eastman at the door.

He did not want to explain anything to Hanson Eastman. He dabbed his face with the napkin, rose haltingly from his chair, feeling greatly overfed, and excused himself quickly from Drucker. Though he felt distress from having overeaten, he lumbered out of the dining room just in time to head up the hall when Grace and Hanson walked in.

The door to the room he had occupied last night was the first to the right, and he took it without hesitation. The lock was still broken. Horace Hull would be back tomorrow. He would never need to know what had taken place in this room while he was gone. Regi shuddered at the sight of the deceased Mrs. Adamson and thought that after he cleaned up here he might ask Julia if there were any extra rooms. Though he would be tight for two weeks, he would settle up with her when he got paid in the morning. They should be able to conduct their business early at the bank and be on their way to Salt Lake City tomorrow afternoon.

Many things troubled him. However, one of them was how he would retrieve his things from the Eastmans. He knew he had left most of what he owned in the bedroom at the Eastman house. The last thing on earth he wanted to do was to face these people who had been so kind to him, to go to their place, to explain to them anything at all, to suffer their questions of concern. He would never have been able to live up to the phantom ideal they had trumped up of a small cousin who had left them years ago who somehow belonged to them in a way he himself would never understand. They were religious people, refined, gracious people. He was not like them in any way. He allowed his appetites to rule his body. He was a victim of his weaknesses in ways he could never explain, even to himself. It seemed he often had no control, his life a vicious cycle. As soon as he overindulged his body, his soul seemed to back away into the remote corners of himself and cower undernourished, subdued by his abuse. What kind of care was he taking of himself? That was it. He did not care for himself.

Feeling heavy and stretched to the limit, he stood in front of the mirror in the bathroom, dabbed water on his face and dried it with a towel. For a moment he leaned over the sink, feeling for an instant as though he could not hold everything he had put into his stomach. And then he heard voices outside the door.

Quickly he closed the bathroom door and locked it. Someone grasped the door to the room as though they were thrusting a key into it. Then it suddenly opened. "Oh, it's not locked!" someone said. It was Julia Hull. "It's broken," he heard more dimly. She must have been at the door, bent over it. He heard people come into the room.

He thought he heard murmuring. Then crying—anguished wracking sobs, and heart-rending cries for, "Mama, Mama." Close to the cries he heard, "Shhh, Laura. I'm here. Everything is going to be okay." Alex's voice.

Most of the time all he could hear was sobbing. Finally the door rattled again and someone inside the room stepped across the floor to open it.

"Father!" Laura said.

Through all of it, there was nothing but darkness for Regi. He could only imagine what took place in the small room now filled with people. Weary, he sank to the cold tile of the bathroom floor. There was just enough room to spread out if he put his feet in the space in front of the small toilet bowl. He pulled the towels from the rack, his eyes barely adjusting to the pitch black darkness. Even though he wore his coat, he was freezing. Although it was too dark in the room to see what was hanging on the hook above his head he pulled it down to cover his shoulders. It smelled of formaldehyde. The pockets, stiff with rags and paper, grazed his legs. He pushed a thick towel under his head. Without wanting to, without really expecting to, he began to doze.

"Yes, yes, you and I are related through Scott Hunt," the deeper voice of Robert Adamson said slowly. "Yes, yes."

"Alex and I are more than cousins," Laura was saying. But the rest of the words were muffled and indistinguishable.

"Those funds? They are my father's funds. Well, yes, yes. I'm ready with the money." Alex's voice.

Then the door opened. Reginald thought he could hear someone in the hall again. The walls rocked as though someone were walking swiftly into the hall.

"Not yet, Laura. But soon."

Regi had begun to fall into a deeper sleep now. He could barely hear the voices outside the bathroom door. "Tomorrow, then," Adamson called down the hall. He had gone to the door, but Regi thought he could still hear someone in the room. "I'm sorry, my darling." It was Robert Adamson. "Oh, heaven above," his deep voice throbbed. "It was only money. It was not as important as having you . . ."

He woke in the deep night, feeling cramped on the cold floor. Where was he? At first he did not know. When he remembered, he had no idea of the time or place. Was he really in either? He clamped his fists and felt the blood vessels swell against his head. In a sudden flash, he believed he saw the heavenly figures again as in a dream. They were no longer reaching for him. They stood back, though he felt their warmth. "I am coming, but not now," he said in silence to himself. He had the distinct impression in his mind that now was the time for him to free himself.

He listened and could hear no one in the room. He put his hand on the lock, but it involuntarily froze. To be sure he heard nothing, he did not breathe. His heart pounded and he broke into a cold sweat. He pushed the lock out of its hasp. It slipped noisily. He was so relieved to break out of this prison he had made for himself by his own choice, that when he gasped and let his breath go, he felt sudden tears in his eyes.

But then his breath caught in the room—because although he could see that Mrs. Adamson lay exactly as he had first seen her, the odor of death had intensified.

He did not use the lights. Through the open door of the bathroom, enough starlight shone that he could see to move about. Before he left the room, he used the lavatory. He washed himself thoroughly with the cloths and towels available to him and pulled his hands across his wrinkled clothing, smoothing it down as best he could. Feeling his way in the dark, he hung the towels on the racks; he hung the muslin coat on the back of the door. Feeling heavy and still unclean, as though touched by decay, he paused at the door to hear what he could of the occupants of the hotel. There seemed to be no sounds from any of the other rooms. He fumbled toward the clock and turned the face of it to the fading light in the window. It was three in the morning. For a long time he stood with his ear against the door, but he could hear nothing. So he dared to move the knob. He grit his teeth trying to be quiet. He wanted to be out of this room, this place of death, forever.

The electric light from the halls blasted his eyes. Moving quickly forward, he shut the door to the room of death and shuddered. Tonight he would be gone from here. In the lobby he sat down on the sofa that faced the front window. He gazed at the dark street, empty and as quiet as a tomb.

He sat for a long time watching the deep night fade into dawn. He was a man without a home. No place to lay his head. That was something you paid a price for, Ethel had told him before he left her in Salt Lake City, a place to lay your head. But he had ignored her. He had found the other woman lying on a bench in the park in San Jose, her eyes black with bruises and blood because her husband had beaten her. She had lived with Regi for six weeks at the rooming house until Reginald had abandoned her, hoping she would go to her abusive husband who might want her, and show kindness to her. "Why did you marry him?" Regi had asked her over and over again. She had sobbed, "To belong to someone. To have a place to call home. You pay a price for everything you get in this life." The price had finally been too great for her.

But Regi had never listened to the beat of his heart that urged him to settle down. Sometimes he thought it was because what he really loved was the excitement of the initial attraction. And he had loved and loved and loved. But was it love? He had found himself without a place to lay his head, imprisoned by his own choice, with no place to go. Mrs. Summerfield had told him that real love was to make a place for yourself and bring something more to it than just your heart: commitment, planning, effort, long-suffering, patience.

"There is always a price on everything in life," Ethel had told him through her tears. "How much and what are you willing to pay?"

Finally Regi could sit no longer and he stretched out on the sofa and slept until dawn.

He pulled himself together when he woke because he heard

Drucker's voice in the hall. He saw Adamson with him, and Barrington. They ducked into the dining room with Drucker. Regi tightened his belt, smoothed his collar and ran his hands through his hair. He looked in the mirror in the hall. As a boy he had followed Hawk in the Tree to the River. They had both looked into the water and Hawk in the Tree had said, "Looks like us." He still looked like the Reginald Summerfield he knew, but he had experienced something he had never experienced before, and something in his heart had changed.

He took his portfolio from the safe where Barrington had always insisted it was kept overnight. At the table in the dining room over coffee, Barrington and Drucker and Adamson chatted about the documents Drucker had drawn. Adamson indicated he was ready. He was waiting for Laura, and for the funds from the other party. They were here. While he had been gone to Salt Lake City to get his wife's money, Alex and Laura had gone to Idaho over the weekend to get an amount from Alex's father.

Regi's back was to the door of the dining room and he did not see Laura and Alex enter. But the others saw them. When Alex came into the room, the others looked up. Regi turned, and Alex grinned.

"We thought you were dead," he said. Barrington looked to Regi as if for an explanation.

"Maybe I was," Reginald said wryly.

"Well, you look alive enough for me." Alex flipped his coat and sat in an empty chair. He was holding Laura's hand.

Laura tossed Regi a look of steel. She returned her eyes to gaze at her father. "Good morning," she said to her father, or to everyone and no one in particular. But her mouth was set in a tight determined line. Reginald felt sick.

"Are we ready, then?" Alex Hunt said, drawing a large leather wallet out of his coat. His face was drawn into a daring gesture of reckless authority. He hit the edge of the wallet against the table and looked around the circle at the others.

"The bank doesn't open until nine o'clock," Adamson said.

"It don't hurt to be there right at nine," Drucker said. "I understand there is another party drawing funds, and Harper at the First Security thought they were also interested in purchasing the hotel."

Adamson looked at Drucker cautiously. "Our agreement has already been made with Mrs. Hull," he said.

"Finish your coffee," said Barrington. He leaned back in his chair and sat up stiffly, as though he had been thinking differently about things during the night. "Aren't you a bit inexperienced to take over the management of a hotel?"

"Mrs. Hull is his cousin."

"Cousin? Seems everybody around here is cousins. So what does that mean?" Barrington kept his eyes steady. "Does business sense pass through the genes like blue eyes?"

"She is going to help us for as long as we need it," Alex Hunt defended himself, holding back the irritation he felt toward Barrington.

"I'm still not convinced you won't need a good deal more than a cousin to give you pointers," Barrington said smoothly, rifling through the folders.

"It's too late to change any of the agreements, Mr. Barrington," Alex suddenly said in a straightforward, open way. "I'm announcing my marriage to Laura Adamson. We're getting married in March."

Barrington drew back, surprised.

"Say, that was sudden!" Drucker slapped the table with his hands. He leaned back and laughed, pitching his chair on its back legs. "Can you be certain that fast?"

"That fast?" Alex leaned forward and grinned. "We've spent every waking moment for hours with one thing in mind since we found out the Adamson money and the Hunt money are essentially one and the same. That's half of it. And you've already agreed to the other half."

Barrington was slower than Drucker. He leaned forward and

looked at Alex with a very slow, penetrating gaze. "Is that so?"

Adamson leaned back in his chair and tucked his thumbs into his waistcoat. He wasn't smiling, but his gaze was distant. "Didn't they surprise us, though," he said. "That money is the money from my wife's family, and I believe that is exactly what she would want."

"Well, I'll be bamboozled," Drucker said, letting his chair fall forward. "If that doesn't take the cake. Mr. and Mrs. Hunt. Congratulations." He put his hand out and Alex slowly took it.

Reginald Summerfield sat without saying a word.

"Do you want more coffee?" Julia came by and smiled.

"I'll have some more," Barrington said. He looked up at her and watched her turn away. "So that's what you are going to be doing—running a hotel, eh, Miss Adamson? Until this money is brought back into the steel?" He said it with a diffident candor, not reproachfully, not accusingly. But he waited for her to answer him.

"Of course Alex will help me," she said, glaring at Barrington with her clear blue eyes.

"And that's something I'm willing to do, Mr. Barrington," Alex shot back without a pause. "You can trust us. Besides, my father's funds . . . I wouldn't let my father down." He said this leaning forward and leveling his eyes into Barrington.

"Ha ha! The kid's a natural-born businessman." Drucker laughed and hit the table again.

"We have plans," Alex added.

Barrington waited for a long moment. "What kind of plans, Mr. Hunt?"

"Additions, promotions, advertising," he smiled. "For one thing, we plan to change the name of it to the Royal House Hotel."

There was a hush at the table. Only Drucker moved. He nodded to Reginald. "Say, don't that have a ring to it?" he said.

Barrington dared to smile. He leaned back again and looked steadily at Alex. He took a moment to appraise Alex, to wait until he could register this young man's spirit against his own experience. He paused. His words were measured when he finally spoke. He was turned in Alex's direction, but it was as though he looked through Alex Hunt. He finally said slowly: "Tonight is Christmas Eve, and I'm not in the mood to argue. I'm going to trust you, Mr. Hunt."

There was another hush at the table.

"You can trust me," Alex said. "Julia's my cousin. She's signed without even looking at the offer. I'll get her to finish signing. She assures me her husband will approve. I'll get any help they can give me."

Laura took Alex's hand and pressed down on it. Her face seemed to glow with light, and she rose quickly. She leaned toward his cheek and whispered into his ear. Then she left the room.

"She's . . . not feeling well," Alex excused her.

Drucker laughed again. "We've got a wedding on our hands, is it?" he said. "We've got a wedding, and a hotel. And we'll be home on Christmas Eve! Well, let's get going then."

33

Mara Eastman Jones

Mara woke, startled. She thought she heard a crash. She rose from her bed, looked out the window. Outside in the poplar trees, the light was still very dull in the gray sky. There seemed to be no stars. It was barely morning. What had she been seeing? She had been dreaming. She had been standing on a cliff above the valley. Mountains stood all around her. She could see for miles. The rim of blue peaks in the distance swam in a smoky mist while everywhere the sound of wind made a strange music in the tops of the trees.

She was standing with a large crowd of people behind her, and she held her arms out to keep them from pushing her. It seemed she was holding a book in her hands—Sobe's journal! Carried by the crowd to the edge of the cliff, when she leaned over the edge, she was caught up by a wind and began to fly, the pages of the book fluttering in the wind. She leaped over the cliff and soared. Below her was the valley where she had first come with her father and mother, her brother, sister, and the Indians—Spirit of Earth and Rain. They met Chief Angatewats on that first sunny day in March when the yellow of early wild forsythia had bloomed along the hills. He had taken them to see his people who had sat stony-faced when the Mormon leader Dimick Huntington told them in their language: "We are going to build our homes here."

When she looked back, she saw the crowds on the precipice run to the edge of the cliff and though she cried out to them, "Please! Watch where you are going!" they pressed over the edge and fell like so many small bones scuttling along in the wind.

And there was a great sound of crushing below her, and crying, and great gulps of sobs that tore out her heart. Now suddenly awake, Mara thought she heard a crash outside of her dream somewhere. She looked out of the window. She thought there was something out in the dark dawn that had fallen—a tree, a shingle from the roof. But she felt a presence in the room and she turned swiftly. Someone had shut the door and stood in the semi-darkness.

"Aunt Mara?" a voice said. It was Grace.

With a leap of fear in her heart, Mara breathed heavily. When she first opened her eyes, she saw Sobe's journal lying open, face down on the bed beside her. She had been fortunate to retrieve it from Reginald before he disappeared. When she moved in the bed, it slipped, and she reached to clutch it. "You startled me."

"I'm sorry. But we want you to come with us. Please." Grace was dressed in her warm scarlet cloak with the gray rabbit hood. As soon as she saw that Mara was awake, she came swiftly to the bed and reached for her. She took the journal out of her hand and laid it on the table. Mara let it go. There were the old precious words, but there was today, now.

"I've never seen Hanson so excited," she whispered. "Oh, please, Aunt Mara. This could be the most important and wonderful day of our lives."

"My goodness!" Mara said. "That serious? You are here early." She gathered her senses about her, checked the clock beside her bed and frowned. "What's the hurry?"

"Hanson is waiting. And I agree that we should talk to Julia this morning."

Mara was a little taken back. Granted, she had started the ball rolling, but she suspected Grace and Hanson had been giving it a substantial push every moment since then. "Before we go to the bank?" Mara asked, feeling frumpy and indisposed.

"Please, Aunt Mara. Hanson has had a premonition that we should talk to Julia early."

"A premonition," Mara said, sitting up on the edge of the bed. "What kind of premonition?"

"He doesn't want to talk to me about it," Grace said.

Mara thought she could hear the wind of her dream, the whistle of space in her mind. "Well, I suppose a premonition is a premonition." She hunted for her slippers on the cold floor.

"They're here, Aunt Mara." Grace knelt at her feet and found them for her. Mara slipped her feet into them while she steadied herself on Grace's shoulder. Her heart leaped up in her throat when her fingers touched the shiny dark curls. "This is Rain's hair," she whispered in her inner heart. It rippled against her touch in solid strands.

"Here are your slippers, Aunt Mara. Oh, I'm so glad you'll come now. Can I help you get ready?"

When Mara rose from the bed she felt light-headed and she leaned on Grace's arm. She looked at the black eyes and the white skin as though she had never seen them before. "You also look like Rain," she whispered inside her heart.

"Here, which dress do you want to wear?" Grace opened the wardrobe door and pulled aside the curtain over the clothes.

"Let's see. Tonight's the Christmas party! I'll wear my red dress all day and blind everybody!" Mara's eyes twinkled. "Tonight I'll add the holly and my white collar. Do you think Julia likes red? Do you think Mr. Harper at the bank will step it up when he sees red?" She winked at Grace.

Grace tolerated Mara's teasing. She pulled the dress from the closet rod and opened it above her Aunt Mara's head. Mara stood without moving and accepted her help. The dress fell over her hair and around her shoulders. Grace pulled it into place, helping Mara to find the sleeves.

"I remember a time when I helped to dress your Grandmother Rain," Mara whispered. "That was so long ago." They had pulled the old Indian mother and her daughter Rain into the log cabin and shown them the dresses they had prepared for the holidays. The two looked with stolid faces as

Mother Eastman had gently tugged on their skins. "We'll remove these and wash you," she had whispered. The old mother had frowned and held down her leather skirt with her palms. But Rain had touched the white dress with the lace and smiled. They scrubbed them down in the large tub in the middle of the room. The old mother would not sit. She stood and let them handle her, all the while frowning and holding her arms to her sides.

Grace's eyes met Mara's eyes for a brief moment.

"So much has happened, my darling. So much has happened since then."

Grace's hands flew nimbly over the buttons while Mara smoothed her own wiry hair.

"You have been here longer than any of us," Grace said. "You will know what to do."

"You just think so," Mara grinned at her. "You just keep thinking somebody else is always going to be around to keep you from jumping off a cliff. But you're going to be Mrs. Hanson Eastman on your own for a long time," she winked.

Grace finished the buttons. She tied the sash. She took the hair brush from the table and ran it through Mara's tough little hair.

"Your hair needs curls," Grace said.

"It needs a lot more than curls," Mara laughed. "How about life?" She pulled the ends out on her head and both she and Grace laughed at the image in the mirror over the wardrobe— the little dried-up old woman with hair that stood on end.

Grace slipped a pair of alabaster combs at the sides by Mara's temples. Mara let her do it. She smiled at the results. "You have succeeded in civilizing this wild person in the mirror," she smiled. "Let's go."

Hanson waited for them below in the foyer. He was standing with heels together, his hat in his hand. He looked anxious and sheepish as though he was aware that getting a woman up at 6:30 A.M. on the day of the Christmas party was expecting a lot, especially if she was over eighty.

"No earthly influence could have removed me from the gravity of my bed," she said, leaning on Grace down the stairs. "Only you two heavenly angels—you swoop down and I'm at your command."

"Come on, Aunt Mara, you're doing fine." Grace held her, wobbling, when she took time to expound.

Hanson tried to smile, but the anxiety was carved deeply under his eyes.

"This is an awful time to raise an old woman. And you're not touching my old Will at this hour, are you?"

"No, we're not touching Will," Grace shook her head.

The clock began chiming. "It's seven," Hanson said. "Come on, Aunt Mara. That isn't so bad for an old farm hand."

"You been reading too much of *Poor Richard's Almanac*," Mara smiled. "All right, lead the way."

"We'll go to pick up Father, and then we'll go to talk to Julia. Did Grace tell you?"

"She told me, and I think you two are about as subtle as a couple of elephants."

But Ashel was ready, also. He said he had not slept much last night. "Remember when we were children, and we couldn't wait until Christmas? That's how it was for me. And I kept dozing off and dreaming. Then I would wake and all I could see was the sky with stars. And I saw the moon."

"What did you dream, Ashel?" Mara asked him when he settled her into the front seat of the Chevrolet.

"I dreamed there was a large army coming down out of the east canyon—coming to get us."

"Humph. That wasn't a dream. There was a large army came out of the east and coming like a big bird to eat the carrion of our little culture." She was talking about the United States Army, when they had come that spring to accompany Governor Cumming from the east. They had camped in the park, their horses snorting and stamping in the mud, the flies as thick as fog.

"But we fooled them! We were still alive, weren't we?" Ashel said, clutching the wheel in his hands. "We were alive and well, and we sold them peas and a few onions and cucumbers. I'll tell you what happened to me in the dream. I was flying over the valley."

"Hmm," Mara said. "You were flying?"

When Grace and Hansen had settled in the back seat, Mara said, "Did you call her?"

"No," Ashel said. "We'll surprise her in the dining room."

"I don't think she likes surprises very much," Grace ventured.

"But I think she might be pleased by this one," Hanson said.

The moon scudded across the west in the morning sky. It was very bright, and the gray roofs and walls of the city lay bathed in the glowing light.

"I feel like my life is just beginning," Hanson said. "I've dreamed about coming home while I was over in Europe. When I thought about Grace and about all of you, you seemed very far away, as though you were in another world. I wanted to live in your world instead of the world I lived in. I could see your world, and now it is around me and I am really amazed to be at last living in my dream."

"It is like a dream, isn't it," Grace said, laughing and tightening her hands on his. There was a music in the morning that seemed to harmonize with the music of the universe. It was like the music in the wind.

"We have everything we want right here," Mara said. "Each other. That's all we need, all we want. Forever each other."

"You're an old dreamer, Aunt Mara. What kinds of things do you dream for the Royal House Hotel?"

"I've got an idea for a white Spanish castle and a Castillian garden," Aunt Mara said, pleased and almost giggling. "I see that old boarding house faced with gleaming white stucco, an arched walkway and arbor in the north, smooth arches, and heavy gleaming Spanish tile. And large handsome heavy wood windows."

"Oh, that's a romantic dream, Aunt Mara. What do you see, Uncle Ashel?" Grace gleamed.

"I see what Mara saw first because I've had time to think about it: a series of rooms fit for kings and queens, princes and princesses, and every guest is one."

"You're original, Ashel," Mara teased.

"We're original," Ashel mused. "First we have the East House Hotel on the east side of Main and the town suddenly moves east and we never bother to rename it the West House Hotel. We simply sit there on the West side with the East House Hotel and wait. And the world passes us by."

"But now they'll stay in a Castillian castle with arches, an arbor, and a fountain."

"You have an imagination, Aunt Mara," Grace laughed.

"It is in your imagination that you create the world you will live in," Aunt Mara said as she raised her oratorical finger. The Chevrolet bumped along the road, and they suddenly found themselves in reality in front of the Hull House Hotel with its little sign and the gold lights shining from the lobby.

"She'll be serving breakfast," Grace said.

Ashel and Hansen opened the doors for the girls. Mara placed a hand on Ashel's arm and began to hum "Pomp and Circumstance" when she leaned on him up the walk.

When Ashel opened the door of the hotel, Julia was standing in the center of the foyer in her white apron with her glorious dark hair piled up on top of her head and her arms full of a tray of white cups and saucers. "Oh, hello," she said to them, repressing her astonishment. "Grace, Hanson, how nice to see you again. Hello, Mr. Eastman and Mrs. Jones." Her eyes darted from one to the other. "I'm sorry, my husband is not here, though he should be here any minute. What can I do for you?" Behind her, the doors of the dining room gleamed with light. The room looked crowded for this time of day. Mara saw the time—ten minutes to eight o'clock—on the large old clock in the lobby, and on the small one over the desk where the thin, curly-headed clerk carefully added and subtracted figures in a large leather-bound account book.

Ashel did not seem aware of Julia's discomfort. "Now, Julia. I'm not sure you know what has been happening with us the last week since Hanson came home, except that of course you were with us to bury Grace's Grandmother Rain. But there is more. And I'm not sure you haven't guessed what that is."

Ashel's approach seemed wordy and cumbersome. Mara put a hand on Ashel's arm.

"Julia, honey, we hadn't made an appointment. We know we need to talk to your husband. But do you have a minute someplace where we could first talk to you?"

Julia stood very straight, and her eyes reflecting the light looked startled and large. She balanced the tray in her arms and indicated with a nod of her head that they should follow her to the rooms that she and Horace kept at the end of the long hall. She excused herself to take the cups into the kitchen where her cook labored over some hot rolls and muffins.

"Would you like some breakfast?" Julia asked them.

"Oh, that won't be necessary," Ashel said in a kind voice. "We'll be just a moment."

"I can have some bread brought in."

"Well, that's very sporting of you," Hanson said.

Mara regarded him with a sharp look.

"The Hulls are famous for their bread!" Hanson said.

Julia looked back at him and smiled. "I believe we got the recipe from the East House Hotel."

Their banter cast a little silence over the party. Julia left them seated in her rooms and in a few moments brought a basket of muffins and a little pot of herb tea. She set the muffins and the tea on the low table and began asking who wanted lemon, who wanted sugar.

Ashel leaned forward. He didn't eat. He sat and looked at the cloud of steam in his hands. And he spoke as though he spoke to the tea. "You've known for a long time that the East House Hotel has needed refurbishing. It should have been renamed the West House Hotel several years ago." He cleared his throat. "We have been very short on money, but we sold some stock because of a desire to somehow move our business to the east part of town."

Julia's eyes softened. She had always been Grace's friend. She gazed at Ashel with a very patient look. She gave the tea all around and passed a little dish with lemon wedges.

"You have fixed up your rooms so beautifully," Mara said, admiring the rosebuds at the curtains. "How do you find time for everything, Julia? You are a talented girl. What will happen when you have your baby?"

Julia looked at Grace. She had told her not to say anything to anyone. Mara saw the look. "Honey, you can't hide it any longer. You can see it in your eyes if you can't see it on your body. But even there . . ." She leaned her head back a little and grinned. She put her fingers up to make an inch. "I can see it there, too, honey. You can't hide it from an old woman who has seen too many babies grow for too many years!"

Julia was a beautiful woman. She was still smiling through all of Ashel's speech and through Mara's twinkles and grins. After she passed the sugars in a little dish, she put the basket of muffins back on the tea table. Hanson took one, and Grace held one on her lap in a white napkin.

"You have told us the price of purchase for several months. You knew we wanted to purchase the Hull House Hotel," Ashel said gravely. "We wanted to do it for a long time. We have received word now that we can sell our Tintic mining stocks. And we will have the funds this morning." His words were measured.

Julia was watching him guardedly. "Oh," she finally said, the breath escaping from her. She sat down in one of her dining chairs. She clutched the seat of it in her hands as though she would fall if she were not careful.

"I could never say anything about it without my husband."

"When will he be here?" Hanson asked, breathless with excitement.

"He should be here some time very soon this morning—on the early train," Julia breathed. Her face seemed numb as though she was taken back. Mara had expected her to be happy at the full price offer, that the offer would be cash, that the dream for both seller and purchaser had come true.

"Isn't it wonderful," Grace whispered to her, holding very tightly to her gloves in her hand.

Julia looked at Grace as though she were looking through a wall. "Yes. Yes, of course. I knew you were thinking of it. But . . . but of course my husband should be here. I am so very sorry . . ."

"Do you mind . . . I think I'd like to go and meet him at the train," Ashel smiled at her. He put the tea, which he had never touched, on the table.

At the same time he was about to rise, Julia turned her head to the door. After a soft knock, the door opened, and the head that peered into the room belonged to Alex Hunt. As he opened the door, he also revealed behind him a blushing Laura Adamson. Seeing the others in the room, Alex froze. "Oh, my gosh!" he exclaimed. "Well . . ." he stammered. Julia went to the door and opened it fully to reveal his sharply pressed blue waistcoat, starched white collar, and a pair of polished boots. Behind him, Laura pulled a fox stole around her shoulders and up on the nape of her neck that had been shorn of curls.

"Well, hello . . ." Hanson got up from his chair and turned toward them. "Alex! I . . ."

"Well, hello!" Alex said, recovering from his surprise. "Really, I never expected to see you at it so early." He almost laughed.

"At it? Where have you been?"

There was a painful moment of suspenseful silence. Finally

Alex answered, making an effort to shut down the color that was rising in his face. "You wouldn't believe me if I told you!" He stood very tall, as though his height might provide a form of escape.

"It looks like you two are getting along splendidly," Mara said.

Alex looked at her from a great distance. He laughed. "Meet the Mrs. Hunt-to-be. Laura, the Eastmans."

Grace gasped almost inaudibly.

"I believe we have the honor to be acquainted—at least we have met," Ashel said with a cool look. "Your father, Robert Adamson, was to take the place of the Williams brothers at the Academy?"

Laura did not answer. She gazed at him from beneath the crown of her bright hair.

"That's the one. And we intend to be married as soon as possible, if not sooner," Alex spoke for her.

Hanson turned toward his father and away from them, his hands deep in his pockets. "Alex, I thought . . ."

"You were acting fast yourself! You told me you were ready to do something this weekend. Did you do it?" he grinned.

"I've known Grace all of my life. But I thought . . . you and I . . . you didn't say a word to me."

"Hey, love is love," Alex grinned. "You can't stop love, eh, Laura?" He reached for her hand. When she slipped it into his, she tossed the bobbed hair out of her face and thrust her chin forward. The light on her white cheeks gleamed.

"Did you need something?" Julia asked. She was standing now behind the coffee table, twisting a tea towel.

"Ah, well . . ." Alex was stammering, but he maintained his presence with a kind of raw masculine power. He leaned toward them. "Just dropped by to tell you . . . I had in mind some additional . . . uh, nights in this hotel, but I wished to let you know we will probably be leaving this evening at about seven. Can you hold our . . . effects?"

Julia looked puzzled at his words. "Of course we can. If you'll pack them and remove them at noon, we'll lock them in the closet of the vestibule."

Of course Mara knew Alex could not have had many "effects" at this place, if any. Something about his speech seemed strange.

"Thank you, we'd be so grateful."

"Alex," Hanson began, "I thought we might talk. Do you have a minute? I wanted to . . ."

Alex stared at him, losing possession of himself for only a split second. "If you're busy, that's not my fault. I phoned Saturday but you were out riding," he laughed. "It's Christmas, and Laura and I have some Christmas shopping to do. Don't we, pet?" He searched for her other hand. She clung to him.

"This early in the morning?" Mara said.

"We have lists to make, private vendors to contact. Don't we, pet?"

The room seemed hot, the fire in the grate so stifling, Mara fanned her face with the end of her glove. She had drawn her lips into a narrow line.

"So we'd better get going, hadn't we, pet?" Alex was smooth as melted butter. He steered her out the door into the hall by her elbow. She tightened the fur piece around her neck as she left. "It's nice to see you. I'll probably be coming tonight for my things at your house. Sorry, my man," he addressed Hanson.

Hanson was not done. "I wish you would have told us. At the very least you owe us an explanation about your position at the hotel," Hanson said.

Alex paused at the door. "Hey, I'm telling you now, aren't I?" Then he shut the door.

"Even his eyes look a little like the eyes of a . . ." Mara said. But when she saw Hanson's face, she did not say more. He was pale. The heat in the room had brought beads of sweat along his brow.

"I never was that impressed with him. I'm sorry," Ashel said quietly.

But Hanson would not say anything negative about his friend. Mara was not sure he could see there had been anything negative to say.

"He's in love. He doesn't want to think about letting us down. He'll come around when he marries Laura," Hanson said. "This is just temporary, Father. I know he still wants to work it out at the hotel. He said he likes the hotel business, at least what he saw of it. He'll be back. He just needs some time . . ."

Grace had no words.

Mara pulled forward and began slipping on her gloves. "Thanks, Julia. We may try to intercept your husband at the train station. There are some urgent matters about this transaction we should discuss with him." She turned. "Are you coming, Ashel?"

"I'm coming."

Julia followed them out of the room. The foyer was still lit by very dim light. There was no trace of Alex and Laura. They had gone. The hotel seemed empty. No one sat in the lobby or the dining area. The boy who worked with Julia was at the desk filing bills.

"He should be on that 9:00 A.M. train," Ashel said, slipping his watch fob out of his pocket and checking the time. "It's 8:00 A.M. We could go back to the East House for something to eat."

"All right," Mara said, looking back at Julia. The girl was standing at the window, pulling the curtains back and tying them with rope. In the electric light, a dark silhouette, she revealed the bloom of her figure. Mara was surprised at how far along Julia really was. As she turned back to the window to look out into the street she thought she saw two people—a man and a woman—coming toward the hotel in the dark. She thought it was Alex and Laura returning. However, when their eyes met Mara's in the window, they suddenly disappeared around the corner of the block. She was puzzled. They had been so quick.

At the East House Hotel Maggie Hammond served high stacks of hotcakes, adding extras like blueberry syrup and cream. Dawes hurried in and out of the kitchen hustling for his employers, Ashel and Hanson. Ashel made notes about the menu and the service, or his thoughts in general, in a little black book he stored in his breast pocket. Grace ate quickly and stared at her empty plate. She did not speak much to Hanson. Quiet for a long time, they seemed apart. Mara ate nervously, and Ashel watched the time.

The railroad station looked like an electric toy blazing in the dark morning. A row of small black birds sat on the telephone wires outside in the street. Above the blackness a gray sky was just beginning to come alive with the dawn. Inside the station, Christmas candles and pine boughs twinkled in the windows. Mara stood by Ashel inside the station while the porter and the engineer moved quietly about. The world seemed hushed this day more than on other days. The station lights looked red, gleaming like starlight. So many years ago, Mara remembered, there were lights in the sky while Mary and Joseph came to find a place in the inn.

"Is there anything I can do for you?" The porter finally hobbled to them. He was Ernest Freeman, one of the members who had dropped out of the Church when the issues of plural marriage had been unresolved. He had preserved his second wife ("She is my wife, after all") by moving to Mexico, and he had returned to Provo when she died.

"As a matter of fact, do you know when the Bamberger is due?"

"It should have been here by now," the porter smiled. "Must have been delayed on account of the holiday."

Mara smiled and Grace and Hanson nodded warily, as though they were not really paying attention. A young boy clinging to his mother's hands kept peering around at them from under his flannel cap. He smiled at them from behind his mother's hat box. If he made the least sound, she tapped him with her lorgnette.

At last, as the bells in the tabernacle chimed nine o'clock, the semaphores began flashing and bells clanging. The tracks rumbled as the cars rolled in, ending in a roar almost deafening, a great screech as metal ground against metal when the train came to a halt.

The porter put up the black stepping stool to a crowded Pullman car where several people stood jostling one another behind the windows.

Mara saw Horace Hull inside the glass. "There he is," she said.

Grace and Hanson stood holding one another close in the cold air. Their breath made clouds of steam.

"I'll speak to him," Ashel said in soft words. "Please don't overwhelm him. Perhaps it would be best if you stand back out of the way."

Grace and Hanson turned around and stepped back as several people in fine hats and greatcoats carrying large portmanteaus or pieces of luggage stepped off the cars and onto the platform.

"Mr. Hull! Mr. Hull!" Ashel called to him as the man stood between the cars, his head above the others. He wore a deerskin top hat with a black and white feather. He had leaned over to see the step and at Ashel's call looked up suddenly and squinted his eyes as though he could not see.

"Mr. Hull! Here!" Ashel guided his gaze to himself by waving vigorously.

The man did not seem to recognize Ashel, but when he saw Mara at his side he nodded and smiled. He lifted his hand and stepped to the ground. Then he vigorously shook hands with Ashel. "Well, to what do I attribute this honor to be met at the station three blocks from my hotel?"

Ashel bowed slightly from the waist. "If it's all right with you, Mr. Hull, we'd like to drive you home."

Hull looked perplexed. He laughed. "Such a few blocks?"

Mara reached for Hull's hand. "We'd like to talk to you, Horace." She recoiled a bit, remembering her feelings less than a week ago in the room with Rain under the sheet. "At our home not long ago you mentioned—"

Ashel glanced at her with the silent message that he would approach the subject. "Do you have your bag, Horace?" he said.

Horace Hull took a moment to make his way through the station yard, the people. The Eastmans followed him. The crowd was thinning out now. With the help of the porter, he found his piece of luggage on the baggage cart. He walked through the station then, looking about as though he were making sure he was in the right place, he assessed the lights, the small tree in the corner of the station trimmed with lopsided ribbons and tipped candles. Attached as decorations were a few paper birds, their wings looking very much touched by human hands.

"Where is your car, Mr. Eastman?" Horace said, tearing his eyes from the tree and making his way through the station door to the street.

"Right out here, Mr. Hull." Hanson pressed against the door and held it open until his family had passed through.

"It smells like Christmas Eve," Hull said. "It smells cold and crisp, but with a tang of pine in the air."

Hanson kept up with them. "It smells that way because tonight it is Christmas Eve," he said.

Mara walked beside him and put her hand in his arm. "Julia does such a lovely job at the hotel," she said to ease the conversation. "Your little home inside the back parlor looked so cozy with the pine boughs and the tree."

"Yes, she knows how to do things right," Horace said. Ashel opened the car door for him. He ducked into the front seat.

Ashel settled himself into the driver's seat before he began. "We wanted to talk to you." He turned to Hull before he started the car. "Last Tuesday you mentioned to Hanson that you're still interested in selling the hotel."

Mr. Hull looked at him. The early morning light barely revealed his face. "Yes, I'm planning to sell it."

"Well, we are ready to buy," Ashel said slowly.

Hull turned to the window and looked out. "I've had some other interest last week," he said.

Mara paused. This was exactly what she had feared. "Is it Barrington and his group?" she asked, anxiously leaning forward from the back seat where Hanson and Grace sat beside her, holding to one another.

"I believe he's in on it," Horace Hull said, uncertain, turning to the front and gazing out at the street.

"We can pay you this morning at eleven o'clock," Ashel said. "Full price. Cash. We decided to sell our stock in the Tintic mine."

Horace turned to look at him, surprised. A grin began at his mouth. "Both an East House and a West House, eh?"

"East and West. There really should be no division," Mara said.

Ashel's gaze seemed dark, even in the growing light. He was warning her not to reveal too much about changing the name of the hotel. "We knew there was another interest. But we have the cash this morning at eleven A.M. We wanted to talk to you before the bank opened. That's why we are here to meet you at the station."

"I'll need to talk to Julia first." Horace Hull seemed very ponderous, slow, as though he were thinking of something else.

We're on our way there now," Ashel said, leaning into the steering wheel.

The quiet seemed ominous for a long time. Mara tried to diffuse it with a word of praise for Julia's housekeeping. Though light was coming up in the east, the hotel looked dark. The lights had been turned off; the shadows still lurked in the eaves. Ashel stopped the car at the south entrance which gave easy access to the Hulls' apartment.

Horace very slowly took his bag and climbed out of the

auto. "We'll see what she has done," he said on the walk.

"What she has done?" Mara asked as they reached the door.

"I gave her authority to act in my behalf until I returned," he said under his breath. It sounded like a lame excuse.

Mara heard his soft words as she came to the doorstep and lifted her skirts. Her heart raced. "Was she to do something?" she asked.

But Hull did not answer her. When he tried the door and found it locked, he put down his valise and fumbled for the key. "Would you like to come in?" he said.

The morning was still cold. "Thank you, Horace," Mara said. "I hope we're not causing you a problem. Julia did indicate we should just return with you."

Ashel came into the apartment behind her. Grace and Hanson huddled just inside the door.

"Julia," Hull called out. But there was silence. He turned on the electric lights. They blazed overhead and in the corner a red lamp illuminated the heavy wreath woven with silk ribbon and pine boughs, and the small tree.

Julia was not there. Once inside the dining area, Horace Hull found a note on the buffet. It read, "I went to the bank with Mr. Hunt."

At Mr. Hull's elbow, Mara saw the writing just as Horace tucked it into his waistcoat. "Mr. Hunt," she said to herself. Mr. Hunt. She thought this morning in the dark that she had seen Alex Hunt and Laura turn back toward the hotel. Her heart stopped in her throat.

Ashel did not see the writing on the note. "She's not here?" he said, disappointed.

"She's gone to the bank," Horace said, going into his room with the valise. From the dark recesses of the apartment they could hear him putting things away, opening drawers, shutting them up again. "You were on your way to the bank yourself, weren't you?"

Ashel's face grew white. "Julia's at the bank?" he said. He

looked at Mara, his eyes gray with shock.

Hanson moved forward swiftly, still gripping Grace's hand. "What is it, Father?" he said. "What is it? Where'd she go? The bank?"

The blazing dining room walls seemed to back away from them, to diffuse as though they were transparent. Mara felt thousands of other imaginary eyes on all of them for a time, as though she were standing in a room filled with hundreds of people—perhaps spirits of those who lived inside the walls of these rooms. Unimaginable eyes, the eyes of hundreds of those who had lived in this hotel. For a moment, she thought she would black out. She leaned against the doorway of the small parlor and put herself between Hanson and the dark apartment behind her.

Hanson stopped. "Is everything all right, Aunt Mara?"

Mara gripped her hands together. She watched his eyes. "Hanson," she began. "You knew there was another party interested in buying the hotel?"

Hanson moved back; his eyes flashed. "Yes . . . Has something happened?"

"We don't know," Mara said with a measured tone.

Ashel came back from the bedroom. "Let's get in the car."

Hanson stood firmly in the hallway. "Tell me what has happened."

"We're taking Mr. Hull with us to the bank," Ashel said in a harsh voice.

Grace looked up at Hanson. She held tight to his arm. "Hanson, please," she said almost inaudibly. "Please don't worry. Everything will turn out as it should."

But her words were lost in the rush to get out the door—Ashel's turning so quickly that he flipped his scarf as he pulled it round his neck. The large flaps on the pockets of his greatcoat thumped like wings.

"Then let's go," Mara said, following him. And Hanson turned and followed them. They waited at the door for a moment, holding it open for Hull, who seemed close behind. In a moment the red and gold light in the apartment shut out and there was blackness in the hotel. Hull was beside them and they climbed into the car.

Mara felt she could not breathe. She felt all of her blood in her body closing off in her nerves. No one wanted to speak. Even Hull said nothing as the car swerved around to the left and stopped to curve north onto J Street where the lights faded out in the waxing day. Only Grace tried to ease the tension. The pine boughs draped over the gas lamps looked frosted in the morning light. "I'd love for Christmas to last all year," Grace said.

In only a moment they were in front of the bank, where Hanson jumped out and opened Hull's door. He opened Mara's door. As she rose, she whispered, "Hanson, let your father do the talking. I'm not sure . . ."

Hanson did not wait for her warning of uncertainty. He pulled Grace out of the car, tucked her hand in his arm, and walked quickly to the bank behind Hull, who stayed with Ashel until they made their way through the large doors.

For such an early hour, the bank looked busy. In a corner, under the lights at the loan officer Harper's desk, were a ring of people seated on folding chairs. Mara did not want to look, so she watched Hanson's eyes. He peered over her head at the group, and his eyes narrowed. Mara knew without asking him, or hearing the breathy rasp in his throat, who it was seated in the circle of chairs, and her nerves tightened. She cringed, watching the lights fall off overhead, feeling the cold of the marble floor under her feet and the distance of the cavernous hollow room of the bank where every sound—the sound of a coin against the cash box, the sound of a pen scratching on paper, seemed multiplied in a thousand other remembered moments screaming in her mind. Horace Hull stood between them and the gate that swung into the officer's quarters. He looked at them dolefully. "It may already be too late," he said.

"I'm sorry."

"Will you see?" Ashel said, controlling his voice.

All of them faced away from the group at the table, hoping to remain unseen, except for Hanson. He ducked slightly when Harper looked his way. All of the others were facing Harper, their backs to the Eastmans. Hull walked through the gate purposefully, his shoulders back, his head forward. There was silence in the room while the group turned their heads, and Harper glanced out into the open foyer where the Eastmans tried to look obscure.

They waited for what seemed like a long time. The cashier smiled at them, and Mr. Carver, the comptroller, asked if there was anything he could do for them. Blushing, Mara said no, they were waiting for Mr. Hull.

Hanson's eyes narrowed. He set his mouth in a forced line.

"What is it, Hanson?" Grace whispered.

"I . . ." He could barely speak, overcome by surprise and betrayal. "I can't believe it. Julia Hull and Alex Hunt."

"They are cousins," Mara said softly. "Hanson, I thought you knew."

"I knew. But I never believed . . ." Hanson's shocked eyes rested on Mara's face, but he was not seeing her.

Ashel was standing at the rail behind a large cabinet so that he could look in, but not be seen. He seemed lost in his thoughts.

"Who are they?" Grace asked, her face very pale.

"Barrington's people," Ashel said without moving. "The man Drucker, the man Barrington, Mr. Adamson, Julia Hull, and Alex Hunt."

Grace breathed in sharply and clutched Hanson's sleeve. "Please, Hanson, it will be all right."

Hanson jerked his arm from her, clutching the gate with his hands, and Grace backed away.

"That was fast," Ashel said under his breath as he remained to look at the group. "Very fast." He was grasping the rail so tightly that his arms shook. The veins stood up along the backs of his old hands. "It's hard to believe." He turned to Hanson. "He was your friend, Hanson." His words seemed measured, and his head lowered. Then he whispered, "I would sooner have been his enemy."

Hanson was stunned. He did not speak.

As Ashel watched, the assistant banker, Harper, rose from his chair at the desk as Hull approached him. The group greeted Hull amicably enough. Alex Hunt cast a glance back as they spoke, but not enough to see the Eastmans standing a bit out of the way in the hall.

Ashel ducked when he saw Hunt's gaze. "It would be best not to make a fuss," Ashel said in tight words between his teeth.

Harper came out from behind the desk and called a clerk to bring some papers. A young man with a flat head and curly hair ducked into the cubicle where the purchasers sat. He began to shuffle papers and point to places on the page.

"Is there any way to stop them?" Mara whispered. "Ashel . . . ? I'll go . . ."

Ashel raised his arm to hold her back. "No. It's too late, Mara."

When Harper came toward them, his size cut off the view of the group at the desk. He was a tall man with a very thin face and small tufts of gray over his ears. His sallow cheeks sagged with gray lines.

"Mr. Eastman. I'm so sorry. Miss Julia signed an agreement with her cousin Mr. Hunt not twenty minutes ago. And now that Hull is here . . ."

"What has happened?" Ashel seethed.

"It is a very firm agreement. Drucker and Hunt have furnished the money."

"Hunt?" Ashel asked.

"Alex Hunt's father and mother, James and Hilary Hunt, owners of the Granite International Cement and Asphalt of Salt Lake City. It was done before they came in this morning. Julia signed on the way here."

"Is it legal?" Ashel said.

Harper looked very long-faced. "I'm afraid so, Mr. Eastman. They are now owners of what they want to call the Royal House Hotel."

Mara started forward. "What did you say?" she asked. Her head was spinning as though she were spiraling down some darkness where she had never been. She was aware of Hanson—of his private grief.

"They are changing the name to Royal House Hotel."

Hanson looked at Mara, shocked. "Why, that . . ."

Mara put a hand on his arm. "You are still the owners of the East House Hotel," she whispered. "Act accordingly."

"I'm sorry," Mr. Harper said. "I would have let you know early this morning of the direction of the transaction, but I could not reach you by telephone at the hotel."

"Did you try?" Ashel asked.

"I had one of my secretaries try," Harper said solemnly, looking very much like a liar.

Ashel looked at Mara and put a hesitant hand on her arm. "Do they know of our interest in making the purchase?" he asked.

"They may have had some idea—for it has been hurried forward."

"If we can leave gracefully," Mara whispered to Hanson who had already begun to walk back inside the hall to Grace.

"You've already sold the stock. Would you still like to withdraw the funds?" Harper asked.

"No," Ashel said. "We'll refurbish the East House in the spring."

"I'll keep them for you," Harper said.

Ashel was silent, looking forward into the foyer and into the large room where the parties remained seated with their backs toward the hall. They were busy signing documents with the clerk.

"Now, if you'll excuse me," Mr. Harper said kindly, "I have some business regarding this transaction to attend to." He bowed slightly and turned back to the desk. For a long moment Ashel and Mara did not move.

Mara took Ashel's arm and whispered, "Let's go before they have completed the business."

Ashel agreed.

White-faced, Hanson followed Ashel and Mara without looking up as they left, hoping Alex would not turn to look at him. He dug his hands deeply into his pockets, leaving them unaccessible to Grace. He moved rapidly, moved with the appearance of hoping to disappear into the street without being seen.

But Mara gave a last look into the room to see Alex grinning at them. He dared to wave to her! She caught her breath. Yet she smiled civilly in return and briefly nodded her head to him. Still grinning, he saw all of them leave the front door and walk into the dim morning.

"And this is the friend that we still must befriend," she said out in the cold air to Hanson and Grace and Ashel.

"I feel cheated," Ashel spoke. "I overheard them saying the Tintic stock has already gone up! Our sale was good for them! And for us an unfortunate piece of timing."

"We must somehow be larger in spirit than we may feel," Mara whispered. "We still do have the cash, remember. The world is sometimes full of violence to our fondest hopes and dreams."

Hanson moved forward on the walk away from her words to the car, still bent forward with his hands in his pockets and his head down. Grace followed him at a distance, not knowing what to say. They were all silent as they drove home.

34

Caroline Eastman

When Caroline heard the knocking, she thought it was the wind in the loose shingles. Suddenly waking, she felt that she was alone—that Ashel had gone somewhere, and when she reached out for him, fished for him in the huge sea of the bed, she discovered she had been right. He was not there.

She always seemed to know where he was. Always, though, he disappeared into the outside world of hurrying and exchanging, a world Caroline saw only in dreams. And her dreams of that world were of shadows of noises, shadows of figures as though they became a hum behind a veil draped over her eyes—a veil that blew only slightly like silk in a wind. And Ashel had always stood between her and the cords that might have lifted the veil.

She lay awake in the bed for a long time. She knew only hazily the direction of their money—of the fortune her father had left them—of Papa Eastman's involvement with the mill, its destruction, the assets of the hotel and some other rental properties, and the purchase of building lots on Center Street against the possibility of their increase in value some day.

What she never knew was how much care Ashel took to protect everything, and to protect her from knowing everything—for it was in an oasis of calm that he wanted to come to her every night to a quiet rest in which the vagaries of the marketplace were phantoms and her smile the most beautiful reality of his life. He came to heal in a place of his own, furnished by her love: the needlepoint, the afghans, the small rococo paintings in the gilt frames, the oil landscapes above the landing on the stairs, the richly-papered walls, the sunlight streaming into the darkness from cut glass. All of these things and Caroline's smile of peace—a haven for himself that Caroline knew he would never have disturbed if he could have kept it always apart from what he knew of his other worlds.

The removal of the center of town to the east side had only tilted the ship of their estate as far as Caroline knew. She knew the details of the difficulties, but she had been protected in the continuing richness of their lives, the fine roasts, the good fruit and breads, the small gifts they gave to one another, and the continuing offerings of charity they showered upon others who had so much less. It was in this realm of her distribution of their goods that her concentration was sharpest, and though she knew that Ashel and the others had gone to the bank this morning to purchase another hotel, her world continued to revolve around the moments of delight she took in creating the miracles of their finest event in the year—their large Christmas Eve.

This morning, while she lay in and out of sleep, she dreamed for a moment that the knocking announced the arrival of their guests. But she consciously knew it was not yet time. She lay for a moment in her quilts, passing over the details of the buffet in her mind: the turkey, the sweetbreads, the herb-laced croissants, the cranberries, minted pears, the fine yams in glazed sweet sauce, the basted beans, the dressing with onions, celery, apples, walnuts, parsley, and thyme. She picked through the details of the table decorations, the Waterford candelabrum, the bursts of lilies and baby's breath, crystal, red ribbons and pine, and baby red plums, and with the help of the men, the transportation of all of it to the large house on the corner. It was in her mind that she saw the laden tables tied with garlands of Oregon grape, and after her dreams, the reality usually like magic, somehow took place.

If there were an arena of figures, numbers, the collection of paper, and the challenge of profits and losses, all of these moved in an orbit totally removed from her dreams where there were candles, lightly-browned pie crusts with tempting sweet fruit fillings, chestnut torte, linen napkins, fluted vases, and silver spoons.

That her world depended upon the world of the exchange of paper was a given—a fact taken for granted, but never hauled out to look over or worry over like a wounded mouse the cat might keep alive for sport. They were worlds moving in twin tracks across the vast elegance of their lives in a place where everything, though it was born of the most dedicated effort and labor, came to them from their concentration on loyalty, beauty, and love.

For a few moments there had been no knocking, but suddenly it began again. Now, as she continued to hear it, she knew it was at the front door. She slipped easily from her silk sheets into the wheelchair beside her bed, a practice made easier by time. She drew her silk robe around her shoulders and the woolen afghan over her knees. She had not dressed yet. Whoever it was would understand.

But she was not able to wheel herself from the room before the large door swung open and a voice rang in the dark hallway.

"Mrs. Eastman! Are you here?" It was Sissy Corey's voice. She had often been used to coming in if Caroline slept soundly. "Hello, Mrs. Eastman!" she called again. "Do you mind if we come in?"

Caroline's immediate question was "Who is *we?*" But she did not say it. She called out: "Sissy, is that you?" There was then a flurry of bumping and scraping, the sound of hard leather against the wood floor, large bumps against the doorjamb, the sound of scraping against the screen door, large sounds of fists jamming and pumping against the front door.

"May we come in?"

Caroline wheeled her chair through the door and into the hall. "Yes, of course, Sissy." When she saw the girl her heart fell inside of her. The girl's face was wrapped in a torn scarf plugged with burrs. It fell away from her cheeks to reveal a series of raw scratches as though someone had dragged a sharp set of fingernails into her sad eyes. "Sissy, what has happened?" Caroline cried out. "You are hurt!"

"It's him," Sissy said softly. "It's him." Him was her younger brother, Chub Corey, who was leaning against his sister, dragging at her coat, his leaden feet hunkered down by the heavy boots and dragging along the floor.

"He's sick," Sissy said. "And my pa will kill him if he finds out."

Caroline at once assessed the problem and her heart froze inside of her. "Of course, Sissy. Let him come in. Take him to Grace's room behind the kitchen and let him have the bed. Take off his boots."

Sissy knelt to the floor and pulled at the heavy leather gunboats on her brother's feet. The boots were so large for him—probably cast-offs from his father—that they slipped off easily. Under the boots were ragged socks that looked more like a few holes strung together with yarn.

The boy fell back against the floor—his fists flailing wildly about his head and knocking against the wood like bobbins thrown off the spindles. He groaned, and spittle dribbled from his mouth.

"On my way to work I heard somebody groaning inside the screen door of the Freshwater Hardware. It was Chub. He's awful sick, Miss Caroline, and I know how Mama would feel."

Caroline also knew. It was obviously a sickness he had brought upon himself—the reeking odor of alcohol climbed into her nostrils and spun into the top of her head. Caroline knew. But there was much she did not understand. "How old is he now, Sissy?" She leaned forward in the chair to push the large boots aside.

"He's only twelve, Mum."

"Twelve?" Caroline repeated the word. Her voice trailed off. Her eyes followed the boy's fists above his head as they pounded against the floor. "Who does he know, Sissy—to end up like this? Who does he know who would . . . ?"

"I don't know, Mum. The boys he goes with. There's a man down by the tracks . . ."

Caroline gripped the edge of the chair and stared through Sissy into the front rooms. "Never mind," she choked back her words. "Ashel isn't here. Grace isn't here. Just take him to Grace's room, Sissy. Then start up the fire in the stove." Tonight would be the party, Caroline thought to herself. So much to do today.

She tried to wheel close to the boy to help Sissy lift him, but she could not help. Sissy curled the child's hands in her fists and dragged him inch by inch into the back hall and through the door to Grace's room. "He'll be all right," she said.

"Has this happened before?" Caroline wanted to know.

"Once," Sissy said, closing the door. "Once before, and Papa nearly beat him to death."

"Once before." Caroline's heart ached. She had reached the point where her very own heart tightened in her body when she saw suffering. Ashel had told her she must learn to separate herself from the suffering of others in a world of their own choosing, but Caroline had said, "As long as there is anything I can do to encourage them to make better choices, I will do it. I must do it." She saw Sissy's face, and the blood rose against her cheeks now. Sissy had come to her and there was something she could do. She would hire Chub to work with Sissy. She would look after Chub. She would see that he learned to work and to think well of himself, and to perform some position for Ashel at the new hotel. They would be tight for a while. Chub could learn to paint. He could learn to clean and to weed flower beds. He was so young, and she would make a difference in his life as she had made a difference for Sissy and Cherry—as the Eastmans had made a difference for her.

"Did you put him on the bed?" Caroline asked.

"No'm. He is too heavy. I left him on the rug there. He is

asleep."

Very well. Caroline would leave well enough alone. She began to discuss the day's activities with Sissy. The Christmas Eve was to be held at the big Eastman house, but Caroline was to furnish the pies and the hors d'oeuvres, and Sissy must help her. Sissy wheeled her into her bedroom, and Caroline dressed quickly as the light coming up in the East chased the shadows out of the house. They began together on the food while Sissy chatted about Cherry's skirt she had sewn up out of a flour bag, about the other boys and the two little girls who could talk of nothing else but being at the Eastman house on Christmas Eve.

"That is where they'll be," Caroline said thoughtfully, all the time in her mind anticipating what tragedy would color the air with darkness when Frank and Lida Corey found that Chub was not in his bed, and that he had been on the street in the cold all night long, and that he had given himself over to the untrustworthy Reb Stuart, who often sat with the popcorn wagon on the street. And she did not really know what to do, except to bring the boy out of his stupor and discuss it with Ashel when he came. That it might be a long morning at the bank, she knew. The clock said nine forty-five. She believed they had anticipated receiving the funds at eleven. But at that moment she thought she heard the distinct sound of the Chevrolet.

It was hard to believe they would have returned so soon. Worried, she wiped her buttery fingers on the dish towel and wheeled back from the table. "Sissy," she said, hesitating. Sissy turned back from the stove where she was warming the yeast.

"Yes, Miss Caroline? What is it you want? Can I do something?"

"Yes, Sissy. Will you please go to the front window for a moment and see who it is that is driving up to the house this time of day?"

"Yes'm." Sissy dashed back to the front room wiping her hands on her apron. "It's Mr. Eastman," she called back. "And

Hanson and Grace, and . . . your Aunt Mara." She stayed for a moment at the window, peering through the pine wreath and grape berries to make certain. "It's your folks, Mrs. Eastman," she said, coming back. "Do you want me to move Chub out of Grace's room?"

Caroline grimaced. Something was wrong. It was too early for them to return. They forgot something, or the bank was sending them back for something.

"No, Sissy," she said with patience. "Don't worry about Chub. I just . . ."

"What is it, Miss Caroline?" Sissy looked concerned. "Miss Caroline" was determined to wheel out of the kitchen. Sissy helped her negotiate the table and the door.

Inside the foyer, Caroline waited, wringing her handkerchief in her hands. She heard the voices on the stoop. She saw the top of Mara's hat bobbing in the door window. When the door opened, Mara was the first to enter, followed by Grace and Ashel. Hanson, who had been holding the door, waited for a moment before he quietly stepped in.

"Is something wrong?" Caroline said to Ashel. "Why are you back so soon?"

Without answering her, Ashel moved to the dining room and put his portfolio on the table. "Somehow, there have to be things of more importance in this world."

"Hanson and Grace are more important," Mara said, pulling the hat out of her hair and peeling off her gloves.

"Well, that was it—Hanson's future," Ashel said. "That was the entire point."

"Their future is just as bright without the Royal House Hotel."

"It didn't work out," Caroline said, her face strained.

Ashel came to her and kissed her hair. He stayed for a moment with his lips in her curls. Then he leaned down to her cheek and leaned his weight on the handles of the wheelchair behind her. "No, it didn't work out, darling."

Caroline next looked at Hanson, whose eyes were narrow and sharp in his pale face.

"Darling," she said. "Hanson . . . honey, I'm sorry."

He looked at her with the look of surprise he had conveyed to all of them at the bank.

"Darling," she said, uncertain as to what she should say to his hurt look, to the pain that was so visible in his eyes.

Ashel took the silence for his own opportunity to break things down slowly to Caroline. "It was how it happened that hurt us all the most . . . although perhaps any way it might have happened would have hurt . . ."

While they gathered in the dining room around the table, Ashel wheeled Caroline in to be with them. Though she knew out of the corner of her eye that Grace had ducked into the hall, she did not think about it, or she would have offered a warning—that Chub lay on her bedroom floor.

In a moment Grace was back with them in the dining room and peeling off her gloves and her hat and looking very concerned. "Aunt Caroline," she whispered. "Can I talk to you?"

"What is it, honey?" Caroline asked.

Grace was quiet when she leaned down against Caroline's hair. "Did you know that the Corey boy is . . ."

"Oh, yes!" Caroline drew back and directly met Grace's eyes. "Yes, honey. I'm sorry. This morning Sissy brought him in. Do you need your room?"

"What is it, honey?" Mara said, folding her gloves into her purse.

"The Corey boy. Sissy found him at Freshwater's across the street on her way to work," Caroline said, turning in the chair by herself to face Ashel. "I wanted to talk to you, sweetheart," she whispered.

"Was he . . ."

"Yes," she said swiftly. "He is only twelve."

"I've been concerned about the boy ever since he and his

friends have been going down to Stuart's hovel down by the tracks. The man is not a good influence on any of them," Ashel said.

Caroline wheeled closer to him and stopped in front of him at the table. "I want to hire him, Ashel, to tell Frank and Lida we'll hire him here to work with his sister."

Ashel looked at her. He reached for her hand. "My little Florence Nightingale," he said softly. "You want to save all the world." He never flinched, knowing how serious it would be to pay for all of this now.

Caroline smiled, but her concern could not be tossed off. "Just the little piece of it I can help—if I can."

"He must be cold," Grace said, taking up the spirit of Christmas that she herself had wished would begin to last all year. "I have that extra quilt in the top of my closet. Sissy didn't cover him . . ." She had turned back by now. She called back to Mara and Grace: "Get Sissy to make up some hot peppermint tea."

"It seems like the beginning of the end for the Coreys," Ashel said. "They had child after child after child, never thinking how they would garner the resources to care for them."

"Yes, but they are here now," Mara said, following Grace into the hall. "They are here now, and our only choice is to do for them what our conscience begs us, what our hearts tell us is our sacred trust."

Caroline wheeled behind them and watched through the open door as Grace picked the boy up in her arms and placed him on the bed. Grace next leaned over him, pulled his hair out of his eyes, and with her gloved finger wiped the spittle off of his cheek. Mara covered him with the quilt she pulled out of the cupboard at the top of the wardrobe.

"Sissy says he will be all right," Caroline said. "Thank you. Perhaps if he works around here . . ."

Mara's face flickered with a sad light. "He is such a child, still," was all she said, leaving the room.

In the dining room again, the women found Hanson pacing around Ashel at the table, his hands in his pockets. He was looking down at the floor, his eyes still dazed.

"The best thing we can do now is to do the shopping for the girls and start moving the party to the house on the corner. What was it you needed for tonight that we haven't been able to purchase elsewhere? Most of the markets will close at noon for Christmas Eve."

Caroline turned to him, grateful for his business-as-usual tone of voice. Hanson took note of his words. He stopped walking about at the other end of the table, stopped at the candelabra and began to pick at the wax drippings on the candles, putting them carefully into his left hand.

Ashel looked up at Hanson. "Son," he said quietly. "It's Christmas Eve. It's Christmas Eve."

35

Grace Tuttle

When Grace returned from covering the boy on her bed and opening the window to let the cool air in on his cheeks, she wanted to tell Sissy she would go to tell their mother and father—to talk to them now. She wanted to straighten it all out before the party. But Caroline needed their help at the market. And she needed help with the food, and moving the silver and dishes to the big house. She needed everyone. Everyone would be pressed into service for the party. She knew there wasn't time to get her own house ready, and she submitted herself to the needs of the family.

Mara bustled over to her place to get her mop bucket and soap, and Uncle Will offered to come over "until I bust my back wide open." And they began the job that needed to be done on the house to make it ready for the big Christmas Eve.

Grace tried to forget about Hanson's dark anger. She worked with Mara and Will. Hanson went to the market with Ashel, and when he came back he seemed in a better temperament. All of them—even Caroline, who finally, after all the pies, breads, and puddings had been moved to the big house, had come to help set the tables and finish last-minute details—all of them were doing better as the day progressed.

They sent Sissy home with a letter Caroline wrote which said, "We are so glad the Corey family can be with us at our home tonight. We have kept little Charles with us to help Sissy. He wasn't feeling well—said he did not tell you where he was. But he is here—and not to worry."

At last, at about 4:00 P.M., Grace went into her room for the last time. The Corey boy was awake. He sat up on his bed, and he was rubbing his eyes.

"Hello, Charles," Grace said to him. "We were worried about you. Do you know what happened last night?"

The boy's face fell. His hair stood up all over his head and the skin on his cheeks was flaccid. Dark rings stood under his eyes. He shook his head. "I don't know," he said.

"You came here early this morning. You had been drinking alcohol," Grace said.

He looked frightened.

"Charles," she said, putting her arm around him. "We've let you sleep it off. But it is very bad for you. Your father won't like it. Why don't you help us with the party. Do you want to help?"

"Sure," he said.

"We're going to talk to your father and tell him what happened and that we need you to work here for us."

His black eyes widened. "My father will kill me," he said.

"He won't like what you have done, but if you work for us, you will make money and be able to help him," Grace said.

He was very pale.

She brought him with her to the big house where he chopped wood. He started fires in the fireplaces and kept them going. He did willingly whatever she asked him to do. She also asked him to help her carefully pack the valises that belonged to Alex Hunt and Reginald Summerfield. They put the valises in the upstairs wardrobes, made the beds, and cleaned the rooms. He was slow and sometimes he did not concentrate on what he was doing. But he stayed with the tasks and Grace gave him fifty cents.

His eye widened. "This is mine?" he said.

"It's yours."

Hanson came to the house after he went to the market, and he put new candles in all of the candlesticks, in the candle dishes on the Christmas tree, and in the candelabra. He draped the candelabra with garlands of grape leaves and boughs of pine.

It was 5:30 P.M. when Grace heard the brakes of the car. She left her post at the stove where she was heating the apple butter while Mara was cutting the apples and carrots into strips. When she looked out of the curtains, she dropped quickly back from the fading light. She put a hand on her throat. No words came from her, but her surprise roused the attention of the others, who were setting the table in the front room. Hanson was lighting the candles on the mantelpiece. It was Caroline who had the presence to wheel to the front door just in time to see the top hat of Alex Hunt, and to hear his knock and the cheery tenor of his voice.

"Hello!" Alex shouted through the door. He opened the door and revealed not only himself in his huge raccoon coat, but Laura huddled face down behind him, clasping her own fur cape about her shoulders, curling it close around her ears under the blond waves of her bobbed hair.

"Well, well, what have we here!" Alex said, grinning from ear to ear. "I thought the party was to be at Mara's house. But I find you here!"

There was dead silence. Alex could not have helped but know. But he continued as though everything was just fine. "I saw you at the bank this morning. But you wouldn't stop for me. I waved. I tried to get your attention."

Mara was quiet, standing in the kitchen door. Ashel stiffened. He stayed behind the French chair in the front room. Hanson turned abruptly from the fireplace with the match sticks still burning in his hands.

When he saw Hanson, Alex's face blanched. "I wanted to surprise you, Hanson."

Hanson's brows knit. He blew out the fire in the match and shook his fingers. "You surprised us."

"I guess I already told you I got engaged," Alex said. "Laura Adamson and I."

There was such a silence that his cheery words fell as though hurtling into a blank chasm. Alex looked at Mara, still standing in the kitchen door. "Say, I tried to wave you down this morning. I have some news to tell you people." He stood uncertainly, but his manner still seemed one of unaffected confidence. "You may have guessed." He paused and gazed at the faces around him—as though testing the atmosphere. "Now we can go into business, Hanson! My father gave a great idea to my cousin Julia!"

Hanson's eyes flashed. All the pain that had settled in them today came to the surface now. "You bought the Royal House Hotel."

"You knew?" Alex said flippantly. "My, news gets around!"

Ashel drew up to his full height. He drew closer to Alex. He was very pale. "Alex, you knew we were planning to buy it," he said evenly.

"Yes, and I talked to Julia and she said she'd rather it stayed in the family. And Drucker was putting up half the money. He knows my father and he was happy to have him as a partner. Laura and I went up to Idaho and got the money so we could all—I kept the name you wanted for it. I mean, we could still work with it together. I wasn't trying to . . . I did what Julia thought would be best." He paused, seeing the silence in the stony face. "She's my cousin, sir."

Hanson's eyes were still piercing and dark.

"Say, don't look at me like that."

"Did you leave your things here, Mr. Hunt?" Ashel asked.

The others were very still, standing in the room around Alex Hunt. He looked uncomfortable in the candlelight—the evening light that began to descend on them, over the candles winking on the mantelpiece, the few large candles hanging in the threaded dishes from the tree.

36

Mara Eastman Jones

Mara stepped out from the kitchen door. She was still holding the paring knife in her hand. When she saw all of the people gathered in the room, in a flash of remembering, she saw the Eastman family on a day they had taken their picnic to a place beside the river. They had been standing around the fire, moving together in rhythm as though they were part of each other. They seemed to be here in the room—all of them now once again.

Mara saw the river as though it were in this room. The river moved on. When she stood in the middle of the room, she said to all of them, covering the blade with her fingers and slipping the knife into the pocket of her apron. "It's Christmas Eve. Tonight the Christ child will be born."

The room fell dead quiet. In this startling moment, Aunt Mara turned to Alex and Laura. Her eyes twinkled; her lips seemed unusually slow, but her words sounded as natural and warm as always. When she began in a soft tone, everyone in the room drew a difficult breath. "Mr. Hunt and Miss Laura." She drew a breath of her own, and then bent over Laura, her hand reaching. "Laura, we were so sad to read about your mother. Oh, I am so sorry." She pressed Laura's hand. "But we are happy to hear the news of your engagement. My, everything happens at once, doesn't it?" She paused for only a short time. "And you are very welcome to stay with us for the party. Would you please do that?"

Grace heard Hanson audibly gasp. He turned sharply away from them. Grace thought she saw burning blotches on his cheeks. Mara continued as if she didn't notice. "We have our own engagement to rejoice in. Hanson and Grace are to be married in February."

Alex made a great showing of surprise. "Is that right? You did it, then!" He put out his hand.

But Hanson did not move.

"We have so much to be thankful for. Would you stay to celebrate with us?" Mara continued.

"Oh, no, we couldn't do that, Mrs. Jones," Alex Hunt said quickly. "No, no. That's nice of you, but we are on our way back to Laura's home in Salt Lake City, and the others with the Barrington party will be right behind us on their way to Salt Lake City tonight, also." He broke away from his volley of words to look at Hanson. "Hey, Hanson, I thought you'd want to see me."

Hanson still did not speak.

"We drove here first. They are following us. I needed to pick up my things. That's why I came. Business is done. There's the funeral. We have to get to Salt Lake City soon."

"It's a long drive to Salt Lake City," Mara said. "You're getting an awfully late start."

The others in the room seemed to be holding their breath in awe. Ashel was glaring at Mara with a deeply disturbed gaze. "Let them go," he said between his teeth. He could not say it, but he knew she understood the message he was casting with his eyes.

"We have plenty. You are welcome to a hot meal," Mara said. "The guests will be coming shortly."

Laura looked up at Alex. "I guess we could stay until they come."

"Until who . . . ?" Ashel asked.

"The others," Alex said. "They are behind us."

"Are they coming here?"

"They were to follow us."

"Then they are all welcome to stay as well," Mara said.

Hanson gave her a sharp look, but she ignored it.

"It's our pleasure. Why don't you have a seat? And we'll be ready when the other guests arrive."

When Mara turned toward the kitchen, she knew Hanson followed her, and that Grace followed him closely. "Aunt Mara," Hanson said to her tightly between his teeth, "you don't know what you are doing! Mara, I cannot believe you would do this to us!"

Mara turned to him. She drew the knife out of her pocket and began again on the carrots and the turnips. "Help me, Grace," she said, and Grace took another knife out of the block and also began to cut the vegetables.

"You can't . . ." Hanson began.

"You can't what, Hanson?"

"You can't have everyone in the world to dinner."

Mara put the knife down on the sideboard. She looked at Hanson slowly with her old eyes. "They are still not home. None of these people are at their homes, and it is Christmas Eve."

"And they have just taken our dreams out from under us and trampled them like so much garbage under their feet. Alex is so smooth you don't even know he is lying."

For a moment Mara was very still. "It seems they were just quicker. There was nothing illegal or unfair."

Hanson stood in burning quiet. "How could you?" He paused, and the sound of Grace's knife against the wood cut the silence like fireworks. "Aunt Mara, I don't understand."

"It would be easy to have them to dinner if we didn't feel they had wronged us, if they were our friends."

"Must you always want to do something difficult?"

Mara moved the knife to the center of the sideboard now and wiped her hands on her apron. "It is always difficult to give when you do not want to give."

"But Christmas is a family time . . ."

"We are all brothers. We are all cousins. Alex is young. He

has energy and he has aggressively moved in where a more honorable man would never go."

"Then we are doing a disservice not to teach him."

"We are teaching him."

"He'll never learn. He always gets away with murder. He is a snake."

"He is a human being. He was your friend," Mara smiled. "Was that so long ago?"

"He was my friend. He is no longer my friend."

"Who are your friends?"

"I'm not sure. My true friends would not ask me to dine with my enemies."

"They are only your enemies if you make them your enemies," Mara smiled.

By now Ashel was in the room with them. "What are you doing, Mara?" Ashel said.

She turned and smiled at him. "We're in the same town with them. We'll be in the same church building with them on Sunday. Ashel," she whispered, slowing them all down with the calm in her voice, "you and I have had long years of learning to pacify whatever is savage in our own hearts, and to calm the hearts of whatever is savage in others. Remember our Indians?"

Ashel stood at the sideboard closely examining the turnips. He shook his head. "I can't believe it, Mara. You always took them in, every potential homeless waif or 'savage' who ever came. You even stood up for Squash and took food to him in the jail."

"I didn't stand up for what he did. I stood up for his right to be treated like a human being," Mara smiled. She wiped her hands again on her apron. "Well, now we need some help here. Do you want to mash the potatoes, Hanson, while I drain the turkey and make the gravy?"

At that moment the Coreys came with six of their children. And behind them the Eggertsons and the Russells and their three young sons.

There was some disturbance when Mr. Corey found Chub in the chimney corner still chopping small kindling for the fire. Grace went quickly to them and drew them toward the window seat. "Mr. Corey, Chub has been a wonderful help to us today. Please forgive him for his indiscretion. We wish to hire him along with Sissy and Cherry."

Sissy came up to them from the kitchen and hugged her mother. "Mum, Chub is going to work with me now."

Mr. Corey's eyes softened. "I don't know. We already owe you so much, Miss Tuttle."

Grace smiled and held his hand for a long moment. "No, you owe us nothing but your love," Grace said softly. "Now I want you to meet some friends of ours."

37

Grace Tuttle

Amid the general noise of children's voices, the conversation of adults meeting one another and striking up conversation, the clatter of dishes about to come to the table with the help in the kitchen of Sissy, Cherry, Caroline, and Mara—amidst all of this confusion, Grace slipped onto the stool in front of the piano and began to play. She played very softly at first, finding the chords of old timers: "Silent Night," "While Shepherds Watched Their Flocks by Night," "Hark, the Herald Angels Sing." Some of the young children came to stand beside her at the keyboard. One of them tried to play the top notes and his brother slapped his hands. Grace stopped playing and took the baby's hands in her fingers. She put his fingers one by one on the keys and played the melody of "What Child Is This?" The haunting sound of the keys filled the room.

Hanson came close to her and brushed his lips against her hair. "Play 'Oh, Come, All Ye Faithful.' I will get everyone to sing."

He gathered the men and women in the room in groups around the two hymn books that were available. He picked up the small Russell boy in his arms and held his plump face against his cheek. "Oh, come, all ye faithful, joyful and triumphant."

At the end of the first verse, Ashel raised his arms to quiet everyone. "Once again we are so fortunate to have our friends and family with us on Christmas Eve." He paused. "For the last five years we have not had our son." There was a hush in the room. "I want especially to welcome Hanson and announce our greatest blessing—the coming marriage of Hanson and Grace, to be held in February. We wish to dedicate this evening to them. And ask Hanson to offer our prayer."

A little rumble of excited voices and parents quieting children rippled through the group. Hanson gave the Russell child to his mother and stood tall in front of the tree. He looked around the group and began to bow his head. But at that moment there was a strong bump against the front door, and then a knock, and a face in the window.

Sissy, who had just come into the room holding a tureen of soup, set the soup down so quickly on the table she almost burned her hand. Laura and Alex turned when they saw the visitor. Laura held tightly to Alex's sleeve.

Hanson walked forward through the group gathered in the living room and to the foyer. For the most part the group was hushed, though a few whispers buzzed through from the mothers still quieting their children.

Hanson stopped in front of the door. Mara moved forward quickly. The crowded room fluttered with whispers. Mara opened the door. "It's our cousin! Hello, Regi. You're just in time. We didn't know where you were. I'm so glad you could come!" She opened the door very wide. "Oh, it has started to snow!"

Great heavy flakes had begun to twist down out of the black sky. With the door into the foyer open, the cold and ice flew into the hall behind the large dark-haired man.

"Come in. Please come in."

The giant figure paused like a huge cold animal from another world, then stepped into the foyer and stood shaking downy snow from his black shoulders. The face under the cap was drawn and tense, the eyes narrow. The cheeks seemed gray with soot.

"Regi, you must stay for our meal with us," Mara said warmly, and reached for his hat and scarf. "We missed you. Where have you been?"

But she faltered momentarily as tension sputtered in the room. His eyes darted around to the others. He did not begin to touch his hat, but kept his bulky hands in the pockets of his greatcoat. He seemed to look through her as though she did not exist in the room—as though if no one were there at all, he would not feel the embarrassment that might be more than he could bear.

But Mara did not let the tense moment rest. "Come in, Regi. This is our cousin, everyone, Reginald Summerfield." She turned to Regi. "You know Alex Hunt and his new fiancé, his cousin Laura?"

Regi's eyes looked bloodshot as he gazed at Hunt and Laura. Laura's eyes flashed, but she remained poised.

"The Russells, Kathryn and Jim, the Coreys, Lida and Frank and their children, the Eggertsons, Bob and Sarina, and their children—I'm so glad you could finally meet." As she named them all, each person smiled or fidgeted. "Regi is our own Sully Tuttle's Mathew Eggertson." The Eggertsons nodded surprise. They were cousins to his father, and were also related. Mr. Eggertson came forward and took Regi's hand. "We heard about you. We thought we'd missed you. We did not know where you were."

"Regi, I'm really glad to see you. I'm glad you are all right." Grace took his hand. She noticed that Sissy was still backed up against the sideboard, her eyes darting nervously at the sight of this man. Grace came forward and tried to encourage Regi to remove his hat and coat.

"I . . . can't stay," Reginald said in a gruff voice that seemed hidden in his throat. "I . . . I . . . they are waiting for me out in the car. For you also, Mr. Hunt." He looked up. His eyes seemed to swim in the bright lights of the foyer. "I just came to get my things."

Mara was beside him in a moment again, raising her arms to help Grace with his coat. "Oh, but we'll invite them also to come in," she said. As she passed him she looked once more into the swirling snow. "It's looking pretty bad. At least come in and have a hot meal. Ashel," she called, "go out and invite the others to come in."

Ashel gazed in disbelief at Mara's performance. He stood for a moment watching her. By now the others, particularly the Eggertsons, had come to ask questions of Regi. Mr. Eggertson elicited Regi's responses with careful dignity. Ashel moved as Mara had bid him, toward the hall coatrack where his wool coat hung. He slipped into it and left to invite the others to come in.

Mara leaned after him, looking out into the dark. "Tell them to bring their overnight valises." And she turned to Reginald, who stood helpless in her wake, looking at her and wondering at her efficient kindness. "Not a one of you ought to try to travel tonight."

Reginald stood steaming in the heat of the rooms. Still he did not move to take off his coat.

But Alex moved. He was at once in his scarf. "I'm afraid we ought to be going, Mara."

Laura was trying to hide her look of embarrassment from Regi's eyes, her look of anger and dismay. Regi looked down to the floor.

"We ought to be going."

But Mara stopped them. "In this weather? Alex, we will be fortunate if our own neighbors get to their homes. The storm is bound to pass. Stay for a few moments at least."

"It's Laura. She's . . . she's not feeling well."

"Then we shall take care of her here," Mara said. "Sissy, get some soda and make some raspberry tea."

There seemed no use to protest. The woman's presence was impregnable. She moved through the crowded room of people like an angel on fire. Everything she touched turned to warmth. Grace tried to follow her, but nothing she did seemed to match Mara's finesse.

"We are about to have prayer," Mara said. "As soon as Ashel and the men come in, we'll let Hanson deliver the prayer."

Grace saw Will's old eyes then, his face taut and narrow. He was watching Ashel who had just come to the front door, and behind him the hated steel king, Barrington, and his assistant Drucker. Will's eyes flashed, and he grasped the sideboard, nearly slipping a tray of turkey to the floor. He stayed in the dining room and would not come out from behind the table.

When all three men had entered, Mara greeted them warmly. "We are honored to have you in our home on Christmas Eve," she said.

Out of sorts, Barrington looked a little off into the hot rooms, his eyes half closed. He did not smile when she offered to take his coat.

But Drucker smiled profusely and removed his wrap readily. "A warm house and food!" he said with genuine relish. "I want you to know, Mrs. . . . ." and he bent over her.

"Jones," she said.

At that moment Barrington looked sharply at old Will standing frozen in the distant room. He knew of him and the woolen mills. They were not friends.

"Mrs. Jones," Drucker said. "One cannot see for a yard in front of his eyes in this storm, and I was afraid we were going to have to spend the night in a parked car."

"It is dreadful." Mara looked out on the whirling mass of flakes. "We have plenty of food for you here, and if the storm doesn't stop—a warm place for you to sleep."

A small sound of distress came from Barrington. He looked off into the distant stairwell at the landing, at the window above the stairs. An electric bulb on the outside of the house was swimming in a flurry of flakes.

"There wasn't no way to see five inches in front of your face," Drucker repeated.

His words worried Mrs. Russell, who hurried to look out the window into the black sky. Mr. and Mrs. Corey followed her.

Mara's voice was calm. "We'll see that all of you have a place to stay if the storm continues. Please don't worry a minute about it. Ashel and Hanson, get the chairs from the upstairs bedrooms. And Sissy and Cherry, set the places."

But there was a wrenching cough from Alex, who had tried to get out before the prayer. "We shouldn't stay," he said to Mara. "We really should be going."

Mara was patient with him. She stood with Alex and Laura in the hall while everyone else was looking on and said "We'll help Laura, but she's not going to be any better in a cold car that cannot move in the snow."

"It's . . . she hasn't felt well . . . we just can't stay." His eyes were riveted upon the huge body of Reginald Summerfield.

Mara looked at Regi. She ascertained the darkness in Laura's eyes. Alex had agreed to stay before Regi had arrived. She knew what had passed between Barrington and their family.

She cleared her throat. "I don't know what has happened, Mr. Hunt, but we are all family here," she said simply. But the words were level and sharp.

"It may be your family," Alex said unevenly. "But we have some of our own to see this Christmas Eve."

At these words, Mara glanced out into the blinding weather. "Alex, I have not told you or Grace, but . . ."

Alex turned at the sound of the slight distance in her voice. "What's that?"

"You do remember that you are related to Laura—you are cousins. You are both from the family of Scott Hunt. I think you have already discovered that Laura's mother, who inherited half of her grandfather Scott Hunt's fortune, was sharing that fortune with your own grandfather Caleb and your father William. You are aware of this, aren't you?"

He was quiet, but he moved stiffly forward. He listened as Mara continued.

"Well, I didn't want to complicate things, but I happen to know that you and Grace are also cousins."

Suddenly Alex's eyes widened. "What?"

"Both of you have the same great-grandfather, Scott Hunt."

Alex's mouth dropped. He looked at Grace. His face was immobile as it registered shocked surprise. He could not take his eyes from Grace. "I had no idea . . ."

Grace looked at Mara with a puzzled gaze and shifted uneasily.

Then Mara looked at Reginald Summerfield standing very still in the room. "Of course we are all related to each other," she said. "One way or another we are all cousins."

A luster went out of Alex's eyes as he gazed at Regi. He backed away. He stayed still at the door of the room.

"We're brothers and sisters," Mara said. "We all belong to each other. We can have a lovely dinner together." There seemed to be a visible change of light in the room. "Now we'll hear Hanson's prayer."

She deferred to Hanson. His face tense with the shock of the revelation, he stood, irresolute, looking over the crowd as they settled down into quiet. "Dear Father in Heaven," he began. "We are so grateful to be in this free country this Christmas season. We have everything to be thankful for. We are a blessed people: for this bounteous feast, for our friends and neighbors, for life itself and all the," he paused, ". . . challenges," he continued, "it brings to us to help us to grow. Please forgive us for our weaknesses. We have many." He paused again. Listening to him, Grace close beside him, heard the strain in his voice. He shifted his feet and began again. "Help us . . . to renew our friendships, to make new ones, and to treat one another with kindness and love. We are all in thy family. We love thee, our dear Father. We honor thee. We give to thee all honor and gratitude for the gift of thy dear Son who taught us all to live in peace. In the name of thy son Jesus Christ, amen." After the murmur of "amen" from everyone, for a time there was absolute silence. No one moved. Grace believed she saw a glow in the room. A shimmering of unusual light.

After a moment, Mara began to speak. "Take a plate from

your place and go through the line at the buffet. There are several tables. You are welcome to stop at all of them."

Suddenly the room became a flutter of movement. The women checked the hands of their children, the men took their places in line behind the buffet, and Cherry and Caroline, wheeling carefully around everyone, lifted the lids from the hot dishes. The warm turkey and yams, the hot dressing, clouded the air with delicious odors. There was a ceremonious pause when Ashel wielded the knife to cut the one bird they left whole for the purpose. All the other fowl and ham and meats lay in uniform slices on the silver and Spode trays. There was hot mustard and cranberry, apple-raisin dressing, glazed carrots, the fluffy white mashed potatoes, the steaming gravy, and the Yorkshire and pumpkin pudding. On each table there were fronds of dried flowers Caroline had leaned from her wheelchair to gather from her own garden and hung upside down in the anteroom from the ceiling to dry: phlox and baby's breath and little bitter waxweed flowers with spiny stems, a couple of fat violet thistles whose flaming petals, though dry, still felt as soft as goose's down. The babies were tempted to touch the center-pieces—to rake their fingers through them. But their mothers pulled them into their chairs on cushions and tied napkins round their necks. There was hot cider with spirals of cinnamon and floating clove, and there were hot breads fit for a king: the white potato flour and rye from Caroline's kitchen, the poppy seed and the fat pads of real butter, and Caroline's sparkling berry jams.

There was enough for everyone to fill their plates several times and to spare. The meal went smoothly. Everyone enjoyed it. The Coreys were grateful many times during the course of the meal, and the children, who generally stayed quiet as mice, said "please" and "thank you" when they asked for something to be passed.

There were good manners all around. Reginald was quiet as he ate, and did not take enormous amounts on his plate. Mr.

Barrington, who sat at the table opposite Uncle Will, wiped his mouth often with his napkin and said perfunctorily: "This is a rare treat. A windfall." Once he said, "I must really compliment your Mormon women. They do know how to cook."

Caroline blushed and passed him the raspberry jam.

"I never thought I'd be inside a Mormon home." He glanced at Drucker and received a nod of agreement. "The Mormon hotel was very fine: Julia was very good at her hotel. But I never thought I would be inside a Mormon home. It's the same scene of hard work and sacrifice as any other lovely American home."

"Well, you are welcome any time," Mara said.

"We took longer than we thought we would take today." Barrington leaned back in his chair, pushing it slightly from the table. "If the storm permits, we really must try to go. Our families are expecting us for Christmas."

At his words, Ashel wiped his mouth, rose from the table, and moved to the door. As he peered out into the black porch, he saw nothing but a whirl of flakes. The fury of the storm had increased rather than decreased. By now the snow had blown into corners and filled up the walkways with drifts up to more than a foot deep. The trees seemed loaded with the heavy ribbons of ice. Everywhere the blackness swallowed up the swirling fury of the wind. There was only a small core of light from a gas lamp in the street, or an insect point of light from a window in the vast distance. The lights from across the street seemed like flickering fireflies, dimming and dimming with a feeble flutter, about to die out. The gale swept a glaze of gray ice like huge canopies over each of the automobiles standing in the street. They were buried far above their wheels, looking like biers—carriages of death draped in funeral clothes.

When Ashel returned from the window, Barrington pushed his chair back from the table and walked to him. "We may have to go back to the hotel."

But Ashel's eyes looked very dark. "I'm concerned you

would even find your way back to the hotel. I'm concerned for all of you except perhaps for our very near neighbors." The Russells and the Coreys would be able to tromp through the heavy snow to reach the Corey home nearby. The Eggertsons also were not far away. The Eastman Hotel, for that matter, was not far away, either.

Alex's face looked very pale. Laura still seemed angry, holding her head down close to her plate. She did not look up from the table.

"I'm afraid we'll have to try the car. We need to get out of here," Alex said, obviously nervous again.

Mara laughed, "Well, I certainly don't want you to feel you are the captives of a prison. But we are happy to put you up in the upstairs rooms. You may think of yourselves as part of our family. We are all in this together. You will be treated like royalty." She paused. "The truth of the matter is," she dared to say, "you may think of this as the Royal House Hotel."

It was perhaps a brazen statement to make. Alex shifted uncomfortably in his chair.

Barrington returned to the table and stood contemplating the situation while he shifted from one foot to the other, and then distributed the weight evenly on both feet. "This has been a lovely meal, but . . ." He looked at Mara. "It is the inconvenience. This is really quite inconvenient." Then he walked to the window again. "Drat it. But look at that storm. Are you sure . . . ?"

"I am sure, Mr. Barrington," Mara said brightly. "Please. It would be an honor."

"Well, then, I don't mind staying if you are serious about the offer."

Drucker nodded congenially and spooned more bread pudding on his plate. "I'm in agreement," he said. "I was the one who tried to drive that car."

Alex took Laura's hand and backed away from the table toward the door. He was watching Reginald's bobbing head, and his empty plate. Reginald Summerfield at about the same time tipped his head back to drain his glass of water. He glanced at Alex and Laura with shaded eyes. Sissy was watching, also. She was clearing the table of dishes now, and in a moment she asked Caroline if she would mind terribly if her family could be excused to get through the storm.

Caroline nodded in agreement, but on their way into the other room, they found Aunt Mara and Uncle Will seated on the divan with the small children, the parents at the window seat and on the chairs, and some on the floor. Though they were still standing, Alex and Laura were listening, too.

"Before you leave," Mara said, holding her hand palm up to Sissy who was untying her apron, "we'll just read a few passages together. Listen, and see if you can hear something very beautiful and true. *And she brought forth her firstborn son, and wrapped him in swaddling clothes and laid him in a manger; because there was no room for them in the inn.*"

Mara felt the peace fall on all of them as she read. The room was silent. Outside while the dark snow raged, there was nothing but the crack of the fire and the words of the holy book open on her lap as she read to all of them the story of the first Christmas. While she read the words she had read a thousand times, she let her thoughts move back in time to the wooden house on the river. The Eastman family had been racing against the cold to prepare for the winter. When the wind whistled through the chinks in the walls, they used the meadow grass they had saved for the cattle to stuff into the openings. When the wind continued to whistle through, they used handkerchieves and pieces of worn-out underwear to stop up the gaps. But the wind had still been so loud when her Papa Eastman read the Christmas story, they barely heard a knock at the door. Mrs. Allen was standing in the door with a lamb in her arms.

"Is this your lamb, Brother Eastman?" she said over the sound of the wind. "My son found it caught in the ice on the river."

Its haunches were filthy with black ice, its coat matted and torn. Papa Eastman looked up from the firelight, and went to talk with her at the door. The Eastmans had never owned a lamb. "No, but if you haven't room, we can take it in until we find the owner," he said.

"I'd be grateful, since we have a new baby in our house," Mrs. Allen said. "It's awfully dirty. Do you have a box?"

While Papa took the wood out of the box on the hearth, Rain had lifted her arms and stretched out her hands. Mrs. Allen looked at Papa with questioning eyes. Papa nodded. Hesitantly, Mrs. Allen dropped the dirty lamb into Rain's lap. Buckling its legs, it settled down in her leather skirt between her knees. She stroked its head. She leaned over the lamb and touched it with her cheek. It slept.

While she read from the Christmas story, Mara noted that Reginald Summerfield stood silently by the doorjamb of the large opening into the dining room. He stood with his face against the wood looking into the fire ahead of him. The orange light of the flames danced in his dark eyes. He had not said anything during the meal except to answer in one or two words a few polite questions.

Mara thought to herself that she knew very little about him. When the others left she would like to have a chance to speak to him, to invite him to open up his heart and tell of his difficulties, his trials. During the entire meal he had insisted on keeping his waistcoat buttoned. He was hot, she knew, because great beads of sweat broke out on his brow. When she drew close to him, she smelled the strong odor of his body and knew he had probably not bathed for some days. He was embarrassed. With his large size he could not really hide anywhere. He seemed lonely as he stood beside the door—as lonely as a displaced Indian might have seemed in this world not of his own choosing. His eyes were lost in the deep piney branches of the candle-laden Christmas tree. Where had he gone? she wondered.

*Glorifying and praising God for all the things they had heard
and seen as it was told unto them.*

She thought she saw more in him than the others would
have found. She would speak with him as soon as she could.

Ashel said the family prayer. All the little children and the
parents knelt around the room in the crisp, bright firelight.
Even Barrington and Drucker stood reverently in the vestibule,
stiffly holding to a chair or the hall tree.

Ashel prayed for the snow to stop so that their friends might
be able to reach their homes safely in time to spend Christmas
with their loved ones. He prayed for the power of God's love to
lift them all to better purposes in life, to help them find kind
words for all men, to guide them to greater love and greater joy
with every action of their lives. "To reach out to others always,
our Father. Help us to be thy children in every way."

Though Barrington and Drucker did not say "amen," both
of them looked up with subdued eyes.

"It's been lovely," Barrington said to Mara as he dressed in
his greatcoat and tied his scarf around his neck. "But really, we
must try to get the cars to move."

But when they went to the door and looked out the
window, they could see that the blizzard was impossible. By
now the Coreys and the Russells and the Eggertsons had dressed
and had begun to wind their ways down to the end of the
street. But even walking a few steps was difficult. To help out
the Eastmans, Mr. Eggertson and Mr. Russell folded Caroline's
wheelchair while Caroline waited on a chair in the hallway for
Ashel. They carried the wheelchair with them when they left.

"It's been wonderful," Lida Corey said, embracing Mara for
a long time. "You can't know how much your family has done
for ours."

The children lined up one by one and shook Aunt Mara's
and Uncle Will's hands. The others put their arms around Aunt
Caroline and kissed her.

Chub took Grace's hand and held it for a long time. "Thank

you, ma'am," he said.

"Remember our promise," Grace said.

"I will."

"Have you been good so that Saint Nicholas can come to your house?" Caroline said to the little ones.

"We are setting out our shoes," Cherry said.

Caroline smiled because she had given a few bags of candy and nuts to Lida and Frank to fill the shoes should they seem empty on Christmas morn.

As Cherry and Sissy left, they leaned over and held Aunt Caroline in their arms for a long time. "We love you," they whispered.

"Next time you will perhaps be bringing Mr. Hammersly as your young man?" Caroline grinned to Sissy.

Sissy blushed. "I hope so," she smiled.

As she passed Reginald Summerfield in the hallway, she stepped a little wide to avoid him. But he turned to her and filled the hall so completely she could not pass. Afraid, she kept her eyes down, while he said softly—Mara could hear him— "I'm sorry, Miss Corey. Please forgive me."

Sissy looked up with frightened eyes. She nodded. Then she turned quickly and followed Cherry into the snow behind her parents.

Mara watched Regi carefully. As the house began to empty, as the guests began to leave, he removed his waistcoat and folded it over his arm. His shirt looked dark with days of grime. He let Drucker and Barrington go first up the stairs. Grace helped situate Laura in her own back bedroom where there would be enough room for both of them together. It looked as though Alex wanted to follow the girls to the back room, but Grace closed the door. After Alex left, she slipped out to say good night to Hanson.

Regi waited for Alex to follow Drucker and Barrington before he began climbing the stairs.

When Ashel picked Caroline up in his arms to carry her

home, Will followed them to the door. Mara came to them as they left and put a hand on Uncle Will's arm. "I just have a feeling, Will," she began, then she paused and did not speak for a moment. "I . . ." she began again. "I want to stay with the young people here," she whispered. "I just have a feeling."

Uncle Will did not like to be inconvenienced. He liked his own bed. He knew it was a hop, skip, and a jump from there, he said, a little out of sorts.

"Just let me stay with them. There's the small bedroom at the top of the stairs."

"Well, it's your Royal House Hotel," Will said. "Looks like you just christened it. Want to make a night of it, eh?"

"I will feel better if I stay with them."

"Suit yourself. I'm going to bed," Will said, and, following Ashel and Caroline, he tottered out into the icy wind.

The last to leave was Hanson. Grace stood by him as he pulled on his gloves. He was hesitant as he approached Mara. "Will you be all right, Aunt Mara?" Hanson asked.

Mara looked up at him, surprised at the subdued tone of his voice. He no longer seemed to be the Hanson so concerned about his own losses and himself. Mara did not speak for a moment, gathering the evidence of his quiet. Finally she looked into his eyes. "If you two are all right, everything is all right," she said honestly. She felt her heart beginning to beat hard in her chest. She thought her heart would burst with love.

Grace looked up at Hanson as she held to his arm. "We're all right," she smiled.

"There are plenty of people here, and Grace will be here to help you, so I'll stay with my parents," Hanson said.

"If you want to stay . . . " Mara began, but she drew back sensing something level in his eyes. He was different somehow from the Hanson who had come at the beginning of the evening. And then in a moment of surprise, he took Mara's hand in his. "God bless you for your example of kindness." He pressed her hand. His unrest seemed to have vanished. When she looked at him she saw a tenderness in his eyes. Her own heart raced when he slipped his arm around Grace and whispered, "I have something I want to tell you, Mara. There are so many who need you." He stood very still in the amber light of the fire, the flakes dancing at the window behind him. "I'm afraid I have had tunnel vision in the wrong tunnel. I learned something tonight. I need very little else but our loved ones— our home. I know if I stay close to Grace I'll learn to know everything is going to be all right. You'll help me, won't you, Grace?"

Grace's smile was tender.

"Everything is going to be all right?" Mara asked.

"Everything is going to turn out all right," Hanson said.

As Mara watched the two young people, they drew close to each other. Grace slipped into her cape and followed him for a brief moment out into the swirling snow. Mara watched them from the stoop. They were laughing and throwing snowballs at each other. In a last affectionate moment, Hanson buried his face in Grace's hair.

It was not long before Grace was inside, cold and wet, but smiling. Mara waited for her. After Grace hung her cape on the hall tree, she turned and saw Mara. There was a pause as though all the angels were singing. She put her arms around Mara. She stood with her in her arms for a long time. "Thank you, my dear Aunt Mara," she whispered. "I love you, you know."

Though Mara felt the snow on Grace's cheeks, she had never felt so warm.

38

Mara Eastman Jones

After Grace had gone to the room she would share with Laura, Mara stood in the hallway for a quiet moment. She let the events of the evening flow through her and sing inside of her for what seemed like a long time. In a daze of happiness, she walked back into the kitchen to clear away a few more details that Sissy and Cherry had left undone. Then she passed up the stairs to the bedroom in the front hall.

She could hear the men fussing with their valises in their lighted rooms. The halls sounded warm with people in them— and such a variety of people she never dreamed would be staying in the old Eastman home on Christmas Eve! But there was plenty of room. Hanson would stay at his parents' house tonight. She was glad he had decided to spend his first Christmas at home with his mother and father. It was a good decision. They had discussed the fact that it was possibly their last Christmas in the mansion, as Ashel had decided to tell Caroline the details of their finances, and gently suggest to her that it might be wise to rent the houses to someone else now, and move into the home on the corner with Hanson and Grace.

Mr. Drucker and Barrington took the large room with two beds and the large fireplace, and Regi and Alex Hunt each had a small room to themselves.

As Mara lay on the bed in the tiny front closet bedroom, listening to the rumble of voices in the hall, she held Sobe's journal in her hands. Long ago she had listened to the voices of the family in the downstairs rooms at Christmas time. That first year they had bathed Rain and her mother Spirit of Earth, and dressed them in clean clothes. Rain had looked at herself in the mirror. With her hair washed clean, she was beautiful. Mara had given her a small comb made of wood sticks tied with leather. Rain had bit the comb with her teeth, and smiled. Then she had taken the comb and wrapped her hair around it again and again. With her hands she had patted the large knot in her hair. All evening, smiling, she had held the comb in her hair. When they had knelt to pray, Rain took the comb out of her hair and held it between her hands. She had never stopped smiling. When she lay down on her cot beside the hearth, she had turned her face to the wall and found her bag of treasures. She took the blue beads out of the bag and tied them one by one on the comb with a thong of leather. She laid the comb with the beads beside her cheek and held to it with her hand, but she did not sleep. From her own bed at the end of the room, Mara saw Rain's eyes open in the firelight for a long time. She was smiling and her eyes were filled with light. In the morning, she took the comb and put it in Mara's hand. Mara shook her head. Rain took two of the beads off of the comb and put them in Mara's fingers. She closed her fingers.

Still holding the journal in her hands, Mara felt a calm. She repeated to herself in her heart, "Everything is going to be all right. Everything is going to be all right."

After a few moments Barrington and Drucker were quiet, and there was no sound from the girls, or from Alex's room. She opened Sobe's journal and began to read:

When I asked for a message from heaven, I saw a light. It was in the smoke of the fire in the furnace at the mill, but brighter than I had ever seen before, and in the light were words I felt. If my people had asked for visions all these years, I was understanding what they saw. I did not hear them with my physical ears. The words told me I must write these things in my own hand, to keep them for the others to remember how I had decided to live—to live the best of everything.

She smoothed the pages with her fingers. But in that

moment, she believed she could hear sobbing somewhere in the deep corners of the house. A deep sobbing. And she believed she knew where it was. Cautiously she rose from the cot in the room, put the journal back on the nightstand, and found her slippers on the dark floor. She lit the oil lamp on the dressing table and replaced the glass flue. The spiral of smoke rose on the air like the substance of a dream. The words of Sobe's vision washed over her. She remembered the Indians believed that smoke was a spirit. It connected earth with heaven like a link that locked them together in a powerful mystic rite. She stood over the smoke and watched it for a moment. How many thousands of the Indian people had seen the smoke rise to heaven and believed it was a spirit connecting heaven and earth with power? The belief itself had empowered their gaze. She believed God lived. That belief empowered her and those she loved. She believed God was a father, and if she lived worthy of his love he would overshadow her with light, take her in his arms, and love her with an overwhelming love. Because he was her father, when he asked her to do his work on this earth, she wished to do all she could do.

She slipped out of the tiny room and into the cold hall that seemed colder since the dark storm raged around them. How many years had she walked the heart of this house—these very halls—even as a young girl. She had bounded down these stairs to see Bret Hunt, Bret who had never really loved her. She had seen her parents live and die here. She loved this place like an old friend. On the shelves of the bookcase she saw the objects of the memories of their lives collected like small monuments: Charles's trophy for winning the boat races, a tiny china piano on a music box given to Jenny when she sang for the Academy, the volumes of Shakespearean plays and poets—Coleridge, Wordsworth, and Keats—that leaned between Eastman's old pine cone bookends like watchful guards of their love for culture. A large volume of Milton's *Paradise Lost* was one of her favorites—with the drawings by Gustave Doré. It was a volume of angels with wings which the doctrine of the Church eschewed, but which Mara kept in her heart, imagining the spirit of every man and woman with wings that were visible only in drawings but would serve the spirit of each man and woman to fly someday. She would fly, she knew that. She would see worlds, she would see Sobe and Rain again—and all of the Indian spirits who had seen the visions that time had made significant and measured. She would see angels, and she would see her Heavenly Father and cry against his cheeks and rest in his arms.

She set the oil lamp down on the sewing machine in the hall. Though the walls of Papa Eastman's big old house were very thick brick and stone, there was always a chill in the wind. When it blew through from the river she again heard the sobbing in the room. When she stopped beside Reginald's door, she listened. He could have been unaware of his own gasping and of the tears in his breathing. He might have been sleeping. But she did not know.

Tap tap tap. She tapped softly on the door, hoping no one in the other rooms would hear her. She listened again. The sobbing seemed quiet. She tapped again softly on the door. This time she heard padded steps to the door, and a body leaning heavily against it.

"It's me, your Aunt Mara, Regi," she said softly. "May I come in?"

For a moment there was nothing. She too was quiet, not wanting to startle him or cause him embarrassment. "Please?" she said once more.

The lock moved in the hasp and the door opened slightly. His face seemed very white, even though there was no light except from the oil lamp she had set down.

He was still in his clothes. Wrinkled and filthy, they hung about him like rags. He looked bent and very old. When she followed him into the room he leaned down and sat against the bed.

"I wish you would talk to me, Regi. Even though . . ." she paused, "even though you have had a life away from us, you are our people."

His eyes looked blank. His face still caught the light from the hall, and he looked very pale. He looked at her and then he shook his head slowly. "You don't know me, Mrs. Jones," he said. "I don't deserve all the kindness you show me."

His voice was low. "I am not worthy," he repeated. And he leaned down against the bed, his shoulders shaking with the painful wrack of his mind and body. "What have I done with my life?" he said.

Mara watched him with her own heart tearing in two. She would suffer his pain for him, if she could.

As he bent over and his body continued to shake, she heard his soft wail: "I don't even know God's name. Tawa, God."

Mara could not bear to see his body and spirit so shaken. "His name," she whispered, "is just language, sounds. He is always the same." She sat near to him on the bed and touched his shoulders and held his thick arm with her hands. "Regi, please. Your God, my God, loves you," she said softly.

"Yes, he loves me," he said from far away against the bedding. "And I continue to turn the other way."

"Regi, Regi," Mara said, softly stroking his shoulder. "This is just the beginning of doing better. Can you take your life now and make him proud of you? You can change—you can become as pure as the snow."

As if in answer, a sharp wind drove the snow against the window and the pane rattled—a cold sound in the black night. Regi's tears broke fresh on his hands and he let them fall. "Oh God, how could I continue to do what I do? There are some needs in me that are never filled."

Mara stayed with him while the wind roared in the chimney. "Regi, I wish you would stay. You were a lonely child. How can you live with love in your heart when no one has ever taught you love? If I had never experienced love, I would not know where to look."

Now he sobbed again against his hand, but he wiped his tears away from his cheek.

For a long time, Reginald did not move. He was very large and very dirty on the bed. Mara winced for a moment, feeling in her bones the energy it was going to take to launder this bedding and clean the mire of his boots from the small rag rug at her feet, but she disciplined her thoughts. It was not always easy to love those who needed it the most.

"I have left someone in California. Ethel," he was saying through his tears. "How could I have left her?"

Mara continued to rub his shoulders. "Reginald, you can make your life over," she whispered. "Send for her."

Reginald's sobs began to slacken. He shifted his head to the wall side where his eyes could not be seen.

"Please, I am honored to hear your tears. Go ahead and cry," Mara said. "There is hope for you if you can grieve."

She soothed his hair with her fingers. "We love you, Reginald. We want your happiness. If we can help you, we are here to help you."

Without a word, he turned toward her again and grasped her fingers with his hand. With his face still turned away, he held her hand for a long time in a tense grip that was almost painful. He still lay on the bed, his breathing uneven.

Mara saw Sobe again in her arms, hidden on the dark bed in the blind woman's basement. He had turned to her then, and she had never forgotten the words he had said in that moment, nor would she forget how she felt when she saw what he had later written in the pages of his journal:

I am indebted to the only mothers I will ever know. Both Mara and Rain have taken me under their wings as birds hover over their starlets. These are my inheritances: a long life, a glad heart, a straight way . . . I must write these things in my own hand, to keep them for the others to remember how I had decided to live—to live the best of everything.

"All of us will be truly free and happy together only if we are all free and happy," she said softly. "As long as one person is in trouble, it is our charge to do all we can to help. That is God's will. Do we go through life causing others pain, or bringing them into our love to help them to heal? It is our choice."

Reginald's rough breathing began to wane. Mara would stay with him until he began to rest more easily. She continued to rub him and to soothe him with her free fingers while he continued to grip her hand.

Finally, he raised his head from the pillow and turned toward her. "Aunt Mara," he whispered now. "I saw him," he finally said.

Mara heard the words in the background of her thought. She did not hear them in the context of this moment. She did not answer him until the words had moved around for a moment in her mind.

"What, Regi?" she asked.

He was not ready to be misheard again. With difficulty he sat up on the bed beside her and took her fingers in his hands. "I saw him, Aunt Mara. I'm sure it was him."

She had heard him correctly. She stopped massaging the dark skin. She turned to him. "You saw him, Regi?" She did not question his words. And she knew of whom he was speaking.

"I saw him, and I felt his love, too," he said.

"Oh Regi," Mara whispered. "Oh Regi. He came to you?"

"Yes. And I want his love."

Mara pressed his hand. "He loves you, Regi."

"I've made up my mind. I will find out where Ethel is and go to her. I want us to . . . build something."

Mara saw Regi's life as though it passed before both of them in that instant. The little child Mathew stood on the stool beside her in the kitchen once again, his small brown hands on the edge of the table in the flour. She saw his face—it flashed through her memory so clearly, she was startled. She drew back. The little boy Mathew had looked up at her and he said, "Aunt

Mara, why are you using a shaving mug?" He had reached out to touch it, but she took it quietly out of his hand.

Patiently she had told him, "Someday when you are a man you will use a shaving mug."

Mara smiled. "It's not easy," she said. "It's not the end, but only the beginning. It's a commitment."

He understood her. But he was quiet.

"A commitment means not wavering."

He laid her hand against his cheek. "Will you stay with me for a few more moments?"

"As long as you need me," Mara said. She stayed with him while he settled back down against the bed. She covered him with the quilt. She continued quietly to rub his arms with her hand. In a few moments he was asleep. She sat hearing the storm shuttle the branch of the poplars against the glass. The light in the hall began to flicker.

She thought about the house filled with people she had never dreamed she could love—harder to love even than the little dried-up old Spirit of Earth and her daughter, Rain, who came to them so many years ago when all of this began. The people in this house tonight were people who had wronged them, who had seemed to let greed and personal need and appetite rule them to the point of allowing them to hurt others. But she did not have to judge them. How glad she was of that! The Savior loved them all. He had even come to Regi and promised him love. She thought about her mother who had let Spirit of Earth and Rain come in. They were still with them in many ways. It had not been that difficult to let these people also come in. It was Christmas Eve.

The clock in the hall began softly to chime midnight. "It is midnight and our day of celebrating our Savior's birth is here," Mara thought, smiling to herself. She gathered her wool robe more tightly around her shoulders and slipped quietly out the door. She stopped in the center of the hall at the heart of the old house, to pick up the lamp and carry it to her room. "Royal

House. That's a good name for a place to stay," she thought, musing to herself.

Before she lay down to sleep, she pulled the curtains to the side of the window and curled the wick of the oil lamp into the oil until it sputtered out. She could see that now the sky was not in darkness. Now the snow was not so heavy, but fine, like particles of light falling. She looked up into the East. Under the clouds, she could see a bright star shining.

About the Author

Marilyn Brown was winner of the 1991 Utah State Fine Arts novel prize, BYU's first Mayhew fiction prize, and the first novel award given by the Association for Mormon Letters. She holds a master's degree from BYU and a Master of Fine Arts degree from the University of Utah. Two of her previous novels, *Thorns of the Sun* and *Shadows of Angels*, have been published by Covenant.

Marilyn, who has six children and six grandchildren, lives in Springville, Utah, with her husband Bill and a friendly assortment of animals including four ducks, three horses, two cats, and a beaver.